# Shadows of Ambition

Elizabeth Campbell

Published by Elizabeth Campbell, 2024.

This is a work of fiction. Similarities to real people, places, or events are entirely coincidental.

SHADOWS OF AMBITION

**First edition. October 1, 2024.**

Copyright © 2024 Elizabeth Campbell.

ISBN: 979-8227585721

Written by Elizabeth Campbell.

# Chapter 1: The Arrival

The lively streets of downtown Brampton pulse with a frenetic energy that sends a jolt through my veins as I step from the cab and onto the sidewalk. The air is thick with the aroma of freshly baked pastries and the sharp tang of gasoline, mingling in a fragrant chaos that feels electric. I clutch my portfolio—a leather-bound testament to my aspirations and late nights spent pouring over every detail—tightly against my chest, as if it were a shield against the world I'm about to dive into. This is it, my debut as a PR consultant at Nexus Communications, a firm as glamorous as it is ruthless, and my heart races with both exhilaration and anxiety.

The glass façade of the Nexus building looms overhead, a sleek behemoth reflecting the bright blue sky and the bustling city below. It's a structure that seems to have been designed to intimidate, its sharp angles and polished surfaces glimmering like a promise of success for those brave enough to enter. I straighten my blouse, smoothing it down as if that might somehow ground me, and step into the expansive lobby. The space is awash with marble and chrome, a testament to wealth and ambition, where echoes of heels clicking against the floor harmonize with the soft murmur of conversations—a symphony of ambition that fills me with both hope and uncertainty.

As I make my way to the elevator, I pass clusters of sharply dressed professionals engrossed in discussions, their voices rising and falling like the tide. The atmosphere hums with competition, each word exchanged carrying the weight of unspoken aspirations. I take a deep breath, absorbing the atmosphere as I stand before the polished metal doors, my reflection staring back at me with wide eyes. Am I really ready for this? Before I can dwell on that thought, the elevator doors slide open, and I step inside, my pulse quickening.

"Twenty-sixth floor, please," I murmur, pressing the button with a practiced confidence that belies the butterflies fluttering in my stomach. As the elevator ascends, I watch the numbers light up one by one, each digit an inch closer to my dreams. The rush of air as we rise feels like a mini-victory, a reminder that I am moving forward, away from the mundane and into the thrilling unknown.

When the doors open, I'm greeted by a bustling office, a hive of activity that instantly envelops me. My gaze sweeps across the room, taking in the open layout filled with sleek desks, collaborative spaces, and the constant click of keyboards. Brightly colored art pieces adorn the walls, adding a splash of creativity to the professional atmosphere, while large windows offer a breathtaking view of the city, the skyline punctuated by the iconic CN Tower in the distance.

"Welcome to Nexus!" a voice calls out, breaking through my awe. A woman strides toward me, her presence commanding yet warm. She has auburn hair that falls in effortless waves, and her emerald green dress is a striking contrast to the neutral tones of the office.

"I'm Leah, the head of your department," she says, extending her hand with a smile that could light up the room. Her handshake is firm, infused with an energy that immediately puts me at ease.

"I'm so excited to be here," I reply, trying to match her enthusiasm. "I've heard great things about the firm."

"Great things, indeed! But don't let that fool you; it's a jungle up here," she says with a mischievous grin. "But if you can handle it, there's no limit to what you can achieve. Let me introduce you to the team."

As we navigate the maze of desks, I catch snippets of conversations, laughter, and the occasional heated debate. My heart swells with a sense of belonging, despite the undercurrent of competition. I meet a variety of colleagues—each one more vibrant than the last—each introduction laced with shared hopes and subtle rivalries. They're a tapestry of personalities, each thread adding depth to the workplace fabric, and I can't help but wonder where I will fit in.

After a whirlwind of introductions, Leah leads me to my own desk—a cozy corner adorned with a potted plant that seems to thrive despite the fluorescent lighting. It's a small space, yet it feels like a promise of my own place in this dynamic world. I set my portfolio down, the weight of my ambitions pressing against the polished wood, and look around, feeling a spark of excitement.

"Your first assignment is to develop a campaign for one of our new clients," Leah explains, her tone serious yet encouraging. "They're a tech startup launching an innovative app, and they're looking to make a splash. I trust you'll bring fresh ideas to the table."

"Absolutely," I say, my mind already racing with possibilities. The thrill of creating something impactful ignites a fire within me, and for the first time today, my nerves settle into a determined resolve.

As the day unfolds, I dive into brainstorming sessions, poring over market research, and sketching out ideas on sticky notes that soon cover my desk like a colorful mosaic of creativity. The energy of the team is infectious, and I find myself lost in a rhythm of collaboration, laughter, and the occasional moment of friendly banter.

Yet amidst the whirlwind of activity, a figure catches my eye—a woman perched in a sleek chair, her dark hair framing her sharp features. She watches the room with an intensity that sends a shiver down my spine. There's something in her gaze, an unyielding strength wrapped in an air of mystery. I can't quite place it, but I feel the stirrings of rivalry before I even know her name.

The day slips by in a flurry of ideas and interactions, my excitement growing with every passing moment. As the sun begins to set, casting a golden hue across the cityscape, I realize I'm not just entering a new job; I'm stepping into a vibrant tapestry of aspirations and challenges, where every thread weaves a story that is waiting to unfold. With my heart racing and a spark of ambition igniting within me, I can't help but wonder what this new chapter will hold.

The days unfurl like pages of an intriguing novel, each one filled with a blend of excitement and uncertainty. I find my rhythm at Nexus Communications, where the constant buzz of creativity serves as both a soundtrack and a backdrop to my aspirations. With each sunrise, the kaleidoscope of the office reveals new characters, their ambitions weaving in and out like actors on a stage, all while I learn my lines in this fast-paced play of public relations.

My desk quickly becomes a sanctuary of sorts, cluttered yet inviting, adorned with vibrant sticky notes and half-finished sketches of marketing strategies. I've taken to arriving early, the quiet of the office in those first moments a welcome reprieve from the vibrant chaos that follows. It's a chance to sip my coffee—a rich blend that hints at dark chocolate—and gather my thoughts before diving headfirst into the whirlwind of the day.

Just as I settle into this routine, the presence of that enigmatic woman looms larger. Emma, I learn from whispered conversations, is as sharp as the suits she wears. She carries herself with an air of confidence that borders on intimidation, yet there's a magnetism about her that draws others in. I often catch her in the corner of my eye, discussing strategies with the upper management or engaging in debates that leave even the most seasoned veterans nodding in admiration. She's a force, and it's impossible to ignore the electric tension that crackles between us, an unspoken competition that feels almost palpable.

One afternoon, as I huddle with my team over an open presentation, a light-hearted discussion turns into a challenge. Someone proposes a brainstorming session for the upcoming tech startup campaign, and the words tumble from my mouth before I can censor them: "How about we think outside the box, maybe even break a few rules? What if we brought in a live demonstration at a public event?"

Leah's eyes spark with interest, and before I can finish articulating my vision, Emma's voice slices through the room. "Public events? That's a risky play, and the last thing we need is to tarnish our reputation on a whim." Her tone is clipped, yet there's an underlying curiosity, as if she's gauging how far I'm willing to push.

I can feel the heat rising in my cheeks, the familiar pang of self-doubt clawing at my insides. But this isn't the time to retreat; I can't let my nerves overshadow my ambition. "Sometimes the biggest risks yield the most extraordinary results," I respond, my voice steadier than I feel. "Imagine capturing the attention of our target audience not just through marketing, but through an experience that they can feel and touch."

The room grows quiet, and I hold my breath, waiting for Emma's response. She arches an eyebrow, a smirk dancing on her lips, and I can see the gears in her mind turning. It's a challenge, one that I can't help but rise to meet, and for a fleeting moment, a spark of camaraderie flares between us—a mutual respect born from the fire of competition.

As the week progresses, my ideas take root and blossom. I find myself working late, the dim office lights casting shadows on the walls, accompanied only by the occasional hum of fluorescent bulbs and the soft rustle of paper. One evening, I notice Emma lingering by her desk, her brow furrowed in concentration as she types furiously, her jaw set with determination. It's a rare glimpse into her world, and for a moment, the rivalry seems to fade, replaced by an understanding of the passion we both share for our work.

"Burning the midnight oil?" I venture, leaning against the partition that separates our workspaces.

She glances up, her expression softening just a fraction. "Trying to keep up with the pace around here. You're not half bad at stirring the pot, you know." There's a hint of challenge in her tone, yet her eyes glimmer with something akin to admiration, and it takes me by surprise.

"I'm just trying to make a mark," I admit, feeling emboldened by her acknowledgment. "This place is full of incredible talent. I want to bring something fresh to the table."

Emma nods, a flicker of respect crossing her face. "Keep pushing. Just don't let your ambition cloud your judgment. Nexus has a way of chewing people up and spitting them out."

Her words linger in the air, a reminder of the stakes we're playing for, but there's a warmth behind her warning, an unspoken acknowledgment that we're both navigating this intricate dance of ambition and survival together.

As days turn into weeks, I begin to find my footing in this bustling ecosystem. My campaign for the tech startup evolves into something tangible, and the thrill of watching my ideas take flight is intoxicating. Each meeting brings new insights, new opportunities to refine my vision, and I soon discover that the very competition I once found daunting is now a driving force pushing me to excel.

With every successful brainstorming session, my confidence blossoms, and I can feel the subtle shift in the dynamic between Emma and me. Where once there was palpable tension, there now exists a burgeoning respect that hints at the possibility of collaboration. I catch her shooting me approving glances during meetings, and her playful jabs become more frequent—each one a reminder that I am earning my place among these formidable professionals.

One Friday afternoon, as the week winds down and the office buzzes with anticipation of the weekend, Leah gathers the team to share the preliminary feedback from our pitch presentation. As she praises the energy and creativity of our ideas, I glance over at Emma. To my surprise, she's smiling—a genuine, unguarded expression that makes her seem almost approachable. It's an invitation, perhaps, a sign that our rivalry is evolving into something more complicated and layered.

After the meeting, I approach her, the adrenaline of success still coursing through my veins. "So, what did you think of the presentation?" I ask, a teasing lilt in my voice.

"It had potential," she replies, tilting her head slightly as if weighing her words. "But we can always make it better."

"Better how?"

Her eyes sparkle with mischief. "I'll show you. Meet me here tomorrow at ten. I have a few ideas."

The unexpected invitation leaves me both thrilled and apprehensive. What does this mean for our dynamic? I can't quite grasp where this partnership might lead, but one thing is clear: the intricate web of our lives at Nexus is growing tighter, drawing us both deeper into the exhilarating chaos that is our new reality.

The morning light spills through the floor-to-ceiling windows of the Nexus office, bathing the room in a soft glow that belies the frenetic energy that pulses within. My heart races as I prepare to meet Emma, the enigmatic woman who has become both my rival and, strangely, my unexpected ally. I set my coffee down on my desk, the rich aroma a comforting reminder that today marks a new chapter, a fresh beginning in this dizzying world of PR.

As I approach our designated meeting spot, a sleek conference room with glass walls that offer a panoramic view of the bustling street below, I can feel my excitement bubbling just beneath the surface. The air hums with possibility, and I can't help but imagine the myriad ways our ideas might take flight, transforming our initial concepts into a campaign that captivates and enchants.

Emma is already seated at the large oval table, a laptop open in front of her and a collection of documents neatly arranged. She glances up as I enter, a sly smile playing on her lips, as if she's been waiting for this moment—this potential collision of minds. "I hope you're ready to elevate this project," she says, her tone both teasing and sincere. "I have a few thoughts that might just blow your mind."

"Bring it on," I reply, matching her energy.

She leans forward, her eyes glimmering with excitement. "So, I was thinking we could integrate a social media challenge into the launch. Something interactive, maybe tied to the app's features. It'll create buzz, and we can engage directly with our target audience."

I nod, enthusiasm igniting within me. "That's brilliant! We could use influencers to amplify the reach. Imagine the user-generated content that would pour in!"

As we brainstorm, the boundaries of our rivalry begin to dissolve. Our ideas flow effortlessly, merging like streams converging into a river, each concept propelling us further into uncharted territory. Emma's creativity complements my boldness, and together we sculpt a campaign that feels innovative and daring—a reflection of our combined talents.

The hours slip away, punctuated by laughter and a few playful jabs that only strengthen the bond we're forming. We dive deep into the nuances of our campaign, discussing target demographics, media channels, and potential pitfalls. Each revelation feels like a triumph, a testament to our hard work and shared vision. I can't help but admire the way Emma thinks; she possesses a brilliance that challenges me to raise my own game, pushing me further than I thought I could go.

Just as we're wrapping up, Emma leans back in her chair, her expression turning contemplative. "You know, for all the competition and tension, I didn't expect us to work this well together," she admits, her tone surprisingly earnest. "It's nice to collaborate with someone who actually brings fresh ideas to the table instead of just recycling the same old tactics."

Her words resonate deeply, filling me with a sense of validation. "I feel the same. You've got this incredible energy that makes me want to push harder."

As the afternoon sun casts long shadows across the table, we finalize our campaign strategy, a vibrant tapestry of creativity woven from our unique perspectives. The moment feels monumental, an intersection of ambitions that could lead us both to greater heights. With a shared sense of purpose, we decide to present our ideas to Leah, eager to showcase the potential of our collaboration.

When the time comes, we stride into Leah's office, buoyed by our shared enthusiasm. Leah greets us with a raised eyebrow, a hint of skepticism lingering in her gaze, but as we unveil our proposal, that skepticism melts away. Her expression shifts from curiosity to approval, and she leans back in her chair, nodding along as we elaborate on our vision.

"This is impressive work, both of you," Leah finally says, her voice steady and confident. "I love the fresh angle you've taken. If you can pull this off, it could redefine how we approach campaigns for tech startups."

The praise sends a rush of adrenaline through me, a euphoric affirmation of our efforts. Emma and I exchange a glance, a shared moment of victory that solidifies our newfound partnership.

As the days roll on, we immerse ourselves in the project, our connection deepening amid the whirlwind of deadlines and late-night brainstorming sessions. Together, we navigate the unpredictable landscape of the PR world, meeting with clients, pitching ideas, and facing challenges head-on. The office transforms into a second home, a space filled with laughter and shared triumphs, each moment forging a bond that is undeniably electric.

Yet, beneath the surface, the intensity of our rivalry still flickers, a constant reminder of the stakes involved. I catch myself comparing my progress to Emma's, wondering if I'm doing enough to prove myself in this high-stakes environment. She continues to excel, her natural charisma and intellect shining through in every interaction.

One afternoon, as we work late in the office, I watch her as she effortlessly navigates a tricky conversation with a client over the phone. She possesses an innate ability to charm and persuade, weaving through objections with the grace of a dancer. I'm struck by a pang of admiration mixed with envy, and it ignites a fierce determination within me to elevate my own game even further.

"Emma, that was incredible," I say once she hangs up, my voice laced with genuine respect. "How do you do that?"

She shrugs, a modest smile gracing her lips. "It's all about reading the room and adapting. You'll get there. Just trust your instincts."

Her encouragement stirs something within me—a flicker of confidence that begins to take root. With each passing day, I learn more about myself and my capabilities, and it's thrilling. I start to embrace the competition, not as a threat, but as a catalyst for growth.

As the launch day approaches, anticipation electrifies the air. Our campaign takes on a life of its own, bubbling with energy as we coordinate every detail—from social media teasers to event logistics. The pressure mounts, but so does my excitement; I can feel the adrenaline coursing through my veins as I envision the impact we'll have.

The night before the launch, we gather with the team for a final run-through, the atmosphere charged with nervous energy. I glance at Emma, who stands at the center of the room, her confidence radiating like a beacon. It strikes me then, how far we've come from those initial, tense encounters. We've transformed from rivals to partners, our connection forged in the fires of ambition and creativity.

After the meeting, I linger behind, watching as Emma gathers her things. "We did it," I say, feeling a rush of gratitude for our shared journey.

"Yeah, we really did," she replies, her eyes sparkling with excitement. "Whatever happens tomorrow, I'm glad we did it together."

With those words, a weight lifts from my shoulders, a sense of camaraderie that transcends the competition. Together, we stand at the threshold of something monumental, ready to face whatever comes next. And as I leave the office, my heart swells with hope and determination, knowing that this adventure is just the beginning.

## Chapter 2: A Rivalry Ignited

The conference room felt like a shrine to ambition, its glossy mahogany table reflecting the sharp edges of a world poised for success. As I stepped in, a wave of polished shoes and tailored suits flooded my senses, each personality distinct yet layered within the fragrance of expensive cologne and freshly brewed coffee. I took a deep breath, my heart thudding in sync with the ticking clock mounted on the wall, a constant reminder that every second counted in this arena of sharp minds and sharper tongues. Today marked the beginning of my new journey, and the stakes were set sky-high.

I barely had time to adjust my blazer when I noticed him—the firm's golden boy, Ashton Parker. He stood at the far end of the table, illuminated by the afternoon sun that streamed through the expansive windows, casting him in a golden hue that seemed almost otherworldly. His tousled dark hair fell effortlessly over his forehead, and his deep blue eyes sparkled with an intensity that made the air around him vibrate. He had that smile—the kind that could melt a glacier but also seemed to cut through the air like a knife. It was infuriating how he commanded the room, his presence a potent cocktail of charisma and charm.

As our team lead began to outline the objectives of our project—a high-stakes campaign for a luxury skincare brand—I couldn't help but steal glances at Ashton. His confidence was magnetic, yet I felt an electric tension coursing between us, something raw and almost competitive. Every time our eyes met, it was as if we were playing a game where neither of us had agreed on the rules. I was drawn to him, yet simultaneously pushed away by the audacity of his gaze, which felt like a challenge, daring me to keep up.

As the meeting progressed, the discussion swirled around branding strategies and consumer psychology, but all I could focus on was Ashton's laughter—a rich sound that seemed to reverberate within the walls. It punctuated the conversation like the perfect note in a symphony, drawing attention back to him. He threw out ideas with effortless finesse, weaving them into the tapestry of the campaign with the grace of a master storyteller. Meanwhile, I felt the pressure mounting, a swirl of determination igniting within me. I had to prove myself, not just to him but to everyone in the room.

It was during a particularly heated discussion over market demographics that the rivalry truly sparked to life. Ashton leaned back in his chair, arms crossed, his expression amused as he observed me laying out my strategy. "You really think we can target the millennial market with just Instagram ads? That's a bit... basic, don't you think?" he teased, his voice laced with playful condescension.

A flush of annoyance crept up my neck, but I forced a smile, ready to volley back. "And you think a high-budget commercial will resonate with a generation that thrives on authenticity? The world has changed, Ashton. It's not about the glitz anymore; it's about connection." The moment the words left my mouth, I felt the adrenaline rush through me. There was something exhilarating about standing my ground, challenging the golden boy's glimmering facade.

As the meeting wrapped up, the energy shifted, and I could feel Ashton's scrutiny intensifying. I caught him glancing at me from across the room, his expression inscrutable. Beneath that veneer of charm, I sensed a flicker of respect mingling with his competitive spirit. The rivalry had begun, but beneath that simmering tension, there was something more—an unspoken understanding that we were two sides of the same coin, destined to push each other toward greatness.

With the meeting behind us, the team was tasked with brainstorming sessions in smaller groups. I found myself paired with Ashton, much to my mixed feelings. Part of me wanted to bask in the glow of his brilliance, to learn from him, but another part burned with the desire to outshine him. Our discussions danced around creative concepts, our banter weaving a fabric of competition that felt both invigorating and exhausting. I found myself enthralled by his ideas, yet furious at how easily he turned even the most mundane suggestions into captivating proposals.

"Okay, I'll give you this," he said one afternoon, leaning over a stack of marketing reports, his breath sending shivers across my skin. "You have a knack for thinking outside the box. But I still think we should focus on influencer partnerships to reach the younger audience." His words, spoken with that infuriating charm, made my stomach flutter and my resolve harden.

"Influencers? Please," I replied, rolling my eyes for effect, though my heart raced. "It's all about authenticity now. If we can get the brand's voice to resonate with real people, we'll hit our target. Let's build a community, not just a following."

I could see the challenge flare in his eyes as he leaned back, folding his arms across his chest, a smile tugging at his lips. "I like your fire, but we need something flashier. Let's merge our ideas; it could create the perfect balance."

Despite myself, I couldn't help but smile. Perhaps there was a hidden potential in our rivalry. It was a game of chess played with ideas instead of pieces, a clash of ambition and creativity that felt like a duel in a coliseum. The thrill of it was intoxicating, and I realized that this rivalry might not just ignite my passion but could fuel something even deeper between us.

Every day in the office felt like stepping onto a stage, a performance where I could either shine brightly or fade into the shadows. I was determined to rise, to carve my place among the stars, even if it meant battling against the golden boy who seemed to capture the attention of everyone around him. This was not just about the project; it was about proving that I belonged, that my voice mattered in a world that often drowned out the whispers of those like me. The tension lingered, and with each passing day, I felt the flames of rivalry ignite into something that could burn brilliantly—or consume us both whole.

Every morning as I entered the office, the air was thick with possibility, each day a new chance to elevate the campaign. The sleek, minimalist design of the space was as crisp as the ideas that bounced around the room. Glass walls divided the teams, allowing us to peek into the vibrant chaos of creativity that thrummed through the firm. My heart raced as I walked past Ashton's team, who, with their whirlwind of discussions and animated gestures, seemed to pulsate with energy. Despite my earlier resolution to not let him distract me, I could feel his presence like a moth drawn to flame.

Our rivalry had turned into a dance, one that I couldn't help but engage in. There was a rhythm to it: the way he would offer a bold idea, his voice rich with confidence, and I would counter with something unexpected, catching him off guard. Each encounter brought its own thrill—a mixture of exhilaration and irritation that sent adrenaline coursing through my veins. I was becoming addicted to the challenge, to the way he pushed me to think beyond my usual bounds.

One afternoon, we found ourselves huddled over a whiteboard, markers in hand, mapping out a marketing strategy. The room was silent except for the soft scratching of our pens and the occasional hum of conversation from other teams. It was as if the world had narrowed down to just the two of us, our energy crackling like static electricity. I was determined to present my best ideas, to make a mark that would resonate.

"Okay, picture this," Ashton began, leaning in closer, his voice low, almost conspiratorial. "What if we create a series of short films that showcase the transformative effects of the products? We can blend storytelling with visuals that really capture the essence of the brand." He turned to look at me, eyes glinting with enthusiasm.

I paused, considering the potential. "That could work," I admitted, "but what if we also include customer testimonials, real stories that highlight authenticity? It will add a layer of trust. The beauty market thrives on the narrative of real experiences."

His brows shot up, and for a split second, surprise washed over his features before he nodded slowly, contemplating my suggestion. "That's actually brilliant," he conceded, his expression shifting from competitive to genuinely impressed. "A perfect marriage of your idea and mine."

The realization sent a thrill through me. In this competitive dance, I was starting to see the value in collaboration. We were no longer just rivals; we were beginning to weave our ideas into something far more compelling than either of us could have achieved alone. Each time our eyes met, there was a flicker of understanding, a hint of camaraderie buried beneath our competitive banter.

As days turned into weeks, the project took shape, and our rivalry evolved into an exhilarating partnership. Late nights spent crafting presentations and the adrenaline of brainstorming sessions fueled a growing connection between us. We became the dynamic duo of the office, our synergy undeniable. Colleagues began to notice the chemistry, commenting on how well we played off each other. I would catch glimpses of Ashton's thoughtful glances as I spoke, his genuine interest adding a softness to our exchanges that I hadn't anticipated.

One evening, as we worked late, the fluorescent lights cast a soft glow over the office, creating an almost intimate atmosphere. The usual bustling energy had quieted, leaving only the sound of our laughter echoing in the hollow space. Ashton leaned back in his chair, his expression contemplative. "You know, I was warned about you," he said, a teasing lilt in his voice.

"Warned? About me? What did they say?" I shot back, feigning offense, though curiosity piqued within me.

"That you were ruthless and wouldn't hesitate to trample over anyone who got in your way." He chuckled, his eyes sparkling. "But I think they were wrong. You're fierce, yes, but you're also driven by something deeper."

The admission caught me off guard, my breath hitching. "Driven? By what exactly?" I pressed, intrigued.

"Passion. You genuinely care about what you're doing, and it shows," he replied, his tone earnest now, peeling back the layers of our rivalry to reveal a deeper understanding. "That's rare in this industry. It's easy to get lost in the glitz and glam of it all, but you remind me why we're here."

His words resonated within me, sending warmth flooding through my chest. The intensity of our rivalry had evolved into something far more complex, and while the competitive spark was still there, it was now infused with mutual respect and a hint of admiration. I found myself wanting to impress him not just as a competitor but as a collaborator.

The campaign launched, and the response was overwhelming. Social media buzzed with excitement, and the feedback from the client was nothing short of ecstatic. I could feel the adrenaline surging through me, the sweet taste of success a heady concoction. In those moments of triumph, I realized how much I relished working alongside Ashton.

In the midst of our celebration, we were invited to a high-profile launch event for the skincare brand, a lavish affair set in a sprawling mansion overlooking the city. As I donned my favorite navy dress, I caught my reflection, the confidence swirling within me as palpable as the fabric that clung to my skin. I wanted to make an impression, not just on the guests but on Ashton, who would undoubtedly be the center of attention.

The night was a spectacle of opulence, with golden chandeliers cascading light over elegantly dressed guests sipping champagne and exchanging pleasantries. Ashton's presence in the crowd was magnetic, his laughter ringing out like a siren's call, drawing everyone toward him. I could see the glances he received, admiration mixed with envy. Yet, there I was, a flicker of defiance in my heart as I strode toward him, determined to shine in my own right.

"Look at you," he remarked, his gaze appraising yet sincere, a playful grin splitting his face. "You clean up well."

"Coming from you, that's quite the compliment," I replied, matching his smile with my own.

As the evening unfolded, we mingled with influential figures, our banter flowing seamlessly as we navigated conversations. Each shared laugh seemed to deepen the bond we were forming, and I reveled in the dynamic that had developed between us—a combination of rivalry and undeniable chemistry.

As the night drew to a close, I felt a spark of something more lingering in the air, an undercurrent that swirled just beneath the surface. This rivalry, once a mere competition, was morphing into a connection that could lead to unforeseen possibilities. With each glance exchanged and each teasing remark, I couldn't shake the feeling that we were on the brink of something entirely new, something that could ignite the spark of creativity in both our professional and personal lives. In this vibrant tapestry of ambition and allure, Ashton and I were woven together, two opposing forces drawing closer as the allure of success ignited a flame neither of us could ignore.

The weeks that followed the campaign launch were a whirlwind of activity, each day blurring into the next with the frenetic pace of an office that thrived on ambition. Our project had taken off like a rocket, catapulting both Ashton and me into the spotlight. The whirlwind of late nights and endless brainstorming sessions had not only fueled our rivalry but had also woven a complex tapestry of camaraderie that left me exhilarated and bewildered. I had never anticipated that a competition could feel so much like collaboration, that the spark of our antagonism could ignite a deeper connection.

As the buzz around our campaign continued to grow, the firm decided to host a celebratory gathering at a trendy rooftop bar, a glittering oasis perched high above the city. The evening sky was painted in hues of lavender and gold, the sun setting behind the skyline, casting long shadows and transforming the ordinary into the extraordinary. The view was breathtaking, but it paled in comparison to the energy thrumming between Ashton and me as we navigated the mingling crowd.

The atmosphere crackled with excitement as laughter mingled with clinking glasses. I felt a rush of adrenaline, heightened by the anticipation of what this night might bring. The moment Ashton appeared beside me, his playful grin framed by the shimmering city lights, my heart skipped. He leaned in closer, his voice barely above the music. "Ready to celebrate our success?"

"Only if you promise not to hog all the attention," I quipped, nudging him playfully. The banter felt natural, easy, as if we had been dancing this dance for years rather than just weeks.

As the night unfolded, we moved through the crowd like a well-rehearsed duet, exchanging witty repartees while effortlessly charming those around us. The shared glances, the casual brushes of our hands as we reached for the same hors d'oeuvre, ignited a heat between us that felt tangible, almost electric. Yet, just beneath that playful surface, I felt the sharp edge of competition simmering, an undercurrent that kept me on my toes.

When it came time to make a toast, the room quieted, the vibrant energy coalescing into a single, expectant moment. Ashton raised his glass, his gaze sweeping over the gathering. "To teamwork," he began, a teasing smile gracing his lips, "and to the fierce competitor who kept me on my toes."

Laughter erupted around us, and I could feel heat rising to my cheeks, caught between embarrassment and pride. I lifted my glass, responding, "To collaboration, and to the golden boy who's surprisingly not as infuriating as I thought." The toast drew a chorus of cheers, and I relished the connection we had forged, the lines of rivalry blurring into something far more complicated.

The evening morphed into a series of shared stories and laughter that wrapped around us like a warm blanket. As the night wore on, the laughter gave way to deeper conversations, and I found myself drawn to Ashton in a way that felt both thrilling and terrifying. We sat together, the cacophony of voices fading into the background, the city skyline shimmering in the distance.

"Why do you really do this?" he asked, his expression suddenly serious, cutting through the playful facade we had built around ourselves. "What drives you?"

I hesitated, the question unearthing layers of vulnerability I hadn't expected to confront. "Honestly? I want to make a difference, to create something that resonates with people. The beauty of this industry is in its potential to connect, to tell stories that matter," I confessed, the words flowing more freely than I anticipated. "What about you? You always seem so... at ease."

Ashton ran a hand through his hair, his gaze distant for a moment. "I think it's about the thrill of the chase for me. The competition, the rush of seeing ideas come to life. But there's also a part of me that wants to prove something—not just to others, but to myself. That I can create something meaningful."

The honesty in his voice caught me off guard, revealing a depth that contradicted the confident facade he often projected. In that moment, I realized that beneath the layers of charm and charisma, Ashton was just as driven and passionate as I was. Perhaps this rivalry wasn't just about competition; perhaps it was a mirror reflecting our own insecurities and aspirations.

As the night wore on, the space between us began to shrink, the laughter softening into a comfortable silence. I could see the flicker of curiosity in Ashton's eyes as he leaned in closer, the energy between us shifting from playful rivalry to something that felt dangerously intimate. It was in that moment that I understood the stakes had escalated.

Our connection was undeniable, and yet, the fear of crossing that invisible line held me back. I could sense Ashton's hesitation, too, a shared understanding that we were both standing on the precipice of something profound. The vibrant cityscape stretched out behind us, a kaleidoscope of lights that mirrored the chaos and excitement of our burgeoning relationship.

As the event came to a close, I found myself lingering, reluctant to part ways. Ashton caught my gaze, a flicker of mischief dancing in his eyes. "Want to grab a late-night snack? I know a place that serves the best tacos in town."

My stomach rumbled at the mention, and I nodded, eager to extend our evening. We slipped away from the bar, the cool night air brushing against my skin as we made our way to a small food truck parked around the corner. The neon lights flickered overhead, casting a warm glow that made everything feel more vibrant.

As we munched on tacos, the conversation flowed effortlessly. We swapped stories of our childhoods, revealing glimpses of vulnerability that felt refreshing amidst the competitive landscape we had navigated. I learned about Ashton's upbringing, the pressure to excel in a world that expected perfection. He listened intently as I shared my own journey, the struggles and triumphs that had shaped my path.

As the hours slipped away, the boundaries between rivalry and companionship began to blur. In the laughter, the shared stories, and the easy camaraderie, I felt a shift within me. This was more than a competition; this was a partnership, a connection that had the potential to grow into something beautiful.

Yet, as we finished our tacos and stepped back into the night, I felt a familiar pang of uncertainty. What did this mean for us? Could we maintain our professional rivalry while exploring this unexpected bond? The world around me shimmered with possibility, but beneath it all lay the reality of our ambitions and the very real fear of losing the spark that had ignited between us.

In the days that followed, our relationship deepened as we continued to navigate the challenges of the campaign, each brainstorming session infused with a newfound warmth. I could sense that the tension had transformed; we were no longer simply competitors but allies who inspired each other to reach new heights. The stakes were still high, but now we faced them together, our shared aspirations creating a bond that felt unbreakable.

As the campaign reached its zenith, I found myself standing on the cusp of something extraordinary. With Ashton by my side, I was ready to embrace the journey ahead—both the challenges and the unexpected turns that would shape our paths. In a world that thrived on competition, we had discovered the power of connection, a vibrant collaboration that ignited not just our careers but our hearts as well. Together, we would navigate the chaos of ambition and passion, forging a path that was uniquely ours, filled with promise and possibility.

# Chapter 3: Breaking the Rules

A steady hum of anticipation filled the air as we gathered in the sleek, glass-walled conference room that overlooked the vibrant heart of downtown Chicago. The sun poured through the floor-to-ceiling windows, bathing the space in a warm golden glow, illuminating the sharp edges of the sleek furniture and the glossy surface of the long conference table. My team, a motley crew of creatives and analysts, buzzed with energy, their voices mingling like the sounds of a bustling café. I leaned back in my chair, the cool leather wrapping around me like a comforting embrace as I gazed out at the urban tapestry below—the honking taxis, the rhythmic footsteps of pedestrians, and the tantalizing aroma of street food wafting through the open windows. The city felt alive, pulsing with possibilities, much like the campaign we were about to unleash.

Then there was Ashton, the thorn in my side, sitting at the head of the table with his signature smirk plastered across his face, the very embodiment of confidence. He wore his dark hair slightly tousled, as if he'd just stepped off a film set where he played the lead in a romantic comedy. He thrived on the tension he created, his charisma wrapping around him like an alluring mist. I could sense the competitive electricity crackling between us, a dance of attraction tangled with irritation. It was maddening yet undeniably intoxicating.

As the clock ticked steadily toward noon, he finally broke the ice. "Ladies and gentlemen, I present to you the opportunity of a lifetime," he announced, his voice smooth like velvet, sending shivers of both excitement and dread down my spine. "We're going to do something no one expects. We're going to disrupt the entire market."

His proposition hung in the air, an uninvited guest at a dinner party. I could feel the collective breath of my team hitch. "Ashton," I interjected, the words tumbling out before I could restrain them, "we can't just waltz into this and throw caution to the wind. What you're suggesting is reckless."

He leaned forward, eyes glinting with a mix of challenge and amusement. "Reckless? Or revolutionary? Sometimes, you have to break the rules to make a mark. We have to stand out, Riley. You know that better than anyone."

I felt my heart race, the rush of adrenaline mixing with an undeniable thrill. He was right, but there was a line between ambition and folly, and I wasn't sure I was ready to dance on it. I had always prided myself on my integrity, the unyielding belief that creativity should be both innovative and ethical. But here he was, tempting me to let go of the reins, to abandon my cautious approach for a taste of the exhilarating unknown.

The room buzzed with murmurs, the other team members caught between their loyalty to me and their intrigue toward Ashton's audacious proposal. The stakes had never been higher, and the tension was palpable. My stomach churned as I shifted in my seat, the weight of their expectations pressing down on me.

"I get it, Ashton. But there's a reason why these rules exist. They keep us grounded," I replied, my voice firmer than I felt. "If we take this risk and it backfires, we lose everything."

"Or we gain everything," he countered, his gaze unwavering, like a magnetic force drawing me closer. "Imagine the headlines, the buzz, the clients we'll attract. We can't just play safe; we need to redefine the game."

For a fleeting moment, I entertained the idea, picturing the vibrant billboards lighting up the skyline, our campaign emblazoned across social media feeds. It was thrilling, the thought of pushing boundaries, yet terrifying, the fear of losing everything I had worked for. Ashton's passion ignited something deep within me—a yearning to break free from the constraints of conventional thinking and step into the exhilarating chaos of the unknown.

"Riley?" His voice cut through my thoughts, pulling me back to the reality of the room. The team watched me expectantly, a mix of excitement and apprehension etched on their faces. "I can see you're tempted. Let's think about what we could achieve if we combine our strengths. You're the visionary; I'm the risk-taker. Together, we could create something truly revolutionary."

The challenge in his eyes stirred something within me, a concoction of frustration and longing that I couldn't ignore. I wanted to scold him for being so reckless, yet I was equally drawn to his audacity. The line between admiration and irritation blurred, leaving me dizzy.

"Okay, let's say we entertain this idea," I relented, my heart racing as I spoke. "What's the plan?"

His grin widened, infectious and reckless. "We'll create an immersive experience that pulls people in, something that feels like a secret club—a community. We'll launch a guerilla marketing strategy that invites our audience to participate in the narrative. It's about creating a buzz, Riley, making them feel part of something bigger."

I could almost feel the pulse of the city syncing with the heartbeat of our ambition. The thrill of the unknown called to me, a siren song echoing through the vibrant streets outside. I was teetering on the edge of a precipice, and Ashton was holding out his hand, urging me to take the leap.

"But," I pressed, my voice barely above a whisper, "if we do this, there's no turning back. We'll have to be fully committed. Are you ready for that?"

The smirk faded for a moment, replaced by a serious glint in his eyes that sent a shiver down my spine. "I was born ready."

In that moment, standing at the crossroads of ambition and caution, I felt a surge of daring swell within me. Perhaps it was the intoxicating blend of the Chicago skyline beyond the glass or the thrill of challenging norms alongside Ashton, but the idea of letting go of my reservations beckoned me. I took a deep breath, bracing myself for the thrilling chaos that awaited.

The afternoon sun shifted, casting long shadows across the conference room as we dove deeper into the labyrinth of brainstorming and strategizing. I felt a whirl of emotions—an intoxicating blend of anxiety and exhilaration—swirling in my chest like the winds that whipped through the streets of Chicago on a crisp autumn day. Each idea tossed around felt like a precarious dance, teetering on the edge of brilliance and recklessness. The buzz of the team, normally a comforting hum, now felt electric, heightened by the stakes of the audacious campaign we were about to unleash.

Ashton had a way of making the ordinary feel extraordinary, transforming mundane meetings into an arena of innovation and excitement. With each proposal, he flicked at the edges of my comfort zone, urging me to step beyond the safe boundaries I had meticulously erected. I watched him, captivated and irritated in equal measure. His enthusiasm was contagious, sparking a flicker of rebellion in my own heart. Yet, a voice in the back of my mind warned me of the fine line between creativity and chaos.

He leaned back in his chair, a playful glint in his eyes as he surveyed our team. "Imagine this," he said, his voice low but charged with enthusiasm. "We set up pop-up experiences across the city—places where people can not only engage with our brand but become part of the narrative. We could have a flash mob in Millennium Park, a scavenger hunt leading to our main event, and a massive reveal that will have everyone talking."

My mind raced, grappling with the thrilling possibilities, but a nagging doubt lingered. "Ashton, that's a lot to orchestrate in such a short time. What if it flops? We'll have invested so much time and energy for a gamble that could backfire."

"Or we could capture the city's imagination," he countered, leaning forward, his voice thick with conviction. "Look at the brands that have become household names—what do they all have in common? They dared to take risks. They didn't play it safe, Riley. They made people feel something."

His words echoed in my mind, like a mantra urging me to abandon my cautious tendencies. I imagined the vibrant scenes he painted—people laughing, engaging, sharing. The thought of transforming our campaign into an exhilarating experience sparked a fire within me, a yearning to let go of the reins and allow creativity to soar. Yet, with every heartbeat, the worry gnawed at my insides. Was I truly ready to dive headfirst into this chaotic adventure, risking everything I had worked for?

"Okay," I finally said, my voice steady yet tinged with uncertainty. "Let's brainstorm a little more. If we do this, we need to ensure that every aspect reflects our brand's values. We can't lose sight of that."

Ashton nodded, a triumphant grin spreading across his face. "Exactly. We'll create an experience that not only captivates but also resonates. It will be memorable and meaningful. We can have local artists, musicians, and influencers collaborate with us. It'll be a celebration of community."

The room hummed with energy as we bounced ideas off one another, our voices intertwining like the lively conversations that filled the cafés below. Each suggestion built upon the last, and I found myself swept up in the momentum, my initial hesitations slowly melting away under the warmth of our shared ambition. Ashton's passion ignited something dormant within me, a willingness to embrace the chaotic beauty of creativity.

But amid the excitement, a part of me remained cautious, an inner voice whispering reminders of the possible repercussions. I could already hear the critics, the naysayers, questioning our decisions if this bold venture didn't pan out. My thoughts flickered back to the quiet evenings I spent alone, meticulously crafting strategies that had always kept us grounded. I had earned my place here, and now, with Ashton leading us down this uncertain path, I questioned whether I was losing sight of my own values.

As we finalized the details of our plan, the adrenaline coursing through my veins surged, tinged with uncertainty. I couldn't deny the thrill of working alongside Ashton, the rush of creativity that bubbled between us as we pushed the limits of our campaign. There was something undeniably magnetic about his presence, the way he drew out my passion while simultaneously aggravating my meticulous nature.

Later, as the sun dipped below the skyline, painting the city in hues of orange and purple, we gathered for a quick dinner in a cozy bistro nestled on a quiet street, its rustic charm a comforting contrast to the modern chaos outside. The intimate setting felt worlds away from the corporate environment we had just left. I watched as Ashton animatedly recounted tales of past campaigns, his gestures lively, his laughter infectious. The room pulsed with an energy that felt alive, a celebration of our newfound camaraderie.

"Do you ever worry about the fallout if this doesn't work?" I asked, my fork pausing mid-air, curiosity gnawing at me. I couldn't help but wonder how someone so effortlessly daring could dance so freely with the risk of failure.

"Every time I take a step into the unknown," he admitted, his tone shifting, revealing a glimpse of vulnerability beneath his bravado. "But that's the beauty of it, isn't it? The thrill of pushing past our limits, of tasting the possibility of greatness. It's worth it to me, even if it means falling flat on my face."

His candor struck a chord, resonating deep within me. I admired his audacity, the way he made risks feel like opportunities rather than threats. Yet, the fear of losing everything still lingered in the shadows of my mind, a constant reminder of the stakes at hand.

As our plates cleared and the laughter continued to flow, I felt the magnetic tension between us thickening, an undeniable chemistry igniting the air around us. Each shared glance, every accidental brush of our hands sent jolts of electricity coursing through me, intensifying my internal struggle. Was I truly willing to blur the lines of professionalism for the sake of this reckless endeavor and my growing feelings for him?

The evening faded into a warm, inviting twilight, the city bustling with life outside the windows, unaware of the conflict brewing within me. I had willingly chosen to leap into this chaotic whirlwind alongside Ashton, and as my heart raced with both excitement and trepidation, I couldn't shake the feeling that this journey would reshape not only our campaign but also the very fabric of who I was becoming. In this vivid tapestry of ambition, fear, and undeniable attraction, I was determined to find my way, even if it meant dancing dangerously close to the edge.

The days leading up to our campaign launch unfolded like a well-timed symphony, each note resonating with a mixture of anxiety and exhilaration. I found myself caught in a whirlwind of late-night brainstorming sessions, coffee-fueled debates, and the intoxicating chaos that only comes from pushing the envelope. The excitement in our office had reached fever pitch, the air thick with creativity as our vision began to take shape. Every time I glanced at Ashton, leaning against the wall with that unshakeable confidence, I felt a thrill ripple through me—a heady blend of admiration and frustration that seemed to bind us together.

We had decided to meet after work hours to fine-tune our strategy. The city outside transformed into a mosaic of twinkling lights, casting an enchanting glow across the conference table where we spread out our sketches, ideas, and fervent aspirations. It was a raw and vulnerable moment, an unveiling of dreams, and I found myself immersed in the electricity of the room.

Ashton flicked through our visuals, his brow furrowed with a mix of concentration and excitement. "This is it," he said, the intensity in his voice palpable. "We're not just selling a product; we're selling an experience. We'll have people participating in our story, engaging with our brand on a visceral level. Think of it as a narrative arc—each touchpoint leading them deeper into the plot."

I leaned forward, drawn into his vision, the fervor in his voice igniting my own passion. "But we have to be careful. We can't lose sight of our values. Each experience must be authentic and aligned with what we stand for." I felt a flicker of uncertainty as the pressure mounted, a weight pressing against my chest, threatening to suffocate the excitement that had been building.

"Authenticity is key," he agreed, nodding vigorously. "We'll partner with local artists and influencers who embody our brand ethos. It's not just a campaign; it's a celebration of the city and its culture. And trust me, when people feel the pulse of their community in our brand, it will create an undeniable connection."

His enthusiasm was contagious, washing over me like a warm wave. As we dissected each element, I became increasingly entranced, the tension between us shifting from frustration to an exhilarating synergy. The ideas flowed freely, and for every suggestion I offered, Ashton met it with fervor, weaving our visions into a tapestry that felt both daring and deeply resonant.

But amidst the whirlwind of creativity, doubts continued to lurk in the back of my mind. The closer we drew to the launch, the more I found myself grappling with the balance between professional integrity and the intoxicating thrill of pushing boundaries. I didn't want to be swept away entirely by Ashton's reckless abandon, yet his magnetic energy pulled me closer, enticing me to embrace the chaos.

The night before our grand reveal, we gathered for a final run-through in the office. The air was electric with anticipation, each member of our team buzzing with nervous energy. As I glanced around the room, I could see the sparks of creativity igniting in everyone's eyes, a collective belief in the vision we were about to share with the world. The coffee cups stacked precariously on the table became a makeshift shrine to our late nights and relentless determination.

"Alright, team," I announced, standing to address everyone. "Tomorrow is not just about what we're selling; it's about how we make people feel. We're creating an experience, a moment they'll carry with them. Let's remind them that our brand is not just a name; it's a community."

Applause echoed in the room, a sound of unity and shared ambition that warmed my heart. Ashton caught my gaze, a flicker of admiration sparking in his eyes. The connection between us felt stronger than ever, a silent agreement that we were about to embark on an unforgettable journey together.

As the clock inched closer to midnight, I gathered my things and prepared to head home, the city still alive outside the window. The moon cast a silver sheen across the streets, illuminating the world in a surreal glow. I paused to take it all in, my heart racing with excitement and uncertainty. The boundaries we were about to cross felt exhilarating, like standing on the edge of a precipice, ready to dive into the unknown.

The next morning arrived with a cacophony of sounds—honking cars, laughter spilling from coffee shops, and the vibrant energy of a city awakening. My heart raced as I made my way to the venue, anticipation coursing through my veins. The space was transformed, a kaleidoscope of color and sound that invited passersby to step inside our world.

Ashton was already there, moving with a frenetic energy as he directed the setup, a whirlwind of enthusiasm and charisma. The moment I stepped inside, I was enveloped in the infectious spirit he had ignited in everyone. "Riley!" he called, his face lighting up as he spotted me. "Look at this place! It's perfect!"

I smiled, the excitement bubbling within me. "It really is. You've outdone yourself." The decorations danced around us, a playful mix of bold colors and captivating displays that captured the essence of our brand and the city itself.

As the hours sped by, the space filled with laughter and chatter, people eagerly engaging with the immersive experiences we had created. I watched in awe as participants dove into our narrative, sharing their stories and connecting with one another. The buzz in the air was intoxicating, a symphony of joy and celebration that transcended mere marketing. It felt alive, pulsating with the heartbeat of the city we loved.

As the evening sun began to dip below the horizon, casting a warm glow through the windows, Ashton and I found ourselves on the terrace overlooking the skyline. The city glimmered like a treasure chest beneath us, and in that moment, I felt an overwhelming sense of accomplishment and connection. The boundary between us, once defined by irritation and rivalry, had begun to blur into something deeper, more intricate.

"Can you believe how well this is going?" Ashton asked, his voice barely above a whisper as he leaned against the railing, eyes fixed on the vibrant scene below. "We did this, Riley. Together."

"I know," I replied, my heart racing, caught in the whirlwind of emotions swirling between us. "It's more than I ever imagined."

He turned to me, his gaze intense, a flicker of vulnerability shining through. "You know, I couldn't have done this without you. You kept me grounded when I was tempted to fly too close to the sun."

For a heartbeat, everything else faded into the background, the city below us becoming a blur as I focused solely on him. The connection we shared, once riddled with tension and uncertainty, felt as if it had blossomed into something rich and profound. In that fleeting moment, I realized that we were no longer just two competing forces; we had become partners in a dance, weaving our dreams into the very fabric of the city.

But the question loomed—what would this mean for us? As I looked into Ashton's eyes, I could feel the intensity of the moment pressing down, inviting me to take a leap into the unknown. I had embraced the chaos of this campaign, but could I also embrace the unpredictability of my feelings for him?

As the sun set, casting the city in a magical twilight, I knew that the adventure had only just begun. Whatever awaited us beyond this campaign, one thing was clear: I was ready to navigate the uncertain waters of ambition, integrity, and undeniable chemistry, hand in hand with Ashton, even if it meant bending the rules along the way.

# Chapter 4: The Unexpected Proposal

The sun dipped low over the shimmering expanse of Lake Evergreen, casting a golden hue across the water that mirrored the colors of a forgotten postcard. The air buzzed with the sounds of summer, cicadas chirping a melodic symphony while the gentle breeze rustled the leaves of towering pines. I had barely stepped out of my car, a dusty old hatchback that clashed with the beauty surrounding it, when I felt the weight of the weekend press against my chest. An unexpected proposal had landed me in this picturesque retreat—a cabin cloaked in tranquility, far removed from the frenetic energy of the city.

Ashton stood by the dock, hands shoved into the pockets of his faded jeans, the sun glinting off his unruly hair, giving him an almost ethereal glow. He looked out at the water, and for a moment, I dared to believe he was contemplating something profound. Perhaps he was thinking about our rivalry, which had always been a fiery, competitive dance—each of us vying for the top spot, a battle of wits and relentless ambition. But now, here we were, together, in a space that felt too intimate for two rivals and yet charged with possibilities that made my heart race.

I hesitated at the edge of the cabin's porch, the scent of pine and earth grounding me, urging me to tread carefully. The soft creak of the wood beneath my feet seemed to echo the uncertainty rippling through me. Was this retreat simply a strategic move on Ashton's part, a way to gain an advantage? Or was there something more lurking beneath his confident façade? My instincts told me to keep my guard up, but the allure of the setting, coupled with the magnetic pull I felt towards him, made it hard to resist.

Inside, the cabin exuded rustic charm. Sunlight poured through the tall windows, illuminating the pine furniture and the inviting stone fireplace. A woven rug lay spread across the wooden floor, softening the otherwise stark edges of the room. The kitchen, a warm heart of the cabin, beckoned with the promise of shared meals and late-night discussions. As I stepped inside, the warmth wrapped around me like a comforting blanket, erasing the chill of doubt that had clung to me since I had agreed to this absurd weekend.

Ashton turned towards me, his eyes reflecting the sunlight with a twinkle that felt both familiar and unsettling. "I hope you're ready to dive in," he said, his voice rich and smooth, reminiscent of the sweet tea I always craved on sweltering afternoons. "We've got a lot of brainstorming to do, and I don't intend to let you off the hook."

"Is that so?" I countered, crossing my arms, a playful smirk creeping onto my face. I had to remind myself that this wasn't some romantic getaway, but rather a battleground cloaked in the guise of collaboration. "Just don't expect me to hold back. I'm not about to let you run the show."

As we began our work, a tension settled between us—one that was both electric and unnerving. We sprawled on the plush couches, surrounded by notes and charts, the competitive spirit igniting every idea we tossed around. With each laugh that escaped my lips, every playful jab exchanged, I felt the carefully constructed walls around my heart begin to soften. The evening stretched before us, the darkness wrapping around the cabin like a velvet cloak, and the flickering light from the fireplace danced shadows across our faces, creating an ambiance that was too intimate for mere colleagues.

The chemistry between us was palpable, igniting every shared moment with a spark that left me breathless. As we debated strategies, I couldn't help but steal glances at Ashton. He was animated, his gestures grand as he spoke, and I felt a rush of admiration. There was something undeniably charming about his passion, a spark that drew me in and made me momentarily forget that I was supposed to be focused on our competition.

After hours of discussion, we decided to take a break, venturing outside to inhale the crisp night air. The stars were scattered across the sky like a million tiny diamonds, and the lake shimmered under their glow, whispering secrets only the night could hold. I leaned against the railing of the porch, soaking in the serenity, when I felt Ashton's presence beside me.

"Beautiful, isn't it?" he murmured, his voice low, almost reverent.

I nodded, unable to articulate the jumble of emotions swirling inside me. "It really is," I said finally, my gaze still locked on the lake. "It's easy to forget how stunning nature can be when you're buried in spreadsheets and meetings."

For a moment, silence enveloped us, and I could feel the weight of unspoken words hanging in the air. Ashton shifted slightly, and I stole a glance at him. His expression was thoughtful, almost vulnerable, as if he were grappling with something heavy on his mind. The light from the cabin flickered, momentarily illuminating the shadows of uncertainty that danced in his eyes.

"Listen, I know we've always been at odds," he began, his tone shifting. "But I think there's more to what we can create together than just competition."

My heart skipped a beat. His words hung between us, thick with implication. I wanted to dismiss them, to focus on the strategies we had mapped out. But the sincerity in his voice and the way he looked at me made it hard to ignore the possibility that he was hinting at something deeper—something that could unravel the careful fabric of our rivalry and weave a new, unexpected narrative.

The chemistry thickened, blurring the lines we had drawn in the sand, and I couldn't shake the feeling that this weekend held more than just plans and strategies. It was a turning point, a precipice from which we might either leap into something uncharted or retreat back into the safety of our competitive roles.

The night deepened, wrapping the cabin in a cocoon of silence punctuated only by the gentle lapping of waves against the shore and the occasional rustle of leaves. It was intoxicatingly serene, the kind of environment where whispered secrets felt sacred, and I found myself reveling in this unexpected escape from the relentless pace of our daily lives. I leaned against the railing, letting the cool wood press against my back, drawing strength from the earthiness of the cabin. Ashton was beside me, his gaze lost somewhere in the depths of the lake, and I couldn't help but wonder what thoughts were flickering through his mind like the stars above.

The stillness felt like a pause, a breath held in anticipation of something profound. A sudden breeze swept through, tousling my hair and carrying with it the faint scent of pine and something sweet—maybe the lingering hint of marshmallows from earlier. I could almost taste the memories we were crafting. Each moment was a stitch in a tapestry that felt richer than the one we had meticulously woven in the boardroom, filled with competition and rivalry.

"You know," I ventured, breaking the spell of quiet, "I didn't expect to enjoy this as much as I have. I thought it would be all work and no play."

Ashton turned his head, a smile creeping across his face, one that transformed his serious demeanor into something almost boyish. "Oh, you thought I would let it be all work? You clearly underestimated my ability to distract."

"Distract?" I echoed, raising an eyebrow. "Is that what you call this?"

He laughed, a sound so rich and genuine that it filled the night air, softening the edges of the tension that had lingered between us all weekend. "Maybe I'm just trying to win you over with charm instead of spreadsheets."

I rolled my eyes, but the flutter in my stomach betrayed me. "It's not working, you know."

"Isn't it?" he countered, stepping closer, his warmth radiating like the heat from the fireplace inside. "You're here, aren't you? You could have easily backed out, but you didn't."

Caught off guard, I faced him fully, the distance between us shrinking in the soft glow of the moonlight. "I came here because I didn't want to lose," I admitted, my voice barely above a whisper. "But now? Now, I'm starting to wonder if I should be worried about more than just our competition."

He held my gaze, those vibrant eyes searching mine, as if trying to decipher a code. "What do you mean?"

For a moment, I considered deflecting, retreating behind my carefully constructed defenses. But the truth spilled out before I could second-guess myself. "I mean... I didn't think we could connect like this. I didn't expect to enjoy your company, let alone find myself... drawn to you."

Ashton's expression shifted, the playful glimmer replaced by something deeper, more serious. "I feel it too," he confessed, his voice low and steady. "But this weekend was supposed to be about collaboration, not feelings."

"Collaboration? Or maybe it was just an excuse to get me alone," I teased, but the playful edge to my voice was waning, replaced by an undeniable vulnerability.

He smiled faintly, the shadows of doubt flickering in his eyes. "Maybe a bit of both."

Before I could respond, he turned, moving back towards the cabin, the moment stretching like the silence that followed. I hesitated, heart racing, knowing that whatever had just passed between us was not just a fleeting spark; it was something electric, begging for attention. The retreat had morphed from a strategic meeting into a deepening connection that left me bewildered.

Inside, the cozy ambiance enveloped us once again, our discussions resuming with a sense of urgency. We sketched plans across the coffee table, brainstorming ideas as laughter echoed off the cabin walls. The more time we spent together, the more the lines between competition and camaraderie blurred. Ideas flowed like the wine we poured, each sip loosening the gravity of our rivalry, allowing creativity to flourish in a way that felt both exhilarating and dangerous.

As the hours slipped away, we found ourselves huddled close on the couch, maps and charts strewn around us like confetti. I had lost track of time, the night draping us in its velvety embrace, and in this cocoon, I felt an inexplicable sense of comfort. Our knees brushed against each other, and every accidental touch sent a ripple of awareness shooting through me.

"Okay," I said, my fingers tracing the edge of a plan we had just developed, "what if we incorporate some unconventional tactics? Something that feels... unexpected?"

"Like what? Flash mobs?" Ashton quipped, his eyes twinkling with mischief.

"Maybe not flash mobs, but think about it—if we shake things up, we could grab attention in a way our competitors won't see coming."

"Now you're talking," he grinned, leaning forward, enthusiasm igniting his features. "I like where your head's at."

As we fleshed out our ideas, the conversation flowed naturally, punctuated by laughter and the kind of chemistry that felt as intoxicating as the wine. Each plan became an anchor, pulling me deeper into a realm where our rivalry transformed into something richer, more layered. I could feel the air between us thickening, a tension wrapped in excitement, like the moments before a storm.

Eventually, we sank back into the cushions, spent from our brainstorming session. The world outside was cloaked in shadows, and the only light that filled the room was the soft glow of the fire. I felt a sense of peace settle around us, a calm after the storm of ideas, and in that stillness, I caught Ashton watching me.

"What?" I asked, my heart thudding loudly in the quiet.

"You just look... different," he said, his voice soft, the intensity of his gaze unwavering. "Less competitive, more... relaxed."

"Maybe you've finally worn me down," I teased, though inside, I was wrestling with my own emotions. "Or maybe I'm just drunk on the lake air."

"No, it's not that," he insisted, the weight of his gaze pressing on me, a seriousness breaking through our playful banter. "I think you're letting your guard down."

The words hung in the air, thick with unspoken implications. I could feel the butterflies in my stomach fluttering wildly, and suddenly, I was acutely aware of everything—the warmth of the cabin, the flicker of the flames, and the intensity of Ashton's gaze piercing through the shadows. The moment felt suspended, as if time had folded in on itself, allowing us to exist in this little bubble away from the world outside.

But the tension was laced with something unnameable, something that felt like it could shift at any moment, and I couldn't shake the feeling that Ashton was holding something back, a secret waiting to unravel beneath the surface of our newfound connection.

The glow from the fireplace flickered, casting playful shadows on the cabin walls, and I found myself lost in the rhythmic crackling of the wood as we sat in a cozy silence. I could feel the warmth radiating from Ashton beside me, an inviting presence that made it difficult to ignore the swell of feelings I had tried to suppress. It was a peculiar dance we were performing—two competitors caught in a game of strategy that had morphed into something more intimate, a hesitant exploration of uncharted territory.

Just then, a playful breeze blew in through the open window, rustling the loose papers scattered across the table. I grabbed a stack, attempting to corral them, but one stubborn sheet slid off and fluttered to the floor. As I bent down to retrieve it, my heart raced at the proximity between us. Our shoulders brushed, and a spark ignited, sending a jolt of awareness shooting through me. I could feel the heat radiating from him, a palpable energy that twisted the atmosphere into something thick and electrifying.

"What are you thinking about?" Ashton asked, breaking the silence, his voice low and filled with a curiosity that mirrored my own.

"Just how this weekend turned into something completely unexpected," I admitted, straightening up and meeting his gaze. "I mean, here we are, supposed to be strategizing, and instead, we're... well, whatever this is."

His lips curved into a wry smile, and for a moment, the tension that had settled over us transformed into something lighter. "You make it sound like we're plotting a coup. It's just brainstorming."

"Right," I scoffed, a smile tugging at my own lips. "Because 'brainstorming' always involves secret glances and accidental touches."

"You say that like it's a bad thing," he replied, an eyebrow raised, his expression both playful and contemplative.

"I didn't say that. But we're here for work, remember? We can't afford to get sidetracked."

"Can't we?" he challenged, leaning in slightly, the firelight flickering across his features. "What if the best ideas come from moments like this? From being... real?"

His words hung in the air, heavy with possibility. I found myself drawn closer to him, the space between us shrinking until it felt almost magnetic. The world outside faded, leaving only the cabin, the warmth, and the undeniable pull we were both beginning to acknowledge.

As the evening wore on, we fell into an easy rhythm, our laughter punctuating the air as we tossed around wild ideas, each more outlandish than the last. The tension shifted, morphing into a sense of camaraderie that felt both exhilarating and terrifying. We imagined ridiculous marketing campaigns, concocted fantastical business strategies, and entertained the absurdity of hosting a product launch in a hot air balloon. Each suggestion added another layer to our connection, and I began to wonder if this was what teamwork felt like—a blending of minds and spirits that transcended the competition.

But beneath the surface, a current of anxiety tugged at me. I sensed a depth in Ashton that he had yet to reveal. Despite our shared laughter, there lingered an unspoken weight between us, an acknowledgment of something he was keeping at bay. I felt the urge to reach out, to uncover whatever truth lay behind those piercing eyes. Yet the instinct to preserve my own heart held me back.

As if reading my thoughts, Ashton shifted, turning to me with a more serious expression. "I know we've been dancing around this weekend, trying to navigate the thin line between competition and cooperation. But I want to be clear about something."

"What is it?" I asked, curiosity piqued as I leaned in, my heart racing.

He hesitated, a flicker of vulnerability flashing across his face. "I think there's more at stake here than just our business plans. We've built this rivalry, but I can't shake the feeling that we're both capable of something greater."

"What do you mean?" I pushed, feeling the weight of his words settle over me like a blanket, warm yet heavy.

"I mean, I don't want this to just be about work. I see potential here—between us. I don't know if you feel it too, but…" He trailed off, the words hanging between us like a delicate thread, ready to snap at the slightest provocation.

"I do," I admitted, surprising myself with the honesty. "But it's complicated, isn't it? We're supposed to be rivals."

"Are we?" he challenged gently, the corners of his mouth twitching in a knowing smile. "Or are we just two people who have found common ground in our ambition and drive?"

The cabin creaked around us, and I suddenly felt that the very walls were privy to our unguarded conversation. I took a breath, steadying myself against the whirlwind of emotions swirling inside. "You're right. We could make a fantastic team. But what does that mean for our rivalry? For our careers?"

"I think it means we get to redefine it," he said, his voice firm yet inviting. "We could be something more than just competitors. We could challenge each other, inspire each other."

As the fire crackled, I found myself drawn into his vision, the prospect of a partnership that transcended the traditional notions of competition. A rush of excitement coursed through me, blending with the fear of the unknown. "You really believe that?"

"I do. But we need to be honest with each other. No more secrets," he insisted, locking his gaze with mine, his expression earnest. "I want to know what you're truly thinking, and I want to share what's been weighing on my mind."

It was a bold invitation, and as the flames flickered, I felt a knot of tension in my chest. Secrets were like shadows, creeping around corners, waiting to be brought into the light. I could sense that Ashton's heart held truths he had yet to share, just as mine did.

With a sudden rush of courage, I leaned in closer, the world around us fading into insignificance. "Fine. If we're being honest, I've been struggling with the weight of our competition. I didn't want to admit how much I admired your work, how much I respected your drive. And it terrified me."

"Terrified?" he repeated, a slight smirk tugging at his lips. "Why would you be scared of that?"

"Because admiration complicates things," I murmured, my voice barely above a whisper. "It makes me question everything we've built, every interaction we've had. I didn't expect this connection, and it leaves me feeling exposed."

He reached out, fingers brushing mine, a gentle contact that sent a tremor through me. "You don't have to be exposed with me. This can be a safe space for us both, a chance to explore what's next without fear."

The softness in his voice wrapped around my heart, inviting me to take that leap of faith. I wanted to trust him, to believe that this weekend could lead us down a path of discovery.

As the fire danced in the hearth, casting shadows on our faces, I made a choice. "Okay, let's explore this. Together."

Ashton smiled, the warmth of his expression lighting up the room. "Together."

And with that single word, the tension broke, giving way to a new chapter that would forever change the narrative of our rivalry. Outside, the stars continued to twinkle, indifferent to our unfolding story, while inside the cabin, we began to chart a course that would redefine who we were—not just as competitors, but as partners standing on the precipice of something beautiful and unexpected.

# Chapter 5: Defining Happiness

The sun hung low in the sky, casting a golden hue over the city as I stepped into the bustling heart of Manhattan. The streets pulsed with life, the sounds of honking horns and chattering pedestrians blending into a chaotic symphony that somehow felt familiar. Each corner I turned revealed an ever-changing tapestry of humanity: the barista expertly crafting lattes that steamed like a soothing balm, the businessman striding confidently in tailored suits that glinted in the sunlight, and the street performers who added bursts of unexpected melody amidst the urban cacophony. Here, in this vibrant metropolis, where ambition swirled like autumn leaves caught in a whirlwind, I searched for clarity, but instead found myself entangled in the echoes of our recent retreat.

Ashton's laughter still danced in the corners of my mind, a sound that ignited a firestorm of emotions I wasn't ready to face. The thrill of competition had once fueled my drive, each day an exhilarating race to outshine my colleagues, yet the thrill had morphed into something unrecognizable. The mere thought of his playful smirk sent a ripple of warmth through my chest, making it clear that something had shifted, even if I refused to acknowledge it. The truth was, I had stumbled upon a different kind of victory during our time together—one that threatened to dismantle the fortress I had built around my heart.

With every click of my keyboard, I dove into the depths of our PR campaign, seeking refuge in the familiar cadence of emails and strategy sessions. The office buzzed with the frenetic energy of deadlines approaching like storm clouds on the horizon. My team was fueled by coffee and determination, brainstorming ideas that fluttered like fireflies in the twilight of our conference room. I meticulously crafted pitches, my thoughts flowing as seamlessly as the Hudson River beneath the George Washington Bridge, but my focus kept drifting back to him.

It was a subtle transformation, like watching a caterpillar emerge from its cocoon. My initial disdain for Ashton had given way to a curiosity that gnawed at me, relentless in its pursuit. He was no longer just a rival; he had become a paradox, a puzzle I was desperate to solve. Every interaction blurred the line between friendly banter and unspoken tension, igniting a dangerous spark that lingered in the air between us. I found myself stealing glances across the room, searching for the flicker of his gaze that sent my heart racing. It was maddening yet intoxicating, this blend of rivalry and something deeper, something I could hardly name.

The sound of laughter erupted from the open office space, pulling me from my reverie. I looked up to find Ashton regaling our colleagues with a story, his hands animatedly slicing through the air as he punctuated each point. The room erupted in laughter, but it felt different to me—charged, electric. It dawned on me that the real competition wasn't about outdoing each other in the boardroom; it was about who could navigate this tangled web of feelings and still emerge unscathed. The thrill of victory paled in comparison to the thrill of connection, and it terrified me.

My gaze was drawn to the city outside, the sun setting fire to the skyline, transforming steel and glass into a kaleidoscope of colors. The world seemed to shimmer, reflecting my inner turmoil as I grappled with my evolving feelings. Was this happiness? Was it merely the high of competition, or was it something more profound? I questioned the very fabric of my aspirations, each thread woven with ambition yet now frayed with uncertainty. It was as if the city itself understood my dilemma, urging me to redefine my own narrative amidst the chaos.

As the sun dipped lower, the golden light bathed everything in warmth, and I found solace in the soft glow of the office lamp flickering to life beside me. I needed clarity, a moment of respite to sift through the whirlwind of thoughts clouding my judgment. I had always believed happiness was tied to success, to accolades and recognition, but here I stood, questioning everything I thought I knew.

"Hey, earth to Amelia," Ashton's voice broke through my contemplation, pulling me back to the present. He leaned casually against the doorframe, a playful smile tugging at his lips. "You okay? You've been staring out there like it holds the secrets of the universe."

I chuckled, attempting to mask my racing heart. "Maybe it does. Or maybe it's just the sun setting."

"Or maybe you're just overthinking," he shot back, his tone teasing but his eyes searching mine, as if he could see straight through the façade I had carefully constructed.

In that moment, with the world outside dimming to a soft twilight, I felt the urge to lay bare my thoughts. The walls that had shielded me from vulnerability began to tremble, and I struggled against the tide of honesty surging within me. What if happiness was, in fact, this moment? Not just the thrill of our campaign but the genuine connection sparking between us. What if true victory lay not in the accolades we fought for, but in the connections we forged along the way?

But I couldn't let myself entertain those thoughts too long, could I? This was Ashton—my rival, my competitor. A man who thrived on challenges and relished the taste of victory. The lingering scent of his cologne enveloped me, intoxicating and familiar, stirring emotions I wasn't ready to confront. As I stood there, lost in his gaze, I felt the boundaries of our rivalry begin to blur, leaving me dizzy and unsure of where I truly stood.

In this world of high stakes and relentless ambition, perhaps the truest challenge lay in navigating the complexities of the heart. As I took a deep breath, preparing to respond, I felt a shift—a quiet acceptance that maybe, just maybe, happiness was waiting for me right here, intertwined with the unpredictability of emotions and connections I hadn't anticipated.

The office was a labyrinth of glass and steel, each cubicle a miniature kingdom filled with dreams and desperation, all competing for space in the New York City skyline. As the days unfolded after our retreat, the tension in the air seemed to crystallize, thickening the atmosphere until it was almost tangible. I caught myself stealing glances at Ashton more often than I cared to admit, the rhythm of our banter becoming a soundtrack I couldn't escape. Each quip and every sly smile blurred the boundaries I had carefully erected, leaving me grappling with the realization that I was no longer solely competing with him; I was yearning for something deeper.

In the evenings, the city transformed into a dazzling jewel, its streets alive with the rush of nightfall. I often found myself walking the winding paths of Central Park, the towering buildings framing the horizon like sentinels watching over my solitary reflections. The trees swayed gently, whispering secrets to the cool breeze that danced across my skin, and I couldn't help but feel a strange sense of freedom amidst the chaos. Here, under the dappled moonlight, I allowed my thoughts to wander, pondering the essence of happiness.

On one particular evening, the stars peeked through the city's haze like shy children hiding behind their parents, and I decided to treat myself to a little indulgence. A quaint café nestled between a row of brownstones called to me, its warm glow spilling onto the sidewalk, beckoning passersby like an embrace. As I stepped inside, the rich aroma of freshly brewed coffee mingled with the sweet notes of pastries cooling on the counter, creating a cocoon of comfort that wrapped around me. I ordered a mocha—my guilty pleasure—and settled into a corner, relishing the ambiance while flipping through the pages of a well-worn notebook.

The words poured from my pen like a river freed from its dam, thoughts swirling into sentences that spoke of desire and uncertainty. I scribbled about the thrill of competition, the way Ashton challenged me, igniting a fire within that I hadn't known existed. But as I wrote, I couldn't shake the feeling that these moments were fleeting, like smoke dissipating into the air. Happiness, I realized, was not just about the adrenaline rush of victory; it was about finding beauty in the mundane, the connection between two souls navigating the complexities of life.

Lost in my musings, I almost didn't notice when Ashton walked in, his tall frame silhouetted against the café's soft light. He spotted me almost immediately, his face breaking into a grin that sent butterflies spiraling in my stomach. It was maddening how one glance could disarm me so thoroughly, making my heart race like I was caught in the middle of a competitive sprint.

"Fancy seeing you here," he said, his voice smooth like the coffee I cradled in my hands.

"Just taking a break from the glamorous world of PR," I replied, attempting to sound nonchalant, but the playful glint in his eyes made it difficult to keep my composure.

"Ah, yes, because staring at spreadsheets all day is truly exhausting," he teased, sliding into the seat opposite me without waiting for an invitation. "What's got you so deep in thought?"

My heart thumped, caught between the desire to share my reflections and the instinct to guard my feelings. "Just pondering the nature of happiness, you know, the usual." I smiled, feigning lightness even as I felt the weight of truth pressing against my chest.

"Deep thoughts for a Wednesday night. Care to elaborate?" he prodded, leaning forward, genuinely intrigued.

And just like that, the dam broke. I found myself opening up about my struggles, the realization that I had tied my worth to achievements for far too long. As I spoke, the weight of my words lightened in the warm glow of his attention. I spoke of the connections I had forged over the years, moments that brought genuine joy amidst the chaos. The laughter shared during late-night brainstorming sessions, the camaraderie built through shared triumphs, and even the heartbreaks that taught me resilience.

Ashton listened intently, his expression shifting from playful banter to something more earnest. "You know, I've always admired how you bring people together. Your passion is contagious," he said, his voice steady and sincere. "I think that's what makes you truly remarkable—not just your drive, but your ability to connect with others. That's what happiness really is, isn't it? Building those connections, finding joy in the people around you."

His words hung in the air, heavy with meaning, and for a moment, the noise of the café faded away, leaving only the two of us suspended in our conversation. My heart fluttered with the realization that perhaps, amid the competitive landscape of our careers, I had found a companion in him, someone who understood that happiness transcended accolades and awards.

But as the moment lingered, I felt the familiar tension creep back in. I had let my guard down, and vulnerability felt like a double-edged sword, exposing both my heart and the risks of uncharted territory.

The café door swung open, allowing a chill to sweep through, breaking the spell. Ashton glanced over his shoulder before turning back to me, a spark of mischief lighting his eyes. "Want to grab a drink at that rooftop bar down the street? I promise the view will be worth it."

I hesitated, heart racing with anticipation and fear. A casual drink could easily spiral into something more—an unintentional deepening of the bond we were already forging. Yet the allure of that possibility was hard to resist, a siren's call promising an adventure in the evening air.

"Sure," I finally replied, the thrill of spontaneity igniting a spark of excitement.

As we stepped out into the cool night, the city wrapped around us like a comforting blanket. The lights twinkled like stars fallen to earth, and I couldn't help but think that perhaps happiness was not a destination but a journey—a dance between rivalry and romance, connection and competition, leading me into uncharted waters where the possibilities were as endless as the skyline before me.

The rooftop bar was a hidden gem, perched above the relentless rhythm of the city. As we stepped out into the crisp night air, the ambiance shifted dramatically. The chatter of the streets below faded, replaced by the gentle clinking of glasses and the soft hum of conversation that danced above us like a warm embrace. Strings of twinkling lights crisscrossed overhead, casting a soft glow that illuminated our faces, enhancing the allure of this unexpected adventure. The skyline stretched before us, a constellation of dreams made concrete, each tower reflecting stories of ambition and aspiration.

I found a spot near the edge of the terrace, where the city unfurled below us in all its chaotic beauty. The faint smell of roasted chestnuts wafted from a nearby vendor, mingling with the tangy scent of sea salt from the pretzel cart a few blocks away. It felt as if the universe had conspired to create this moment—a perfect intersection of time and space where anything could happen. Ashton leaned against the railing, his silhouette framed by the city lights, and I could hardly suppress the flutter of excitement that bubbled up within me.

"Isn't it amazing?" he mused, his voice low and reflective, drawing my gaze from the horizon back to him. "Every light down there represents a story, a life being lived. Sometimes I wonder if we're just passing through these moments, or if they actually mean something."

The sincerity in his words sent a shiver down my spine, making the city seem less like a mere backdrop and more like a living entity, pulsating with energy and secrets. "I think they mean something," I replied, my own voice barely above a whisper. "Every connection, every laugh, every heartache—it all shapes us in ways we might not even realize."

He turned to me, his expression shifting from contemplative to something more playful. "You're getting philosophical on me now. Next, you'll be quoting Aristotle or something."

I laughed, relieved to shift the tone, but inside, a knot of vulnerability tightened. "Philosophy was never my strong suit. I'm more of a 'how to' girl."

"Then let's write our own manual," he said, raising an eyebrow with that charming smirk that made my stomach flip. "How about 'How to Navigate Happiness in the Concrete Jungle'?"

The banter flowed effortlessly, each quip a step closer to dismantling the walls I had so carefully built around my heart. We sipped our drinks—his choice of an Old Fashioned, and my sweet mocha from earlier, surprisingly complimentary in their contrasting flavors—and as the evening deepened, so did our conversation.

With each passing moment, the boundaries of rivalry faded like shadows at dawn. We spoke about everything and nothing, our laughter mingling with the symphony of voices surrounding us. He shared stories from his childhood, recounting the adventures of growing up in a bustling household where chaos reigned supreme, his anecdotes laced with warmth and nostalgia. I found myself entranced, hanging on every word, my heart racing at the thought that he had invited me into his world.

"I was the youngest, always trying to prove myself," he confessed, a hint of vulnerability creeping into his tone. "I think that's why I gravitated toward competition. It felt like the only way to be seen."

His admission resonated within me, echoing my own struggles to find my place amidst the noise of ambition. "I understand that," I said softly. "For me, it was about proving that I could stand out in a sea of talent. But sometimes, I wonder if I lost myself in the process."

He met my gaze, the warmth of his eyes sending shivers through me. "You didn't lose yourself. You just found different pieces of you along the way. Maybe that's what this journey is all about—discovering who we are in the midst of all the chaos."

The sincerity of his words wrapped around me like a soft blanket, comforting yet challenging. The rooftop bar faded into the background as the world narrowed to just the two of us, and in that space, something new blossomed between us. The line separating friendship from something more began to blur, and I felt a thrill of anticipation ripple through me, igniting a longing that had been dormant for far too long.

As the night wore on, the city lights flickered like stars, and the world below us continued its relentless pace. The weight of unspoken emotions hung in the air, a palpable tension that buzzed like electricity. I found myself leaning closer, the distance between us shrinking, and for a moment, the chaos of the city faded into a soothing hum. My heart raced as I searched his eyes, wondering if he felt the same magnetic pull, the unacknowledged connection that danced on the edges of our conversation.

Just as the moment threatened to tip into something more, the bartender called out a round of shots, breaking the spell. I chuckled, feeling a mix of relief and disappointment at the interruption. Ashton grinned, a sparkle in his eye, and raised his glass. "To new connections," he declared, a hint of mischief in his tone. "And to the journey ahead."

"To new connections," I echoed, clinking my glass against his, the sound ringing like a promise in the air.

We downed the shots, the warmth spreading through me, igniting a flicker of courage. I knew this was more than just a night out; it was a turning point, a moment that could redefine everything. As the evening continued, we danced around our feelings, the air thick with possibilities, each shared laugh and lingering glance drawing us closer together.

The bar began to fill with the late-night crowd, and I could feel the energy shift as people moved in and out, their laughter echoing against the backdrop of the city. The world felt alive, yet somehow we remained in our own bubble, untouched by the chaos swirling around us.

As we shared stories and dreams, the realization settled deep within me. Happiness was no longer a distant goal, but a collection of moments strung together, fragile yet beautiful. In Ashton, I found a kindred spirit, someone who challenged me, who saw beyond the competitive facade I wore so proudly. I could see him for who he truly was—a man grappling with his own ambitions, seeking connection in a world that often rewarded solitude.

But even as I allowed myself to embrace this connection, a lingering fear whispered in the back of my mind. What would happen when the competition resurfaced? Would our bond withstand the pressures of our careers? I wanted to believe in the possibility of something more, but the shadows of doubt hovered like storm clouds, threatening to rain on the beautiful night we had crafted.

As the evening drew to a close, and the last remnants of twilight faded into the depths of night, I found myself wishing for just a little more time—a fleeting moment to savor the connection that had blossomed between us. Ashton reached for my hand, the warmth of his touch igniting a spark that sent shivers coursing through me. "Let's not let this be just a night out," he murmured, his gaze intense and searching. "Let's make it a beginning."

The words hung in the air, heavy with possibility. In that instant, I knew I stood at a crossroads—between the familiar safety of competition and the exhilarating unknown of connection. And as the city pulsed around us, I felt a surge of hope wash over me, urging me to take the leap.

Maybe happiness wasn't just a destination, but a journey I could navigate alongside him—a dance of rivalry and romance, filled with laughter, connection, and the promise of something extraordinary waiting to unfold.

# Chapter 6: The Unexpected Twist

Rain drummed against the windows, a symphony of chaos that mirrored the whirlwind in my mind. The familiar hum of the coffee shop, nestled between the crumbling brick buildings of downtown Denver, felt oddly soothing against the backdrop of a brewing storm. I cradled my warm mug between trembling hands, seeking comfort in the dark roast as I watched droplets race each other down the glass. Each splash of rain on the pavement outside seemed to echo the tumult inside my heart, where conflicting emotions waged a relentless battle.

Ashton stood across the café, leaning casually against the counter, his frame silhouetted against the amber glow of the overhead lights. The way he tilted his head, a playful smirk dancing on his lips, made my heart flutter and twist simultaneously. His messy dark hair fell just over his brow, and for a moment, I let myself forget the tension simmering between us, the rivalry that had defined our relationship for so long. But just as I thought I could relish this moment of peace, my phone buzzed violently on the table, a reminder that nothing in my life seemed stable for long.

I glanced down, my heart sinking as I read the breaking news alert. The headline screamed scandal, bright and accusatory against the muted café ambiance. My stomach churned as I recognized the name—the very client whose campaign we had been meticulously crafting. It was a name that had held promise, a name that now brought with it a wave of questions and doubts. What had started as an ambitious partnership teetered precariously on the brink of ruin, and with it, my precarious feelings for Ashton threatened to collapse into the abyss of betrayal.

The moment I looked back up, Ashton had abandoned his cool demeanor, now standing straight, tension etched into his features. His eyes narrowed as he scanned the article on his own phone, brows furrowing deeper with each passing second. I could feel the atmosphere shift, the air thickening with unspoken thoughts and fears that neither of us dared to voice.

"Did you see this?" he asked, his voice low and urgent as he approached my table. He leaned in closer, the scent of his cologne enveloping me like a warm blanket, a stark contrast to the chilling news. I nodded, unable to find my voice.

"What are we going to do?" I finally managed, the words spilling out before I could stop them. I couldn't tell if I was referring to our professional predicament or the storm brewing between us. "This could ruin everything."

"Yeah," he replied, his jaw tightening. "We need to act fast. If this gets out, our entire strategy will implode."

As he spoke, I couldn't help but notice how the shadows danced across his face, highlighting the determination that flickered in his eyes. Despite the swirling chaos, there was something magnetic about him—something that pulled me closer, even when I knew I should step back.

"Okay, let's regroup," I said, pushing aside the treacherous feeling creeping into my mind, the doubts about his intentions and our shared history. "We can't afford to panic. We need a plan."

We spent the next hour strategizing, our voices rising and falling in a rhythm that felt almost familiar. The café buzzed around us, the clatter of dishes and the murmur of patrons blending into a symphony of normalcy that felt out of reach. But as we mapped out potential responses, the gravity of the situation pressed heavier on my chest. This was no longer just about our client's reputation; it felt personal, as if every decision we made now had the power to either forge a path forward or lead us both to ruin.

Then the call came, a jarring interruption to our frantic brainstorming. It was our supervisor, her voice crisp and laden with authority as she relayed the news: an emergency meeting had been called, and we were expected to present our revised strategy. The weight of her words settled heavily in the pit of my stomach, an anchor pulling me down.

"I guess we'll need to prepare for the worst," Ashton said, the gravity in his tone pulling me back from the edge of my rising anxiety. I looked up to meet his gaze, and for a brief moment, I caught a glimpse of the man behind the calculated strategist—a flicker of vulnerability that made me wonder if he too was struggling beneath the surface.

The drive to the office was a blur, my thoughts racing ahead to the confrontation that awaited us. The streets of Denver, usually bustling with life, felt like a mere backdrop to the turmoil in my mind. Neon signs flickered to life in the early evening, but they paled in comparison to the storm brewing between us. What had started as innocent rivalry had become something else entirely, a connection tinged with complexities I had never anticipated.

Arriving at the office, the tension was palpable. Colleagues exchanged furtive glances, the hushed whispers and anxious laughter a testament to the chaos that loomed over us like a storm cloud. As we gathered in the conference room, I felt the weight of Ashton's presence beside me, a constant reminder that our lives were now intertwined in ways I could never have imagined.

And then, the door swung open, and the meeting commenced. Our supervisor's voice cut through the air, outlining the stakes and the expectations that lay ahead. But as she spoke, my gaze drifted toward Ashton, who sat with an intensity that both intrigued and terrified me. It was then that I realized the true depth of our situation—not just the impending disaster, but the intertwining of our pasts that loomed like a specter between us.

A scandal involving our client was just the tip of the iceberg. I sensed that Ashton held secrets, fragments of his past that threatened to unravel everything we had built, and as the tension mounted, so did the uncertainty. In that moment, the question became not just about trust in our professional capacity but in the fragile connection we had begun to forge. Would I find the strength to navigate this storm, or would I allow my doubts to drown us both?

The conference room buzzed with a strange mix of urgency and disbelief, like the moments just before a storm when the air is thick with anticipation. As I settled into my chair, the tension in my body mirrored the electric atmosphere. Colleagues shuffled papers, and the murmur of hushed conversations bounced off the stark white walls, creating an almost surreal backdrop to the impending crisis. I could feel the weight of every gaze, the collective anxiety palpable as we awaited our supervisor's assessment of the chaos unfolding beyond our office.

Ashton sat beside me, his presence an anchor and a storm all at once. I stole glances at him, trying to gauge the turmoil beneath his calm exterior. His brow was furrowed, a crease of concentration running from his temple to his cheek, making him look older, more serious. He caught my eye and gave me a quick, reassuring nod, but I felt the tension coiling between us, a taut line that threatened to snap at any moment.

"Thank you all for coming on such short notice," our supervisor began, her voice slicing through the air like a knife. "As you know, the situation with our client has escalated dramatically. The allegations are serious, and the media is already on the hunt. We need to respond, and we need to respond now."

Her words were like a drumbeat, pushing me deeper into my thoughts. I couldn't shake the feeling that Ashton's past was somehow tangled in this mess. A part of me itched to confront him, to demand answers in the harsh light of day, but I stifled that urge, opting instead to focus on the matter at hand. The meeting dragged on, filled with plans, strategies, and contingency measures, but each time I attempted to concentrate, my thoughts spiraled back to Ashton.

Finally, as the meeting concluded, our supervisor assigned teams to tackle various aspects of the crisis. I found myself paired with Ashton, our names tethered together by an invisible thread of fate. The weight of the impending task loomed large, but the more pressing issue lay in the uncharted territory of our relationship—a delicate dance of unspoken feelings and rivalries now layered with suspicion.

As we retreated to a quieter corner of the office, the noise of the bustling room faded into a distant hum. I looked at him, a mix of frustration and curiosity bubbling within me. "We need to talk," I said, my voice barely above a whisper.

"Yeah, we do," he replied, running a hand through his hair, his gaze steady and intense. "But first, let's figure out what we're going to say to the team."

As we laid out our thoughts, our ideas intermingled, forming a tapestry of potential responses to the media frenzy. I could feel the chemistry between us, an undercurrent of tension that made my heart race. Yet, each time I thought about reaching across that divide to connect with him on a personal level, doubt gnawed at me like a persistent rat. Could I trust him? Did he harbor secrets that would unravel our tentative bond?

Hours turned into a whirlwind as we worked side by side, the office transforming into a war room of sorts. I found solace in the rhythm of our collaboration—the way our minds clicked together, each idea sparking another, illuminating the dark cloud hovering over us. For every laugh we shared, there were moments of silence, pregnant with meaning, where unspoken words danced just beyond reach.

In the midst of it all, a break in the storm emerged, a brief respite from the chaos. We stepped outside for a breath of fresh air, the cool Denver evening enveloping us in a gentle embrace. The city was alive, the streets illuminated by flickering neon lights and the distant sounds of laughter spilling from nearby bars. I inhaled deeply, allowing the crisp air to clear the cobwebs in my mind.

"Do you ever feel like everything's falling apart?" I asked, breaking the silence as we leaned against the cool metal railing of a nearby balcony.

Ashton chuckled softly, the sound warm against the cool night air. "Every day. But that's just part of this business, right? Learning to navigate the chaos."

I glanced sideways at him, wanting to read the emotions flickering across his face. "And what about you? I know this isn't just business for you. You seem...different."

He hesitated, his eyes flickering with something—was it fear, regret? "Let's just say my past has a way of catching up to me. I'm trying to keep my head above water, but it's hard when the tide keeps rising."

The hint of vulnerability in his words pulled me in, urging me to probe deeper. "What happened? With your past, I mean. It's not just this scandal, is it?"

He sighed, the sound heavy with unspoken stories. "You wouldn't believe me if I told you. I've made choices that...let's just say they haunt me."

My heart raced at the implications of his words, a sudden urgency igniting within me. "You don't have to tell me if you're not ready, but if we're going to work together, we need to be honest with each other."

He turned to face me, the intensity of his gaze capturing my attention. "You deserve to know. Just...give me time. Once this is all over, maybe I can share."

As I studied his expression, a mix of concern and admiration filled me. The spark of connection between us flickered brighter, igniting a longing I hadn't anticipated. I wanted to pull him closer, to bridge the chasm of uncertainty that lay between us, but the looming crisis held us in check, a reminder of the chaos waiting to erupt.

When we returned to the office, the atmosphere had shifted again, a thick blanket of tension pressing down on us. News had broken about our client, and the wave of media scrutiny was cresting, threatening to crash down around us. Our phones buzzed incessantly with notifications, each one a reminder of the impending disaster we were racing against.

As we sat back down, the weight of the world felt heavier. I glanced at Ashton, who was now frowning at his screen, the lines of concern etched deep on his face. The comforting rhythm we'd found earlier seemed to fracture, replaced by the harsh reality of what we were up against. I realized then that we were no longer just teammates or rivals; we were two individuals entangled in a narrative much larger than ourselves, caught in the undertow of uncertainty and the echoes of our pasts.

And as the storm loomed closer, I couldn't shake the feeling that our fates were intertwined in ways neither of us could yet comprehend.

The atmosphere inside the office shifted dramatically as the news about our client spread like wildfire. The once-familiar hum of keyboards and soft conversations turned into a cacophony of panic and speculation. I could see the fear in my colleagues' eyes, the weight of uncertainty pressing down on them as they scurried about, grappling with the implications of the scandal that had just erupted. It was a wildfire, and I was caught in the blaze, desperately trying to avoid getting burned.

Ashton and I huddled together, strategizing at a table strewn with papers, half-empty coffee cups, and hastily sketched-out plans. The frantic energy was palpable, each whisper and sidelong glance laden with suspicion. "We need to get ahead of this," I insisted, my voice steadier than I felt. "If we let the media dictate the narrative, we're done for."

Ashton nodded, the determination in his eyes mirroring my own. "You're right. We need a statement—a strong one. Something that shows we're in control."

I leaned closer, my heart racing at how easily our thoughts aligned. "What if we emphasize our commitment to transparency? If we show that we're addressing the issue head-on, maybe we can quell some of the media frenzy."

"Exactly," he replied, the tension between us momentarily shifting to a shared sense of purpose. "But we need to be careful. Any misstep could make things worse."

In the midst of our intense discussion, the door swung open, and our supervisor strode in, her expression a mix of resolve and concern. "I need everyone's attention," she said, silencing the room with her authoritative presence. "We have a plan of action, but I need you all to understand the gravity of the situation. This isn't just about our client; it's about our reputation as well."

As she outlined the strategy, my thoughts drifted to Ashton. Could I really trust him as we ventured into this storm together? His past, tangled in this mess, left me grappling with questions that swirled in my mind like a tempest. The flicker of vulnerability I had seen earlier haunted me. Was he the man I thought I was beginning to know, or was there a darker truth lurking beneath the surface?

Once the meeting concluded, Ashton and I retreated to our makeshift war room—a small conference room with a glass wall overlooking the city. Outside, the sun dipped low, casting an orange glow across the horizon that clashed starkly with the turmoil brewing within us. The room felt suffocating, the walls closing in as the pressure mounted.

"Are you okay?" Ashton asked, his voice tinged with concern, pulling me back from my spiraling thoughts. I appreciated his attention, but it only amplified the confusion swirling in my chest.

"I will be," I replied, forcing a smile that didn't quite reach my eyes. "It's just... overwhelming."

He took a step closer, the distance between us shrinking. "I know this is a lot, but I promise I won't let anything happen to you—professionally or personally. We're in this together."

His words struck a chord within me, resonating like a familiar melody. I wanted to believe him, but the doubts lingered like shadows, whispering warnings of potential betrayal. "What if your past is more tangled in this than you're letting on? I need to know if I can trust you."

Ashton inhaled sharply, the vulnerability I'd glimpsed earlier flickering back to life in his expression. "I want to tell you, but I can't right now. This isn't just about me. If I reveal my past, it could endanger everything we're trying to build here. Please, just give me time."

I nodded, caught in the whirlpool of his gaze. Part of me wanted to push for more answers, to demand he open up fully. But another part, one more cautious and strategic, recognized the need for unity in the face of our challenge. "Fine, but know that I'll be watching you. We can't afford any surprises."

As we settled into our roles, the day turned into a blur of phone calls, drafting press releases, and constant monitoring of social media feeds. The clock ticked away, the hands moving with a maddening slowness, and the world outside seemed to carry on, blissfully unaware of the chaos unfurling within the walls of our office.

Night fell, and the city lights flickered to life, casting an ethereal glow across the room. I could see the strain on Ashton's face, the way his jaw clenched as he navigated the tension of the moment. Yet, in the dim light, I also saw the spark that had drawn me to him in the first place—a fierce dedication to his work, a desire to succeed that mirrored my own.

"Let's take a break," I suggested, the weight of the day pressing down on me. "We can't think straight if we're running on fumes."

Ashton's eyes brightened, and for a moment, the tension dissipated. "You're right. A quick walk might clear our heads."

We stepped outside into the cool night air, the city alive with a vibrant pulse. The streets buzzed with energy, laughter spilling from nearby bars and restaurants. The aroma of street food mingled with the crispness of the air, reminding me that life continued even as we faced our own turmoil.

As we strolled, the rhythm of our footsteps fell into sync, a silent acknowledgment of the bond forming between us. "You know," I began, glancing sideways at him, "this whole situation is beyond messed up, but I'm glad we're in it together."

Ashton's lips curled into a small smile, the corners of his eyes crinkling with warmth. "Me too. I never thought I'd find myself in a crisis and be glad about it, but here we are."

We shared a laugh, the sound of it breaking through the tension that had suffocated us earlier. It was a moment of connection, a fleeting glimpse of the camaraderie we could build despite the chaos around us. I felt the walls between us begin to erode, but as we turned a corner, the sight of a group of reporters huddled outside our building slammed the door shut on that momentary escape.

Panic surged through me. "They're here," I breathed, my heart racing. "We need to get back inside."

Ashton grasped my arm, a firm but gentle hold that sent a jolt of electricity through me. "Stay close to me. We'll get through this."

We navigated through the throng, reporters vying for a glimpse of us, questions flying like bullets. I focused on Ashton, his presence grounding me amid the chaos. The closer we got to the building, the more resolute I became. We would face this together, whatever this storm had in store.

Inside, our team was already buzzing with activity, strategizing for the media onslaught. I quickly scanned the room, spotting our supervisor, her brows furrowed in concentration as she coordinated responses. "We need to project strength," she said, her voice firm. "Show them that we're not afraid to tackle this head-on."

Ashton and I fell back into the rhythm of brainstorming. The atmosphere buzzed with a newfound determination, every suggestion and rebuttal sharpening our strategy. As we worked, I felt a shift—something inside me began to blossom. The connection between Ashton and me was no longer just a rivalry; it was a partnership, an alliance forged in the fires of crisis.

As the night wore on, we crafted our responses, weaving together facts and figures that painted a picture of integrity and transparency. The adrenaline surged within me, igniting a fire I hadn't felt in a long time. I glanced at Ashton, our eyes locking in mutual understanding, and for the first time, the weight of doubt began to lift.

With every challenge we faced, I found myself believing in the strength of our alliance, in the possibilities that lay ahead. The world outside might be a tempest of scandal and scrutiny, but within these walls, we were forging our own destiny. Together, we would weather this storm. And as I felt the warmth of his presence beside me, I knew that perhaps, just perhaps, this partnership could evolve into something far more profound than either of us had anticipated.

## Chapter 7: Facing the Truth

I leaned against the cool metal railing of the rooftop terrace, the pulsating city below me alive with a cacophony of sounds—car horns blaring, laughter spilling out of nearby bars, and the distant hum of trains rumbling beneath the asphalt. The skyline loomed like a jagged teeth against the twilight, skyscrapers reflecting the hues of orange and purple that splashed across the evening sky. It felt like a world brimming with possibilities, yet here I stood, ensnared by the gravity of a conversation that loomed larger than the buildings that surrounded me.

Ashton was inside, pacing like a caged lion, his hands shoved deep into the pockets of his tailored trousers. He always managed to look impeccably put together, even when the weight of the world pressed down on him like an anchor. Tonight, however, his impeccable appearance felt like a façade, a mask hiding the turmoil I knew was brewing beneath the surface. The campaign hung by a thread, and the air felt thick with uncertainty and the acrid scent of potential betrayal.

When I stepped inside, the atmosphere shifted palpably. It was a cramped room filled with the scattered remnants of our campaign—posters half-tacked to the walls, blueprints of our strategy sprawled across the dining table like a war map. But it was the tension between us that felt like the most pressing issue of all. I took a deep breath, my heart racing as I approached him. I could feel the heat radiating from his body, the pulse of his anger, or perhaps shame, crackling in the air like static electricity.

"Ash, we need to talk," I said, the words tumbling out before I could second-guess them. My voice sounded steadier than I felt, as if the gravity of the situation momentarily buoyed my confidence.

He turned to me, his blue eyes darkened by shadows, a storm brewing within them. "I know what you're going to say," he replied, his tone sharp but low, as if he were afraid of shattering the fragile silence. "But you don't understand—"

"I don't understand?" I interrupted, the words slipping out before I could rein in my frustration. "You're at the center of a scandal, and we're supposed to just ignore it? How can you expect me to stand by while you play the victim?"

He stepped closer, invading my space, his expression shifting from defensive to something more desperate. "I didn't ask for any of this. You have to believe me. I was trying to do the right thing, to expose the corruption. I never meant for it to blow up like this."

"Then tell me what happened," I urged, the intensity of my need for answers knotting my stomach. "Tell me everything, Ashton. I deserve to know."

He raked a hand through his dark hair, frustration flickering across his features. "I didn't want you to get involved. It was supposed to be a clean operation, but I got too close, and things spiraled. Now, it's a mess, and I... I don't know how to fix it."

His admission struck me like a physical blow, leaving me breathless. I could see the turmoil etched on his face, but it was hard to reconcile that with the man I had come to know. My heart tugged at me, fighting against the rational part of my mind that screamed for caution.

"Are you saying you were involved with the other side? The very people we're fighting against?" My voice wavered, disbelief tinged with betrayal. "What were you thinking? You can't just justify this!"

"I'm not trying to justify it!" he snapped, frustration boiling over. "I'm trying to explain that sometimes you get too deep into something, and you can't just walk away. They were playing a dirty game, and I thought I could outsmart them, but... it didn't work. Now, I'm the one left holding the bag, and I can't let you take the fall with me."

The vulnerability in his words made my heart ache. There was a part of me that wanted to comfort him, to reassure him that we could weather this storm together. But could I trust him? The foundation of our relationship felt fragile, like an intricate glass sculpture that could shatter with the slightest touch.

"Are we even on the same side anymore, Ashton?" I asked, my voice softer now, laden with the weight of my doubts. "Or are you just trying to save yourself?"

He flinched as if I had struck him, the hurt flashing across his face for a split second before he steeled himself. "You have to understand, I never wanted to drag you into this. I care about you too much."

"Care? Is that what this is?" My laughter came out harsh and incredulous. "Because it feels like you're hiding behind excuses, and I'm the one standing here with my heart in my throat. I deserve more than half-truths, Ashton."

His gaze dropped, and the walls he had built began to crumble, piece by piece. "You're right. You deserve more. But I'm terrified of what's happening. I can't lose you, and I can't let them ruin everything we've worked for."

The sincerity in his voice resonated within me, drawing me closer to him, even as my heart wrestled with the echoes of doubt. I wanted to believe in him, to feel the strength of our connection amidst the chaos. But the truth loomed over us like a dark cloud, threatening to unleash a storm that could wash away everything we had built together.

In that moment, I realized the truth: love and loyalty were a delicate balance, one that required trust forged in honesty. Would we emerge from this turbulent chapter together, or would it tear us apart? The answers felt just out of reach, suspended in the air, waiting for us to confront the reality of our choices and the bond we had crafted amidst the backdrop of an iconic city teeming with dreams and hidden dangers.

As the evening wore on, the city below us continued its relentless rhythm, an intoxicating blend of hope and despair weaving through the streets like a living, breathing entity. My heart pounded a relentless beat in my chest, mirroring the chaotic energy surrounding us. The air was thick with uncertainty, and the scent of impending rain mingled with the musk of warm asphalt, a fragrance that felt both familiar and unsettling.

Ashton's eyes darted away from mine, tracing the patterns of light that danced across the cityscape, illuminating his face in flickers of gold and silver. Each reflection seemed to reveal fragments of the man I thought I knew—intelligent, ambitious, fiercely dedicated. Yet, the weight of his secrets hung over us like a thunderhead, threatening to break apart the delicate threads of our connection.

"Ash, you need to understand how serious this is," I insisted, my voice breaking slightly, a desperate plea cloaked in the veneer of authority. "We're in the spotlight now. If you have any connections to the people behind this scandal, it could destroy everything we've worked for. Not just the campaign but you, me, everything."

He turned back to me, his expression resolute yet vulnerable, a complex tapestry woven from both confidence and fear. "I didn't choose this. I thought I could play both sides without getting burned. I thought I was strong enough, that I could make a difference."

I could see the passion igniting within him, but there was an undeniable flicker of desperation behind those fierce blue eyes. "You can't think that anymore," I urged, stepping closer, needing to bridge the emotional chasm that threatened to pull us apart. "It's not just about you anymore. There's a whole campaign at stake, and I can't just stand by while you navigate this alone."

He swallowed hard, the tension in his jaw tightening as he processed my words. "I never wanted to drag you into this. You're too good for this mess." His voice dropped to a whisper, the weight of his admission wrapping around us like a heavy fog. "But here you are, and I can't lose you."

"Then let me help you," I said, a quiet determination creeping into my tone. "We can figure this out together. But you have to promise me no more secrets. No more half-truths. I can't operate on anything less than full transparency."

For a heartbeat, he was silent, and in that silence, I saw the battle raging within him. The city's lights flickered outside, and the hum of traffic faded into the background as we stood on the precipice of something monumental. "Okay," he finally breathed, the admission heavy but resolute. "You deserve the truth."

His confession hung in the air, and I nodded, encouraging him to continue. He took a deep breath, the way one prepares for a plunge into icy waters, and then began to speak, his voice low but steady. "I was approached a few months ago by someone who claimed to have information on the corruption we've been trying to expose. They wanted me to work with them to uncover it from the inside, but it turned out to be a trap."

As he unraveled his story, the room faded, and I was drawn into his world, where shadows lurked in every corner and trust was a commodity far too expensive. "I thought it was an opportunity to take down the people who were ruining this city, but instead, I walked right into a web of deceit. They knew I was involved in the campaign and tried to leverage that against me."

My heart twisted with sympathy and anger. "So they've been manipulating you this whole time? What do they want?"

"They want to discredit me. They want to make it look like I was in cahoots with them all along, using the campaign as a smokescreen." His frustration flared, and his fists clenched at his sides. "They've been spreading rumors, planting evidence. They're playing a game with my life, and I thought I could outsmart them. But I was wrong."

Ashton's gaze pierced mine, searching for understanding, and I felt the weight of the world settle heavily on my shoulders. "And what about us?" I asked, my voice trembling slightly. "What does this mean for us? For what we're building together?"

He hesitated, the moment stretching out like a taut string, and I could see the myriad of emotions warring within him. "I want this to work. I want you in my life, but I don't want you to be a part of this chaos. You deserve better."

"Better?" I scoffed, frustration bubbling to the surface. "What's better than fighting for something we both believe in? If we don't stand together, then we're both going to fall alone."

He sighed, running a hand through his hair again, a gesture I'd come to recognize as a signal of his inner turmoil. "You're right. I just—" He paused, searching for the right words, and I felt a flicker of hope. "I just need to know that you're safe. That you're not going to get hurt because of my mistakes."

"Then let me help you make this right," I urged, my resolve strengthening. "We can dig into this together. We have resources, contacts, people who believe in us. Let's turn this around."

The spark of determination in my voice seemed to ignite something in him. His posture relaxed slightly, and the storm in his eyes began to clear. "You really think we can do this? That we can fight back?"

"We don't have a choice," I said firmly. "If we let them win, we lose everything. And I refuse to let that happen."

As we stood together, the city pulsing with life outside, I could feel the weight of our shared commitment settling around us like a protective cloak. Trust began to weave its way back into our connection, despite the shadows that loomed over us. In that moment, the chaos outside felt less daunting, a challenge we could face as partners, united against the tide.

The realization settled in, warming my heart: this was no longer just a campaign; it was a battle for our future, a chance to forge something greater than ourselves amidst the chaos, and I was ready to fight for it all, side by side with Ashton.

The night deepened around us, a velvet blanket punctuated by the flickering lights of the city that felt like a million eyes watching our every move. My heart raced with a mix of apprehension and determination as I and Ashton turned toward the task ahead. With every second that passed, the urgency of our situation loomed larger, wrapping around us like the humid air that thickened with the promise of a summer storm.

Ashton began to pace again, his fingers dancing along the edges of the table cluttered with campaign materials—outdated flyers, coffee-stained strategic plans, and crumpled notes that whispered of sleepless nights spent planning our attack against a system that had become increasingly corrupt. "We need to dig deeper," he said, the gravity of his voice grounding us in the reality of our predicament. "There's more to this than just the scandal. It's about the people pulling the strings. We need to find out who they are and what they really want."

"I can help with that," I said, my mind racing through our contacts, the potential allies we might tap into, and the resources we could mobilize. "We've built a network of supporters who believe in our cause. If we leverage that—"

"Leverage it how?" he interrupted, his brow furrowed with concern. "We need concrete evidence, not just good intentions. We need to expose their vulnerabilities before they can crush us."

The intensity in his eyes ignited something within me—a sense of purpose that melded with the anxiety swirling in my chest. "Then let's create a plan," I urged, feeling the adrenaline surge as I spoke.

"We can set up meetings, gather intel, and get ahead of this narrative before it spirals out of control."

Ashton nodded slowly, his expression softening as he recognized the determination in my voice. "You're right. We can't allow them to dictate our story. We'll start by reaching out to our contacts in the local media and see if they have any information on the people behind this."

I felt a spark of excitement dance through me at the prospect. The idea of taking control of our narrative invigorated me, transforming the fear into action. "And I can work on gathering the social media chatter around this scandal. If we can pinpoint the origin of the rumors, we might be able to trace them back to their source."

The plan took shape between us, the tension of the previous moments fading into a camaraderie rooted in shared purpose. I moved to grab my phone, eager to set things in motion, when Ashton's hand caught my wrist, his touch sending a shiver up my arm.

"Before we do anything," he said, his voice steady yet soft, "I need to apologize. I brought this on you, and I never meant for you to get caught in the crossfire. I care about you more than I can express, and I should have trusted you with the truth from the beginning."

My heart swelled at his words, a mixture of gratitude and longing coursing through me. I had never doubted his feelings for me, but hearing him articulate them in the face of our chaos felt like a fragile thread woven into the fabric of our shared journey. "I appreciate that," I replied, meeting his gaze with a steady resolve. "But we can't dwell on the past. We need to focus on what's ahead."

With our intentions aligned, we spent the next few hours brainstorming and strategizing. The city outside transformed into a canvas of lights, a vibrant testament to the energy we were channeling into our mission. The adrenaline coursed through me as we plotted our course, each idea igniting more enthusiasm than the last, our laughter mingling with the rush of ideas.

It wasn't long before the sun began to dip beneath the horizon, casting a golden hue that danced across the skyline, an ephemeral reminder that even amidst the turmoil, beauty could emerge. I pulled out my laptop, fingers flying over the keyboard as I began to draft a message to our supporters, outlining our stance and calling for unity. The words flowed easily, infused with the passion I felt for our cause and for Ashton.

"Let's do a public statement," I suggested, glancing up to see him nodding in agreement. "We need to be transparent about the challenges we're facing, but we also need to galvanize our supporters. They need to know we're still in this fight together."

Ashton leaned closer, his shoulder brushing against mine, sending a warm thrill coursing through me. "That's a solid idea. If we can frame this as a rallying call, it could help us regain some of the control we've lost."

The energy in the room crackled as we crafted our message, pouring our hearts into the words we would share with the world. The stakes felt impossibly high, but with each keystroke, I felt the weight of uncertainty begin to lift. We were no longer just two individuals swept up in a scandal; we were partners in a shared mission, bound by our passion and resolve.

As I hit send, a wave of exhilaration washed over me, a tangible reminder that we were choosing to fight rather than submit. I turned to Ashton, who wore a look of determination mixed with a hint of disbelief, and it struck me just how far we had come in such a short time. The night was still young, and our campaign had a pulse once more.

"Now we wait," I said, a mixture of anticipation and anxiety swirling within me. "But we won't sit idly by. We'll keep working, keep digging until we uncover the truth."

He smiled, the warmth of his expression igniting something inside me, a beacon of hope amid the storm. "You're incredible, you know that?"

"Flattery won't get you everywhere," I teased, nudging him playfully. "But I'll take it for now."

We shared a moment of lightness, laughter ringing out like a melody against the heavy backdrop of our circumstances. Yet, beneath that laughter lay a shared understanding that the road ahead would be fraught with challenges. Trust had to be rebuilt, and our vulnerabilities laid bare before us.

As the night deepened, we settled into a rhythm of research and outreach, fueled by a potent mix of coffee and determination. The stakes felt higher than ever, but we were no longer alone in this battle. The connections we forged within our community, the unwavering support we gathered, formed a foundation upon which we could rebuild our campaign and our relationship.

With each new piece of information we uncovered, the sense of urgency shifted into a palpable energy that propelled us forward. The rhythm of the city outside mirrored our newfound resolve, and together, we were determined to turn the tide.

In the face of adversity, we would rise, not just as individuals but as a united front, ready to fight for the future we envisioned. With every obstacle, we would uncover deeper truths and forge a path lit by resilience, hand in hand, determined to reclaim what was ours amidst the chaos.

# Chapter 8: The Collapse

The sun hung low in the sky, casting long shadows across the glossy glass facade of Nexus Communications. I leaned against the cool steel railing of our office balcony, the hum of New York City's evening traffic a constant backdrop to my spiraling thoughts. Below, the streets pulsed with life, a stark contrast to the suffocating atmosphere that had engulfed our team. Just days ago, we were riding high on the wave of a campaign launch, our collective energy ignited by the promise of success. Now, everything felt fragile, like a carefully constructed glass tower on the brink of shattering.

Inside, the air was thick with anxiety. The office, once a vibrant hub of creativity and laughter, had transformed into a war zone. Colleagues whispered in hushed tones, their faces drawn and tense. I could hear the sharp click of heels echoing down the hallway, a sound that had once signaled purpose and ambition but now heralded impending doom. Our team was unraveling, and I could feel it in my bones, a slow creeping dread that something vital was slipping away.

Ashton stood nearby, his brow furrowed in concentration, running a hand through his tousled hair as he pored over a report that seemed to weigh heavily in his hands. The glow of the computer screen illuminated his chiseled features, casting an ethereal light around him that only heightened my awareness of his presence. The tension between us crackled like static electricity, an undercurrent that threatened to pull me under if I let my guard down. We had always shared a fiery connection, a rivalry that fueled both our ambition and our passion. Yet now, as the walls around us began to close in, I wondered if we would emerge together or be consumed by the very forces that had once united us.

"How did it come to this?" I murmured, my voice barely above a whisper. I could see Ashton's shoulders tense at my words, as if he were bracing for a blow. He turned to me, his eyes searching mine for answers we both knew we didn't have.

"We thought we were untouchable," he replied, his voice steady but laced with an undercurrent of frustration. "But the moment you put everything on the line, it becomes that much easier to lose it all."

His gaze shifted to the skyline, where the sun had dipped below the horizon, leaving a haze of pink and orange that painted the clouds in vibrant hues. It was beautiful, a stark contrast to the turmoil swirling within me. I longed to reach out, to close the distance between us, but the weight of the impending collapse held me back. I could feel the tremors of uncertainty ripple through the air, an unspoken acknowledgment that our lives had changed irrevocably.

As the chaos deepened, I found myself retreating into the recesses of my mind, replaying every moment that led us here. The late-night brainstorming sessions filled with laughter, the wild ambition that fueled our every decision—it all seemed like a distant memory, overshadowed by the scandal that had erupted like a volcano, spewing molten lava into our lives. Each accusation that surfaced felt like a dagger aimed directly at our campaign, each headline more damning than the last. The very foundation we had built our hopes upon was crumbling, and I was terrified of what would rise from the ashes.

Days passed, each one marked by urgent meetings and frantic phone calls. Our team's morale was plummeting, and whispers of betrayal echoed through the hallways. The faces of my coworkers morphed into shadows, their once-bright spirits dulled by the suffocating reality of our situation. I felt like a ghost haunting the very place that had once been my sanctuary. In the midst of the chaos, I sought solace in the most unexpected of places—Ashton's presence.

Despite the tension that crackled between us, there was a comfort in knowing we were navigating this storm together. I often caught him stealing glances at me when he thought I wasn't looking, a silent communication that reminded me of the bond we shared. But the fear of what lay ahead loomed large, threatening to eclipse everything we had fought for. As we worked late into the night, I would catch him leaning back in his chair, staring at me with a mixture of admiration and uncertainty. It was a look that sent shivers down my spine and ignited the flames of hope within me, though I could not yet grasp what that hope entailed.

One particularly fraught afternoon, I found myself wandering the streets of Manhattan, seeking a reprieve from the suffocating atmosphere of the office. The scent of roasted chestnuts filled the air, mingling with the crisp autumn breeze that danced through the crowded sidewalks. As I strolled past storefronts, each window gleamed with holiday displays, a reminder of joy and warmth that felt worlds away from our grim reality. I paused to watch a street performer, a saxophonist pouring his heart into a soulful melody. His music wove through the air, wrapping around me like a comforting blanket, urging me to forget my worries, if only for a moment.

I closed my eyes, letting the rhythm envelop me. It was in these fleeting moments of beauty that I found clarity, the cacophony of my thoughts quieting as I surrendered to the music. But as the last note faded into the cool air, reality crashed back in, reminding me of the looming crisis and the decisions I needed to face. I could not run from it forever.

Returning to the office, I found Ashton waiting for me, a look of determination etched across his features. The shadows of our rivalry and unspoken emotions loomed large, but as he stepped closer, the distance between us seemed to shrink. In that moment, I knew we were at a crossroads, one where the choices we made could define not just our careers but the fragile connection that had blossomed between us. We could stand together and weather the storm, or we could let the pressures of our rivalry tear us apart. The world around us was crumbling, but perhaps, just perhaps, there was still a chance for us to rise from the ashes.

The rain drummed a relentless rhythm against the windows, blurring the skyline into a watercolor dream. It was as if the universe, in all its chaotic splendor, was echoing the turmoil in my heart. I sat at my desk, surrounded by the ghosts of our ambitious plans, the air thick with the scent of damp paper and fading optimism. Every droplet cascading down the glass felt like another unspoken word, another truth hidden beneath the surface of our unraveling lives. The once-sleek office now felt like a dilapidated ship caught in a storm, the crew scrambling to salvage what remained.

Ashton sat across from me, his face illuminated by the soft glow of his laptop screen, yet the light couldn't penetrate the shadow that hung over him. The tension between us had transformed into an unwieldy beast, twisting our conversations into tightrope walks where one misstep could send us tumbling into the abyss. I wanted to reach out, to touch his hand and reassure him that we could still find a way through this storm, but fear of shattering the fragile peace kept me anchored in place.

"Did you see the latest headlines?" Ashton broke the silence, his voice a low rumble that reverberated through the silence. I looked up, meeting his gaze—a mixture of frustration and defiance sparking in his eyes. I nodded slowly, the weight of the articles pressing down on me like a heavy fog. Each new story seemed intent on tearing us apart, exposing our weaknesses for the world to dissect and ridicule.

"The world thinks they know us," he continued, a bitter laugh escaping his lips. "But they have no idea what it takes to keep this place running. They don't see the sleepless nights, the sacrifice, or the sheer will it takes to fight through the chaos." His passion ignited a flicker of something deep within me—a reminder of the fire that had first drawn me to him, that intoxicating mix of ambition and vulnerability.

I inhaled sharply, memories flashing through my mind like a slideshow of our shared experiences—the late nights fueled by caffeine and hope, the shared dreams painted in broad strokes of ambition, and the simmering rivalry that had always danced at the edges of our relationship. "We have to find a way to turn this around," I said, my voice barely above a whisper, as if speaking too loudly might shatter the last remnants of our resolve. "We can't let them win."

Ashton's eyes narrowed, the determination etched on his face morphing into something softer, almost wistful. "You're right. But we can't do this alone. We need the team to rally behind us, to believe in the vision we had before all this blew up." The sincerity in his voice stirred something deep within me, a reminder that beneath the chaos lay the promise of something beautiful, if only we could find a way to grasp it.

We spent the next hours crafting a plan, pouring our hearts into a strategy that would revive our campaign and reinvigorate our team. The rain outside intensified, a symphony of chaos that matched the storm raging within me. I could feel my heart racing as we sketched ideas on the whiteboard, brainstorming ways to shift the narrative. Each suggestion brought with it a rush of adrenaline, the kind that made me feel alive, almost giddy with the possibilities.

But beneath that thrill lay a gnawing uncertainty. What if it wasn't enough? What if the damage was irreparable? I glanced at Ashton, his brow furrowed in concentration, the lines on his face deepening as he weighed our options. The flicker of ambition in his eyes ignited my resolve, and I knew we couldn't afford to falter now.

"Let's call a team meeting," I suggested, my voice steadier than I felt. "We need everyone's input, their voices in this. If we're going to fight back, we need to do it as a united front." Ashton nodded, a spark of enthusiasm igniting in his eyes as he grasped the urgency of my words.

When we gathered the team in the conference room, the atmosphere was charged with a palpable mix of anxiety and anticipation. Colleagues exchanged wary glances, their faces reflecting the strain of the past few days. I took a deep breath, reminding myself that hope could flourish even in the darkest moments. I looked around the table, seeing not just a group of professionals but a family bound by shared dreams and aspirations.

"Thank you all for coming," I began, my voice breaking slightly as I fought against the swell of emotion. "I know things have been tough, but we can't let this scandal define us. We have a vision, and I believe we can still achieve it if we come together as a team." I could see the tension in the room begin to shift, a tentative nod here, a shared glance there, as my words sparked a flicker of hope among my colleagues.

Ashton chimed in, his voice strong and unwavering. "We've faced challenges before, and we've come out stronger every time. This is just another obstacle, and together, we can overcome it." The camaraderie began to bubble to the surface, igniting a passion that had been dulled by uncertainty.

Ideas flowed like a river, each one more ambitious than the last. We debated strategies, brainstormed fresh approaches, and shared our fears, allowing vulnerability to create a space where innovation could thrive. I could feel the energy in the room shift, a collective resolve forming as we stood together, shoulder to shoulder, determined to fight for what we believed in.

Hours slipped away as we crafted a revitalized campaign, breathing new life into our vision. Laughter broke the tension, as if the storm outside had finally begun to clear, giving way to a bright horizon. I felt a warmth spreading through my chest, a reassurance that we were not alone in this fight. With Ashton by my side, and our team united in purpose, it felt like we might just emerge from this chaos, stronger and more resilient than before.

As the meeting drew to a close, I caught Ashton's eye, a silent acknowledgment passing between us. The storm outside had calmed, the rain reduced to a gentle patter against the glass. Together, we had rekindled the flames of hope amidst the wreckage of our ambitions, and I realized that perhaps, just perhaps, love and resilience could flourish even in the most uncertain of times. The path ahead was fraught with challenges, but in that moment, standing side by side with the people who believed in us, I felt a surge of optimism that sparked the flame of possibility deep within my heart.

The days melted into a blur of frantic energy, each moment straining against the weight of our collective uncertainty. Despite the resolve that had blossomed during our team meeting, the pressure continued to mount as the scandal cast its shadow over everything we worked for. Nexus Communications, once a beacon of creativity and innovation, felt like a deflated balloon, its potential smothered beneath the weight of public scrutiny.

In the aftermath, I found myself drawn to Ashton even more, his presence a comforting anchor amid the chaos. We would work late into the night, side by side, sometimes in silence, letting the weight of our thoughts settle around us like a warm blanket. Other times, we would engage in lively debates, pushing each other's ideas to their limits, the rivalry that once felt suffocating now igniting a flame of inspiration. In those moments, we seemed to dance along the thin line between competition and collaboration, each challenging the other to rise above the noise.

One late evening, as the city below shimmered with life, I glanced over at Ashton, his brow furrowed in concentration. He was hunched over a stack of papers, scribbling notes with a fervor that reminded me of our first brainstorming sessions. "What do you think?" he asked, lifting his gaze from the chaos on his desk.

The moonlight streamed in through the window, illuminating his features and casting an almost ethereal glow around him. "Can we really turn this around?"

The question hung in the air, heavy with possibility. I leaned back in my chair, allowing myself to consider it fully. "We can," I said finally, my voice steady. "We just need to own our narrative. If we can show our clients that we're still the same passionate team, maybe we can turn this storm into something that strengthens us."

Ashton smiled, a flicker of hope igniting in his eyes. "That's the spirit." He leaned forward, his enthusiasm palpable. "Let's brainstorm how we can engage our audience, maybe create a campaign that shows our resilience. It could highlight our journey, the hurdles we've overcome, and the community we've built."

A wave of exhilaration surged through me at the thought. The idea of transforming our crisis into a story of triumph filled me with renewed vigor. Together, we tossed ideas back and forth, the energy in the room crackling with possibility. We envisioned a series of videos featuring team members sharing their personal journeys, the challenges we faced, and the passion that fueled our work. Each story would serve as a thread, weaving a rich tapestry of resilience and determination that would resonate with our clients.

The next few weeks became a whirlwind of activity as we mobilized our team to bring this vision to life. I coordinated with our marketing specialists, designers, and videographers, each step intertwining our individual strengths into a cohesive effort. Ashton worked tirelessly alongside me, our late-night brainstorming sessions morphing into deep conversations about our aspirations, our fears, and, most importantly, what lay ahead.

We filmed testimonials in the heart of our office, the walls echoing with laughter and determination as our colleagues opened up about their experiences. The energy was infectious, sparking a renewed sense of camaraderie among us. I watched as the shadows of doubt began to lift, replaced by the vibrant hues of optimism and resilience. The campaign was evolving into something more profound than I had imagined—a testament not only to our abilities as professionals but to our capacity as a community to weather the storms together.

One evening, while reviewing the footage, I felt an unfamiliar flutter in my chest as I glanced at Ashton. The way he passionately critiqued each clip, his eyes alight with inspiration, drew me in. I realized that our partnership had transcended the realm of mere competition; it was transforming into something deeper, a shared vision grounded in trust and admiration. The tension that had once marked our interactions had shifted, replaced by a palpable connection that lingered just beneath the surface.

Yet, even as we poured our hearts into this new direction, the outside world remained a constant reminder of the storm brewing beyond our carefully curated bubble. Articles continued to appear, each one casting shadows on our efforts. I could feel the undercurrent of worry ripple through the team, a stark contrast to the enthusiasm that had ignited our campaign.

As we prepared for the launch of our new initiative, I decided to host a gathering, inviting our team and a few key clients to celebrate the progress we had made. It would be a chance not only to showcase our renewed vision but to reinforce the bonds we had forged during this tumultuous journey. As the evening approached, excitement and apprehension twined around me like ivy, each twist bringing with it the hope of what might unfold.

The event unfolded against the backdrop of the city's vibrant skyline, twinkling lights casting a warm glow over the rooftop terrace. Laughter and chatter filled the air, weaving a tapestry of connection and camaraderie. I mingled with our clients, sharing snippets of our journey, their faces lighting up as I recounted our stories of resilience. It felt good to showcase our strength, to remind ourselves—and them—that we were not defined by our failures, but by how we rose from them.

Ashton stood nearby, engaging with a group of colleagues, his laughter ringing out above the din. I caught snippets of their conversation, the warmth radiating from him almost magnetic. It drew me closer, and I found myself gravitating toward him, the space between us collapsing as we fell into easy banter, a natural rhythm emerging that felt both exhilarating and familiar.

"Are you ready for this?" he asked, his voice low enough for only me to hear. His eyes sparkled with excitement, and I felt a surge of courage as I met his gaze. "Tonight is a pivotal moment for us."

I nodded, my heart pounding in my chest. "More than ready. We've worked too hard to let this moment slip away."

He smiled, a genuine warmth radiating from him that ignited something deep within me. In that instant, the world outside faded away, and all that mattered was the connection we shared. The pressure of the past few weeks melted under the weight of possibility, and I felt a flicker of hope ignite between us—a fragile flame that dared to dream of something more.

As the evening progressed, we unveiled our campaign, the videos we had painstakingly crafted playing against the backdrop of the city skyline. The response was overwhelmingly positive, the energy in the room shifting as people rallied around our vision. It felt as if the storm that had once threatened to drown us had finally given way to a clearer sky, our community banding together in support of our resilience.

As the last video ended, applause erupted, and I glanced at Ashton, our eyes locking in an unspoken moment of triumph. It was as if, amid the chaos, we had created something beautiful—an embodiment of hope, ambition, and the undeniable power of connection.

That night, as the city lights twinkled like stars above us, I felt a new chapter begin to unfold, one filled with endless possibilities and the promise of a love that could weather any storm. In the midst of chaos, we had discovered a sanctuary, a shared vision that transcended the noise of the world. And for the first time in a long time, I dared to believe that love could not only survive but flourish amidst the ruins.

# Chapter 9: A Leap of Faith

The sun hung low in the sky, casting a golden hue over the bustling streets of New Orleans. The air was thick with the sweet, intoxicating aroma of beignets dusted in powdered sugar, mingling with the earthy scent of damp cobblestones after an unexpected afternoon rain. Each droplet glistened like a tiny diamond, sparkling under the rays of the setting sun. I stood at the edge of Jackson Square, heart racing as I surveyed the vibrant scene around me. Musicians played lively jazz melodies, their tunes swirling through the warm air, urging my nerves to settle. Yet, the excitement only heightened the urgency in my chest, for I was about to confront Ashton, the man who had become both my greatest rival and an unintentional muse.

The square was alive with laughter and animated conversations, the kind that made you feel a part of something larger. Families strolled by, their children chasing pigeons as artists captured the essence of the moment on canvas. The iconic St. Louis Cathedral loomed in the background, its steeples piercing the sky, a sentinel watching over the countless stories unfolding below. I took a deep breath, inhaling the city's essence—freedom wrapped in a melody, a chaotic harmony that felt like home. Today was about to change everything.

Ashton stood by a weathered iron fence, his figure silhouetted against the fading light. There was an intensity in his posture, a tightness that spoke of his own inner turmoil. I had come to recognize the ways he carried his emotions like a weight, always ready to spar yet so deeply affected by each exchange. My heart thudded against my ribs, each beat urging me to approach him. I took a hesitant step forward, the crunch of gravel beneath my shoes barely audible over the distant strumming of a guitar. He turned at the sound, his sharp features softened by the golden light, yet his eyes remained guarded, flickering with uncertainty.

"Lena," he said, the single word infused with a mix of surprise and something else—something deeper. I wished desperately to believe it was hope, but we had danced around that for too long, circling each other like wary animals, fearful yet drawn to the promise of connection.

"Ashton," I replied, my voice steady even as my insides quivered. There was a storm brewing between us, and I was determined to meet it head-on. "We need to talk."

He nodded, the weight of my words settling between us like the humidity in the air. I motioned for him to follow me to a quieter corner of the square, away from the ebullience of the crowd. I could feel the pulse of the city around us, a reminder of the life we had woven together in this vibrant tapestry, filled with threads of competition, passion, and an undeniable spark that neither of us had acknowledged until now.

In the shade of an ancient oak tree, I faced him fully, the shadows playing across his face, highlighting the tension in his jaw. "Ashton, this rivalry—it's consuming us. I'm not just talking about the campaign. I mean everything. I can't stand the way we push each other away while holding on so tightly." Each word felt like a truth I had finally unearthed, an excavation of buried emotions that had lingered beneath the surface.

His gaze held mine, an electric connection that made the world around us fade into oblivion. I could see the gears turning in his mind, the conflict warring within him. "I know what you mean," he said slowly, his voice low and raw. "But it's complicated. You and I...we were never just competitors. There's more."

The confession hung between us, heavy and charged. I stepped closer, my heart pounding in a rhythm that echoed through my entire being. "What do you want, Ashton? What do you feel?" The question hung there, suspended in the air, demanding an answer.

For a moment, silence enveloped us, broken only by the distant laughter of children and the fading notes of a trumpet. I could see the vulnerability in his eyes, a flicker of something genuine beneath the bravado. "I want to win, Lena. But I also want you." The words tumbled out, raw and unfiltered, each syllable igniting the air between us.

I inhaled sharply, my heart racing as the truth unfurled within me. "Then why are we fighting this? Why are we allowing the competition to drown out what we both know is real?" The realization washed over me like the warm breeze that rustled the leaves overhead. The stakes had never just been about the campaign or accolades; they had always been about us.

Ashton shifted closer, the warmth of his presence radiating like sunlight filtering through the branches. "I guess I've been scared. Scared of losing—of losing you." His admission was like a balm to my frayed nerves, a softening of the armor we had both donned.

"Sometimes," I said, my voice barely above a whisper, "taking risks is the only way to find clarity." I stepped even closer, daring to breach the last barrier that stood between us. "What if we stopped fighting? What if we embraced whatever this is, together?"

His eyes searched mine, the uncertainty melting into something softer, more profound. In that moment, I felt a flicker of hope. Whether we succeeded or faltered, I knew my happiness was intrinsically linked to the connection we shared. This wasn't merely a confrontation; it was a leap of faith—a daring plunge into the unknown that felt more exhilarating than any competition we had faced.

I reached for his hand, our fingers intertwining as the sun dipped below the horizon, painting the sky in hues of pink and orange. Together, we stood on the precipice of a new beginning, ready to embrace whatever awaited us.

The world around us shimmered in the aftermath of our unguarded moment, the hues of the sunset melding into a soft twilight. The laughter of children faded into the background, replaced by the soft hum of conversation drifting from nearby cafés. As I stood there, hand in hand with Ashton, an exhilarating blend of hope and trepidation swirled within me. The weight of our past rivalry was still palpable, yet it felt lighter somehow, as if we had shared a secret that only we understood.

Ashton's thumb brushed across my knuckles, an unspoken promise lingering in the air. I searched his face, wanting to decode the emotions flickering behind his piercing eyes. They had always been a puzzle to me, filled with ambition and bravado, but now they reflected a depth I had yet to explore. It was as if the façade he wore had cracked just enough for me to glimpse the man beneath—the one who was equally terrified and thrilled by the leap we were taking.

"Can you imagine what everyone will say?" he asked, a hint of mischief in his tone, breaking the tension. His lips curled into a wry smile, and I found myself mirroring his expression. It was a playful challenge, a reminder that we weren't merely stepping into the unknown; we were also about to rewrite the narrative of our lives. I could picture the surprised faces of our peers, the whispers trailing behind us like ghostly echoes.

"Let them talk," I replied, feeling a surge of confidence. "At least we'll be living our truth instead of pretending. Isn't that worth the risk?"

He chuckled, a sound that sent warmth cascading through me, chasing away the lingering doubts that had haunted our every interaction. "You're right. I guess it's about time we stop being characters in our own drama and start writing the story we actually want."

With that, we stepped away from the oak tree, our fingers still intertwined, and began to navigate the narrow paths of the French

Quarter. The cobblestones were uneven underfoot, a testament to the city's rich history, and I found myself reveling in the sensation of our footsteps echoing against the old buildings. Each storefront was a little treasure chest, displaying an array of art, jewelry, and trinkets that celebrated the local culture.

As we wandered, I couldn't help but marvel at the colorful facades adorned with wrought-iron balconies draped in lush greenery. The vibrant colors seemed to pulse with life, mirroring the tumult of emotions swirling in my chest. This city had always felt like a character in its own right, an ever-present backdrop to my evolving journey. Now, standing next to Ashton, it felt as if the very essence of New Orleans conspired to bless this new chapter.

We eventually found ourselves drawn to a small café tucked away on a quiet side street. The aroma of freshly brewed coffee wafted through the air, wrapping around us like a comforting embrace. As we settled into a cozy corner, I leaned back in my chair, observing Ashton as he gazed at the bustling street outside. The way the light caught his features made my heart skip—a warm glow that accentuated the contours of his jaw and the playful glint in his eye.

"So, what happens now?" I asked, the question hanging between us like a delicate thread. It was both a challenge and an invitation, a chance to carve out our future together or retreat into the safety of competition.

He turned to me, his expression contemplative. "I think we start by being honest. No more hiding behind our careers or the rivalry. We tackle this together, whatever this is."

His words washed over me, a wave of relief and excitement merging into a heady concoction. It felt so easy to slip into a comfortable rhythm with him, as though our conversations had always flowed in tandem. "I want that," I admitted, my voice barely above a whisper. "But I also want to win this campaign. I want us both to shine, not just one of us."

"Agreed," Ashton replied, leaning forward, a newfound determination sparking in his gaze. "Let's put everything we have into it, but this time, let's do it as a team. If we're going to fight for this, we fight together."

The proposal hung in the air, electrifying and dangerous, yet it felt utterly right. I envisioned our collaboration, our talents intertwining, our strengths amplifying one another. The possibilities stretched before us like the city's winding streets, rich with promise and adventure.

We spent the next hour strategizing over steaming cups of coffee, our initial trepidation melting away as we devised plans and tossed ideas back and forth. Laughter erupted as we recalled our past clashes—moments that had once felt so significant but now seemed trivial in the face of this new alliance. Each shared memory was a thread that wove us closer, reinforcing the bond we were forging.

But as the sun sank lower, casting shadows that crept into the café, a sobering realization settled over me. The campaign was more than just our ambitions; it was also a test of trust. Trust that we could navigate this uncharted territory without losing sight of our connection. I studied Ashton, noticing the flicker of doubt that passed through his eyes, a mirror of my own.

"Hey," I said softly, reaching across the table to place my hand over his. "No matter what happens, we'll be okay, right?"

His gaze shifted to my hand, and he nodded slowly, his voice low and steady. "Yeah, we will. This is different. I don't want to lose you in this. Not now."

The sincerity in his words filled the space between us, stitching together the remnants of fear with threads of hope. I squeezed his hand, anchoring myself to this moment. The café began to empty, the gentle clatter of chairs and laughter fading into the night. Outside, the streetlamps flickered to life, illuminating the path ahead.

We left the café, stepping out into the warm embrace of the evening air. The sounds of the city wrapped around us like a comforting blanket, and I felt a renewed sense of purpose. Together, we would navigate this maze of competition, but more importantly, we would explore the depths of our connection.

As we strolled through the vibrant streets, I stole glances at Ashton, my heart swelling with a sense of belonging. Each step we took resonated with promise and potential. Tonight marked the beginning of something profound, a leap into the unknown that felt less like a risk and more like a homecoming. The streets of New Orleans would bear witness to our journey, and I was ready to embrace every twist and turn that lay ahead.

The night deepened around us as Ashton and I continued our walk through the French Quarter, the air thick with the sounds of laughter and the sultry notes of a saxophone drifting from a nearby bar. Neon signs flickered to life, casting colorful reflections on the cobblestones, while the aroma of Cajun spices wafted through the streets, beckoning us toward culinary adventures. It was a city alive with stories—each alley, each corner holding secrets waiting to be unraveled. And here we were, two reluctant protagonists in our own unfolding tale, ready to seize our narrative instead of letting it slip through our fingers.

We wandered aimlessly, our feet guided more by instinct than intention, our earlier strategy session transforming into an impromptu exploration. Ashton pointed out a quaint gallery displaying vivid canvases that captured the essence of the city's spirit. Each painting told a story—of musicians playing their hearts out, couples dancing in the streets, and the wild celebration of Mardi Gras, where life itself seemed to explode in a riot of color. I felt an electric thrill at the thought of what we could create together, not just in the campaign but in everything that lay ahead.

"Do you remember that time you nearly convinced me to dress up as a giant banana for the Halloween party?" Ashton teased, a playful glint lighting up his eyes. I couldn't help but laugh, my heart swelling at the memory. He had looked so incredulous, caught between his sense of pride and an overwhelming desire to avoid total embarrassment.

"You still owe me for that," I shot back, nudging him playfully with my shoulder. "But let's be real; you'd have rocked that costume."

His laughter echoed in the warm night air, a sound that mingled perfectly with the melody of the saxophone and the occasional pop of fireworks celebrating some local festivity. The moment felt almost cinematic, the kind of perfect evening where time lost all meaning.

Yet, beneath the surface of our jovial banter, a flicker of uncertainty remained. I could sense Ashton grappling with the weight of our uncharted territory, the stakes now higher than ever. He was still the ambitious strategist I had competed against, yet he was also the man I was beginning to care for deeply. The tension in the air was palpable, a mixture of anticipation and fear that swirled around us like the fragrant mist rising from the nearby café.

"Lena," he said, his tone shifting to something more serious as we paused near a fountain. The soft trickle of water mirrored the fluttering in my stomach, both soothing and unsettling. "What if we don't win? What if this whole thing goes south?"

His vulnerability cracked through the bravado, and I felt a wave of empathy wash over me. "Winning isn't everything," I replied, my voice steady. "We've already accomplished so much by deciding to be honest with ourselves and each other. This is about more than just a campaign; it's about our journey."

He studied me intently, his expression revealing the internal battle of his ambition against the burgeoning feelings we were nurturing. "You're right. But it's hard not to think about the consequences of failure, especially when we've both worked so hard."

A hush fell between us, the only sounds the gentle splashes of water and the distant echoes of laughter. I felt the weight of the moment pressing down, urging me to articulate the truth that had been growing inside me, an ember waiting to ignite. "Ashton, if we fail, at least we'll have each other. We'll still have this connection."

He smiled then, a soft and genuine expression that made my heart flutter. "You really believe that?"

"I do," I affirmed, stepping closer, allowing our surroundings to fade into a mere backdrop. "We're building something together, and that's what matters most. I've spent too long focusing on competition, but I don't want that to define me anymore. I want to grow, to explore. With you."

Our eyes locked, the connection between us igniting like fireworks in the night sky, illuminating everything that had once been shrouded in doubt. It was as if the world around us had paused to take note of our admission, the stars glimmering overhead in approval.

"Then let's make a pact," Ashton suggested, his voice low, intimate. "No matter what happens, we support each other. We don't let this become a battleground. We remember that our greatest asset is our ability to collaborate, to create something incredible together."

I couldn't suppress the smile that broke across my face, a burst of warmth that radiated through me. "Deal. Together, we'll make it work."

The agreement settled over us like a comforting blanket, the earlier tension dissolving into an optimistic buoyancy. The night was still young, and we were filled with newfound determination, ready to tackle whatever challenges awaited us.

As we resumed our exploration, the city seemed to pulse with renewed energy. We passed a street performer painting faces in bright colors, and I couldn't resist pulling Ashton toward the booth.

"Let's do it," I urged, excitement bubbling over. "We need to capture this moment."

A few minutes later, I found myself adorned with vibrant butterfly wings painted across my cheeks, while Ashton sported a comically oversized mustache that threatened to overtake his face. We doubled over in laughter, our shared silliness melting away any lingering reservations. The artist captured our playful spirit perfectly, her brush dancing across our faces with an artistry that felt uniquely tied to our evening.

With our newfound looks, we ventured deeper into the quarter, stopping at lively venues where the rhythms of jazz and blues poured into the streets, drawing people in like moths to a flame. We joined a small crowd outside one bar, drawn in by a particularly energetic trumpet player whose skill was both mesmerizing and infectious. I could feel the music thumping in my chest, the beat intertwining with the pulsing energy between us.

As we moved with the music, I caught a glimpse of Ashton in the low light, his carefree laughter melding with mine as we danced, our inhibitions fading like shadows in the bright glow of the streetlamps. The city felt alive, alive like our connection, each beat of the drum underscoring the realization that we had stepped away from rivalry and into a partnership defined by authenticity and joy.

As the night deepened, we found ourselves in a small courtyard, a hidden gem adorned with twinkling fairy lights that cascaded from the trees like stars descended to earth. We sat on a worn wooden bench, the remnants of our paint still vibrant against the moonlit backdrop.

"Lena," Ashton said quietly, his voice dipping into a more serious tone as we both caught our breath. "I'm really glad we did this. I can't remember the last time I felt so… free."

I turned to him, the sincerity in his eyes sending warmth spiraling through my heart. "Me too. It's like we've shed this weight we didn't even know we were carrying."

He smiled, a genuine expression that seemed to light up his entire face. "To new beginnings, then."

"To new beginnings," I echoed, clinking imaginary glasses with him, our laughter ringing out into the stillness of the night.

As we sat there, the world around us continued to hum with life, but for that moment, it felt like we had carved out a little sanctuary, one filled with promise, laughter, and a connection that shimmered brighter than the stars overhead. Whatever challenges awaited us in the days to come, I knew we would face them together, our hearts intertwined in a narrative that was uniquely ours. In that vibrant city, under the watchful gaze of history and possibility, we had found not just each other, but ourselves.

# Chapter 10: Torn Allegiances

The sun hung low in the sky, casting a warm, golden glow over the bustling streets of Manhattan. The air was thick with the scent of roasted chestnuts from a nearby vendor, mingling with the bittersweet aroma of espresso wafting from the café across the street. I paused outside the glass facade of the office building, its sharp angles and mirrored surfaces reflecting not just the light, but the frenetic energy of the city that pulsed all around me. This was my sanctuary, my battleground, and today it felt more like a stage set for a tragic play.

Inside, the atmosphere buzzed with a nervous energy that could only come from whispers shared in hushed corners and glances exchanged over cubicle walls. Each step I took echoed with the silent questions that hung in the air, my heart drumming a staccato rhythm that matched the quickened pace of my thoughts. The scandal had erupted like a summer storm, and the fallout left everyone reeling, especially me. My colleagues scurried past, their faces a blend of concern and curiosity, but I kept my head down, determined to navigate this maze without attracting more attention.

Ashton's office loomed at the end of the corridor, a fortress of glass and steel, its door slightly ajar. I could see the silhouette of his form behind the frosted pane, a tall figure with a strong posture that suggested both confidence and despair. The tension between us had thickened into something palpable, a bond twisted and frayed by the weight of expectations and unspoken feelings. My fingers tingled at the thought of reaching out, of stepping into his space where the air was charged with something more than professional rivalry. But I hesitated, my loyalty caught in a delicate balance.

With a deep breath, I pushed the door open, the sharp creak slicing through the quiet tension like a knife. Ashton looked up, his sharp blue eyes meeting mine, and for a moment, the world outside faded into insignificance. There was an intensity in his gaze that made my stomach flutter, a mix of anger and something softer, something that felt dangerously close to vulnerability. I took a tentative step inside, the door clicking shut behind me, sealing us in a bubble of uncertainty.

"Are you okay?" I asked, the words slipping out before I could stop them. I had meant to sound casual, but my voice trembled, betraying the concern I tried so hard to suppress.

He ran a hand through his tousled hair, the frustration etched across his face morphing into something resembling gratitude. "I don't know, honestly. This whole thing has turned into a circus, and I feel like I'm standing in the center of the ring, waiting for the lions to eat me alive."

I chuckled softly, the sound a fragile lifeline between us, trying to anchor us amidst the chaos that swirled outside. "Maybe you should learn to juggle."

His lips curved slightly at the corners, the tension easing just a fraction. "If only that were the worst of it. This scandal... it's not just a matter of public perception anymore. It's affecting everything. The firm's reputation, my career, and—" he paused, looking away as if the words were a burden he wasn't ready to carry, "and us."

I felt the weight of those unspoken words, heavy and suffocating, yet electrifying. "Ashton, I—"

"Do you trust me?" he interrupted, the intensity of his gaze pinning me in place.

The question hung between us, charged and daring. I could see the flicker of hope in his eyes, battling against the shadows of doubt. Trust was a fragile thing, easily shattered by the winds of uncertainty swirling around us. But as I looked at him, I realized that despite the mess we were in, despite the chaos that threatened to pull us apart, my heart whispered what my mind struggled to acknowledge: I trusted him.

"Yes," I replied, my voice steadying as certainty blossomed within me. "I do. I can't pretend that everything is okay, but I believe in you."

His expression softened, and I could see the guard he had put up slowly lowering, allowing a glimpse of the man beneath the layers of responsibility and ambition. "Then help me fix this," he said, his voice earnest, laden with the weight of his plea. "We can't let them tear us apart."

In that moment, standing in the chaos of his office, surrounded by the chaos outside, I felt a surge of determination. This was not just about the firm or the scandal; it was about us. Together, we could weather the storm, navigate the treacherous waters that lay ahead. But I knew the path wouldn't be easy. Each step would be fraught with challenges, each decision shadowed by the consequences of our choices.

"I'm in," I declared, my heart racing at the realization of the commitment I was making. "Let's figure this out together. We owe it to ourselves."

His eyes sparkled with a mixture of relief and something deeper, something that sent shivers down my spine. The energy between us shifted, crackling with unspoken possibilities as we forged an unbreakable bond, ready to face whatever lay ahead. And in that moment, amidst the chaos of our lives, I felt a flicker of hope, a promise of a future where we could stand side by side, unyielding against the world.

The days that followed our pact felt like navigating through a dense fog, every step uncertain yet exhilarating. The office became a landscape of whispered secrets and sidelong glances, a living organism that thrummed with tension. I had always enjoyed the intoxicating energy of my workplace, but now it felt suffocating, as if the very air around me conspired to remind me of the looming chaos. My colleagues moved about like restless phantoms, the weight of their unsaid opinions heavy in the air, and every time I met a gaze, I braced myself for judgment.

Ashton and I had decided to tackle the mess head-on. We spent evenings pouring over strategy and potential solutions, our conversations laced with urgency and the occasional touch of playful banter. There was a thrill in our teamwork, a connection that made the hours melt away as we combed through endless reports, our focus narrowing to the task at hand. We forged a partnership that was not just professional but deeply personal, each laugh and every shared glance igniting something between us that felt dangerously close to love.

But as much as I relished our late-night brainstorming sessions, I couldn't shake the feeling that we were dancing on the edge of a cliff. I found myself scrutinizing the horizon, wondering when the ground would give way beneath us. The scandal's repercussions hung over our heads like a sword ready to drop, and I felt the tension coiling tighter each day, the anticipation crackling with a volatility that made my heart race.

One afternoon, while the city outside was bathed in a fiery sunset, I found myself in the break room, a sanctuary of mundane distractions. The hum of the coffee machine mixed with the soft rustle of newspapers and the murmurs of colleagues—each snippet of conversation floating around me like leaves caught in a breeze. I stared at the walls decorated with motivational posters, each one proclaiming the importance of teamwork and integrity, and felt a deep sense of irony gnawing at me. Here we were, caught in a web of our making, questioning our values in a place that championed them.

"Hey," a voice broke through my thoughts, dragging me back to the present. Jenna, my friend from the marketing department, leaned against the counter, her brow furrowed in concern. "Are you okay? You've been a bit... distant lately."

I offered her a smile, though it felt as if I were wearing a mask. "Just trying to figure things out, you know? The office is a bit crazy right now."

"Crazy doesn't even begin to cover it." She let out a short laugh, but her eyes remained serious. "Just remember to take care of yourself. This place can swallow you whole if you let it."

Her words hung in the air, echoing my own fears. I appreciated her concern, but I couldn't shake the feeling that I was walking a tightrope. The delicate balance between my loyalty to Ashton and my professional responsibilities was becoming more precarious with each passing day.

Later that week, as we dug deeper into the aftermath of the scandal, Ashton and I found ourselves huddled in his office, papers strewn across the desk like fallen leaves. The tension in the room was thick, and I could feel my heart pounding in my chest as we worked through strategy after strategy. We debated potential repercussions, the tone of our voices shifting from serious to frustrated as we argued and then back to soft camaraderie. I watched him, the way his brows knitted together in concentration and how his jaw tightened when he was deep in thought. Each nuance made my heart flutter, and I cursed the timing of it all.

"How did we get here?" Ashton asked suddenly, his voice barely above a whisper. He ran a hand through his hair, the gesture so familiar it felt intimate. "I mean, this whole mess just spiraled out of control."

"Yeah, it's like a bad dream," I replied, the words tumbling out before I could censor myself. "One moment, we were just colleagues competing for the same promotion, and now…" I trailed off, the weight of it settling over us.

"Now we're fighting for our jobs." His tone was grim, but there was a glint of mischief in his eyes that made me smile. "Who would have thought our rivalry would turn into… whatever this is?"

"Whatever this is," I echoed, my heart racing at the implication. The air shifted between us, charged with an unspoken truth. I longed to bridge the distance that had formed, to tell him that whatever this was, it felt like a leap into the unknown—a thrilling, terrifying plunge that I was willing to take if he was beside me.

But before I could articulate my thoughts, the intercom crackled to life, jolting us both back to reality. "Ashton, we need to see you in the conference room," came the clipped voice of our boss, the words slicing through the fragile moment we had created.

"Great," Ashton muttered, the humor evaporating from his expression. "Just what I needed."

I watched him stand, his posture shifting back to that of the determined executive I knew he was. "Let's tackle this, okay?" he said, meeting my gaze with a fierce intensity. "We can get through this together."

With a nod, I willed the confidence to wash over me. "Together." The word lingered between us, heavy with promise and fraught with uncertainty, but in that moment, it felt like a lifeline.

As he stepped out of the office, I felt a mix of hope and dread coiling in my stomach. The real battle lay ahead, and while I couldn't predict the outcome, I knew I wouldn't have to face it alone. The stakes were higher than ever, and the path before us was shrouded in shadows. But as I looked at Ashton's retreating figure, a fire ignited within me—a determination to confront whatever came next, side by side.

The conference room, a sterile enclave of glass and chrome, felt more like a cage than a space for collaboration. As I took my seat, the atmosphere thrummed with tension, thick enough to slice with a knife. A massive screen loomed at the front, the ominous glow reflecting the concern etched on everyone's faces. The murmurs ceased as our boss, a hawk-eyed woman known for her no-nonsense demeanor, entered the room. She commanded attention, her presence alone making the air feel charged with the weight of unspoken decisions.

Ashton slid into the seat beside me, his demeanor shifting to one of professional focus, a mask he wore well despite the storm brewing beneath. I could feel the warmth radiating from him, a tether anchoring me in the midst of uncertainty. The room quieted, and she began outlining the company's strategy to mitigate the fallout. Every word felt like a stone dropping into a still pond, sending ripples of anxiety across our team. I caught glimpses of Ashton's jaw clenching and unclenching, the tension in his body mirroring my own as we absorbed the gravity of our situation.

"Trust is crucial," our boss stated, her voice steady yet laced with urgency. "We need to restore faith among our clients and within our own team. Communication will be key." She glanced pointedly at Ashton, whose reputation was now marred by the scandal. "Ashton, I expect you to lead this effort."

His eyes flickered with a mix of determination and apprehension. "Of course," he replied, his voice low but resolute. "I'll put together a plan to address client concerns and reassure our team."

As I listened, my heart raced, caught between admiration for his unwavering resolve and the gnawing worry that clung to me. This wasn't just about his career; it was about our shared future, the delicate threads we were weaving together in the face of adversity. I knew what lay ahead would demand sacrifices and compromises, and I was determined to stand by him.

After the meeting, as the colleagues trickled out of the room, I felt the palpable shift in our dynamic. There was a renewed sense of purpose as we gathered in the hallway, and Ashton turned to me, his expression softening. "We need to act fast," he said, urgency lacing his words. "Can you help me draft that communication to our clients?"

"Absolutely," I replied, feeling a surge of adrenaline. "Let's meet later tonight. We can brainstorm ideas and make sure our message is solid."

His eyes lit up with gratitude. "I knew I could count on you." The weight of that simple acknowledgment made my heart swell. It was moments like this that reinforced my belief in him, in us.

The evening air was crisp as I made my way back to the office later, a comforting chill settling around me. The streets were alive with the rhythm of the city, people hurrying past, oblivious to the turmoil that swirled within my chest. I felt the pulse of life in every step, a reminder that despite the chaos, there was beauty in resilience. The lights of Times Square glimmered in the distance, a vibrant reminder of hope amid the shadows.

Arriving at the office, I settled into the familiar surroundings, the scent of freshly brewed coffee lingering in the air. The office was quieter at this hour, and as I waited for Ashton, I let my thoughts drift. I couldn't shake the feeling that the impending storm would test us in ways we couldn't yet foresee. Yet beneath the worry, there was a flicker of excitement at the prospect of facing these challenges together.

Ashton arrived, his brow furrowed with concentration, yet his presence radiated warmth. "Thanks for coming," he said, a hint of relief coloring his voice. "I know it's late, but we need to be thorough."

"Always," I replied, gesturing for him to take a seat. We spread out our notes and reports, the gravity of our task settling in. As we dove into drafting a message to clients, our focus sharpened, and the outside world faded away. We brainstormed tirelessly, each suggestion building on the last, our ideas intertwining like vines, each twist and turn revealing something new.

"This is good," he said, his gaze lingering on me, an unspoken appreciation threading between us. "Your insights are invaluable."

I felt a warmth bloom in my chest, a reminder that I wasn't just a cog in the wheel; I was a vital part of this journey. "It's about clarity and honesty," I emphasized, my hands animated as I spoke. "We need to acknowledge the situation without being defensive."

"Exactly." His eyes sparkled with admiration as he jotted down my ideas. In that moment, I saw the vision of our future take shape, a tapestry woven with trust and collaboration. But as the hours slipped by, the reality of our situation settled like a weight on my shoulders. We were fighting not just for our careers but for the very essence of our connection, each decision a delicate dance on the precipice of uncertainty.

As the clock ticked past midnight, fatigue settled in, but the thrill of our shared purpose kept me alert. Finally, we sat back, our work spread out before us—a carefully crafted message that spoke of accountability and determination, a promise to our clients that we would weather this storm together.

"Let's get some rest," Ashton suggested, running a hand through his hair, the tension finally easing from his shoulders. "We can send this out in the morning."

I nodded, feeling a surge of relief mixed with exhaustion. As we gathered our things, I caught his eye, and in that moment, the world outside faded away. The connection we had forged through this turmoil felt unbreakable.

"Hey," he said, his tone suddenly serious. "No matter what happens, I want you to know how much I appreciate you. I don't just mean work-wise."

The weight of his words settled over me like a warm embrace. "I feel the same way," I replied softly. "We're in this together, right?"

"Always," he assured me, the sincerity in his gaze igniting a spark of hope within.

As I left the office, the city pulsing with life around me, I felt lighter, as if the shadows that had threatened to engulf me were receding. The challenges ahead loomed like distant thunder, but with Ashton by my side, I believed we could navigate the storm. The future was uncertain, but it shimmered with possibilities, and as I walked beneath the streetlights, I felt a renewed sense of purpose. Together, we would weather whatever came next, united by a bond stronger than the pressures of our profession, woven together by trust, resilience, and something deeper that was beginning to take root.

# Chapter 11: The Comeback Plan

The late afternoon sun filtered through the dusty blinds of our makeshift war room, casting slatted shadows across the cluttered table strewn with crumpled papers and half-empty coffee cups. I could hear the hum of the city outside, a symphony of car horns and distant sirens, yet inside our sanctuary, the atmosphere felt electric, charged with possibility. We had retreated to the back corner of the office, a space so nondescript that it had become our haven. The walls, adorned with fading motivational posters that seemed to mock us now, had witnessed many mundane meetings, but today, they bore witness to our quiet revolution.

Ashton leaned back in his chair, a hint of mischief playing on his lips, a stark contrast to the palpable tension that had clouded our team since the scandal broke. He had this way of navigating the storm, steering us into calmer waters with a single, sly grin. He was tall, with dark hair that fell just above his brow, perpetually tousled, as if he had emerged from a whirlwind of ideas. His hazel eyes sparkled with a depth that made it hard for me to focus, each glance layered with meaning and a touch of warmth that lingered long after he looked away. Today, those eyes held something different—a shared determination that stirred something hopeful within me.

"Okay, so what if we flipped the script?" I suggested, leaning forward, my pulse quickening as I embraced the spark of inspiration. "Instead of trying to outrun the scandal, what if we owned it? We could launch a campaign that highlights our commitment to transparency and accountability." My heart raced as I felt the weight of the room shift, the air growing thick with excitement.

Ashton leaned in, his eyes widening. "You mean, like a public confession tour? Let the voters see our humanity?" He paused, a smile spreading across his face. "I like where you're going with this.

We could even incorporate social media, letting people ask us questions live. Raw, real, and unfiltered."

Laughter bubbled up from the team, a sound that felt like sunlight breaking through clouds. There was something liberating about embracing our flaws, acknowledging that we were all too human, each with our own scars and stories. The pressure that had suffocated us just days prior began to lift, replaced by a thrilling camaraderie. I glanced around the table, noting the way my colleagues leaned closer, their brows furrowed in thought, expressions morphing from uncertainty to fervor. We were no longer just a team—we were a family of misfits, battling against the odds, united by a common goal.

Hours slipped by as we volleyed ideas back and forth, a rhythmic dance of creativity that transformed our small room into a cauldron of innovation. The sunlight dimmed, giving way to the soft glow of overhead lights that flickered as if they were sharing in our excitement. The once sterile environment had become alive with the pulse of our collective ambition. Every suggestion felt like a thread, weaving a tapestry of resilience, hope, and a dash of rebellion against the world outside that seemed hell-bent on tearing us apart.

"Let's create a video series," I proposed, my mind racing with possibilities. "We can feature each team member sharing their story—how we got here, what drives us. Authenticity is what people crave right now." The vision formed in my mind like a vivid dream, a montage of heartfelt confessions and shared laughter, all while the skyline of our iconic city glittered in the background. "It could be our way of not just explaining ourselves but also connecting with the voters on a human level."

The team erupted into discussion, each voice building upon the last, ideas spiraling into an intricate web of what-ifs and maybes. The atmosphere shifted once more, now a blend of urgency and creativity, as the reality of our impending presentation loomed large.

I could almost feel the weight of upper management's scrutiny resting on my shoulders, a specter that lingered just outside our door. Their expectations were like a tightening noose, and the idea of presenting our raw, vulnerable approach made my stomach churn.

But amidst that unease, Ashton's gaze found mine, grounding me. In that moment, everything else faded away—the judgment, the fear, even the scandal itself. It was just him and me, our shared vision sparking a light that pushed through the encroaching shadows. I felt an undeniable urge to trust him, not just as a colleague but as a confidant. His laughter had become a balm for my worries, and I couldn't help but wonder if our collaboration could be the catalyst for something far greater than just a campaign comeback.

As we crafted our pitch, transforming each idea into a narrative that resonated with our values, I felt the warmth of hope igniting within me. The very air in the room seemed to thrum with our determination, a force of nature that could challenge even the most entrenched doubts. The world outside continued its chaotic dance, yet here, in our corner of the universe, we were forging a new path, one that could lead to redemption, connection, and ultimately, victory.

With each passing hour, the bond between us deepened, layers of camaraderie and mutual respect unfurling like petals in bloom. Our campaign was no longer just a response to a crisis; it had evolved into a shared mission, one that promised to change us as much as it would the world beyond our four walls. We were a team united not by the weight of scandal but by the possibility of a future filled with hope and authenticity.

The day of the presentation arrived with the kind of brisk clarity that seems to follow the most tempestuous of storms. The morning sun poured through the windows, spilling light onto the worn floorboards of our office, igniting dust motes into a shimmering dance. I sat at my desk, fiddling with the hem of my blazer, trying to shake off the restless energy that buzzed beneath my skin like static electricity. The walls, which had borne witness to our frenetic brainstorming sessions, now felt like they were closing in, a reminder of the stakes that loomed ahead. Today was not just about presenting our ideas; it was about redefining ourselves and perhaps even reclaiming a piece of our dignity.

As I glanced around the office, I spotted Ashton by the coffee machine, his silhouette framed against the bright light flooding in. He was engrossed in conversation with Zoe, our social media strategist, who was using her hands to animate every point she made, her dark hair bobbing with the movement. It struck me how effortlessly he engaged with everyone, his charm like a buoy in turbulent waters, pulling us all to the surface. I remembered how he had joked that morning, saying, "If this goes well, I'll personally bake you all cookies as a reward. If it doesn't, I'll still bake cookies, but you'll have to promise to eat them in silence." Laughter had erupted then, dispelling the tension, if only for a moment.

Ashton turned toward me, catching my eye, and I felt a rush of warmth spread through me. The moment was fleeting, yet it left an imprint—a reminder that we were all in this together, bound by a mission larger than ourselves. I took a deep breath, aligning my thoughts with my resolve. We had crafted something authentic, something that could not only address the scandal but also resonate with the hearts of our audience. This was our moment to show the world who we truly were beneath the headlines.

The conference room was a stark contrast to our cozy brainstorming space. It was clinical, all glass and steel, with the faintest hint of that sterile office scent that makes you want to breathe through your mouth. The long, polished table gleamed under the fluorescent lights, and I could see my reflection staring back at me, a mingling of nerves and determination in my eyes. I took my place at the head of the table, Ashton settling in beside me, his presence a steadying force that bolstered my confidence.

As the door swung open, the upper management filed in, their faces a mix of curiosity and skepticism. There was Harvey, with his ever-present scowl that seemed to be molded into his very features, and Lily, whose sharp gaze flicked over us like a hawk assessing its prey. Their silence was palpable, like a thick fog that clung to the air, and I could feel my heart thudding in my chest, each beat a reminder of the high stakes. I could hear the whisper of my thoughts, a chorus urging me to remain calm and composed.

We began our presentation, the carefully curated slides flashing images of our campaign's vision: a series of raw, heartfelt videos, each capturing the essence of our team and our journey. Each clip was a narrative woven with vulnerability and resilience. As the first video played, I felt my throat tighten. There I was, sharing my story, raw and unfiltered, revealing the insecurities and dreams that had propelled me into this whirlwind of political ambition. I watched as Harvey's eyebrows furrowed, but Ashton's supportive glance grounded me. I was reminding him, and myself, that our authenticity was our greatest strength.

One by one, my colleagues' stories unfolded, their truths illuminated against the backdrop of our campaign. Zoe spoke of her upbringing in a small town, her voice trembling with emotion as she recalled the struggles of her community. Tyler, our data analyst, shared his journey from skepticism to conviction, and I could see the glimmer of pride in his eyes as he articulated the mission that had brought us all together. Each personal story resonated deeply, rippling through the room like a gentle wave, breaking against the hardened facade of our audience.

The final video featured Ashton, his usual playful demeanor softened by a sincerity that made the room exhale collectively. He spoke not just of his professional journey but of the impact of community, the power of connection. "In the end," he said, his voice steady and clear, "we are not just faces on a billboard or names on a ballot. We are people, with dreams, fears, and a desire to serve. We are here to listen, to learn, and to grow together with our community." His words hung in the air like a poignant echo, and for a moment, the stern faces around the table shifted, intrigue flickering across their features.

As the presentation drew to a close, a silence enveloped us, thick and heavy, punctuated only by the soft whir of the air conditioning. I could feel the tension in the room, a blend of apprehension and hope. Harvey was the first to break it, leaning back in his chair, arms crossed, his gaze piercing. "You're asking us to trust you, to let go of the narrative that has been established. What makes you believe this will work?"

I felt the weight of his scrutiny but met it with a resolve that surprised even me. "Because we're willing to be vulnerable," I replied, my voice steady. "We're ready to embrace our flaws and show that we are more than a scandal. We're here to build a dialogue, not just a campaign. People want authenticity; they crave it. And we're prepared to give it to them, even if it means facing our own truths."

Ashton nodded beside me, his unwavering support like an anchor in stormy seas. The atmosphere shifted slightly, the tension easing just enough for hope to slip through the cracks. We had stepped into the fray, our collective vulnerability woven into a fabric strong enough to withstand scrutiny. Whether we would succeed remained uncertain, but in that moment, as I locked eyes with Ashton, I knew we had already begun to change the narrative.

The meeting concluded, and as the upper management filed out, a whisper of promise lingered in the air, sparking a sense of renewal that felt almost tangible. The weight of their judgment still loomed, yet a new energy flickered within me, ignited by the courage we had shown. The world outside our office had not changed, but we had, and in that moment, it felt like the beginning of something extraordinary.

The aftermath of our presentation enveloped me like the comforting warmth of a well-worn blanket. As the day melted into evening, I found myself perched on the edge of my desk, watching the city below transition from the fiery hues of sunset to the cool, inviting glow of city lights. The chaos of the scandal felt a world away, receding like the tide. Ashton leaned against the doorframe, arms crossed, that mischievous glint still lingering in his hazel eyes. "What do you think? Do we still have jobs?" he quipped, the playful inflection in his voice pulling me back from my reverie.

I couldn't help but chuckle, the sound a release of pent-up tension. "We survived, didn't we? That's a start." My heart raced with the thrill of our small victory, yet it was still tethered to the uncertainty that loomed overhead like a cloud refusing to disperse. The decision-makers had left the room with more than just their critical gazes; they carried our hopes and dreams, cradled between the hard edges of their corporate armor.

We gathered our things, the camaraderie we'd built over the last few days still crackling in the air. Tyler nudged Zoe, his voice light with relief. "At least they didn't throw us out of the building." She rolled her eyes but grinned back, the corners of her mouth betraying the seriousness she had donned for the occasion. I caught Ashton's eye again, and we exchanged a silent understanding that we had done something significant together, something that had the potential to reshape our narrative.

That night, as I lay in bed, the sounds of the city pulsing outside my window, I replayed our presentation in my mind. Each moment was etched with raw honesty, our collective vulnerability interwoven with a thread of tenacity that made us human. I could almost feel the ripples of our words spreading through the community we sought to connect with. If we could turn our missteps into a rallying cry, perhaps we could reach those who felt disillusioned by the very system we aspired to represent.

Days passed, and the buzz from our presentation lingered in the office like the scent of fresh coffee. The upper management had remained tight-lipped, but whispers began to circulate. Conversations bubbled with anticipation, each voice tinged with a hope that felt contagious. I found myself drawn to the heart of it all, immersing in discussions that had once felt stifling. Each interaction was a reminder of our shared journey, every laugh exchanged a stitch in the fabric of our newfound resilience.

One afternoon, as I sat in our bustling break room, Ashton slid into the seat across from me, a stack of takeout containers balanced precariously in his hands. "I brought lunch," he declared, grinning as he expertly navigated the minefield of scattered papers and half-empty coffee cups to set the feast before me. "Consider this a victory meal, even if we don't know the outcome yet."

His enthusiasm was infectious, and I couldn't help but smile, grateful for his unwavering optimism. "Victory meal or not, you know I can't resist sushi." I grabbed a pair of chopsticks, eager to dive into the colorful array before us. The flavors exploded in my mouth, vibrant and fresh, a burst of joy against the backdrop of the uncertainty that loomed over our campaign.

As we ate, I shared my thoughts on how we could further engage the community—public forums, interactive workshops where people could voice their concerns directly, and we could respond. "Let's create a space for dialogue," I said, my excitement spilling over. "I want to hear what the voters need from us, not just what we think they want."

Ashton nodded, his brow furrowed in concentration. "That's brilliant. If we can foster genuine connections, it might not just be about winning votes anymore; it could be about winning trust." His expression shifted from contemplation to a boyish grin, and I felt a warmth bloom within me. The way he leaned in, hanging on my words, made it seem like I was sharing secrets with an old friend rather than just a colleague.

As the weeks passed, our campaign transformed. We launched a series of community gatherings, each one brimming with energy and enthusiasm. The atmosphere was electric; people filled the rooms, their voices mingling with laughter and the sound of chairs scraping against the polished floors. Each forum allowed us to showcase our commitment to transparency, our desire to listen and learn from those we aimed to serve. The initial skepticism began to ebb, replaced by a flicker of hope as people realized we were genuinely interested in their stories.

Ashton and I found ourselves spending more time together outside of work. Late-night brainstorming sessions turned into casual strolls through the city, laughter echoing against the walls of buildings steeped in history. We shared not just ideas but pieces of ourselves—our fears, our aspirations, and the quirks that made us who we were. I learned about his obsession with obscure films and how he could recite entire scenes verbatim. He listened as I recounted my childhood, the rollercoaster ride of ambitions and dreams that had led me to this pivotal moment in my life.

The lines between work and personal life blurred, and I found comfort in those moments, a warmth that felt like sunlight filtering through the trees. But with that warmth also came a tension, a simmering awareness that laced our interactions. There was something electric between us, a connection that made my heart race and my palms sweat. I often caught myself stealing glances, wondering if he felt it too.

One particularly crisp evening, as we stood on the rooftop of our office building, the city sprawled out beneath us, he turned to me, the city lights twinkling in his eyes. "You know, I never thought I'd find myself in a position like this, working on something that truly matters," he said, his voice barely above a whisper. "I thought it was just a job."

I felt my heart leap in my chest, the weight of his words resonating deeply. "Neither did I. But it feels like we're part of something bigger than ourselves, doesn't it?" The stars twinkled above us, and in that moment, under the vast expanse of the universe, I realized that our journey was not just about the campaign; it was about finding a sense of purpose and belonging.

As the days turned into weeks, we grew stronger, our campaign gaining momentum, our message resonating with an ever-expanding audience. The scandal that had threatened to swallow us whole was now a mere footnote in our story, overshadowed by the collective spirit we had ignited. I felt a surge of pride watching our vision take flight, transforming from a mere idea into a living, breathing entity that thrived on hope and community.

With Ashton by my side, I felt unstoppable, ready to face whatever challenges lay ahead. Together, we had woven a tapestry of resilience, strength, and connection, one that promised to carry us forward into uncharted territories. The road was still long, but with each step we took, I could feel the weight of the past slipping away, replaced by a sense of possibility that stretched as far as the horizon.

## Chapter 12: Secrets Unveiled

The day of our presentation arrives, and the boardroom feels like a battleground. The stark white walls, often a canvas for corporate vision, now loom ominously around me. They seem to close in, pressing against my chest like a heavy weight, each tick of the clock echoing a reminder of how high the stakes are. I can see the polished table, a long slab of mahogany that has witnessed countless strategies, deals, and betrayals. Its sheen reflects the overhead lights, but today, it feels less like a beacon of hope and more like a glassy surface hiding the treacherous depths beneath.

As I stand at the front, my heart thrums in my chest, a wild percussion of nerves and determination. I can't afford to let my gaze linger on the executives seated before me, their faces a mix of skepticism and indifference, a judgmental jury poised to decide our fate. Instead, I focus on the presentation, my carefully crafted slides that weave together our plan—a blueprint of ambition and hard work, one that could change everything for our team and our company. The words spill out of me, a steady stream of data and vision, punctuated by anecdotes that add a human touch to the cold statistics. I feel the rhythm of my voice carrying me, the adrenaline pushing me forward, urging me to fight for what we've created together.

But just as I think we might succeed, the door swings open with an unwelcome force, crashing against the wall with a clatter that reverberates around the room. All heads turn, and my pulse quickens at the sight of an old acquaintance stepping into the harsh light. He's tall and imposing, a figure from Ashton's past who carries an air of familiarity tinged with menace. The glint in his eye suggests he knows too much—too much about the scandal that had nearly derailed Ashton's career before it truly began. A chill runs down my spine, and I feel the color drain from my face as I catch Ashton's gaze, his expression shifting from confidence to horror in an instant.

The air thickens with tension, a palpable dread that wraps around us like a shroud. I can almost hear the collective inhalation of my colleagues, the tightening of their shoulders as they brace themselves for the storm. This is the moment I had dreaded, the dark cloud hovering over our sunny aspirations. The meeting was supposed to be our triumph, a chance to elevate our vision and showcase the fruits of our labor. Instead, it threatens to turn into an expose, a dramatic unraveling of everything we've fought to build.

"Is this a private party, or can anyone join?" the newcomer asks, a smirk playing on his lips. His voice drips with mockery, and I can feel the disdain radiating off him, cutting through the facade of professionalism in the room. The air is charged, crackling with the unspoken words swirling around us like an impending storm.

Ashton stiffens beside me, his jaw tightening. I can see the inner turmoil playing out on his face, a battle between the man he wants to be and the shadow of his past that refuses to stay buried. I reach for his hand, squeezing it as a silent reassurance, a reminder that he isn't alone in this moment. The warmth of his skin against mine grounds me, urging me to find my voice amidst the chaos.

"Who invited you?" I hear myself say, my voice sharper than I intended. The words slice through the tension, surprising even me. I refuse to let this man bully us or diminish what we've worked so hard to achieve. The executives look between us, intrigue replacing their initial skepticism, their attention fully captured. It's a risky move, but I can't let fear dictate my actions now.

"I was just passing through and thought I'd check on my old friend," he replies, a glint of malice in his eyes as he locks onto Ashton. "Isn't that right, Ashton? We have a lot of history to catch up on."

Ashton's face pales further, and I can feel the tension in him as if it were a physical entity, a wall of ice. I can't let this moment slip away; I need to shield him, to stand firm in the face of this unexpected confrontation. "We're here to discuss our project, not reminisce about the past," I assert, trying to maintain my composure. "We've put in a tremendous amount of work to present today. Your presence isn't relevant."

The man chuckles, an unsettling sound that makes my skin crawl. "Ah, but the past has a funny way of coming back to haunt us, doesn't it?" He leans in, his voice low and conspiratorial, "Especially when there are secrets involved."

Ashton's expression darkens, and I can see the flicker of fear in his eyes. The room holds its breath, waiting for the dam to break. I know I need to be the one to step in, to confront this specter of the past head-on. I take a deep breath, steadying myself. "We're here to focus on the future," I say, my voice firm. "What's done is done. We can't change the past, but we can learn from it and move forward."

"Such a noble sentiment," the man sneers, his gaze flicking between Ashton and me. "But isn't it a bit naive? You think your little presentation can cover up the truth?"

I can feel the stakes rising, the temperature in the room shifting as the executives lean in, eager for the unfolding drama. I can't let them see us falter; I can't let them see Ashton crumble. "What truth?" I ask, my voice steady despite the whirlwind of emotions swirling inside me. "The only truth that matters is the dedication and effort we've put into this project. We're not here for theatrics; we're here to build something great."

The man's smirk falters for a brief moment, a crack in his confident facade, and I seize the opportunity. "You're here to distract from our accomplishments, to dig up dirt instead of recognizing hard work and innovation. We won't allow that." I lock eyes with

Ashton, a silent pact forming between us, a shared determination to face whatever comes our way.

I take a step forward, driven by a blend of protectiveness and anger. The air feels electric as I confront this unwelcome intrusion into our carefully curated world. "If you think you can undermine us, think again. We're stronger together, and nothing you say will change that."

Ashton's hand squeezes mine, and I can sense the warmth of his gratitude, even amidst the storm swirling around us. Together, we stand at the edge of an abyss, and I feel a fierce sense of purpose swell within me. I won't let the shadows of the past dictate our future. Today, we'll rise, together, amidst the scrutiny of the boardroom and the echoes of secrets long buried.

A heavy silence blankets the boardroom, thick enough to stifle a gasp. As I lock eyes with the intruder, a surreal haze envelops the edges of my vision. It's as if time itself has paused, holding its breath in anticipation of a revelation. The others watch intently, their expressions flickering between intrigue and disbelief, and I can almost hear the gears of their minds whirring, calculating what this unexpected turn of events might mean for our futures. My heart hammers like a war drum, each beat echoing the urgency of the moment.

"Why don't we get to the heart of the matter?" the newcomer suggests, stepping further into the room, exuding a confidence that feels insufferably invasive. His shoes click against the floor, a metronome marking the rhythm of this escalating tension. "Ashton, you and I both know the truth behind your rise and the shadows that followed."

I can see Ashton's resolve wavering, the sheen of sweat glistening on his brow as he clenches his jaw, the very image of a man caught in the crossfire of his past. In the dim light, I can make out the contours of his face—each line etched with worry, regret, and something deeper that I can't quite decipher. It's a cocktail of emotions that leaves a bitter taste in the back of my throat.

"Let's not muddy the waters," I interject, forcing a calmness into my voice that I'm not sure I feel. "Ashton has worked tirelessly on this project, and the focus should be on the success we're presenting today."

The man chuckles, a sound as dry as the desert wind, shaking his head dismissively. "Success, you say? What kind of success is built on the ashes of deceit?" The implication hangs in the air like a noxious gas, suffocating and all-consuming. I feel my cheeks flush, a rush of heat rising to meet the chill of his accusation.

I refuse to let my composure falter. "You may know the past, but you don't know Ashton today. He's transformed, and this project is a testament to his growth." With each word, I feel the armor of conviction solidifying around me. I stand taller, trying to create a barrier of strength not just for myself but for Ashton too.

The tension in the room has shifted, morphing into an electric current that zaps through the air. I can sense the executives leaning forward, their interest piqued, a hunger for scandal dancing in their eyes. A flicker of fear shoots through me—will they believe him over us? What if this man's words spiral out of control, wreaking havoc on our carefully curated vision?

"Transformations are delicate things, often built on foundations of glass," he retorts, taking a step closer to Ashton. The way he looks at him, with a mixture of pity and disdain, sends a chill down my spine. "And your little fortress is teetering on the brink, ready to shatter."

I turn to Ashton, searching his eyes for any sign of a crack. He meets my gaze, and for a brief moment, I see the fire that once ignited his ambition, flickering beneath the weight of uncertainty. "Ignore him," I whisper, more for my sake than his, though the words feel feeble against the roaring tide of doubt swirling around us.

"Am I supposed to ignore the truth?" the intruder presses, feigning a look of innocence. "You see, Ashton and I shared more than just the corporate grind. We were colleagues and... friends. Friends who stumbled into some rather messy situations, wouldn't you say?"

The silence in the boardroom grows heavy again, each breath laden with the unspoken fears of my colleagues. My chest tightens, and I can feel the weight of their scrutiny like a hundred eyes boring into my back. But I can't back down. Not now.

"This isn't about the past; it's about the future," I say, raising my voice slightly to command the room's attention. "We're standing at the precipice of something extraordinary. It's easy to throw stones when you're standing on a pile of rubble, but we're building something solid here. Let's focus on that."

His laughter rings out, harsh and mocking. "Building? Is that what you call it? A foundation built on a lie is destined to collapse." He pauses, letting the words settle, as if enjoying the way they hang in the air, waiting for a reaction. "You're just a pawn in this game, my dear. You have no idea what's really at stake."

I feel a flush of anger surge through me, igniting a fire I didn't know I possessed. "You're mistaken if you think I'm a pawn. I'm a player in my own right, and I won't let you dictate our narrative."

Ashton's eyes widen slightly, a flicker of admiration mingled with surprise. He doesn't speak, but I can feel the surge of gratitude emanating from him, fueling my resolve.

"Is that so?" the man asks, tilting his head slightly, as if considering my words for the first time. "Then tell me, what do you really know about him? About the choices he's made? The sacrifices?"

The question hangs heavy in the air, daring me to stumble. I could answer that, yes, I know Ashton is a man of integrity, that he is steadfast and loyal, a visionary who has inspired me in more ways than I can count. But I also know that every hero has a shadow, and his is larger than most.

I refuse to back down. "I know that Ashton has faced challenges that would break lesser people. He's made mistakes, but who hasn't? What matters is how we learn from those mistakes and rise above them."

At that moment, I realize that I'm not just defending Ashton; I'm asserting my belief in second chances, in the resilience of the human spirit. It's easy to focus on failures, to dwell in darkness, but I choose to shine a light on the journey, on the growth and transformation that can emerge from the ashes.

"Then you're a fool," the man sneers, crossing his arms in defiance. "Because the truth will always surface, and when it does, your fragile little world will crumble."

I turn away from him, a gesture of defiance that I hope is as powerful as it feels. "If the truth is so dangerous, then why are you here? Shouldn't you be in the shadows, lurking like the coward you are?"

His eyes narrow, and for a moment, I see something flicker there—fear, perhaps? But just as quickly, it's replaced by a smugness that sends a shiver down my spine. "I'm merely ensuring that the truth doesn't get lost in your fantasy."

Ashton stands beside me, his presence a steady anchor amid the chaos. The weight of the moment presses down on us both, but I can feel the resolve building within him, an ember igniting into a flame. Together, we face the storm, fortified by our shared purpose, refusing to let this man define our narrative. The boardroom, once a battlefield, now feels more like a stage, and we are ready to reclaim the spotlight, determined to turn this moment of vulnerability into a victory for all we've built.

A taut silence stretches across the room, thick and palpable, as I lock my gaze onto the intruder. The air crackles with unspoken accusations, and I can feel the weight of the executives' stares, their eyes flicking between the old acquaintance and us, like a pendulum swinging between judgment and intrigue. I don't know how long we'll be able to hold this line, how much longer we can withstand the scrutiny that feels both suffocating and electrifying.

"You're mistaken if you think you can unsettle us with whispers of the past," I say, my voice steady, fueled by the surge of adrenaline coursing through my veins. "Ashton has grown from those experiences, and it's time you acknowledge that. This presentation is a reflection of his evolution, not a relic of his mistakes."

The man cocks his head, a smirk tugging at the corners of his lips. "A lovely sentiment, really, but it doesn't change the facts. Facts, my dear, have a way of lurking just beneath the surface, waiting to erupt when you least expect it." His tone drips with condescension, the kind of superiority that turns my stomach.

I feel Ashton shift beside me, his hand tightening around mine, the warmth of his grip a reassuring anchor in this turbulent sea. The strength I draw from him empowers me, and I turn to him, silently encouraging him to reclaim his narrative, to stand firm against the shadows of the past.

"Listen," Ashton says, his voice gaining traction. "I've faced my share of challenges and I've made mistakes, but who hasn't? What matters now is what we do with those experiences. I won't let you manipulate our present with your version of the past."

His resolve hits me like a fresh breeze, and I can sense the shift in the room. The executives' expressions flicker from shock to curiosity, their attention now riveted on Ashton. It's a subtle but powerful change, a crack in the facade of indifference that I can only hope will widen.

The man sneers, his bravado faltering just a hint. "Ah, but your past is never too far behind, is it? The walls may seem sturdy, but they are riddled with cracks. A little pressure, and they will come tumbling down."

I can feel the tension coiling tighter, ready to snap. "We are not here to relive the past," I declare, cutting through his taunts with a clarity I didn't know I possessed. "We're here to showcase the future we've built—an opportunity that can only thrive in a culture of trust and collaboration. If you want to be a part of that, I suggest you drop the theatrics and join us in moving forward."

There's a flicker of surprise in the man's eyes, and for a moment, I wonder if I've hit a nerve. But the moment passes, and his facade quickly returns, more solid than before. "You're brave, I'll give you that. But bravery alone won't save you from the inevitable storm that is coming."

With a deep breath, I channel every ounce of determination into my words. "We can weather any storm. It's not just about surviving; it's about thriving in spite of the winds that try to knock us down."

The executives are watching closely, their pens poised over notepads, and I can see the flickers of contemplation dancing across their faces. Maybe, just maybe, this confrontation will highlight our strength instead of our weaknesses.

"Enough!" The word bursts from one of the executives, a woman whose sharp eyes have been silently assessing the situation. Her voice cuts through the tension like a knife, demanding attention and respect. "We came here to hear a presentation, not to dive into the dramatics of personal history. If you have something to contribute to the meeting, do so. Otherwise, let's move on."

Relief washes over me, an unexpected wave that urges me to push forward, to finish what we started. The intruder's smugness falters, and the air lightens just enough to breathe.

"Thank you," I say, turning to the executive with genuine appreciation. "Now, if we can refocus on our project, I'd like to present the innovations we've developed. Our team has worked tirelessly to create something that not only addresses our company's needs but sets a new standard in the industry."

With that, I dive back into the presentation, the familiar rhythm of my speech flowing through me like a well-rehearsed melody. I can feel Ashton's presence beside me, grounding me as I navigate the intricate details of our plan, from the dynamic market strategies to the cutting-edge technologies we've implemented.

As I speak, I notice the flickers of interest on the executives' faces, their brows furrowing in concentration as they absorb the information. I can't help but glance at Ashton, who is watching me with a mixture of admiration and pride that fills me with warmth. It's a reminder of why we're here—to build something remarkable together.

We flow through the slides, illustrating our journey with vivid images and compelling narratives that showcase our dedication. Each statistic I present seems to dissolve the remnants of doubt that hung in the air, and the energy shifts, transforming from suspicion to appreciation. I catch sight of the intruder, who now leans back in his chair, arms crossed, a scowl etched across his face as he realizes the tide has turned.

"Your projected growth numbers are impressive," one executive says, nodding thoughtfully. "But what about the risks associated with this initiative?"

I take a breath, ready to tackle the challenge head-on. "Every great opportunity comes with risks. We've anticipated potential hurdles and developed strategies to mitigate them effectively. It's not just about the numbers; it's about our commitment to adapt and grow as we navigate the landscape together."

The discussion evolves, with questions swirling around the table, and I relish the back-and-forth exchange, feeling more empowered with each interaction. Ashton adds insights, his voice steady and confident, weaving in the practical applications of our ideas and reinforcing the vision we've crafted together. The atmosphere shifts, the room buzzing with collaborative energy, the executives no longer just spectators but participants in our vision.

As the meeting progresses, I can see the initial wariness fading, replaced by a sense of shared excitement. We delve deeper into the specifics, engaging in dialogue that reveals the strength of our proposal and the passion behind our efforts. Each point we make resonates like a note in a symphony, the melody building to a crescendo that I can almost taste in the air.

But in the back of my mind, I can't shake the nagging feeling that the intruder isn't done. Just as I think we're on the brink of securing our success, he straightens in his seat, eyes glinting with mischief. "I think it's important to remember," he interjects, his tone dripping with disdain, "that public perception is everything. If your past comes back to haunt you, no amount of innovation will save you."

The room hushes again, all eyes shifting toward Ashton, the air growing thick with tension. I feel the heat rising again, but I refuse to let his words pierce through the armor of confidence we've built.

"Public perception is based on transparency and growth," Ashton replies, his voice steady, as if he's been preparing for this moment all along. "I've learned from my past mistakes, and I won't shy away from that reality. Our journey has shaped us into stronger leaders. That's the story we want to tell."

A murmur ripples through the boardroom, a collective acknowledgment of Ashton's bravery in confronting his past. I can see the seeds of doubt dissipating, replaced by respect for his candor. The intruder, though still defiant, seems momentarily taken aback, his bravado fading into uncertainty.

As the meeting winds down, I can feel the tide turning in our favor. The conversation flows freely now, the executives engaging with us, voicing their thoughts, ideas, and even concerns with genuine interest. For the first time, I feel like we're truly a part of something larger than ourselves, a collaboration fueled by shared vision and commitment.

As we wrap up, the atmosphere is charged with enthusiasm and a sense of accomplishment. The intruder sits silently, an outcast in a room that has embraced our collective spirit. I glance at Ashton, and we share a look that speaks volumes—relief, triumph, and a shared understanding of how far we've come.

The meeting concludes, and as the executives begin to disperse, I feel a weight lift from my shoulders. "We did it," I whisper to Ashton, the words barely escaping my lips.

His smile is bright, illuminating the remnants of the earlier tension. "We did. Together."

As we step out of the boardroom, hand in hand, I realize that this moment isn't just a victory; it's a testament to our resilience, to the power of love and loyalty in the face of adversity. Together, we've not only faced the storm but emerged stronger, ready to embrace the future we've built side by side. The past may have shaped us, but it will never define us, and as we walk into the sunlight, I can't help but feel that the best is yet to come.

# Chapter 13: The Aftermath

The fluorescent lights above buzz softly, their steady hum contrasting with the disarray that swirls in my mind. As I settle into my chair, the familiar scent of stale coffee wafts through the air, wrapping around me like a heavy blanket. Each inhale is tainted with the aftermath of the meeting—my heart still races, pounding against my ribcage like a frantic bird desperate to escape. The muted whispers of my coworkers filter through the glass partitions that separate our cramped office spaces, each syllable dripping with judgment, and I find myself wishing for a moment of solace in this open-plan purgatory.

    I glance around, hoping for a smile or a nod, a sign that maybe they understood. Instead, I'm met with a sea of aversion, eyes darting away as if my very presence could taint their productivity. Ashton, the one person whose opinion mattered most in that room, avoids me like a shadowed memory. The very thought sends an icy tendril of dread curling around my stomach. He was my ally, my confidant, but today he appears as though he's been carved from stone, too hurt or too proud to acknowledge the bond we once shared.

    Time seems to stretch, each tick of the clock echoing like a countdown to oblivion. The rhythmic tap of my fingers against the keyboard is a feeble attempt to drown out the chaos brewing in my chest. I can't shake the sensation of being both the villain and the victim, a delicate balancing act I never signed up for. They don't know the backstory—how long I've stood beside Ashton, how fiercely I've defended him against the relentless tide of skepticism. They don't see the nuances of our shared laughter or the late nights spent huddled over blueprints, brainstorming ideas that could change everything.

    I take a deep breath, the air thick with the scent of burnt popcorn and the distant chatter of coworkers discussing mundane weekend plans. This place used to feel like home, a sanctuary where dreams mingled with ambition, but now it's a cage made of glass and steel. I'm acutely aware of the weight of their stares, the whispers that grow like weeds in the corners of our office. "She's lost it," I imagine them saying. "How could she stand by him?" Each word is a tiny dagger, and I'm left to fend off the internal bleeding, the gnawing doubt that eats away at my resolve.

Fingers trembling, I scroll through a sea of emails, searching for anything that could distract me from the tumult. A message pops up from the marketing team, a colorful presentation promising to rejuvenate our brand's image. For a fleeting moment, the vibrant graphics pull me in, an intoxicating mix of blues and greens that dance across my screen. I can almost feel the warmth of the sun, the freedom of the outdoors—but then, reality crashes down again, heavy and suffocating. The bright colors fade to gray as the memory of our meeting resurfaces, a vivid tableau of accusations and betrayal.

I close my eyes, wishing I could turn back time, to that moment when the atmosphere shifted, electric and charged with tension. When the boss slammed her fist on the table, demanding answers I wasn't prepared to give. My throat had gone dry, words caught like fish in a net, writhing for freedom while I stood there, paralyzed. Ashton had looked at me then, a flash of confusion in his gaze, and in that split second, I realized we were not allies but combatants in a war we never wished to fight.

The coffee machine gurgles nearby, a distant reminder of comfort. I stand abruptly, the decision igniting a spark of rebellion in my chest. It's a simple act, but it feels monumental. As I walk toward the break room, each step reverberates with determination, a mantra to remind myself that I refuse to be defined by the murmurings of others. The room is filled with the warm aroma of brewing coffee, and I let it envelop me, if only for a moment, a small comfort amid the turmoil.

I pour a cup, the dark liquid swirling like a tempest in a teacup. A flash of movement catches my eye—it's Mia, her wide-eyed expression betraying the worry that lingers beneath her calm exterior. She has always been the unofficial peacemaker of our office, a gentle soul with an infectious laugh that could light up the dreariest of days. As she approaches, I prepare myself for her well-meaning inquiries, fully aware of the protective walls she tends to erect around her friends.

"Hey," she says softly, her voice a soothing balm against the jagged edges of my thoughts. "I heard about the meeting. Are you okay?"

The concern in her eyes feels like an anchor pulling me down, but it's also a lifeline. I nod, forcing a smile that feels more like a grimace, determined to keep the façade intact. "I will be," I reply, attempting to sound more convincing than I feel. "It's just... a lot."

Mia's gaze sharpens, the way a hawk watches its prey. "You're stronger than this, you know that, right?"

Her words wrap around me, warm and sturdy. I want to believe them, to let them seep into my bones and dispel the shadows of doubt that cling to me like mist. But the memories of whispered conversations and the weight of unspoken judgments loom over my thoughts.

"I just need to figure things out," I admit, the vulnerability creeping into my voice despite my best efforts to remain stoic.

Mia leans against the counter, her expression shifting from concern to understanding. "You don't have to go through this alone. Whatever happens, I'm here for you."

Her promise settles in my chest, igniting a flicker of hope amidst the darkness. As I take a sip of my coffee, I feel a little more grounded, a little more like myself. Maybe the road ahead would be fraught with challenges, but perhaps, just perhaps, I could navigate it with the strength I've been too afraid to acknowledge.

I return to my desk, armed with a renewed sense of purpose. The whispers may continue, the judgments may still linger, but within me, a quiet defiance stirs. I'm not merely a bystander in this tale; I'm a protagonist, and it's time to rewrite the narrative.

The atmosphere in the office thickens as the hours drag on, the fluorescent lights flickering intermittently like the pulse of an anxious heart. My fingers tap rhythmically against the keyboard, a futile attempt to drown out the silence that weighs heavily between Ashton and me. Each click is a reminder of the unspoken words that hang in the air, hanging like low-hanging clouds before a storm. I glance up occasionally, hoping to catch his eye, to find some semblance of understanding, but each time he's absorbed in his screen, the tension stretching between us like a taut string, ready to snap.

The dull buzz of the office is punctuated by the sporadic laughter from the break room, an oasis of camaraderie that feels miles away. I can picture Mia, with her carefree laughter and sunny disposition, bringing light into that space as she shares stories about her weekend adventures. I envy her ease, the way she can slip into casual conversation like a fish into water, while I stand on the sidelines, a reluctant observer in my own life.

Desperation begins to seep in, and I find my thoughts wandering to the future, a terrifying place filled with uncertainty. What if the whispers grow louder? What if my standing in the office is irrevocably tarnished? The specter of gossip haunts me, its claws digging into my confidence, gnawing away at the resolve I had managed to muster. With each passing minute, I feel more like an imposter, a mere shadow of the person I once was, battling against the tide of doubt that threatens to consume me.

Finally, I can't take it anymore. With a deep breath, I push back from my desk and make my way toward the break room. Each step feels like a declaration of intent, a subtle rebellion against the confines of my desk and the weight of judgment that clings to me like a second skin. As I cross the threshold, the rich aroma of freshly brewed coffee wraps around me, soothing my frayed nerves. I grab a mug, the ceramic warm against my palm, and pour a generous helping, allowing the dark liquid to seep into my soul like a balm.

Mia looks up as I enter, her smile brightening the room. "There you are! I was just saying how quiet you've been lately. Everything okay?"

Her words are a lifeline, pulling me from the depths of my spiraling thoughts. I manage a smile in return, though it feels brittle, ready to shatter under the weight of honesty. "Just trying to process everything from earlier," I admit, taking a cautious sip of coffee, the heat igniting my senses.

Her brow furrows slightly, the concern in her eyes deepening. "I get that. But you know you're not alone in this, right? We all stand behind you, even if it doesn't feel like it."

Her unwavering support stirs something within me, a flicker of hope amid the uncertainty. I nod, though the shadows of doubt still loom large. "It just feels like the whole world is watching, waiting for me to fail."

Mia shakes her head, her dark curls bouncing lightly. "That's just the nature of office life. People love a good story, but they're not the ones who define your worth. You're strong, and you've always fought for what you believe in."

I take a moment to absorb her words, letting them seep in like the warmth of the coffee. Mia has a gift for turning insecurity into strength, her presence a buoy that keeps me afloat when the tides threaten to pull me under.

"Thanks, Mia," I say, sincerity washing over me. "I really needed to hear that."

Just as she opens her mouth to respond, the door swings open, and in strides Jeremy, the office manager, exuding his usual air of confidence. The sharp click of his shoes on the tiled floor draws everyone's attention. He glances between us, his expression inscrutable, before settling his gaze on me. "Can we chat for a moment?"

My heart drops. There it is—the moment I've been dreading, the culmination of whispers and judgment, laid bare. I nod, trying to maintain my composure as I follow him out of the break room. The air feels charged as we step into the hallway, the fluorescent lights overhead flickering like the anxious thoughts racing through my mind.

Jeremy leans against the wall, arms crossed, the picture of authority. "I wanted to check in on you after the meeting. There's been a lot of talk, and I know things are tense."

A lump forms in my throat, and I swallow hard, grappling with the mixture of fear and frustration. "I appreciate you reaching out, but I'm okay," I reply, forcing the words out, though they feel like lead on my tongue.

He studies me for a moment, the intensity of his gaze piercing through my facade. "Listen, I know you care about Ashton, but you need to be careful. People are quick to judge. It's not just your reputation at stake; it's the team's morale."

Each word lands like a blow, sending waves of resentment coursing through me. "So, what? I should abandon him? Just turn my back on someone I believe in because it's convenient?"

His expression softens slightly, a hint of empathy flashing across his features. "I'm not saying that. But you have to think about the bigger picture here."

I take a step back, the weight of his words pressing down on me. "The bigger picture? You mean the picture where I stand idly by while the people I care about are pushed aside? I can't do that, Jeremy. I won't."

The tension crackles between us, an unspoken understanding passing through the air. I can see it in his eyes, the recognition of my conviction, and for a brief moment, the chasm between us narrows.

"I admire your loyalty," he finally concedes, his tone shifting to one of respect. "Just tread carefully. We all want what's best for the team."

With that, he turns, leaving me alone in the hallway, the echo of his footsteps fading into the distance. The encounter ignites a flame within me, a surge of determination that pushes aside the fear gnawing at my insides. I will not allow this to define me or the bonds I've built.

I return to my desk, and as I sit down, I notice Ashton looking my way, uncertainty dancing in his eyes. The world around us may be spiraling, but within me stirs a resolve stronger than the whispers that linger in the air. I'll find a way to bridge the gap, to prove that standing by someone is not a weakness but a testament to the strength of conviction.

The afternoon drags on, the clock ticking toward the inevitable end of the workday, but I feel anything but settled. The air is thick with unspoken words, my desk a battlefield strewn with papers and half-formed thoughts. As I glance around, the once-familiar faces of my coworkers morph into a gallery of judgment, each look a reminder of the choice I made to stand by Ashton. I want to believe in the righteousness of my loyalty, but the nagging questions burrow deeper into my psyche. Was I right to defend him? What if I was merely stoking the fires of dissent?

A gentle knock on my cubicle wall draws my attention, and I look up to find Mia peeking in, her eyes softening at the sight of me. She steps inside, the small space suddenly feeling a little less suffocating. "Hey, can we talk?"

"Of course." The words escape my lips almost too quickly, my heart yearning for the warmth of friendship amid the cold winds of office politics.

As she settles into the chair opposite me, I can see the concern etched on her face. "You know, I've been thinking about what you said earlier. About standing by Ashton."

I nod, eager for someone to validate my feelings. "It's like... I want to be there for him, but it feels like I'm carrying the weight of the world on my shoulders. Every time I defend him, it's like I'm inviting more scrutiny on myself."

Mia leans forward, her expression serious yet compassionate. "That's the cost of loyalty, I guess. But it's also a testament to who you are. Not everyone would stick their neck out like you are. You've got a good heart."

Her words wrap around me, a blanket of warmth that staves off the chill of self-doubt. "But what if it all backfires? What if I lose everything—my job, my friendships?"

"Then you pick yourself up and keep moving," she replies with an easy confidence that contrasts starkly with the storm raging inside me. "You can't live your life based on what-ifs. Sometimes, you have to trust your gut."

As she speaks, I find myself absorbing her unwavering strength. I think about the times we've shared, her laughter like music that played through the hard moments, echoing even in the most chaotic days. She has always been a beacon of light, and right now, her light is illuminating a path forward that I hadn't considered.

Just then, Ashton walks by our cubicle, his figure a silhouette against the harsh overhead lights. I catch a glimpse of his expression—one of weariness and resolve—and my heart twists in my chest. What must he be feeling right now?

"Are you going to talk to him?" Mia asks, breaking through my reverie.

The question hangs in the air like a delicate thread, each moment stretching as I contemplate the answer. "I want to," I say slowly. "But what if he doesn't want to talk to me?"

Mia raises an eyebrow, a playful glint in her eyes. "You're not going to know unless you try. You two are like a couple of lost puppies right now—needing each other but too proud to bark."

With that, I laugh, the tension in my shoulders easing just a little. "Okay, fine. I'll talk to him."

Mia gives me a thumbs-up, her enthusiasm infectious. "You've got this!"

After she leaves, I sit for a moment, gathering my thoughts like scattered leaves in a storm. The world outside the office blurs, the sounds of bustling traffic and distant laughter fading as I focus solely on what lies ahead.

I take a deep breath, pushing myself out of my chair. Each step toward Ashton's desk feels like traversing a tightrope, precarious yet exhilarating. As I approach, I notice the small personal touches he's added—a photo of him with his sister, the quirky mug adorned with a quote about coffee and life. These little details remind me of the man I care about, the one whose passion and dedication have always shone through despite the chaos around him.

When I reach his desk, I pause, heart racing. He glances up, surprise flickering in his eyes. "Hey."

"Hey," I reply, my voice steadier than I feel. "Can we talk?"

He nods, and I can see the tension in his shoulders ease just a fraction. We find a small conference room nearby, a space that feels less exposed than our desks, the walls lined with motivational posters that do little to alleviate the weight of the conversation looming before us.

Once inside, I close the door behind us, a soft click sealing us off from the world outside. The silence stretches between us, thick and heavy, but I refuse to let it suffocate me. "I wanted to check in on you," I begin, my voice trembling slightly.

Ashton leans against the table, his expression inscrutable. "I appreciate that. It's been... a rough day."

"I can only imagine," I say softly. "I've been thinking a lot about what happened. About how the team's been reacting."

He nods, running a hand through his hair, the familiar gesture tugging at my heartstrings. "I hate putting you in this position. I never wanted to drag you into my mess."

I take a step closer, the space between us feeling charged with unspoken words. "But I chose to stand by you. I believe in you, Ashton. You're not alone in this."

His eyes flicker with something—gratitude, maybe—but also an undercurrent of sadness. "You shouldn't have to bear the weight of my mistakes. It's not fair to you."

"It's not about fairness," I insist, my voice rising slightly with passion. "It's about loyalty and support. I don't want to abandon you when you need someone to believe in you."

For a long moment, the silence envelops us, the air thick with unfiltered emotions. I can see the struggle in his eyes, the conflict between his desire for my support and the instinct to shield me from the fallout. Finally, he exhales, the tension releasing in a heavy sigh. "I don't want to drag you down with me."

"You're not dragging me down," I say firmly. "You're my friend. And I believe that we can navigate this together, even if it's messy."

His gaze softens, the walls he's built around himself beginning to crack. "It means a lot to hear you say that. I just wish I could make things right."

"I know," I reply, stepping even closer until I can feel the heat radiating off him. "But we can figure this out. Together."

In that moment, the chasm that had grown between us starts to shrink, filled with the shared understanding of two people standing in the eye of a storm. I reach out, placing a hand on his arm, grounding us both in the chaos. "Let's tackle this head-on. We can come up with a plan."

Ashton looks down at my hand, a flicker of hope dancing in his eyes. "You really mean it, don't you?"

"I do," I say with conviction. "We're stronger together. And I refuse to let fear dictate our choices."

A smile breaks through his somber expression, a glimpse of the man I know beneath the weight of doubt. "Okay. Together it is."

With that, we spend the next hour mapping out strategies, brainstorming ideas that could turn the tide and restore not just his standing but our team's morale. Each suggestion feels like a step forward, a brick laid in the foundation of our resilience.

As the sun begins to dip below the horizon, casting golden light through the blinds, I realize that the shadows of doubt that once haunted me are fading. The journey ahead may be riddled with challenges, but I've discovered an undeniable truth: standing by someone you care about isn't just about loyalty; it's about the unwavering strength that comes from connection.

In that moment, as we sit side by side, the world outside fades away, leaving only the bond we're forging anew. Together, we'll face whatever storms lie ahead, fortified by the knowledge that true strength lies in unity, in standing firm against the tides that threaten to pull us under.

# Chapter 14: A Turning Point

The fluorescent lights buzzed above, casting a sterile glow over the chaotic landscape of papers and half-drunk coffee cups that littered the desk. It was in that dimly lit corner of the office, where shadows danced playfully along the walls, that I found myself locked in a battle of wills with Ashton. His usual confidence, the kind that rolled off him like a soft whisper of smoke, had turned brittle under the weight of my questions. I felt like a wild animal cornered by a hunter, desperate for answers, my heart pounding like a drum signaling an impending storm. The scent of burnt coffee mingled with the stale air, wrapping around us, thickening the tension.

"What are you hiding, Ashton?" The words slipped from my lips, raw and unfiltered, each syllable charged with a tremor of betrayal. My heart raced, propelled by a cocktail of frustration and fear, pushing me to the edge of something I couldn't fully understand. I had given him so much of myself, and yet here we were, dancing around the truth like two nervous teenagers at their first prom, both terrified of what would happen if we let go.

He ran a hand through his tousled hair, and in that moment, I saw a flicker of uncertainty cloud his hazel eyes. "It's not that simple," he replied, his voice low and strained, as if the very act of sharing his truth could shatter the delicate balance of our connection. I could feel the vulnerability lurking beneath the bravado, a raw wound wrapped in layers of bravado, begging to be acknowledged.

The air crackled with an energy that felt almost palpable, and I took a hesitant step closer, wanting to breach the chasm between us but unsure of what lay on the other side. "Then make it simple," I urged, desperation coloring my tone. "I deserve to know what brought you to this point. You can't just keep shutting me out."

He hesitated, the muscles in his jaw tightening as he wrestled with the ghosts of his past. The shadows in the room seemed to close in around us, listening intently to the unspoken words hanging heavily in the air. It was a moment suspended in time, a perfect blend of fear and hope, as I stood on the precipice of his past, teetering on the edge of a truth I feared would reshape everything.

"I didn't always make the right choices," he finally admitted, the confession escaping him like a wounded bird. "There were times when I thought I was doing what was best, but I was just running away—running from my mistakes, from my family. It's easier to wear a mask and pretend everything's fine." His voice cracked slightly, and I could see the façade he had built slowly crumbling, piece by piece.

Ashton's words wrapped around me, pulling me closer to him, and for the first time, I sensed the weight of his struggles. It was a world he had been trying to keep hidden, a landscape littered with the wreckage of his decisions. I could almost picture the versions of himself he had left behind—each one a silent echo of the man he had become, a collage of regrets and unfulfilled dreams.

I leaned against the edge of the desk, feeling the cool surface bite into my palms. "You're not alone in this, you know," I whispered, the truth of my own vulnerabilities spilling out alongside his. "I've made my share of mistakes too. I've spent so long trying to outrun them that I lost sight of who I really am. We're both just trying to find our way back."

His gaze held mine, and in that instant, the walls I had built around my heart began to tremble, bricks shifting as I let the possibility of understanding seep in. The memories of late-night conversations and laughter echoed in my mind, a warm blanket on a cold night, reminding me of the bond we had nurtured. It wasn't perfect, but it was ours, and I yearned to protect it from the storms of our past.

"I want to be better," he confessed, the vulnerability in his voice wrapping around me like a fragile thread. "But I don't know if I can." There was a rawness to his admission, a trembling acknowledgment that cut through the air like a blade. I saw the boy who had once hidden behind a mask of bravado, the boy who had faced demons far scarier than the monsters lurking in my own heart.

As the clock ticked away in the background, marking the seconds like a countdown, I felt a shift within me, a subtle understanding dawning. We were both standing at a crossroads, our paths intricately intertwined, and the weight of his confession settled like a blanket of snow, both heavy and beautiful. The fear of jumping into the unknown flickered in my chest, but it was overshadowed by the urgency of this moment—the undeniable desire to leap into the depths of his truth, to immerse ourselves in a world stripped of pretense.

"We can figure it out together," I said softly, letting my resolve cascade like a waterfall. "No more masks. No more running." My heart swelled with a determination I hadn't known existed. I didn't want to be the girl who clung to her fears. I wanted to be brave, to stand alongside him as we navigated the labyrinth of our lives.

He stepped closer, the warmth radiating from him cutting through the tension. There was a flicker of hope in his eyes, a spark igniting a flame we both desperately needed. In that instant, I felt the dam within me crack, and with it came a surge of emotions—fear, hope, vulnerability, and an overwhelming sense of connection that was unbreakable.

As the shadows flickered around us, the room felt smaller, our struggles converging in a symphony of shared experiences and unspoken words. We stood on the edge of something profound, both terrified and exhilarated by the leap we were about to take into the depths of our intertwined destinies.

The silence that followed felt heavy, like a fog rolling in from the coast, thick and impenetrable. I could hear the faint ticking of the clock, a constant reminder of time slipping away, and the weight of unspoken words filled the space between us. The world outside faded, leaving just the two of us suspended in this moment. Ashton's expression was a canvas painted with regret, and as I searched his eyes, I realized how much I craved to understand him.

"What if I told you that I'm scared?" he said, his voice barely above a whisper, as if uttering the words too loudly would make them more real. It struck me how he could stand before me, this man who seemed so effortlessly confident, yet here he was, unearthing fears that mirrored my own. There was something profoundly beautiful in that fragility, a shared humanity that felt like an electric current buzzing between us.

I took a step closer, feeling the warmth radiating from him, drawing me in like a moth to a flame. "You're not alone in that," I said, trying to weave my own honesty into the conversation. "I've been terrified too—terrified of letting people in, of trusting them with the pieces of myself that I keep hidden." My heart raced, the admission spilling out like a secret I had held far too tightly. The vulnerability in my words hung in the air, mingling with the lingering scent of coffee and the faint traces of aftershave clinging to his collar.

"Isn't that the irony?" Ashton asked, a wry smile breaking through the tension. "We spend so much time building walls, thinking they'll protect us, when in reality, they just isolate us." His insight struck a chord deep within me, resonating like a note played on a well-tuned guitar. I had spent years erecting barriers, convinced they were my armor against the world, when all they did was keep me from feeling alive.

The office around us faded further into the background, becoming nothing more than a backdrop for this moment. I could almost hear the rustle of leaves outside, the whisper of the wind carrying stories of distant lives, and the city hummed softly beyond the walls. I pictured the bustling streets of Chicago, where each block was alive with stories unfolding, strangers navigating their paths. Yet here we stood, in this cocoon of honesty, exploring our truths.

"What if we tore down those walls?" I asked, my voice steady despite the tremor of uncertainty beneath. "What if we took the leap together?" The thought of sharing my fears with him, of being vulnerable and open, sent a thrill down my spine. It felt both exhilarating and terrifying, like standing at the edge of a high dive, peering down into the deep blue abyss below.

He looked at me, those hazel eyes glinting with something I couldn't quite decipher—was it hope? Or perhaps a flicker of disbelief? "You make it sound so simple," he replied, a hint of amusement dancing in his tone. "But what if we fall? What if we crash and burn?"

I couldn't help but laugh at the thought, a sound that felt foreign and liberating all at once. "Well, if we do, at least we'll have some great stories to tell," I quipped, the humor serving as a balm for the tension that crackled in the air. The truth was, I was done being scared. Life was a cacophony of moments, and each misstep only added to the rhythm of our existence.

His laughter joined mine, and it echoed off the walls like music, a melody of shared understanding. "Maybe we can build something better," he suggested, his gaze softening, a glimmer of vulnerability shining through the bravado. "Maybe we can create a space where we're not afraid to be ourselves."

In that instant, I felt the tremors of possibility swirl around us, swirling like leaves caught in an autumn breeze. "Yes," I breathed, the word bursting forth, carrying the weight of my resolve. "Let's create that space."

Ashton stepped closer, and I could feel the heat radiating between us, a magnetic pull that sent shivers down my spine. The unspoken promise hung in the air like a delicate thread, binding us together in our shared commitment to embrace the unknown.

The clock continued to tick, each second an echo of our choice to move forward, to leap into the uncertainty together. I could feel the energy in the room shift, the shadows receding as light flooded in. It was as if the universe conspired to support our decision, urging us to break free from the chains of fear that had held us captive for far too long.

"I want to be honest with you," he said, his voice low and steady. "There are things in my past that I've kept buried. Things I'm not proud of." There was a gravity to his words, a sense of weighty histories that clung to him like an old coat. I could see the flicker of pain in his eyes, and my heart ached for the boy who had struggled beneath the weight of his choices.

"Whatever it is, I'm here," I reassured him, my heart swelling with a fierce determination. "We can face it together. You don't have to carry that burden alone." The sincerity in my voice felt foreign yet familiar, a promise wrapped in hope and empathy.

As he stood there, processing my words, I could see the barriers he had erected begin to tremble, the fissures widening as he contemplated the leap of faith we were about to take. There was an authenticity in this exchange that felt both liberating and terrifying—a connection forged in the crucible of honesty.

"I don't know how to start," he admitted, a hint of vulnerability softening his tone. I smiled, feeling the corners of my lips lift in encouragement. "You can start by telling me about your dreams," I suggested, eager to shift the narrative towards something lighter. "What do you really want?"

The question hung between us, a lifeline thrown into the deep waters of uncertainty. Ashton paused, his expression shifting as he searched for the words, and I could almost see the gears turning in his mind, the cogs of self-doubt clashing against the aspirations he had stifled. "I want to be someone who inspires," he finally said, the words spilling out like a secret he had kept locked away. "I want to help people find their voice, to be a guiding light in a world that often feels dark."

The sincerity in his voice sent a rush of warmth through me, igniting a spark of admiration. "That's beautiful," I replied, my heart swelling at the thought of him stepping into that role. "You already have that in you. It's just waiting to be unleashed."

In that moment, I could see the potential glimmering in his eyes, the light of someone who was just beginning to discover the depths of their own capabilities. And as we stood together in that dimly lit office, surrounded by remnants of our fears and hopes, I realized we were no longer just two individuals navigating our struggles. We were allies, partners ready to face the unknown hand in hand, ready to transform our stories into something extraordinary.

The air between us pulsed with a newfound intensity, each word woven into the fabric of our shared reality. The office, usually a sterile environment filled with the clatter of keyboards and muffled phone calls, had transformed into our sanctuary—a makeshift safe haven where secrets could breathe and dreams could stretch. My heart raced, not with fear, but with the thrilling anticipation of possibilities unfurling before us like petals blossoming in the dawn.

Ashton shifted slightly, the way he always did when he was trying to gather his thoughts, and I could sense the storm of emotions brewing just beneath the surface. "You don't understand," he began, his voice steady yet laced with a tremor that hinted at the weight of his truths. "I've hurt people. I've made choices that I can't take back. I used to think I was invincible, but every time I look back, all I see is a trail of destruction." His eyes darkened, and for a moment, the bravado faded, leaving behind a young man grappling with the consequences of his past.

I took a step closer, drawn in by the gravity of his confession. "Ashton, we all make mistakes," I replied softly, my voice a gentle murmur that cut through the tension like a warm breeze. "What matters is how we choose to move forward. We can't change the past, but we can shape our future." The realization hung between us, and as I spoke, a part of me felt compelled to reach out and anchor him to the present.

The faint hum of the city beyond the glass windows served as a backdrop, a reminder of the vibrant life outside waiting for us. The sun had dipped below the skyline, painting the horizon in hues of orange and pink, a kaleidoscope of colors that felt almost too beautiful to exist in conjunction with our shared heaviness. I wanted him to see that beauty, to understand that even in darkness, light could seep through if we allowed it.

"I just don't want to hurt you," he admitted, the vulnerability raw and unfiltered. His gaze held mine, a torrent of emotions swirling within, and in that moment, I understood the depths of his fears. The thought of being the one to break him, to push him past his limits, sent a shiver of apprehension through me. But alongside that fear was a fierce determination—a flame ignited by the bond we were forging.

"You won't," I assured him, every word an oath that bound us together. "We're in this together, remember? I'm not going anywhere." The sincerity of my promise enveloped us, a tether connecting our hearts in this fragile moment.

He nodded slowly, a flicker of hope igniting in those hazel eyes. "I want to believe that," he said, his voice low but steady. "But I need to tell you everything, no more hiding. It's time to confront my past."

As he took a deep breath, I could feel the gravity of what he was about to share. I watched as his chest rose and fell, the light from the streetlamps filtering through the window illuminating the sharp angles of his face, casting shadows that danced across his features. He was beautiful in a way that was disarming, the kind of beauty that stemmed from authenticity rather than superficiality.

"My father was never around," he began, his voice barely above a whisper, as if the admission could shatter the remnants of the walls he had carefully constructed. "He was always off chasing his own dreams, leaving my mother to pick up the pieces. I guess I thought I could be different, that I could rise above the chaos. But I ended up just like him."

The admission struck a chord within me, resonating with memories of my own fractured family dynamics. "Ashton," I said softly, reaching for his hand, my fingers intertwining with his. "You're not your father. You're not defined by his choices."

His grip tightened around my fingers, and I could feel the tremors of his past echoing through our connection. "I know, but it's hard to shake off those expectations," he continued, the honesty laced with sorrow. "I wanted to be the hero, the one who saves everyone, but I ended up being the villain in my own story."

"No one is a villain in their own story," I countered, my voice firm yet gentle. "We're all just people trying to figure things out, making mistakes along the way. What matters is that you're here now, willing to confront it."

The moment hung between us, charged with an energy that felt almost sacred. It was as if we were standing at the threshold of something profound, a doorway into uncharted territory where pain and healing intertwined. The warmth of his hand in mine felt like a lifeline, tethering us to this moment of shared vulnerability.

"I want to change," he confessed, his voice barely above a whisper. "I want to be the person I've always dreamt of being. I want to inspire others, not hurt them."

"Then let's do that together," I replied, my heart swelling with an urgency that felt like a call to action. "Let's carve out a space where we can be ourselves, where our dreams can breathe and take flight. We can help each other grow."

The intensity in his gaze deepened, and I could sense a shift—a subtle metamorphosis unfolding between us. It was in that moment, standing together amidst the shadows of our pasts, that I realized how intertwined our lives had become. The flickering candle of hope ignited within me, illuminating a path forward.

He took a deep breath, releasing the tension that had coiled within him. "I want to share my dreams with you," he said, his voice steadying. "I want to help others find their voice, just like you've helped me."

And there it was—a beautiful symmetry to our connection. In helping him confront his fears, I had also discovered my own strength. "Together, we can build something incredible," I said, excitement bubbling within me.

As the conversation deepened, we explored the dreams that had once felt too distant to grasp. We envisioned a world where we could create workshops, inspire others to share their stories, and help those navigating their own tumultuous paths. The vibrant energy that enveloped us felt transformative, a surge of life that whispered promises of a brighter future.

The sun had fully set, leaving behind a tapestry of stars that twinkled like diamonds against the deep indigo sky. The city beyond our window buzzed with life, a reminder that our dreams were not just wishes cast into the night; they were seeds waiting to be nurtured into something magnificent.

As the night deepened, we leaned into our shared aspirations, mapping out the contours of our journey ahead. With each word exchanged, the invisible threads connecting us grew stronger, weaving a tapestry rich with potential and promise. We were no longer just two souls adrift in the chaos of life; we were co-authors of our own story, crafting a narrative steeped in courage and vulnerability.

In that small, dimly lit office, surrounded by the remnants of our pasts, we made a pact—a promise to navigate the storm together, to lift each other when the weight felt unbearable, and to celebrate the victories, no matter how small. As we sat in that cocoon of possibility, the world outside continued to spin, oblivious to the profound shift occurring within the walls of our sanctuary.

And for the first time in a long while, I felt a sense of clarity wash over me. I was not just a collection of past mistakes; I was a beacon of hope, ready to guide Ashton—and myself—into the light. Together, we could rewrite our stories, transforming the chaos of our lives into a symphony of resilience and growth, a testament to the beauty of second chances and the power of connection.

# Chapter 15: Rediscovering Trust

The air buzzed with the electric hum of summer in Chicago, the kind that wrapped itself around your shoulders like a warm shawl. From my perch in the cozy corner of a local café, the rich aroma of freshly brewed coffee mingled with the sweet scent of pastries cooling on the countertop, creating a welcoming embrace that felt like home. The café, a charming mix of rustic wood and exposed brick, was alive with the chatter of regulars—familiar faces that punctuated the atmosphere with laughter and conversation. I watched as the barista expertly pulled shots of espresso, each movement precise, a dance in rhythm with the bustling backdrop of the city outside.

As I stirred my caramel latte, the world beyond the window offered a vibrant tableau. Bicycles whizzed by, their riders laughing and weaving through traffic, while pedestrians ambled past, their faces lit with the carefree glow of a sun-drenched afternoon. The vibrant colors of blooming flower boxes along the sidewalk added an almost festive air to the scene, a stark contrast to the quiet tumult brewing within me. It had been days since that fateful confrontation with Ashton, our words still hanging in the air like a heavy fog, but there was an unmistakable shift, a softening of edges that hinted at the possibility of healing.

Ashton had always been a force of nature—a whirlwind of ideas and determination that could either inspire or infuriate. In the past, our rivalry had fueled late-night brainstorming sessions, each of us vying to outdo the other, our passions clashing like thunder and lightning in the night sky. But now, the competitive tension was morphing into something more tender, more nuanced. I had caught glimpses of his vulnerability, his relentless drive to prove himself, which stirred something deep within me. I admired his tenacity, even as it pulled at the strings of my own insecurities.

The café's door swung open, and a gust of wind swept in, carrying with it the unmistakable scent of summer rain. I looked up to find Ashton entering, his dark hair slightly damp, framing his face in an artful tousle that somehow made him look even more handsome. His eyes, those deep pools of determination, caught mine as he approached, and I felt a familiar flutter in my chest—a spark of something I couldn't quite name. He slid into the seat across from me, his usual confident grin tempered by a newfound gentleness.

"Hey," he said, his voice warm, breaking through the barrier of silence that had lingered between us. "I figured we could brainstorm a little more today."

"Brainstorm?" I echoed, a teasing smile dancing on my lips. "Isn't that what led to our lovely shouting match last week?"

He chuckled, the sound rich and infectious, easing the remnants of tension that still clung to the corners of our relationship. "Yeah, well, I thought we might try a different approach this time. No shouting. Maybe a bit of compromise?"

"Compromise?" I raised an eyebrow, intrigued. "What's in it for you?"

He leaned back in his chair, arms crossed, a playful smirk playing on his lips. "I get to see you smile again without the impending doom of an argument hanging over us."

His words washed over me, a gentle balm to my frayed nerves. In that moment, I realized how much I had missed our easy banter, the way our conversations could flow effortlessly, sometimes spiraling into heated debates but always circling back to a shared respect for one another's brilliance.

We began to talk about our campaign ideas, sketching out plans on napkins as if we were artists crafting a masterpiece rather than mere colleagues caught in a tumultuous relationship. The café buzzed around us, but in our little bubble, it felt like time had paused. I could see the fire in Ashton's eyes as he outlined his vision—bold strokes of ambition mixed with practical, grounded steps that made my heart race with excitement.

"Imagine this," he said, leaning forward, his enthusiasm infectious. "We combine our strengths—your creative edge and my analytical approach. Together, we could really shake things up."

His passion resonated within me, igniting my own ideas. I leaned closer, eager to dive deeper into our newfound partnership. Our laughter intertwined with the café's symphony, the murmur of voices and clinking of cups fading into the background. Each shared insight, every moment of understanding, began to rebuild the fragile threads of trust that had been so precariously frayed.

As the afternoon wore on, the sun began to dip lower in the sky, casting a warm golden glow through the windows. I could feel the weight of the world lifting from my shoulders, replaced by the lightness of possibility. With every passing hour, the rivalry that once defined us was slowly being transformed into something far more profound. I was surprised to find myself rooting for him, cheering on the very qualities that had once sparked our disagreements.

It was a shift I hadn't anticipated, this gentle drift toward companionship. The barriers that had once seemed impenetrable began to dissolve, replaced by a budding camaraderie that felt almost exhilarating. The thought of intertwining our personal and professional lives no longer filled me with dread but instead painted a picture of shared victories, laughter echoing in the corridors of our successes.

In the growing twilight, as we finally set our napkin sketches aside and gathered our belongings, I looked into Ashton's eyes. There was a flicker of understanding, a silent promise that we would navigate this new territory together. The journey ahead was still uncertain, but for the first time in a long while, I felt a surge of hope.

As we stepped out into the evening air, the city pulsed around us, a living, breathing entity full of potential. I took a deep breath, inhaling the scent of rain-soaked pavement and blooming jasmine. It felt like a new beginning, a chance to rediscover trust in both Ashton and myself, to embrace the tangled threads of our lives as they wove a richer, more vibrant tapestry.

The city wore a different shade of life as we stepped into the busy streets, our conversations spilling into the evening like a colorful thread weaving through a tapestry. Neon signs flickered above, casting a kaleidoscope of colors onto the sidewalks where hurried commuters dodged each other, clutching cups of coffee and cell phones, their lives a chaotic rhythm against the steady hum of the city. Ashton walked beside me, his presence an anchor amidst the whirlpool of activity. It was strange, really, how much had changed in just a few days. A strange alliance was budding between us, tempered by laughter and tentative vulnerability, and I found myself intrigued by the man beside me.

With each step, the energy of the city seeped into my veins. I could hear music spilling from nearby bars, mingling with the chatter of groups enjoying the night. The scent of street food wafted through the air, tempting and tantalizing. As we approached a small food cart serving sizzling tacos, my stomach growled in agreement, reminding me that we hadn't eaten since that morning.

"Are you hungry?" Ashton asked, his brow arched in that familiar way that made it hard to remember why I had ever thought of him as a rival.

"Starved," I replied, my voice laced with mock desperation. "But only if they have those spicy shrimp tacos."

A sly grin broke across his face, one that sent a thrill down my spine. "I'll take that as a personal challenge. Let's find out if they're really as good as you say."

He ordered for both of us, his easy banter with the vendor illustrating how effortlessly he could charm anyone. I watched as he interacted, a natural charisma pouring from him like the vibrant salsa that accompanied our meal. We settled onto a small bench, the world around us fading into a soft blur as we focused on our food. The first bite of the taco was an explosion of flavors—spicy, tangy, and utterly delightful.

"I stand corrected," he said, his mouth full, "these might be life-changing."

"I told you!" I laughed, a genuine sound that felt foreign yet exhilarating. The tension that once simmered between us dissipated with each shared bite, each bite steeped in the kind of camaraderie that could only bloom in the glow of city lights and the shared delight of good food.

As we devoured our tacos, our conversations drifted into more personal territory. We exchanged stories of our college days—mine spent holed up in the library, dousing myself in textbooks, while he recounted wild nights out with friends that now seemed like echoes of a different life. I learned about his first foray into advertising, a humiliating but hilarious mishap involving a giant inflatable gorilla that had deflated spectacularly at a client's event. He laughed at the memory, and I couldn't help but join in, imagining the scene with vivid clarity.

"What about you?" he asked, curiosity sparkling in his eyes. "What's your most embarrassing moment?"

I hesitated, the playful facade slipping momentarily as I reflected on the moments that had shaped me. "Well, there was this one time during a presentation, my laptop crashed mid-slide. I was so flustered that I accidentally spilled coffee all over my notes. Talk about a confidence killer."

His laughter echoed through the air, deep and infectious, wrapping around me like a comforting blanket. "I guess we've both had our share of disasters."

"True," I replied, a smile creeping onto my face. "But we survived. That's what matters, right?"

"Absolutely," he agreed, his gaze intense, as if he could see the resilience hidden beneath my playful exterior. "It's the failures that teach us how to succeed."

With the tacos devoured, we lingered on the bench, the warm summer air wrapping around us like a nostalgic embrace. The laughter had stripped away the remnants of our previous animosity, leaving us vulnerable yet invigorated. I felt a blossoming sense of trust begin to flourish, taking root in the fertile ground of shared experiences.

Ashton leaned back, stretching his arms above his head, the movement causing his shirt to pull tight across his chest. I tried to avert my gaze, but curiosity got the better of me. There was an undeniable appeal in his relaxed confidence, and I found myself captivated by the man I had once thought to be nothing more than an obstacle in my path.

"What's next?" I asked, eager to prolong this moment, to dive deeper into the newfound connection that thrummed between us like an electric current.

"I was thinking we could hit that rooftop bar nearby," he suggested, a hint of mischief in his eyes. "The view is incredible at night, and I hear they make a mean mojito."

The idea thrilled me, the thought of sharing a drink with Ashton under the sprawling Chicago skyline felt both exhilarating and slightly terrifying. I nodded, unable to suppress a smile that seemed to grow from somewhere deep within.

We navigated through the labyrinthine streets, finally reaching the bar, a chic rooftop oasis that overlooked the shimmering skyline. The twinkling lights of the city reflected in our glasses as we settled into a cozy corner, the air filled with laughter and music that created a backdrop of warmth and intimacy.

As we clinked our glasses, I felt a surge of hope. This was more than just a professional partnership; it was blossoming into something profound, a connection built on shared laughter, mutual respect, and the willingness to confront our fears together. The weight of our past began to feel lighter, as if we were stepping into a new chapter—one filled with possibilities that had once seemed impossible.

The evening wore on, our conversations flowing effortlessly, blending dreams and ambitions with the casual ease of two friends navigating uncharted waters. I found myself sharing my hopes for the future, the way I longed to leave a mark in the industry, while he spoke of his aspirations to create campaigns that resonated on a deeper level.

Time seemed irrelevant as the city pulsed below us, the heartbeat of a world in motion. Each moment spent together drew us closer, a tentative weaving of our lives that felt both natural and extraordinary. The laughter we shared, the stories we exchanged, and the trust we began to build became the threads stitching our past and future together. And as the sun dipped below the horizon, painting the sky in hues of pink and orange, I couldn't shake the feeling that this was just the beginning.

As we lingered on the rooftop, the gentle hum of the city below felt like a lullaby, wrapping us in its melodic embrace. The air was thick with the aroma of summer—grilled meats wafting from nearby street vendors mingling with the floral notes of jasmine creeping over the balcony railings. We took our time sipping on our drinks, the coolness of the mojitos a refreshing contrast to the warmth radiating from the setting sun. Each sip became a reason to linger, a reminder of the ease we had discovered in one another's company.

Ashton leaned back in his chair, his gaze sweeping across the skyline. "You know," he began, his voice low and thoughtful, "this city has a way of bringing out the best in people. It's like the energy feeds off our ambitions and dreams."

I followed his gaze, letting the sprawling cityscape consume me—the twinkling lights of the skyscrapers standing tall against the darkening sky like a constellation of aspirations waiting to be realized. "It does," I agreed, feeling the excitement bubble up inside me. "It's like every corner has a story waiting to unfold."

He turned to me, a spark of curiosity lighting up his eyes. "What story would you want to unfold if you could write your own?"

I pondered for a moment, the weight of his question settling on my shoulders. The vision that emerged was vivid—my dreams morphing into colorful images before me. "I want to create campaigns that don't just sell a product but resonate with people's lives," I confessed, my voice steady. "I want to inspire, to connect, and to evoke real emotions. It's not just about marketing; it's about storytelling. I want to be the voice that people remember."

Ashton's expression shifted, a mix of admiration and something deeper lurking behind his eyes. "You're already doing that," he said earnestly. "The way you've approached this campaign has changed how we think. It's not just about numbers; it's about people. You have a gift."

His words washed over me, a balm for my insecurities that had lingered long after our initial confrontation. I could feel the weight of my ambition lifting, buoyed by the realization that my dreams were not so far out of reach. "And you?" I asked, eager to learn more about the man beside me. "What do you want?"

His laughter rang out, a rich sound that seemed to draw the very essence of the city closer. "I want to create something that lasts. Something that makes people think differently about the brands they interact with." He paused, his gaze turning serious. "I want to challenge the status quo."

Our conversation danced between dreams and reality, intertwining our hopes and fears with the threads of our shared experience. The moment was intoxicating, charged with a chemistry

I had never anticipated. The rivalry that had once seemed so daunting was slowly morphing into a partnership rooted in respect and understanding, a bond that felt more meaningful with each passing moment.

As the evening unfolded, the city lights blinked awake, one by one, casting a warm glow that wrapped around us like a protective cocoon. We shared our fears, our dreams, and our aspirations, a mutual unveiling of the layers we had hidden behind professional facades. The walls that had divided us began to crumble, revealing a foundation built on shared values and passions.

When the waiter brought over another round of drinks, I noticed Ashton's fingers absentmindedly tapping against the table, a habit of his I had come to recognize. "What's on your mind?" I asked, intrigued.

He met my gaze, his expression contemplative. "I've been thinking about how much we've both grown since we started this journey. How we've pushed each other, challenged each other, and somehow come out stronger." He paused, his eyes narrowing slightly as he assessed me. "I think we could do something really special together, something beyond just this campaign."

The proposition hung in the air, tantalizing and charged. The idea of joining forces with Ashton, of melding our strengths and creativity into something new and powerful, sent a thrill down my spine. "You mean, like a collaborative project?" I asked, my voice barely above a whisper.

"Exactly," he replied, leaning forward with an intensity that made my heart race. "We both have unique perspectives and talents. If we harness that energy, we could really disrupt the industry."

The thought sent my mind spiraling into overdrive, possibilities unfurling like petals blooming in spring. "What if we created a brand that embodies authenticity?" I proposed, feeling the excitement surge within me. "A brand that tells real stories, connects with people on a personal level, and highlights the values that matter most to them?"

Ashton's eyes lit up, a fire igniting within them. "Yes! And we could leverage social media to amplify those stories, to engage directly with our audience. We could build a community around it—something that feels less like marketing and more like a movement."

A movement. The word hung in the air, filling the space between us with an undeniable energy. I could envision it—the late-night brainstorming sessions, the creative chaos, the unfiltered passion that would drive us to create something extraordinary.

"I'm in," I said, my heart racing. "Let's do it."

With that simple phrase, we sealed our fate. The tension that had once existed between us was replaced by an electric current of potential, intertwining our paths in ways I had never anticipated. As we clinked our glasses together in celebration, the warmth of possibility enveloped us, mingling with the summer air and the city's heartbeat below.

As the night deepened, laughter and conversation swirled around us, the lively atmosphere punctuated by the clinking of glasses and the soft hum of music. I felt a sense of belonging in this moment, a realization that perhaps I was finally beginning to find my place—not just in the city, but with Ashton.

In the days that followed, our collaboration blossomed. Late nights turned into early mornings as we bounced ideas off each other, each conversation igniting more inspiration. We scoured the city for stories, venturing into vibrant neighborhoods and hidden corners where real people lived their lives, eager to capture the essence of authenticity we aimed to portray.

The more time we spent together, the more I recognized the depths of Ashton's character—a passionate idealist wrapped in layers of wit and charm. He became not just a partner in work but a friend, someone who made the weight of ambition feel lighter and the journey more enjoyable. I found myself eagerly anticipating our brainstorming sessions, where laughter flowed as freely as our ideas, and the bonds of trust deepened with every shared moment.

As our project took shape, the boundaries between personal and professional blurred, crafting a narrative that was uniquely ours. Each brainstorming session was infused with laughter, each challenge met with determination. We were no longer just two individuals vying for success; we were a team, united by a shared vision that felt both exhilarating and terrifying.

The city pulsed around us, and in that vibrant tapestry of life, I knew we were crafting our own story—one filled with authenticity, connection, and the rediscovery of trust. It was a tale worth telling, a journey worth taking, and I was grateful to have Ashton by my side as we ventured into the unknown together.

# Chapter 16: Breaking the Cycle

The hum of the city pulsated around me, a rhythmic heartbeat that thrummed through the soles of my shoes as I stepped onto the cracked pavement of Union Square. New York had a way of swallowing you whole, but on that particular evening, it felt as though the world had exhaled, allowing a cool breeze to curl through the bustling crowd. The sun was dipping behind the skyscrapers, casting a golden hue over the park that shimmered like a promise against the concrete jungle. As I wandered through the market stalls, the aroma of roasted chestnuts wafted through the air, mingling with the laughter of children chasing after pigeons, their joy infectious.

I found solace in the mundane chaos, a welcome distraction from the whirlwind that was my life with Ashton. Each fruit vendor, each artisan selling handmade jewelry, felt like a tiny vignette of a story waiting to be told. My fingers brushed against the rough wooden surface of a handcrafted table, and I smiled at the craftsperson who stood nearby, a weathered man with twinkling eyes and a gentle demeanor. In that moment, I wanted to capture everything—the sounds, the smells, the vibrant hues of the world around me—like snapshots of life I could tuck away in my mind to revisit whenever the weight of corporate expectations pressed too heavily on my shoulders.

As I navigated through the throng, the memory of our late-night brainstorming sessions flickered in my mind like a neon sign flashing in the night. Those moments with Ashton had become an anchor, drawing me away from the mundane and plunging me into the depths of my creativity. He had an uncanny ability to peel back the layers of my mind, revealing the raw and often chaotic thoughts that swirled within. Each idea I tossed into the air found its counterpart in his steady gaze, igniting a spark that often left me breathless.

We had taken risks together, challenging the status quo of our corporate lives, and I could feel the thrill of it coursing through my veins. The boardroom had become a battleground where we fought for innovation, pushing against the stifling walls of convention. But it was during those hushed conversations beneath the glow of desk lamps in the late hours of the night that I discovered Ashton's vulnerability. As he shared his fears and dreams, his voice would soften, revealing the boy beneath the polished exterior of a successful entrepreneur. The walls he had built began to crumble, piece by piece, and I found myself mesmerized by the fragments of his soul that shone through.

His laughter became my favorite sound, a melodic chime that echoed through our late-night discussions, filling the void with warmth and understanding. I could see the way his eyes danced when he spoke of aspirations that extended beyond quarterly profits and market shares. Together, we crafted a vision for our campaign that transcended the confines of our jobs, a manifesto of dreams that dared to challenge the world. I reveled in the creativity that flowed between us, each idea a brushstroke on the canvas of our collaboration, vibrant and full of life.

Yet, as the days turned into weeks, shadows from our past loomed larger, creeping into the corners of our blossoming relationship. Just when I began to believe that we could navigate this storm together, the weight of old wounds began to resurface, bringing with it a tension that crackled like static in the air. I could feel the familiar anxiety tightening its grip on my chest, a reminder that love was never without its challenges.

I caught Ashton staring at his phone more often, his brow furrowed in concentration as if the weight of unspoken words hung between us. The once-comfortable silence began to feel heavy, laden with the unsaid, and I could sense the fissures forming beneath the surface. In those moments, I would find myself longing to bridge the gap, to reach out and grasp his hand, to remind him that we were in this together. But the fear of provoking the darkness that lurked within him held me back.

One evening, as we prepared for another late-night session, I decided to confront the tension that simmered beneath our collaboration. I placed a steaming cup of coffee in front of him, the aroma wafting into the air, hoping to draw him back into the warmth we had cultivated. "What's on your mind?" I asked, my voice steady yet soft, trying to penetrate the fortress he had built around himself.

He looked up, and for a fleeting moment, I saw the flicker of uncertainty in his eyes. "Just the campaign," he murmured, though I could tell there was more lurking behind those words. "I think we might need to pivot our approach."

"Pivot?" I echoed, curiosity piqued. "Is this about the data from last week? I thought the feedback was positive."

His sigh was heavy, like a weight that had settled on his shoulders. "It's not just the numbers. There are things—personal things—coming to light, and I don't want them to affect us. This campaign means everything to me, and I don't want my past to interfere with our vision."

As the words hung in the air, I realized that this was the moment where our paths diverged and intertwined, where the fragility of our connection became evident. I leaned closer, willing my heart to speak louder than my fears. "We can face this together. Whatever it is, I'm here, and I'm not going anywhere."

In that instant, I could see the glimmer of hope reflected in his eyes, and I knew that the journey ahead would demand strength from both of us. But love, I understood, was an intricate dance between vulnerability and resilience. We were at a crossroads, and while the shadows of the past threatened to pull us apart, I was determined to weave a tapestry of trust and understanding that would hold us together, no matter the storms that lay ahead.

## SHADOWS OF AMBITION 167

The city seemed to hum a little louder as we dove deeper into our campaign, the vibrant pulse of New York becoming our backdrop, almost a character of its own. Each morning, as I walked into the office, I felt a thrill course through me—a blend of anticipation and nervous energy. Ashton and I had formed an unspoken alliance, a delicate balance of creativity and pragmatism that ignited something within me I hadn't realized was lying dormant. Our brainstorming sessions flowed seamlessly, ideas mingling like the city's cacophony, each suggestion layered with passion and purpose.

The conference room transformed into our sanctuary, where whiteboards filled with scrawled notes and colorful diagrams became a visual representation of our aspirations. I remember one particularly crisp Tuesday morning, sunlight streaming through the tall windows, illuminating the space with a golden glow that seemed to breathe life into our ideas. Ashton stood at the whiteboard, markers in hand, his brows furrowed in concentration. I watched as he sketched out a concept for a promotional event—something bold, something that could capture the city's imagination.

"Picture this," he began, his voice steady yet infused with excitement. "We host an interactive art installation in Central Park, where people can contribute to a collaborative mural. Each stroke, each color represents their interpretation of what our campaign stands for. It's about community, engagement, and creativity."

The vision he painted was vivid and enchanting, sparking a rush of adrenaline that danced through my veins. "And we could have live performances! Musicians, dancers—an entire celebration of creativity," I added, my mind racing ahead as I envisioned the park alive with color and sound.

Ashton turned to me, and for a moment, the world around us faded. His eyes held a glimmer of something—an appreciation for the wild, uninhibited ideas I often feared to share. "Exactly! We'll turn this campaign into an experience rather than just another corporate initiative," he said, the excitement in his voice echoing off the walls.

Those moments became the heartbeat of our collaboration, a rhythm that pulsed between us, allowing both our strengths to flourish. He pushed me to explore the edges of my creativity, while I grounded his lofty ideas in reality, ensuring they were actionable. Yet, despite the exhilarating highs, I could feel an undercurrent of tension lingering, as if we were dancing on a tightrope, each step precarious. The shadows of our pasts loomed large, casting doubts that threatened to unravel the delicate fabric we were weaving.

Late nights had become our norm, the office bathed in the soft glow of desk lamps as we delved into research and revisions. The air was thick with caffeine and possibility, and I often found myself stealing glances at Ashton as he worked, captivated by the determination etched on his face. Those hours were sacred, and in the quiet moments, we'd share fragments of our lives—stories that revealed our scars and our dreams, exposing vulnerabilities that felt almost dangerous yet exhilarating.

One evening, we sat sprawled across the floor, surrounded by a sea of colorful sticky notes and takeout containers, our laughter echoing off the walls. The stress of our jobs melted away as we played a ridiculous game of "Would You Rather," where the absurdity of the questions pulled us further into our own world. "Would you rather fight one hundred duck-sized horses or one horse-sized duck?" I asked, unable to contain my laughter.

Ashton burst out laughing, the sound rich and melodic. "Definitely the hundred duck-sized horses. A horse-sized duck sounds terrifying—imagine the quack! It would be deafening!"

Our laughter faded into a comfortable silence, and I felt a warmth spread through me, an undeniable connection that simmered beneath the surface. I glanced at him, my heart fluttering as I realized how effortlessly our worlds had intertwined. "You know," I ventured, my voice barely above a whisper, "I never expected to find this—this creativity and freedom—in a corporate setting."

He looked at me, his expression softening. "Neither did I. It's like we're breaking the mold together, redefining what this can be."

Yet, just as I began to embrace the magic we were creating, a chill swept through me, a reminder of the walls we had both erected. The following week, a series of meetings unfolded, each one drumming up more anxiety than the last. Ashton began to retreat into himself, his laughter becoming a distant echo, and the connection we had nurtured felt strained under the weight of unsaid words.

During a particularly tense meeting, as the marketing team dissected our campaign strategy, I noticed Ashton's shoulders tense, the familiar furrow reappearing on his brow. The conversation pivoted towards market analysis, and I could see him becoming increasingly withdrawn, the fire in his eyes dimming.

I leaned over, my voice low enough to be heard only by him. "Hey, don't let them get to you. We know what we're doing, remember?"

He shot me a grateful glance, but it didn't reach his eyes. "I know. It's just... I can't shake this feeling that my past is catching up with me. I want to be present, for you, for this campaign, but it's hard."

The confession hung heavy in the air, and my heart ached for him. I reached for his hand, squeezing it gently, wishing I could chase away the shadows. "Whatever it is, you don't have to face it alone. We're in this together."

But the words felt inadequate, mere band-aids on wounds that ran deep. I wished I could show him that love wasn't just about navigating the bright moments but also about weathering the storms. I could see the storm clouds gathering in his eyes, and I knew then that the journey we had embarked upon would demand more from us than either of us had anticipated.

As the week wore on, I became increasingly aware of the fissures threatening to widen between us. Our late-night sessions transformed into quiet standoffs, the air heavy with unspoken fears. Each time I attempted to breach the distance, I found myself met with a wall of silence, a barrier that felt both familiar and frightening. We were teetering on the edge of something profound, yet the ghosts of our pasts threatened to pull us under, and I knew that navigating this terrain would require more than just creativity and passion—it would require courage.

The days morphed into a blur of creativity and tension, a tapestry woven with vibrant threads of innovation and darker shades of uncertainty. I could feel the weight of Ashton's struggle pressing against the walls of our shared space, thickening the air until it felt charged with electricity, as if a storm were brewing just beyond the windows. Our campaign had taken on a life of its own, gaining momentum with the fervor of a New York City subway train, and yet, here we were, standing on the platform, watching it rush past us, leaving a trail of chaos and noise in its wake.

The heart of Manhattan pulsed around us, a frenetic energy that mirrored the conflicts brewing within our partnership. I had always loved the way the city came alive at dusk, with the streetlights flickering on like stars, illuminating the faces of hurried commuters. But now, as I glanced out at the streets below, the magic felt tainted by the shadows creeping into our work and lives. My mind raced, thinking of all the ways I could reach him, all the words I could offer to dismantle the wall he had erected.

One evening, after yet another tense day in the office, I found myself wandering the cobblestone streets of the West Village, seeking refuge among the eclectic cafés and bookstores that lined the narrow lanes. The scent of roasted coffee beans mingled with the sweet aroma of freshly baked pastries, wrapping around me like a comforting hug. I stepped into a small café, the bell above the door chiming softly, and sank into a worn leather chair, hoping to summon the courage to confront the tension that hung heavy between us.

As I sipped my cappuccino, the barista's chatter filled the space, their voices creating a tapestry of life that reminded me I wasn't alone in this chaotic city. It was here, among the mismatched furniture and eclectic art, that I finally let my mind wander back to the night Ashton and I had spent in the office, mapping out our future.

That night, I had peeled back the layers of my own insecurities, sharing stories from my childhood that shaped who I was. I spoke of the relentless pressure to excel, to always be the best version of myself—a drive that had propelled me forward but also left me feeling unworthy of love. I had seen the vulnerability in his eyes then, the way he had listened with rapt attention, absorbing every word as if they were sacred truths. It had felt like a turning point, a moment where the barriers began to crumble.

But now, those moments felt distant, overshadowed by the looming shadows of doubt and fear. I closed my eyes, willing myself to remember the strength of our connection, to grasp tightly to the thread that wove us together. The buzz of the café faded into the background, replaced by the echo of his laughter and the softness of his gaze when he spoke of dreams larger than our corporate ambitions.

Determined to bring back that warmth, I resolved to find the right moment to reach out. I returned to the office with a sense of purpose, crafting my plan in my mind like an artist preparing to paint. I needed to confront the shadows head-on, to pull back the curtain on the fears that had taken root in both of us. When I entered the conference room, I found Ashton already there, his expression a mix of fatigue and determination as he poured over the latest data.

"Hey," I said softly, my heart racing as I crossed the room to stand beside him. "Can we talk?"

He looked up, his brow furrowed, but he nodded. "Sure. What's on your mind?"

I took a breath, gathering my thoughts as I glanced at the whiteboard filled with our ideas, vibrant and hopeful. "I feel like we're at a crossroads, and I don't want the past to dictate our future. I know it's hard, but we can't let our fears control us. We have to face them together."

Ashton studied me, his blue eyes darkened with a storm I had come to recognize. "It's not that simple. My past isn't just a shadow; it's a reality that has shaped me. I can't just sweep it under the rug and pretend it doesn't exist."

I stepped closer, my voice steady. "I'm not asking you to forget. I want you to share it with me. Let me in, Ashton. We've built something beautiful, and I refuse to let old wounds tear us apart."

He hesitated, the tension in his shoulders easing slightly as he absorbed my words. "It's scary," he confessed, his voice barely above a whisper. "Opening up means exposing my weaknesses, and I don't want to drag you into my chaos."

I reached for his hand, intertwining my fingers with his, feeling the warmth radiate between us. "But love isn't about perfection; it's about understanding and supporting each other through the chaos. I want to be there for you, just as you've been there for me."

For a moment, silence enveloped us, thick and heavy with unspoken fears. Then, slowly, the tension began to dissipate, like the fog lifting off the East River on a crisp morning. I could see the fight within him, the desire to trust, to let someone in despite the risk.

"Okay," he finally said, his voice steadying. "But it won't be easy."

"Nothing worth having ever is," I replied, a smile tugging at my lips. "And I'm not going anywhere."

With that small affirmation, the atmosphere shifted, crackling with renewed energy. We spent the rest of the evening laying bare our fears, sharing stories that unearthed pieces of ourselves we had kept hidden. Ashton spoke of his childhood, filled with uncertainty and a longing for stability that felt perpetually out of reach. He shared his struggle to prove himself in a world that often saw him as just another suit in the corporate landscape. I listened, my heart aching for the boy who had fought so hard to become the man he was today.

In return, I opened up about my own journey, revealing the pressures I faced and the scars I carried. The vulnerability felt like a delicate dance, one that pulled us closer with each shared truth. By the end of the night, the weight of our burdens felt lighter, as if we had stripped away the armor we wore to protect ourselves from the world.

With the shadows finally giving way to a newfound light, I realized that our love was not merely a fairy tale spun from ambition and creativity. It was raw, messy, and real—a reflection of the world around us. As we navigated the complexities of our pasts, I knew we could forge a future built on honesty and vulnerability.

Stepping back into the rhythm of our campaign, I could feel the energy shift. Our collaboration thrived as we melded our visions into something greater than either of us could have created alone. Together, we transformed the once-distant goal of an art installation into an immersive experience that invited others to share their stories, their dreams, and their creativity.

With each passing day, we built not only a campaign but also a bond that felt unbreakable. The city buzzed around us, and together, we stepped into its vibrant embrace, ready to conquer whatever challenges lay ahead. Our love had become our greatest strength, a force that would carry us through the chaos of life—a beautifully tangled web of dreams, fears, and aspirations, woven together against the backdrop of the relentless, stunning pulse of New York City.

# Chapter 17: Unraveling Threads

The morning sun cast its golden hue over the vibrant streets of New Orleans, where the air thrummed with the energy of the day. I stepped onto the cracked pavement, my heels clicking in a staccato rhythm that mingled with the jazz drifting from nearby cafés. Each note seemed to tease and tantalize, echoing the sentiment I held within—an exhilarating yet unsettling anticipation of what lay ahead. The familiar scent of beignets wafted through the air, mingling with the sweet aroma of magnolia blossoms that framed the wrought-iron balconies of the old townhouses. I could almost taste the powdered sugar on my lips as I navigated through the throngs of tourists, each one oblivious to the turmoil brewing beneath my composed exterior.

In a city that embraced the absurd and the beautiful, I had carved out my niche. As a campaign strategist for a local nonprofit, my mission was simple: create a groundswell of support for a cause close to my heart. Yet, as I adjusted the strap of my canvas messenger bag, my thoughts swirled with a gravity that threatened to pull me under. The campaign had begun with such promise, the community rallying around us like a vibrant tapestry woven from countless threads of hope and determination. But just as we neared the finish line, I felt the delicate strands of our efforts begin to fray, tugged at by unseen hands.

My phone buzzed insistently, pulling me from my reverie. A new email had arrived, its subject line unassuming yet laden with implication. I opened it cautiously, my heart pounding as I scanned the words. The message was cryptic, a series of veiled accusations and insinuations that suggested hidden agendas lurking within our own ranks. Who was pulling the strings? I could feel the frisson of anxiety ripple down my spine. The thought of betrayal—especially from someone I trusted—set my pulse racing.

With the vibrant backdrop of the French Quarter fading into a blur, I made my way to our office, a quaint little space tucked away on a cobbled side street. The walls were adorned with photographs of past campaigns, each one a testament to our hard work and commitment. Yet today, they felt like ghosts, specters of a past untainted by the current storm. The creaky wooden floors groaned underfoot, and I paused for a moment, taking a deep breath to steady my racing thoughts.

As I entered, the faint hum of conversation filled the air, mingling with the scent of freshly brewed coffee. My colleagues were gathered around the conference table, animated discussions painting a picture of optimism that felt painfully discordant with my inner turmoil. Ashton, my partner in both work and, increasingly, in life, was seated at the head of the table, his expressive features illuminated by the late morning light streaming through the window. I had grown to adore the way he challenged me, pushing the boundaries of my comfort zone while encouraging my ambition.

Yet today, his relaxed demeanor struck me as dissonant, a careless serenade in the midst of an ominous symphony. "Hey, you're just in time!" he called, his voice smooth and warm, like a freshly poured cup of chicory coffee. I forced a smile, the weight of my discovery settling heavily on my shoulders as I slipped into my seat.

"Did you read my email?" I ventured, my voice tinged with urgency. The chatter around the table paused, eyes flickering toward me. Ashton looked up, the easy confidence that usually radiated from him replaced by a fleeting look of concern.

"Which one?" he replied, his tone casual, but I could see the spark of understanding ignite in his eyes. He had sensed my tension, and the gravity of what I was about to share hung like a storm cloud over us.

"The one about possible sabotage within the firm," I said, my heart racing. "We need to talk about it."

He shrugged, dismissing my concerns with a wave of his hand, a gesture that made my stomach drop. "It's probably just some misunderstandings. We're all a bit stressed, you know how it gets."

The nonchalance in his voice only fueled the fire within me. How could he dismiss the possibility of treachery so lightly? I glanced around the table, noting the shifting expressions of my colleagues. Some looked concerned; others appeared skeptical, as if I had spun a wild tale rather than presenting a potential reality. My heart thudded painfully against my ribs, the sensation of unease morphing into a potent cocktail of frustration and fear.

"Isn't it worth investigating?" I pressed, my voice rising slightly. "If someone is undermining our efforts, we can't just sweep it under the rug!"

Ashton's gaze hardened, a flicker of annoyance crossing his features. "You're jumping to conclusions. We have enough to deal with without chasing ghosts."

His dismissal felt like a slap, a sharp crack that resonated deep within my core. Had our growing intimacy become a veneer that masked deeper issues? Doubt crept in, uninvited yet insistent. As I met his gaze, I could see the spark of irritation, a fire that stoked my own insecurities. Did he truly believe I was overreacting, or was there a part of him that questioned my capability? The shadows of betrayal loomed larger, darkening the space between us.

I turned away, suddenly desperate to escape the weight of his gaze. My fingers traced the edges of the table, grounding me even as the chaos within threatened to unearth my carefully cultivated composure. The vibrant world outside beckoned, yet here I sat, ensnared in a web of intrigue and uncertainty. How had we arrived at this juncture, where the lines between professional ambition and personal affection began to blur? I had come to rely on him not just as a partner in our campaign, but as a confidant, someone who understood the nuances of my aspirations and fears.

With every moment that passed, I felt the threads of our connection fraying. I needed to unravel the mystery surrounding our campaign, and I needed Ashton by my side. But if he refused to acknowledge the potential threat lurking in the shadows, how could I trust that our love—so vibrant, so full of promise—could withstand the weight of betrayal?

The day melted into a sultry evening, the kind that settled over New Orleans like a thick, fragrant blanket. The sun dipped low, casting the sky in strokes of orange and violet, transforming the streets into a kaleidoscope of colors that seemed to pulse with life. As I stepped outside, the heat clung to my skin, a reminder that the city was as alive as my racing thoughts. I navigated the labyrinth of the French Quarter, my senses heightening with each step. The distant strumming of a guitar mixed with laughter and the sizzling of Cajun delicacies wafting from nearby food stalls, an irresistible siren call urging me to surrender to the evening.

Despite the vibrant ambiance, my mind churned with the weight of our conversation. I turned the email over and over in my head, each cryptic phrase unraveling another layer of worry. It was as if I had stumbled into a film noir plot, where the protagonist was a reluctant heroine wrapped in suspicion and intrigue. The thought made me chuckle softly, though it lacked any real humor. In reality, I was just a woman trying to save a campaign that felt increasingly precarious, all while wrestling with the shadows that had begun to seep into my personal life.

I slipped into a small café, its rustic charm inviting me to take refuge in its dim light. The walls were lined with vintage posters, and the air was thick with the aroma of freshly baked pastries. I ordered a café au lait, the comforting warmth a balm against the tumult within me. As I settled into a corner booth, I couldn't shake the feeling that I was being watched. Perhaps it was just paranoia, a side effect of delving into murky waters where I feared betrayal lurked. But the thought of Ashton dismissing my concerns gnawed at me, creating a pit in my stomach that no amount of caffeine could fill.

With my coffee steaming before me, I pulled out my laptop, the familiar glow of the screen both comforting and daunting. I opened the email again, scrutinizing each word as if they held the key to some hidden conspiracy. Whoever had sent this message was a master of ambiguity, leaving just enough breadcrumbs to tempt me down a rabbit hole of speculation. As I typed notes into my document, my mind drifted to the people I had come to trust within our organization. Each name conjured images of camaraderie and shared dreams, but now they also sparked a flicker of doubt. Could one of them be orchestrating this chaos from the shadows?

Just as I began to formulate a plan of action, my phone buzzed, jarring me from my thoughts. It was a text from Ashton, a simple question: "Want to grab dinner?" The casual invitation sent a jolt through me, a clash of yearning and uncertainty. The thought of sharing a meal with him—the way his eyes sparkled when he laughed, the warmth of his presence that filled the spaces around us—offered a fleeting comfort. Yet, I hesitated, the turmoil swirling within me whispering that this moment might not be about romantic gestures and easy conversation. It might require something much more complex: the unraveling of truths.

After a moment of deliberation, I responded with a tentative yes, feeling the tension between what I wanted and what I needed coiling tighter in my chest. When I arrived at the restaurant, the ambiance was an intoxicating mix of candlelight and soft music, the air filled with the scent of roasted garlic and fresh herbs. Ashton was already seated at a small table, his posture relaxed, but I noticed the furrow in his brow as he glanced up to greet me. I took a seat across from him, the space between us suddenly feeling like a chasm.

"You look nice," he said, attempting to bridge the divide with a compliment. I offered a tight smile in return, the words hanging between us, heavy with unspoken tension.

"Thanks. I thought a change of scenery might help clear my head," I replied, taking a sip of my drink to buy time, feeling the liquid warmth slide down my throat.

"I get that. It's been a long week," he said, looking around the restaurant, a slight fidgeting of his fingers hinting at his own restlessness. "How's the campaign going?"

There it was—the proverbial elephant in the room. I swallowed hard, fighting the urge to skirt the issue, to protect the fragile bubble we had created together. But the whispers of the email haunted me, refusing to fade into the background noise of dinner chatter. "Actually, I received a concerning email today," I said, my voice barely above a whisper. "It mentioned possible sabotage."

Ashton stiffened slightly, his eyes sharpening as he focused intently on my face. "Sabotage? What do you mean?"

The way he leaned in, his attention fully on me, ignited a flicker of hope that perhaps this time, he would understand the gravity of my concerns. I explained the email's contents, carefully detailing the implications, the unspoken accusation that someone was undermining our hard work. Each word felt like a release, a way to strip away the weight of isolation that had accompanied my worries.

As I spoke, I watched the subtle changes in his expression, the initial concern melting into skepticism. "You really think someone in the team is doing this?" he asked, his voice steady, but the hint of disbelief was palpable.

"I can't shake the feeling that something isn't right," I replied, my heart racing as I laid bare my vulnerabilities. "We've worked too hard for someone to jeopardize it all."

His brow furrowed, but rather than empathy, I sensed a subtle defensiveness creeping into his posture. "You know how competitive this field is. Maybe it's just someone feeling threatened," he said, his voice tinged with dismissal.

I recoiled at the thought, my chest tightening. "Or maybe it's someone who wants to see us fail," I countered, my tone sharper than intended. The realization struck me—his reluctance to engage in my fears felt like a rejection of my instincts, a refusal to confront a truth that could shatter the illusion of our partnership.

The meal arrived, steaming plates of culinary delights, but the food felt insubstantial, a mere distraction from the reality of our conversation. We ate in silence, the air thick with tension. The restaurant buzzed around us, yet our small table felt like a separate universe, one where shadows loomed larger than life, echoing the whispers of betrayal and mistrust.

With each bite, I felt a part of myself withdrawing, shielding my heart from the storm brewing just below the surface. I needed him to stand with me, to be a partner not just in the successes but in the fights, yet it seemed the closer we came to uncovering the truth, the more he wanted to retreat.

As we finished our meal, I realized this was more than a simple dinner—it was a crossroads. Our burgeoning love, which had felt so vibrant, now felt frail, like a glass sculpture poised on the edge of a table, teetering between admiration and destruction. Would we become stronger together, or would the revelations lurking in the shadows of our campaign tear us apart? The questions hung unvoiced in the air, heavy with unfulfilled possibilities, a silent plea for clarity that remained tantalizingly out of reach.

The lingering taste of our half-eaten dinner hung in the air as we left the restaurant, the warm glow of the streetlamps casting a golden light over the cobblestones. I felt the weight of the night pressing down on me, thick with unresolved tension, like a fog settling into the crevices of my mind. The world around us pulsed with life—the laughter of revelers spilling from bars, the sweet notes of a saxophone drifting from a nearby jazz club—but the vibrancy felt distant, as if I were watching a movie from behind glass, unable to reach out and touch the warmth of it all.

As we walked side by side, the silence between Ashton and me was deafening, filled with unsaid words that clung like a stubborn fog. He glanced at me occasionally, his expression a mix of concern and impatience, as if he were waiting for me to lift the weight of this darkness off our shoulders. The reality was that I felt tethered to the uncertainty that had seeped into our lives, a fear that threatened to unravel not only our campaign but the fragile bond we had cultivated.

The shadows deepened around us, elongating like fingers reaching for something they could never grasp. My mind raced with thoughts of the email—who sent it, and what did they want? Every step felt like a descent into a labyrinth, each twist and turn drawing me deeper into a mystery that had no clear exit. I had once embraced the thrill of unearthing truths, but now the exhilaration was overshadowed by the dread of betrayal, a specter that loomed larger with each passing moment.

"Do you think I'm overreacting?" I finally broke the silence, my voice barely above a whisper. The question hung between us, heavy with the weight of vulnerability. I had to know where he stood, what he truly thought. Did he believe in the integrity of our team, or was he merely placating me for the sake of our relationship?

Ashton hesitated, a flicker of something—frustration?—flashed across his face. "I just think we need to focus on what we can control," he replied, his tone measured, almost clinical. "Chasing down shadows isn't going to help us win this campaign."

His dismissal stung, and I felt the sharpness of disappointment twist in my gut. "And what if the shadows are real? What if someone is actively trying to sabotage our work?" I shot back, unable to contain the passion rising within me. "I need you to be with me on this, Ashton, not just in our successes but in confronting the challenges, too."

He stopped in his tracks, his gaze piercing through the dim light. "I am with you, but I won't let fear dictate our actions. It's a slippery slope. We need to stay focused on our goals, not get lost in paranoia." His words, though spoken with conviction, felt like a barricade, creating distance instead of solidarity.

We resumed walking, the city swirling around us, alive and unaware of the storm brewing in our hearts. I longed to bridge the gap between us, to pull him back into my orbit, but with each passing moment, it felt as if our paths were diverging. The doubts I harbored morphed into a monstrous silhouette, looming over our burgeoning love, threatening to overshadow everything we had built.

In that moment, I resolved to seek the truth on my own. The thought flickered like a match struck in the dark; a tiny flame of determination ignited within me. If he wouldn't engage in this battle, then I would shoulder the burden. I would not let anyone destroy what we had worked so hard to achieve.

The next morning, I dove headfirst into research, the flicker of my laptop illuminating the dim apartment as I dissected the email, each line a potential lead. The taste of coffee bitter on my tongue fueled my relentless pursuit. My fingers flew across the keyboard as I combed through old campaign notes, conversations, and interactions, searching for anything that could point me toward the source of the betrayal.

Hours bled into one another, the chaos of the outside world fading into the background as I honed in on the task at hand. My mind sharpened with each discovery, each connection I made between the dots—interactions that felt innocuous at the time suddenly transformed into potential clues. I became a detective in a world that had once been a simple landscape of community outreach and advocacy. Now, it was rife with suspicion and conspiracy.

As the sun dipped low in the sky, painting the room in hues of orange and pink, a chilling realization dawned on me. The sabotage wasn't just a random act of malice; it felt personal, targeted. My heart raced as I pieced together snippets of conversations I'd had with colleagues—moments where trust seemed to falter, where alliances wavered in the face of competition. Each memory added another thread to the web of suspicion I was weaving, tightening around my chest.

That evening, I decided to confront one of my colleagues, Jenna, a close friend and fellow strategist. She had been instrumental in our campaign, her insights and creativity guiding us toward success. But the more I analyzed her contributions, the more I sensed a change—a subtle shift in her demeanor, the way her laughter no longer reached her eyes when she spoke of our goals. It was a whisper of doubt, a lingering thought that demanded to be acknowledged.

As we met in a small, secluded bar tucked away from the bustling streets, the atmosphere felt charged with anticipation. I ordered a glass of wine, hoping the rich, velvety liquid would soothe the tension coiling in my stomach. Jenna arrived, her smile warm yet hesitant, and I felt an immediate urge to put her at ease, to remind her of the camaraderie we had forged.

"Thanks for meeting me," I said, gesturing to the dimly lit booth in the corner. "I've been feeling a bit overwhelmed lately and wanted to talk."

Her eyes flickered with concern as she settled into the seat across from me. "Is everything okay? You seem a bit on edge."

I took a deep breath, the words tumbling from my lips like a confession. "I received a strange email yesterday, and it got me thinking about our team dynamics. I wanted to see how you felt about everything. Do you think someone might be undermining our efforts?"

The moment I spoke the words, I felt the weight of our friendship press down upon us, an unspoken challenge hanging in the air. Jenna's expression shifted, a flicker of something I couldn't quite place flaring in her eyes. "I don't know, but... things have been tense lately," she replied cautiously, her tone cautious but guarded.

"Exactly," I pressed, my heart pounding. "I can't shake the feeling that there's more beneath the surface. Can you think of anything?"

For a moment, silence enveloped us, thick and oppressive. I watched as she toyed with her glass, her gaze drifting toward the bar. "I guess some people feel the pressure more than others," she said slowly, her voice barely above a whisper. "But I wouldn't jump to conclusions. We're all just trying to do our best."

Her words felt hollow, like a damper on the urgency I felt inside. "But what if our best isn't enough? What if someone's actively working against us?" I pressed, desperation creeping into my voice. "We can't afford to be naive."

The vulnerability of that moment hung in the air, and I could see her weighing her response. The truth I was searching for seemed tantalizingly close, but I feared it would shatter everything. Then, with a quiet intensity, she met my gaze. "I've heard whispers... rumors, really. You know how it gets in this industry."

"What kind of rumors?" I asked, my pulse quickening.

"Just... things about how some people feel sidelined, like they're not getting enough credit. It's not just you and Ashton running the show, you know?" she said, a hint of sadness threading through her tone.

A wave of nausea washed over me. The insinuation hung in the air like smoke, distorting our reality. "You think someone is trying to sabotage our work out of jealousy?"

"I don't know," she admitted, looking away. "But you're not the only one who feels it. Just be careful, okay?"

Her words resonated within me, echoing the fears I had tried to shove down. As I left the bar that night, the weight of uncertainty bore down on my shoulders, but I felt a flicker of clarity—a commitment to protect what we had worked so hard to achieve. I wouldn't let anyone tear us apart, not now when the finish line was finally in sight.

Armed with the knowledge that the threads of our campaign were unraveling, I steeled myself for the confrontation I knew I had to have. I needed to rally the team, to bring us back together and face whatever storm was brewing. As I stepped into the night, the air crackled with anticipation, and I knew that the next move would be mine to make.

# Chapter 18: A Heart Divided

The air was thick with the scent of charred burgers and salty ocean breezes as I leaned against the weathered railing of the pier, watching the sunset smear the sky in hues of tangerine and lavender. This was my sanctuary, a place where the rhythm of the waves crashing against the pylons provided a soundtrack to my turmoil. The fading light cast long shadows, mirroring the uncertainty that had nestled deep in my chest, threatening to unravel the delicate threads of my heart.

Ashton stood beside me, hands shoved deep in his pockets, his shoulders squared against the cooling wind. I could feel the tension radiating from him, a palpable energy that seemed to oscillate between frustration and despair. He looked out at the horizon, but I sensed that his mind was miles away, probably wrapped around the very thing that had shaken my world—his betrayal. I wanted to reach out, to bridge the widening chasm between us, but the fear of what I might discover held me captive. The betrayal wasn't just an abstract concept; it was a tangible entity that lurked in the corners of our relationship, waiting for the right moment to strike.

"Beautiful evening, isn't it?" he murmured, his voice low, almost swallowed by the wind. But the words felt hollow, and I knew that neither of us was in a place to appreciate the sunset. It was merely a backdrop to our unraveling.

I forced a smile, though it felt like a mask rather than a genuine expression. "Yeah, the sky looks like a painting." The words tasted bitter, for I longed for the simple joy of admiring a sunset without the weight of suspicion. The light danced on the water's surface, creating flickering diamonds that mocked the storm brewing within me. Each flicker reminded me of the moments we shared—moments now tainted by doubt.

My mind raced back to the day I uncovered the truth. It had been a normal afternoon, the kind where the sun filters through the leaves, and laughter floats on the breeze. I had stumbled upon a series of messages on Ashton's phone—flirty texts that pricked at the edges of my heart, revealing a connection I hadn't known existed. The name of the woman sent a jolt through me, and as I reread the messages, each word felt like a knife carving into the trust we had painstakingly built. I wanted to scream, to confront him with the truth I held in my trembling hands, but I couldn't shake the image of him—his smile, his warmth—disintegrating before me.

I turned my gaze back to the ocean, desperate to drown out the tumult inside. The waves crashed rhythmically, each swell a reminder that life was an unyielding force, indifferent to my pain. I wanted to be brave, to confront the truth, but my heart quaked at the thought of losing him. My friends had seen the change in me, urging caution like the gentle tug of a tide, reminding me that love could often blind us to what was right in front of us. But how could I tear my gaze from the man I had grown to love?

I inhaled deeply, filling my lungs with the salty air. "Ashton, can we talk?" The words slipped out, laden with the weight of all the unsaid things that had swirled between us like the fog rolling in from the sea.

He turned to face me, his expression unreadable. "What do you want to talk about?" The distance in his voice stung, and I felt the warmth of my vulnerability wash over me. This was the moment I had dreaded, the confrontation that could fracture our fragile connection.

The waves roared behind us, a cacophony of sound that seemed to urge me forward. "I found something on your phone," I said, each syllable a boulder tumbling down a mountainside, unstoppable and inevitable. The silence stretched between us, taut like a wire ready to snap.

His eyes flickered with something—panic? Guilt?—before settling into a mask of composure. "What did you find?" he asked, and the weight of his question hung in the air, heavy with the unspoken acknowledgment that everything was about to change.

"Texts. Between you and—" I hesitated, not wanting to utter her name, as if doing so would give her power over the fragile bond we shared. "Between you and someone else."

The ocean roared, a fitting backdrop for the chaos that surged within me. Ashton's face paled, the color draining from his cheeks as he absorbed my words. In that moment, I saw the flicker of the man I knew, wrestling with the shadows of the man I feared he might be.

"Is this how you found out?" he asked, voice strained as if he were grappling for some lifeline in a sea of my disappointment.

I nodded, the simple act feeling monumental. "I thought we were—"

"Happy?" he interrupted, and there was an edge in his voice, a sharpness that cut through the fog of our shared memories. "I thought we were too."

The words hung in the air, and I could feel the icy grip of betrayal tightening around my heart. "Then why?" The question burst forth, fueled by hurt and confusion. "Why would you do this?"

"I didn't mean for it to happen," he pleaded, his eyes searching mine, seeking understanding or perhaps forgiveness. "It was a mistake. You have to believe me."

Mistake. The word reverberated in my mind like a dissonant chord, a note that didn't quite fit into the symphony of what we had built together. "A mistake?" I echoed, incredulity threading through my voice. "You think that's an excuse?"

"I never wanted to hurt you," he said, his gaze pleading, desperate for me to see the truth beneath the surface. But the truth was a shifting tide, elusive and dangerous, and I struggled to navigate its depths.

I wanted to see him as he was, to wrap my arms around the man who had held me close on so many nights, the man whose laughter echoed in my memory. But every attempt felt like grasping at smoke, slipping through my fingers as I stood on the precipice of our relationship, teetering between love and betrayal.

The silence stretched between us, thick as the fog rolling in from the ocean, enveloping the pier in a shroud of uncertainty. I struggled to breathe, my heart pounding a wild rhythm that felt utterly out of sync with the calm waves lapping at the wooden beams below. The air was heavy with unspoken words, and the scent of salt and impending rain clung to my skin, a reminder of how close the storm was to breaking.

"Look," Ashton began, his voice unsteady, as if he were testing the waters of my resolve. "I never intended for any of this to happen. You know how much you mean to me." He stepped closer, his hands coming out of his pockets as he reached toward me, but I recoiled instinctively, as though the warmth of his touch had suddenly turned cold. I needed space, yet the very thought of distance felt like a betrayal itself.

"You keep saying that, but what does it even mean anymore?" My voice was sharper than I intended, slicing through the air like the gulls screeching overhead. I felt a flicker of guilt for the anger spilling from my lips, but it was eclipsed by the overwhelming ache of betrayal. "What does it mean to be in love with someone and then throw it away for a mistake?"

Ashton's expression faltered, and for a moment, I caught a glimpse of the vulnerability that lay beneath his usually confident demeanor. His eyes, usually so full of warmth, now glimmered with a hint of desperation. "It wasn't like that," he said, his voice softer now, almost pleading. "It was a moment of weakness. I never wanted to hurt you."

"Yet here we are," I countered, my heart aching with the weight of his words. The sky was deepening into a palette of dark blues and purples, the setting sun ceding ground to the encroaching night, mirroring the shadows gathering in my heart. "This isn't just a moment. This is a rupture, a crack in the foundation we built. I don't know how to fix this, Ashton."

The waves crashed harder against the pier, a tumultuous backdrop to the chaos within me. I wanted to find a way back to the blissful ignorance we had shared, those carefree evenings filled with laughter and whispered secrets. Yet, each time I closed my eyes, I saw the texts again—her name, the laughter, the flirtation that danced on the edges of their exchanges like a malicious ghost refusing to be exorcised.

"I need time," I finally said, my voice quivering. "I can't pretend everything is okay. Not right now." The truth tasted bitter on my tongue, but it was necessary. The realization was as heavy as the humid air settling around us, clinging to my skin and filling my lungs.

Ashton ran a hand through his hair, a gesture I had always found endearing, but now it felt like a futile attempt to hold himself together. "I understand," he replied, his voice low, an acknowledgment that hung between us like an unwelcome guest. "But please don't shut me out completely. I'll do whatever it takes to make this right."

"Making it right isn't as simple as saying you're sorry," I shot back, the frustration bubbling up again. "I need to know you understand the depth of what you've done. I can't just sweep this under the rug and hope it'll disappear. Love isn't magic, Ashton; it's work. It's trust. And you broke that trust."

The tension coiled tighter, each word twisting into a knot that felt insurmountable. I turned my back to the ocean, desperate to escape the icy fingers of doubt that threatened to drown me. "I need space to think. I'll call you when I'm ready." With those words, I took a step away, needing to put distance between us, a safety buffer to process the onslaught of emotions.

"Wait!" His voice cut through the air, desperate and raw, pulling me back from the precipice of my resolve. I turned slowly, the tide of emotions swirling within me. "You don't really mean that, do you? You can't just walk away. Not after everything."

And yet, the thought of walking away felt more appealing than staying, especially when his gaze bore into me with that mixture of hurt and hope. It was intoxicating and dangerous, like standing on the edge of a cliff, staring into the abyss and wondering if the plunge would lead to liberation or destruction.

"I don't know what I mean," I admitted, feeling the truth spill from my lips. "Right now, all I feel is confused and hurt. I can't do this with you staring at me like that." My voice wavered as I spoke, my heart a confusing mess of yearning and resentment.

"Then let me help you understand," he pleaded, his voice dropping to a whisper that wrapped around me like a warm embrace. "Let me explain. I swear to you, it was never meant to go this far. I was—"

"Being reckless?" I interrupted, the sharpness in my tone betraying the ache in my chest. "That's a pretty easy excuse, don't you think? This isn't just some casual fling; it's our relationship at stake. I thought you understood what we had."

The truth hit me like a wave crashing into the rocks—hard and relentless. I had entrusted him with my heart, my secrets, my dreams, and he had returned with something that shattered it all. The loss loomed large, a gaping hole in the fabric of my existence, leaving me feeling hollow.

"I'll fight for us," he said, his voice thick with emotion. "You can't deny what we have. I know I've messed up, but I'm willing to put in the work. Just give me a chance."

The sincerity in his words pierced through my defenses, unraveling the walls I had hastily erected. I wanted to believe him, to cling to the remnants of our love like a lifeline, but the fear of being hurt again kept me rooted in uncertainty. The darkness of doubt whispered that even if I chose to forgive, I might never forget.

I glanced back toward the ocean, the darkness creeping in as the last vestiges of sunlight vanished. "I wish it were that easy," I replied, my voice barely a whisper. "But right now, I need to figure out what I want. I don't know if I can trust you again, and I can't live like this. Not knowing if you'll hurt me again."

"Just promise me you won't shut me out completely," he said, desperation creeping into his tone. "Let's take it one step at a time. I'll do whatever it takes to prove to you that I'm still the man you fell in love with."

My heart trembled at his plea, the memory of his warmth still lingering in my veins, but the echoes of betrayal were louder. "I'll try," I said finally, feeling the weight of my words as they hung between us. "But it won't be easy, Ashton. I need time to sort through this."

The wind howled softly, rustling through the trees lining the pier as if whispering secrets I wasn't yet ready to hear. The horizon was now a deep indigo, the stars beginning to twinkle like distant promises of hope. But in that moment, the stars felt far away, obscured by the clouds of doubt that loomed over us.

As I turned to leave, my heart weighed down by uncertainty, I glanced back one last time. Ashton stood there, a silhouette against the dying light, the embodiment of everything I both cherished and feared. It felt as if the tides were shifting, the world around us poised for change, and I wasn't sure if I was ready to embrace whatever came next.

The sun had fully surrendered to the horizon, leaving behind a velvet canvas sprinkled with stars that flickered like distant hopes. I walked away from the pier, my heart a paradox of longing and resolve, with the salt air mingling with the dampness of the evening. Each step felt heavy, as if I were dragging the weight of our conversation along with me, tethered to the unresolved feelings that had become a part of my very being.

The quaint streets of our coastal town unfolded like a familiar storybook, with old Victorian homes standing proud, their gabled roofs silhouetted against the deepening sky. The lanterns lining the walkway flickered to life, casting a soft glow that mirrored the tumult within me. I longed for the comfort of my friends, the ones who had always stood by me, ready to lend a listening ear or a shoulder to cry on. Their laughter felt like a balm on my wounds, and I desperately needed that warmth after the cold confrontation with Ashton.

As I reached my favorite coffee shop, its windows aglow with golden light, a sense of refuge washed over me. The aroma of freshly brewed coffee wafted through the air, intertwining with the scent of baked goods, creating an inviting cocoon that promised solace. I pushed open the door, the familiar bell tinkling softly, announcing my arrival. Inside, the cozy atmosphere embraced me like an old friend, the chatter of patrons blending with the soft strains of music that drifted through the air.

"Hey, there she is!" my friend Mia called out from a corner table, her face lighting up with genuine delight. She waved me over, her dark curls bouncing with enthusiasm. "We saved you a spot. We were just talking about our plans for the weekend!"

I managed a smile, though it felt brittle at the edges. "Weekend plans sound great," I replied, sliding into the booth opposite her. The vibrant energy of her presence was a comfort, a balm to the frayed edges of my heart.

"Are you okay? You look like you've seen a ghost," Mia said, her eyes narrowing with concern. She reached across the table, squeezing my hand, and in that simple gesture, I felt the knot of my tension begin to loosen, if only a little.

"I'm just…processing things," I said, choosing my words carefully. "You know how it is with relationships—complicated."

Her expression shifted from concern to understanding, a quicksilver transition that spoke volumes about our friendship. "Complicated, huh? You mean, like, he messed up?"

I nodded, the weight of my emotions surfacing in the warmth of her gaze. "It's just hard, you know? I really care about him, but trust... trust is fragile, and he broke it. I don't know how to piece everything back together."

Mia sighed, leaning back in her seat as she absorbed my words. "You're right, trust is everything. But don't forget that it's okay to take your time with this. You don't have to rush into forgiveness just because he wants you to."

"I know," I said, staring into the depths of my coffee cup, swirling the liquid in circles. The steam rose and danced, almost playfully, and I couldn't help but feel like it was mocking my inability to find clarity. "I just wish things were different. I wanted it to be easy."

"Who doesn't?" Mia replied, her tone lightening. "But let's be real for a second. If relationships were easy, we'd all be sipping cocktails on the beach without a care in the world, right?"

I chuckled softly, the tension in my shoulders easing. "True. But I feel like I'm at a crossroads. Every choice seems like it could lead to a completely different life. It's terrifying."

She leaned forward, her expression serious. "Sometimes you need to make those terrifying choices, especially if you want to protect yourself. You deserve to be happy and not just settled."

Her words settled in my mind, and I found a glimmer of strength within them. I could take control of my narrative, even if it meant embracing uncertainty.

"I guess I just have to figure out what I really want," I mused aloud, feeling a sense of determination blooming within me. "Maybe it's time for a little self-discovery."

Mia smiled, the warmth returning to her eyes. "That's the spirit! And remember, you're not alone in this. I'm right here with you, ready to binge-watch terrible reality TV and drown our sorrows in ice cream whenever you need."

The thought of our late-night escapades brought a flicker of joy to my heart, and I felt grateful for the unshakeable bond we shared. "Thanks, Mia. I really appreciate you being here."

"Always," she said, her confidence washing over me like a soothing wave.

As the evening wore on, the shadows deepened outside, and I lost myself in conversation with Mia and the others, finding moments of laughter amidst the heaviness in my heart. They reminded me of the importance of connection, of the laughter that bound us together like an unbreakable thread.

But even in the light of friendship, the specter of Ashton lingered, weaving through my thoughts like a relentless tide. I wondered how he was coping with the distance I had created, whether he was grappling with his own demons in the solitude I had left him. The thought stirred a mix of guilt and longing, and I tried to push it aside, reminding myself that I needed this time to process.

The coffee shop began to empty as the night wore on, the baristas tidying up while laughter faded into the distance. I felt a gentle tug in my heart, an acknowledgment that tomorrow would be another day filled with choices. As I prepared to leave, I looked at my friends, their faces illuminated by the soft glow of the café lights, and felt an overwhelming sense of gratitude.

Walking back into the cool night air, I inhaled deeply, the scent of the sea mingling with the warmth of the bakery lingering on my clothes. I was ready to face whatever tomorrow would bring, to unravel the complexities of my heart, and to explore the possibilities that lay ahead.

With every step, I embraced the uncertainty, each footfall a testament to my resilience. The stars twinkled above like tiny beacons of hope, and as I made my way home, I allowed myself to dream of the future, knowing it could hold the promise of love, healing, and perhaps even a little magic—if only I dared to reach for it.

Back in the stillness of my room, I sat by the window, gazing out at the undulating waves under the moonlight. My heart was still divided, the echoes of Ashton's words swirling in my mind, but I felt the tiniest spark of hope igniting within me. Whatever the outcome, I was learning to embrace the complexity of love, the beauty in vulnerability, and the strength that comes from facing the unknown.

Tomorrow would be a new day, a chance to reclaim my narrative and step into the light—one cautious step at a time.

# Chapter 19: The Breaking Point

The sun dipped low over the horizon, casting a warm, golden glow across the bustling streets of Chicago. The hum of the city enveloped me, a familiar rhythm that used to be comforting, but now felt suffocating, like a noose tightening with each tick of the clock. My heels clicked against the pavement, the sound sharp and jarring, matching the frantic pace of my thoughts. As the campaign launch approached, anticipation crackled in the air, mingling with the rising tension that had become my constant companion.

Each day felt like a tightly wound spring, the pressure coiling and constricting, ready to snap at the slightest provocation. Secrets loomed like storm clouds on the horizon, dark and ominous, threatening to unleash chaos at any moment. I had thought the campaign was just about selling our vision, but it had morphed into a battleground, where trust was a rare commodity and alliances shifted like the wind. The trust I had built with Ashton was fragile, teetering on the edge of collapse, and I feared it wouldn't survive the storm brewing within our team.

As I pushed through the glass doors of our office, the familiar scent of fresh coffee and polished wood greeted me, but it offered little solace. The office was abuzz with last-minute preparations, phones ringing, and voices rising and falling like the tide. I caught snippets of conversations, words like "strategy," "budget," and "crisis," all swirling around me in a dizzying dance. I felt as if I were caught in a whirlpool, unable to escape the currents dragging me down.

My gaze drifted toward Ashton, standing at the far end of the room, his back turned to me. He was deep in discussion with our project manager, his hands gesturing animatedly, the tension radiating off him in palpable waves. My heart tightened. The man I had come to care for deeply was becoming a stranger, his familiar demeanor overshadowed by an intensity that unsettled me. I wanted to march over, to demand answers, but the weight of uncertainty held me in place, anchored by my doubts.

With a deep breath, I gathered my courage and made my way toward him, weaving through the maze of desks and people, each step fueled by a mixture of hope and dread. As I approached, I could see the tension in his jaw, the way his brow furrowed with frustration. I hesitated, my heart pounding in my chest, unsure of how to breach the chasm that seemed to have opened between us.

"Ashton," I said, my voice barely above a whisper. He turned, surprise flickering in his eyes, but it was quickly overshadowed by the storm brewing beneath the surface. "Can we talk?"

The corners of his mouth tightened, and I could sense the struggle within him, a tempest of emotions fighting for control. "Not now, I'm in the middle of something," he replied curtly, his tone sharper than I expected. The words struck me like a slap, and I flinched, feeling the heat rush to my cheeks.

"I need to understand," I pressed, desperation creeping into my voice. "I need to know what's really going on. The emails, the hidden agendas—it feels like we're all playing a game, and I don't want to be a pawn anymore."

He exhaled sharply, the frustration boiling over as he stepped closer, his presence looming like a thundercloud. "You think I'm hiding something? I'm trying to keep this team together while you're playing the blame game! We have a campaign to launch, and you're focusing on petty squabbles instead of the bigger picture!"

The heat of his words ignited something within me, a fire that had been simmering just beneath the surface. "Petty squabbles? This isn't about that! It's about trust, Ashton! You've been distant, and I can't shake the feeling that there's something you're not telling me."

For a moment, the room fell silent, the air thick with tension. I could feel the eyes of my colleagues on us, their gazes like daggers, and embarrassment washed over me. Yet, I stood my ground, refusing to back down. He took a step closer, the space between us charged with electricity, each heartbeat echoing in my ears.

"I'm not the enemy here," he said, his voice low and intense. "I'm trying to protect us all. This campaign is everything we've worked for, and if you can't see that—"

"Then what? You're just going to keep me in the dark?" My voice trembled, the weight of his silence suffocating. "Do you really think I can just sit back and trust you when everything feels so...so broken?"

He ran a hand through his hair, frustration radiating from him like heat from a fire. "I'm doing my best, but it feels like you're not even trying to understand. You want answers, but I can't give you what I don't have. We're all fighting our own battles here."

A silence enveloped us, a chasm of unspoken words and unresolved feelings. The ache in my chest deepened, and I felt a sharp sting of betrayal cutting through the haze of emotion. The man I had once leaned on for support now seemed so distant, and the warmth between us had morphed into a chilling frost.

"I can't keep doing this," I said, my voice shaking as I turned to walk away, each step feeling heavier than the last. My heart splintered with every stride, uncertainty gnawing at me like a ravenous beast. I wanted to scream, to cry, to let the world know that I was breaking beneath the weight of it all. The love I had nurtured felt tainted, and the trust we had built seemed to crumble like a fragile house of cards, leaving me standing in a storm of doubt and despair.

The city pulsed with life outside my office window, the busy streets below teeming with people who seemed blissfully unaware of the storm raging within me. Each honk of a car horn, every burst of laughter drifting up from the cafes, felt like a cruel reminder of normalcy. Inside, the atmosphere was charged, electric with unspoken words and lingering glances, as if my colleagues sensed the shift in the air but didn't dare to acknowledge it. I sank into my chair, the leather cool against my skin, but the chill spreading through me was something deeper, a bone-deep anxiety that gnawed at my resolve.

Days blurred together as I lost myself in the minutiae of the campaign, focusing on numbers and projections, a futile attempt to drown out the chaos of my thoughts. I crafted email after email, pouring over every detail, but every sentence felt like an echo of my tumultuous encounter with Ashton. His words replayed in my mind, raw and unyielding, like a record stuck on a single note. I was desperate to shake the feeling that we were adrift in separate boats, navigating turbulent waters while pretending the storm didn't exist.

During lunch, I sat with Mia, my closest confidante and a whirlwind of optimism. Her laughter was infectious, her spirit a balm for my frayed nerves, but today, even her brightness felt muted. She noticed my distracted gaze, her brow furrowing in concern as she leaned closer. "You look like you've seen a ghost. Spill it," she urged, her fork poised mid-air, the remnants of her salad forgotten.

I hesitated, torn between the desire to unburden myself and the fear of dragging her into my tangled web of heartache. "It's just the campaign. It's a lot," I replied, forcing a smile that felt like a mask. But Mia wasn't having it; she scrutinized me with an intensity that felt almost like a spotlight.

"It's not just the campaign, is it? It's Ashton," she pressed, her voice gentle but firm. The air thickened, the truth hanging between us like an unspoken confession. I sighed, the weight of my unvoiced fears crashing down on me like a wave.

"I don't know what's happening between us anymore," I admitted, the words spilling out before I could hold them back. "It feels like I'm chasing a ghost, and every time I reach out, he pulls away. I thought we were a team, but now..."

"Now it feels like you're on opposite sides of a battlefield," Mia finished for me, her eyes sympathetic. I nodded, the lump in my throat growing heavier. "Have you talked to him? Really talked?"

"I tried," I said, bitterness creeping into my tone. "But it feels like he's more invested in the campaign than in us. I don't even know what to believe anymore."

Mia reached across the table, her hand warm and reassuring against mine. "You two have something special. Don't let the chaos of work tear that apart. Find a moment—just the two of you. You need to clear the air before it's too late."

Her words resonated with a flicker of hope, igniting a spark within me that I desperately needed. Maybe I had been too focused on the shadows lurking in the corners, too consumed by fear to see the light peeking through. I took a deep breath, nodding slowly. "You're right. I'll talk to him tonight."

As the afternoon wore on, I felt a sense of purpose begin to replace my anxiety. The chaos of the office became a background hum as I refocused on the tasks at hand, each click of the keyboard grounding me in the moment. But as the clock ticked closer to the end of the day, a gnawing anticipation twisted my stomach into knots. I could picture Ashton's face, the way his features tightened when he was deep in thought, and I wondered if he would let me in this time or if the walls he had built would remain impenetrable.

When the workday finally ended, I took a moment to gather my thoughts, glancing around the now-empty office. The soft glow of the lamps created a cozy ambiance, the remnants of the day's chaos fading into the background. I needed to approach this conversation delicately, navigating the jagged edges of our relationship with care.

I found him in the small conference room, hunched over a table cluttered with papers and half-empty coffee cups. The sight of him, so immersed in his work, made my heart clench. I remembered how we used to share those late-night brainstorming sessions, the air electric with ideas and laughter. Now, it felt like we were two ships passing in the night, each lost in our own storms.

"Ashton," I said softly, stepping inside the room. He looked up, surprise flickering in his eyes before it was quickly replaced by a guarded expression. The atmosphere shifted, tension curling around us like smoke, but I pressed on. "Can we talk?"

He nodded, but there was hesitation in his movements, the way he shifted in his chair as if bracing for impact. "Yeah, of course. What's on your mind?"

The words felt heavy on my tongue, a mix of fear and hope churning within me. "I think we need to address what happened earlier. I don't want to keep dancing around this anymore. I care about you, Ashton, but I can't be part of a relationship where I feel like I'm always second to everything else."

His expression softened, and for a moment, the walls began to crumble. "I never meant to make you feel that way. It's just been... overwhelming. The campaign, the pressure—it's consuming everything, and I didn't want to drag you down with it."

"I appreciate that, but I'm already here, right beside you. I want to share the load, not feel like a burden. I need you to let me in."

The silence that followed was thick with unspoken emotions, the air charged with a sense of urgency. I held my breath, praying that this moment would be the turning point, the place where we could either rebuild or break apart. Ashton's gaze met mine, vulnerability creeping into his eyes as he leaned forward, bridging the distance between us.

"I've been scared," he admitted, his voice low and raw. "Scared of failing, of losing everything we've built. I thought I could handle it, but it's been harder than I ever imagined."

In that moment, I saw the boy I had fallen for—the dreams we had spun together, the laughter we had shared, the passion that had ignited between us. I realized that amidst the chaos, there was still a flicker of hope, a chance to reclaim what we had lost.

"I'm here for you, Ashton. We're stronger together," I said softly, reaching out to grasp his hand. The warmth of his skin against mine felt like a promise, a tether pulling us back toward one another. As our fingers intertwined, I sensed the fear beginning to dissolve, replaced by a shared determination to face the storm together.

The warmth of Ashton's hand in mine sparked something that felt both fragile and electric, a flicker of connection in a world that had recently seemed so dark. I watched as he processed my words, his brow furrowing slightly, the wheels of his mind visibly turning. This moment hung in the air like the sweet scent of freshly brewed coffee, rich and intoxicating, but it also carried the weight of uncertainty—like a gusty autumn wind threatening to scatter the leaves before they could settle.

"I've let the pressure get to me," he finally admitted, his voice barely above a whisper, as if the admission itself might unleash a tempest. "I was so focused on proving myself, on making this campaign a success, that I started to push you away. I thought that if I could just stay ahead of the game, everything would fall into place."

I felt a knot in my chest slowly begin to unravel. "But it doesn't have to be that way. We're in this together. You don't have to shoulder all of this alone."

Ashton met my gaze, and in that instant, the barriers that had separated us began to crumble. His eyes, usually filled with determination and drive, glistened with vulnerability. "You make it sound so easy," he said with a soft chuckle, the corner of his mouth lifting in a half-smile that was both apologetic and hopeful. "But I've always felt like I had to handle everything myself. Asking for help feels...weak."

I rolled my eyes playfully, trying to dispel the tension lingering in the air. "If you think admitting you need help is a sign of weakness, then we're all doomed. I mean, look around—everyone here is juggling the chaos. If we can't lean on each other, what's the point?"

A brief silence enveloped us, punctuated only by the distant murmur of colleagues wrapping up their workday. I could see the flicker of realization in Ashton's eyes, as if he was finally beginning to see the power of vulnerability, the strength in sharing the load. "You're right," he said, his voice gaining confidence. "It's just hard for me to let go. I don't want to let anyone down."

With a deep breath, I squeezed his hand tighter, drawing courage from the warmth that radiated between us. "You won't let me down. I'm not going anywhere, but you have to trust me enough to share what you're feeling, even if it's messy. We can weather this storm together, I promise."

As we exchanged hopeful glances, a sense of clarity began to wash over me. The clouds of uncertainty that had shadowed my heart started to dissipate, replaced by a cautious optimism that felt almost foreign but desperately needed.

"I want to make this work," Ashton said, his voice steady now, as he leaned closer. "Not just the campaign, but us. I know I've been an idiot, but I'm willing to do whatever it takes."

His sincerity ignited a warmth in my chest, and I knew this moment was a turning point. The challenges that lay ahead felt daunting, but for the first time, the weight on my shoulders didn't feel so heavy. We had uncovered the cracks in our foundation, but instead of crumbling, we had the opportunity to fortify them together.

The tension in the room shifted, softening as laughter echoed from the hallway, a reminder of the world outside our bubble. I stood, drawing Ashton with me. "Let's get some fresh air. I think we both could use a break from all this intensity."

He nodded, a grateful smile creeping onto his face, and together we stepped into the cool evening air. The city buzzed around us, the golden glow of the streetlights casting a warm embrace over the pavement. As we walked side by side, the ambiance transformed, the chaos of the office receding into the background.

We wandered into a nearby park, the grass still vibrant despite the encroaching chill of fall. The leaves, a riot of colors, crunched beneath our feet, and I felt an exhilarating sense of freedom envelop me. In that moment, I could almost forget the pressures waiting for us just a few blocks away, the looming launch and the shadows of secrets that had plagued our every move.

Ashton turned to me, his expression contemplative. "You know, I never really stopped to appreciate moments like this," he said, gesturing toward the sky where stars began to peek through the twilight. "It's easy to get lost in the grind, to forget the beauty of just being."

"Exactly," I replied, my heart swelling. "This is what life is about—finding joy in the little things. We can't let the chaos consume us. We have to make space for moments that remind us why we do this."

His eyes sparkled with understanding, and for the first time in what felt like ages, we stood in unison, united not just by ambition but by the bond we were beginning to rebuild.

But just as the air felt lighter, a shadow loomed in the form of a notification ping from Ashton's phone, slicing through our moment. He glanced down, the smile fading as he read the message, tension creeping back into his posture.

"What is it?" I asked, instinctively leaning closer, the warmth of our earlier conversation still flickering in my chest.

"It's from Sam," he said, frustration coloring his tone. "He wants to discuss the emails again. The ones we thought were buried."

A pit formed in my stomach as the reality of our situation crashed back over me. The storm we had hoped to outrun was catching up, and we couldn't ignore it any longer. "Do you think it's serious?" I asked, my voice trembling slightly.

"Given how the last few meetings went, I'm not sure we can afford to dismiss anything," he replied, his brow furrowing again. "We need to be proactive about this."

The flicker of hope that had ignited between us felt like it was about to be snuffed out. I could sense the impending dread, the realization that our moment of peace was temporary at best. Yet, amidst the uncertainty, something shifted inside me.

"We'll handle it," I said, determination lacing my voice. "Together. You and I can strategize, come up with a plan. We've come this far; I won't let a few emails dictate our worth."

Ashton met my gaze, the fire in his eyes returning. "You're right. Let's face this head-on."

We stood in the park, surrounded by the rustling leaves and the distant laughter of couples enjoying their evening, and I felt a surge of resilience washing over me. Our relationship had been tested, but we were not defined by our struggles; we were shaped by how we overcame them.

Hand in hand, we left the tranquility of the park behind and walked back toward the office, the shadows of doubt still lurking at the corners of our minds but now illuminated by the possibility of growth. In that moment, I understood that we had taken the first step—not just toward confronting the challenges ahead, but toward forging a deeper connection that would withstand the fiercest of storms. Together, we would navigate the labyrinth of ambition and emotion, and I was ready to embrace whatever lay ahead.

# Chapter 20: The Fallout

The day unfolds with an unsettling hush, the kind that settles in after an intense summer rain, when the world seems to hold its breath, waiting. As I step into the office, the air crackles with unspoken words, a heavy fog of tension wrapping around my shoulders like a threadbare blanket. My colleagues, usually vibrant with chatter and laughter, flit about with wary glances, their expressions an intricate tapestry of concern and intrigue. I feel like a ghost walking among the living, a specter tethered to the earth by the invisible threads of yesterday's confrontation with Ashton.

He sits across the open space, hunched over his desk like a weary sailor navigating stormy seas. The sunlight pours in through the large windows, igniting his hair, and for a fleeting moment, I forget the words that shattered our fragile peace. I remember the way he smiles, a mix of mischief and sincerity that has always captivated me, making my heart dance in ways I can't fully comprehend. But now, that smile is a distant memory, overshadowed by the anger that ignited between us like a wildfire.

I settle into my own space, the familiar scent of freshly brewed coffee mingling with the lingering aroma of last night's takeout. The hum of conversation buzzes in my ears, a constant reminder of the world spinning around me while I remain stuck in place. I can't shake the feeling that everyone knows what happened, as if the walls themselves have absorbed our heated words, ready to spill them out in hushed conversations. Each glance toward Ashton sends a jolt of mixed emotions through me—anger at his stubbornness and longing for the connection we once shared.

Focusing on the campaign feels like trying to catch smoke with my bare hands. My mind drifts, wandering through the chaos of our argument, where each word was a dagger, each silence a chasm between us that seemed impossible to cross. The project we're working on, a vibrant and bold rebranding initiative, should be thrilling. Yet it feels hollow without his input, his sharp insights that used to complement my own creativity. I can't ignore the missing pieces of our collaboration, a puzzle now marred by unresolved conflict.

I find myself tapping my pen against the desk, the rhythmic clatter echoing like the heartbeat of my frustration. It's a futile attempt to ground myself, to pull my thoughts into alignment, but all I can think about is the way his eyes glinted with fire during our argument. It was like watching a thunderstorm gather on the horizon, the air thick with anticipation before it broke free. I had dared to challenge him, to voice the concerns that had been simmering beneath the surface for weeks, and now I'm left with the fallout—a landscape scarred by harsh words and bitter truths.

As the hours creep by, the office continues to hum around me. Laughter bursts from the break room, punctuating the stillness of my thoughts, and I wonder if I'll ever find my way back to that camaraderie. I glance at my watch, willing the minutes to pass faster, but the hands seem stuck in time, mocking me with their slowness. Every tick resonates with my internal struggle, a reminder of the urgency to address the tension between Ashton and me.

Finally, during a brief lull in the chaos, I muster the courage to rise from my desk. I walk toward the break room, my heart pounding a rhythm that feels almost primal. The soft light filters through the frosted glass, creating a halo effect that momentarily distracts me from the storm brewing within. I pause at the entrance, taking a breath that feels like a declaration of war against my insecurities. I need to face him, to strip away the armor of pride and vulnerability that has enveloped us since the argument.

The room is alive with the chatter of my colleagues, but I find my eyes drawn to Ashton. He stands by the coffee machine, stirring a cup of steaming liquid, his brow furrowed in concentration. The sight pulls at my heart, a reminder of how easily we connected over shared moments like this. But now, that connection feels like a fragile glass ornament, teetering on the edge of a precipice, ready to shatter at the slightest touch.

I take a step forward, my pulse quickening as I cross the threshold into this makeshift battlefield. The air is thick with unspoken words, each one lodged like a pebble in my throat. "Ashton," I say, my voice a whisper lost in the hum of the room. He turns, those stormy blue eyes locking onto mine, and I feel the weight of our unresolved issues pressing down on both of us.

"Can we talk?" I manage, though the request feels like a double-edged sword, fraught with uncertainty and the promise of confrontation. He nods slowly, his expression inscrutable as he places his cup down, the clink of ceramic against the counter echoing in the silence between us.

Together, we step away from the cacophony of laughter and chatter, moving toward a quieter corner of the office. The walls seem to close in, an intimate space where we can shed the facades we've built around ourselves. I glance at him, searching for a sign of the boyish charm that used to illuminate his features, but all I see is the weight of the world reflected back at me.

"I didn't mean to push you away," I begin, my voice trembling with the weight of truth. "I just needed you to see things from my perspective." The words spill out like water from a cracked vessel, vulnerable and unfiltered.

The silence that envelops us feels almost electric, charged with the weight of our past interactions and the unyielding present. His gaze drifts from mine, a flicker of something—regret, perhaps—crossing his face before he masks it with a stoic expression. The air between us thickens, laden with all the things we left unsaid, the breaths we'd shared that now hang like uninvited guests at the back of our throats. I take a deep breath, summoning the courage that has often escaped me in moments like these.

"It's not just about the project," I continue, desperate for my words to break through the wall that seems to have risen between us. "I feel like we've been dancing around each other, avoiding the real conversations. This isn't just business for me, Ashton. It's personal." My heart races as I confess, each word trembling on the edge of vulnerability.

He shifts slightly, his arms folding defensively across his chest, and I can't help but notice how he seems to physically retreat into himself. "You're right. I didn't see that," he finally admits, his voice low and laced with a hint of regret. The admission feels like a balm, soothing yet sharp with the reminder of what's been lost. "I thought I was protecting you, but I didn't realize I was just pushing you away."

A flicker of warmth ignites in my chest at his honesty, and I step closer, closing the distance that has felt insurmountable since our fight. "I want to be in this with you, Ashton. Not just as colleagues but as... well, as more." The words spill out before I can catch them, and I brace myself for his reaction.

His brow furrows as he processes my words, the usual spark in his eyes dimmed by the weight of our shared history. "More?" he echoes, the uncertainty in his tone cutting deeper than I anticipated. I can see the wheels turning in his mind, the conflict warring within him.

"Yeah, I mean, we've been through so much together. I thought you felt it too." My heart sinks a little, the truth of our situation flooding in. Maybe I had misread the signals, clinging to the hope that our chemistry could outweigh the turmoil of our recent exchanges.

Ashton runs a hand through his hair, a gesture I recognize as his way of processing the chaos. "I do feel it," he finally admits, but the way he says it makes my stomach knot. "But I don't want to ruin what we have. I don't want to complicate things further."

Complicate. The word hangs in the air, taunting me with its implications. How had we gone from laughter and late-night brainstorming sessions to this fragile dance of hesitance? "But isn't it already complicated?" I counter, my voice firm yet laced with the vulnerability that comes from being exposed. "We're tiptoeing around each other like we're in some high-stakes game, and it's exhausting."

The corners of his mouth twitch, as if my bluntness has struck a chord he wasn't prepared for. "You always did have a way of cutting through the noise."

"Maybe that's what we both need right now," I reply, my resolve strengthening. "To stop dancing and start being honest with each other. No more masks, no more pretenses." The sincerity of my words resonates in the space between us, and for a moment, I think I see a glimmer of hope in his eyes.

But then, as if the weight of the world rests squarely on his shoulders, the moment dissolves. "It's not that simple," he says, the shadows of doubt creeping back into his expression. "We have to think about the campaign, about our jobs."

"Exactly. And I want us to be great together," I implore, stepping even closer, my voice softening. "But we can't do that if we're stuck in this limbo, pretending like everything is fine when it's not. We owe it to ourselves to figure this out."

A silence lingers, heavy and palpable. I can see the conflict swirling in his eyes, the way he grapples with the possibility of letting down the walls he's so carefully constructed. There's a flicker of longing, a fleeting moment where I dare to believe that perhaps he wants this just as much as I do.

"Okay," he finally says, the word barely a whisper. "Okay, let's talk."

Relief floods through me, mingling with the adrenaline that has propelled this conversation forward. We move to a quieter corner of the office, a small enclave with a couple of plush chairs and a coffee table strewn with old magazines. The noise of the bustling office fades into the background, and I find myself soaking in the moment, the reality that we're finally addressing the elephant in the room.

"I just don't want to lose you," he says, his voice low and earnest. "I can't handle the thought of pushing you away for good."

"Then let's stop pushing each other away," I reply, my heart racing as I lean in, wanting to bridge the chasm that has kept us apart for far too long. "We're stronger together. I believe that."

He looks at me, searching for something in my eyes, perhaps the reassurance that I'm not just saying what he wants to hear. I hope he sees the truth in my gaze, the honesty that wraps around my intentions like a warm embrace.

"Alright," he says at last, a small smile breaking through the tension. "Let's do this. Let's be honest with each other."

With those words, the dam begins to break, the floodgates of our unspoken feelings ready to pour forth. In that moment, surrounded by the remnants of our past arguments and the echoes of unfulfilled possibilities, we finally have a chance to rebuild—not just our project, but something far more profound.

As we sit across from each other, the weight of our shared burdens lifting, I can't help but feel the first rays of a new dawn breaking through the storm clouds that had loomed over us. The world outside fades away, and in this intimate moment, filled with the promise of change, we begin to carve out a path that is uniquely ours.

We settle into our seats, the plush chairs absorbing the tension that crackles in the air like static before a storm. I watch Ashton as he leans forward, his brow furrowed, the light catching the edges of his jaw in a way that makes him look simultaneously fierce and vulnerable. The man I've known for so long is both present and elusive, the remnants of our fight still clinging to him like a fog that refuses to lift. Yet, in this moment, the barriers between us begin to dissolve, one breath at a time.

"I don't want to pretend anymore," I say, my voice steady, filled with the conviction that has been bubbling beneath the surface. "This project means everything to me, and I thought it did to you too. I don't want us to just be coworkers who happen to share a desk." My eyes lock onto his, willing him to understand the depths of what I'm saying.

Ashton's gaze softens, a flicker of realization igniting in his eyes. "I've been scared. Scared of what this could mean for us," he admits, his honesty cutting through the remaining tension. "We've built something really special here, and I don't want to mess it up. I didn't want to rock the boat."

"Sometimes, rocking the boat is the only way to keep it from capsizing," I counter, my voice low but firm. "We need to navigate these waters together. You know how hard I've worked to be here. I want to share that journey with you, not just as colleagues, but as something more."

The corners of his mouth twitch up in a hesitant smile, and I can't help but mirror it. The playful banter we used to share bubbles to the surface, the warmth of nostalgia wrapping around us like a beloved blanket. "You always did have a knack for seeing the bigger picture," he replies, a spark of mischief returning to his tone. "But the reality is that we have a lot of work ahead of us."

A cascade of possibilities washes over me, intertwining the professional with the personal in a way that feels both thrilling and terrifying. "Then let's tackle it together. We can be honest with each other about what we want, both in the campaign and in… whatever this is between us."

Ashton nods, the weight of the moment settling between us. "Agreed. But that means we need to set some ground rules. I can't let my feelings cloud my judgment, especially with the launch date looming."

"Ground rules?" I ask, amusement flickering in my chest. "Are we going to draft a contract? Maybe include a clause for pizza on Fridays?"

He chuckles, the sound a sweet melody against the backdrop of the office chaos. "Maybe just a promise to communicate openly. No more secrets or assumptions."

"Deal." The word leaves my lips like a promise, a silent pact binding us together. In this small corner of our bustling office, I can feel the shift, the realignment of our connection, the way the stars might realign after a tumultuous night.

We talk about the project for the next hour, brainstorming ideas as we sketch out our visions on a whiteboard. Each time our hands brush against one another, the contact sends a jolt through me, igniting sparks of something deeper. The laughter flows easily, a testament to our unbroken bond, and for the first time in days, the weight on my chest begins to lighten.

As the conversation flows, I can't help but notice how his confidence seems to swell with every passing moment. He has a way of bringing out the best in me, encouraging me to dive deeper into my ideas while also challenging me to refine them. I marvel at how we can shift from the brink of chaos to a collaborative synergy that ignites our creative spirits.

When the clock chimes, signaling the end of our lunch break, we find ourselves surrounded by a flurry of colleagues returning from their own breaks, the noise enveloping us like a tidal wave. "Let's finish this day strong," Ashton says, determination etched on his face. "We've got a campaign to crush."

We return to our desks, but the atmosphere feels different now, charged with renewed energy and purpose. Each time I glance his way, I catch his eye, and it's as if a silent understanding passes between us—a promise to keep pushing forward, to not only fight for our project but also for the connection that lies just beneath the surface.

The rest of the day unfolds like a whirlwind, our collective efforts propelling us through brainstorming sessions, presentations, and late-night edits. The once-looming deadline transforms into a challenge we eagerly embrace, our collaboration breathing new life into the campaign. I'm astounded by how quickly our synergy rekindles, the easy flow of ideas transforming what could have been a daunting task into a thrilling adventure.

But as night falls and the office empties, I feel the shadows creeping back, whispering the doubts I had tried so hard to suppress. The world outside the window glimmers with the glow of city lights, a stark contrast to the emotional storm brewing within. I wonder how this new dynamic will play out beyond the confines of our work. Will we be able to navigate this newfound intimacy when the stakes become personal?

As we gather our belongings, I catch Ashton's eye again, and a shared smile passes between us, soothing my worries like balm on a wound. "Want to grab a drink?" he asks, an inviting tilt to his voice.

"Yes," I reply, the answer spilling from my lips before I can second-guess myself. "Let's celebrate this victory."

The warmth of his smile ignites a flicker of hope within me, and together we step into the night, leaving behind the shadows of our earlier confrontation. The city wraps around us like a familiar embrace, and for the first time in what feels like an eternity, I allow myself to imagine a future where we can truly thrive together.

As we navigate the bustling streets, the air is thick with laughter and the sweet smell of street food wafting from nearby vendors. The pulse of the city mirrors the rhythm of my heart, alive with possibility. With each step, I feel lighter, buoyed by the knowledge that we're both ready to explore not only the campaign but also the intricate layers of our relationship.

Underneath the twinkling stars, I can see the glimmer of potential in our connection, the exciting uncertainty that comes with daring to dive deeper. And as we find a small, vibrant bar tucked away on a side street, I realize that in this chaos of emotions and ambitions, I am ready to embrace the adventure that lies ahead—together.

# Chapter 21: A Night of Reckoning

The bar exudes a warmth that wraps around me like a familiar blanket, inviting and snug. Its wood-paneled walls, adorned with quirky art and vintage memorabilia, whisper stories of laughter and lost moments. A jukebox hums softly in the corner, its vinyl selections filling the air with a nostalgic energy, perfectly complementing the clink of glasses and the low murmur of conversation. I find a table nestled in a cozy alcove, the flickering candles casting playful shadows that dance across the tabletop, illuminating my thoughts and anxieties with a soft glow.

The amber liquid in my glass catches the light as I nervously twirl it, feeling the weight of the day's unspoken words settle heavily in my chest. I trace my finger along the rim, the cool glass a stark contrast to the warmth of the space around me. My mind races, a carousel of fears and doubts spinning wildly—did I make a mistake inviting Ashton? Is it too late to mend what's been frayed between us? Each question hovers like a specter, threatening to unravel the fragile hope I cling to.

Then, like a breath of fresh air slicing through the fog, I see him stride in, his silhouette framed by the golden glow of the bar's entrance. Ashton's presence has a magnetic quality; it's as if the room tilts slightly in his favor, drawing the attention of those around him. My heart leaps, a small rebellion against my carefully constructed defenses. He's wearing that old navy sweater I once teased him about—the one that clings just enough to his frame, making the rugged lines of his jaw and the faint shadow of stubble all the more enticing.

As he approaches, a smile teases the corners of his lips, and I can't help but smile back, despite the tension thickening the air between us. Our history is like a finely woven tapestry—beautiful and intricate, yet riddled with frayed edges and loose threads. I can almost hear the echoes of our laughter from countless evenings spent sharing dreams over cheap beer and greasy fries. But tonight, those memories are intertwined with the bitterness of our recent silence, making the atmosphere feel electric and charged.

He settles into the seat across from me, the candlelight casting a warm glow over his features, accentuating the twinkle in his eyes that has always sent my heart racing. "Hey," he says, his voice low and smooth, wrapping around me like a caress. It's a simple word, but it carries the weight of all the moments we've hesitated to share since our last argument—the fallout that lingered like a shadow over everything we used to be.

"Hey," I reply, my voice barely above a whisper, as if saying it too loudly might shatter the fragile peace we've managed to create. The waiter arrives, and we order drinks—Ashton opting for a whiskey neat while I stick to my usual gin and tonic. I can sense the tension in his posture, the way his fingers tap rhythmically on the table, a telltale sign of his nerves. The air crackles with unsaid sentiments, each heartbeat echoing the uncertainty of what comes next.

"I've been thinking," I finally venture, forcing the words out like a stubborn cork popping from a bottle, "about us, about everything." I pause, searching his face for any hint of how he feels, any sign that he's still in this with me. "I know things have been... complicated lately."

Ashton leans forward, his eyes intense and searching, urging me to continue. "Complicated is one way to put it," he says, a wry smile playing on his lips, but the warmth of his gaze softens the words. It's as if he's inviting me into a shared space where vulnerability and honesty can coexist.

"I've felt it too," I admit, the weight of my truth hanging heavily between us. "Every time we avoid each other, it's like a knife twisting in my gut. I miss you, Ashton. I miss who we were before everything got messy."

His expression shifts, and I can see the walls he's built beginning to crack. "I miss that too," he confesses, the sincerity in his voice a balm for my anxious heart. "But it's like we're stuck in this loop, and I don't know how to break out of it."

The words hang in the air, heavy with the acknowledgment of our fractured connection. The music swells around us, a slow ballad that wraps itself around my heart, and I can't help but feel the room begin to shrink, leaving only the two of us in this moment, tangled in our shared history.

"I don't want to give up on us," I say, my voice stronger now, fueled by a sudden rush of determination. "But we need to talk about what happened, about how we got here."

Ashton nods, the tension in his shoulders easing slightly. "You're right. We can't keep pretending everything's fine when it's not." The honesty in his words is a salve to my frayed nerves, and I feel a flicker of hope ignite between us, a fragile flame struggling against the winds of doubt.

We begin to peel back the layers of our relationship, sharing the fears and insecurities that had driven us apart. Each revelation feels like a small victory, the barriers between us slowly crumbling as we rediscover the connection that once felt unbreakable. The conversation flows like the bourbon in his glass, rich and smooth, filling the empty spaces left by our silence.

As the night unfolds, the shadows that loomed over us begin to dissipate, replaced by a tentative promise to rebuild the trust that had been lost. Yet, even in this moment of clarity, the lingering uncertainty reminds me that while we're on the right path, the journey ahead won't be easy. It's a risk, stepping back into the light after wandering through the darkness, but as I look into Ashton's eyes, I know it's a risk worth taking.

The conversation flows like a warm current, easing the tightness in my chest as we peel away the layers that had once felt impenetrable. Ashton leans back, his brow furrowed in thought, and the flickering candlelight casts shadows across his face, accentuating the vulnerability that has crept in alongside the honesty. I catch glimpses of his inner turmoil, the flickers of doubt intermingling with moments of clarity, and it makes me acutely aware of the depth of what we're attempting to navigate.

"I always thought we had this unbreakable bond," he says, his voice a mixture of nostalgia and regret. "And then it all just... unraveled. I didn't see it coming."

His admission resonates deep within me, a painful reminder of the gulf that had widened between us. I recall the countless late-night conversations where we dared to dream, where our plans for the future danced just beyond our fingertips like fireflies on a warm summer night. "Neither did I," I reply, my tone steady, though my heart quivers. "But somewhere along the line, I think we both started to put up walls instead of building bridges."

He nods, eyes locking onto mine, and in that moment, we share an understanding that transcends words. It's a silent acknowledgment of our shared culpability, the realization that both of us had been navigating this emotional minefield with trepidation, afraid to tread too close to the memories that burned brightly yet painfully in our hearts.

Ashton reaches for his drink, taking a long sip as he contemplates the space between us. The ice clinks against the glass, and I watch as he swirls the whiskey, a habit that seems to anchor him. "What if we just... started over?" he suggests, the corners of his mouth twitching in a tentative smile that sets my heart racing. "Not forgetting what happened, but maybe treating it like a lesson rather than a scar?"

The thought is like a breath of fresh air, invigorating yet tinged with caution. "You mean like a clean slate?" I ask, intrigued. "Can we really do that?"

"I think we can," he replies, his eyes shimmering with determination. "But it's going to take effort. We'll have to be honest, even when it's uncomfortable."

I feel a thrill course through me at the idea. Starting over could mean recapturing the magic we once had, rekindling the fire that had dimmed over time. The path won't be easy, but the prospect of rebuilding excites me, igniting a spark of hope that had long been buried under layers of doubt and hurt. "I'm willing to try if you are," I say, my heart pounding like a drum in my chest.

Ashton leans forward, his expression serious. "We need to communicate more, and not just about the good stuff. If something bothers us, we need to tackle it head-on. No more avoidance."

"Agreed," I say, a sense of relief washing over me. The idea of addressing our issues feels liberating, like unshackling ourselves from chains that have weighed us down for far too long. "I want us to feel safe enough to be honest. I want to know what's on your mind, even when it's hard."

We sit in comfortable silence for a moment, letting the reality of our new resolve sink in. Around us, the bar continues to hum with life, the patrons lost in their own worlds, but we've created our own bubble, insulated from the outside chaos. I can hear the faint strains of a love song weaving through the air, adding a soundtrack to our delicate truce.

"I never wanted to hurt you," he finally says, breaking the silence. "It was never my intention."

"I know," I reply, feeling the sincerity in his words resonate with my own feelings. "But sometimes it's the things left unsaid that hurt the most. I wish we had been more open."

The admission hangs between us, thick with a shared understanding of the complexities of love and relationships. I can see the wheels turning in his mind, the gears of reflection slowly grinding to a halt as he grapples with our past.

As the conversation deepens, I feel a strange alchemy brewing between us—a mix of vulnerability, honesty, and a dash of that irrepressible spark that once defined our connection. We dive into stories from our past, the quirky moments that made us laugh, the secrets we had hidden away, and the dreams that had seemed so vivid, so possible. Each shared memory feels like a brick lifted from the wall, the mortar of our history binding us together, making our laughter more resonant, our smiles brighter.

With every story, I find pieces of myself in him, the familiar cadence of his voice reassuring, the glint in his eye sparking joy. It's as if we're rediscovering not just each other but the very essence of who we are together. I lean in closer, relishing the warmth radiating from him, the tension from before dissipating like steam in the cool night air.

"Remember that time we tried to cook dinner together?" I tease, a grin breaking across my face. "I swear we almost burned the apartment down."

His laughter fills the space between us, rich and hearty, echoing off the walls like music. "How could I forget? I thought I was a culinary genius, and you were my trusted sous-chef. We ended up with takeout and a fire alarm instead."

"Ah yes, a classic," I chuckle, the memory igniting a warmth that rushes through me. "I think that was the night I realized that maybe I should stick to microwave meals."

"And I should never touch a frying pan again," he adds, his eyes sparkling with mirth. The ease of our banter feels like a lifeline, drawing us back to a place where laughter and joy reigned, a reminder of who we were when the world felt simpler, more vibrant.

As the night wears on, I feel a shift within myself, a renewed sense of hope blossoming in the fertile ground of our shared laughter and vulnerability. The promise of what's to come hangs tantalizingly in the air, the future stretched before us like an unwritten page waiting to be filled with our stories. The clock ticks on, but time seems to bend and stretch, allowing us to bask in the warmth of connection, to savor the beauty of rediscovery, as the city outside pulses with life, oblivious to the quiet revolution taking place within our hearts.

The laughter subsides, and the warmth of the bar seems to cocoon us in a momentary bubble, shielding us from the chaos of the world outside. The jukebox clicks over to a slow, haunting melody, the soft notes weaving around us like an embrace. I glance out the window, catching sight of the bustling street, where life continues unabated, indifferent to the fragile connection we are working so hard to reclaim. But here, in this intimate corner, it feels like the universe has conspired to pause just for us, allowing space for the tender stitching of old wounds.

"Tell me about your dream job," Ashton suddenly asks, his tone curious, as if he's trying to map out my soul. "What would make you wake up every day feeling like you're where you belong?"

The question takes me by surprise, pulling me from the comfortable haze of nostalgia and forcing me to confront the ambitions I'd tucked away. I pause, swirling the ice in my glass, letting the liquid clink against the sides like the heartbeat of my desires. "I've always wanted to be an architect," I admit, the words tumbling out before I can second-guess myself. "Not just in the traditional sense, but to build spaces that resonate with emotion—homes that feel alive, offices that inspire creativity. I want to create environments that shape experiences."

His eyes widen slightly, a glimmer of admiration flickering within them. "An architect? That's incredible! Why haven't you pursued it?"

I bite my lip, the hesitation flooding back. "Life happened. I got caught up in other responsibilities, and... well, I guess I let fear dictate my choices. It feels safer to stay within the lines of what I know."

Ashton leans closer, his intensity compelling me to look into his eyes, to see the earnestness reflected back. "That's not living, though. You're meant for more than just existing in the comfort zone. You deserve to chase what makes your heart sing."

His words resonate within me, striking a chord that reverberates through the walls I've constructed over the years. "And what about you?" I ask, eager to return the favor, to unearth the dreams that perhaps lie dormant in him as well.

"I've always wanted to be a filmmaker," he confesses, the light in his eyes igniting with passion. "Not the blockbuster kind, but the indie films that capture raw emotion and tell stories that need to be heard. I want to shine a light on the human experience, to make people feel seen."

A smile spreads across my face, warmed by the revelation. "You'd be amazing at that. Your perspective on life is so unique; I can't imagine anyone better suited to tell those stories."

Ashton leans back, his expression a blend of vulnerability and hope. "But I've been stuck in a corporate job, chasing numbers and deadlines instead of dreams. It's exhausting."

The realization hits me, a soft slap of clarity that we've both been running on empty, chasing roles that don't feed our souls. "So, we both have a lot of rebuilding to do," I say, the words wrapping around the air between us, bringing a sense of unity.

"Yeah," he replies softly, his gaze unwavering. "But I think we can do it. We just have to commit to being there for each other, even when it gets tough."

The depth of his commitment resonates through me, and I realize how desperately I've missed this—being seen, being heard, being understood. The intimate atmosphere of the bar, with its soft glow and warm scents of aged wood and rich spirits, feels like a sanctuary where anything is possible. I raise my glass, my heart swelling with a mix of courage and optimism. "To new beginnings," I toast, the words heavy with significance.

"To new beginnings," he echoes, clinking his glass against mine, the sound sharp and bright, slicing through the tension that had suffocated us for so long.

We sip our drinks, the flavors dancing on our tongues, a tangible reminder that change is within reach. As we linger over our newfound commitments, I notice the way Ashton leans in closer, as if the distance between us could be measured not just in physical space but in the emotional gravity pulling us together. I can feel the sparks flying, the energy surging as the atmosphere shifts, rich with possibility.

The conversation continues, flowing effortlessly as we dive deeper into our aspirations, our fears, and the myriad of experiences that have shaped us into who we are today. I share stories of my childhood, recounting moments spent with my father sketching designs on napkins in diner booths, the smell of greasy fries and coffee thick in the air. Each memory becomes a brushstroke on the canvas of my life, vivid and colorful.

Ashton shares snippets of his upbringing in a small town, where he would gather with friends to shoot short films on a camcorder, their laughter echoing through the empty streets. "I remember one time we tried to reenact a famous scene from a movie, and we ended up covered in mud from head to toe," he laughs, his eyes sparkling with the humor of it. "We had to hide from my mom when we got home; she'd have killed me if she'd seen the state of my clothes."

Our laughter intertwines, filling the space with a lightness that feels refreshing after the weight of our earlier conversations. It's as if we're peeling back layers of ourselves that had grown dull over time, revealing the vibrant colors beneath.

As the night deepens, we venture outside into the cool air, the city buzzing with life around us. The streets glimmer under the streetlights, each puddle reflecting the night sky, a mirror of the stars that twinkle overhead. I feel a shift, a sense of possibility swirling in the atmosphere. "What if we did this more often?" I suggest, my breath visible in the chill. "Not just drinks but... outings that remind us of who we used to be, who we could be again."

Ashton smiles, a slow, genuine grin that spreads warmth through me. "I'd like that. Let's not just talk about our dreams; let's chase them together."

With that promise hanging in the air, we set off down the street, side by side, our steps aligning as if guided by an unseen force. Each footfall feels lighter, buoyed by the understanding that while the road ahead may be fraught with challenges, we have chosen to face them together. It's a leap of faith, but the exhilaration of the unknown propels us forward, each moment steeped in the vibrancy of possibility.

In this dance of rediscovery, the shadows of our past begin to fade, replaced by a vivid tapestry of hope, laughter, and the promise of what lies ahead. The night is ours, and with every heartbeat, I can feel the vibrant threads of our connection weaving back together, stronger and more resilient than before. The journey may be long, but for the first time in a while, I feel ready to embrace whatever comes next, hand in hand with the man who has become not just a part of my past but the cornerstone of my future.

# Chapter 22: Finding Common Ground

Evenings in the heart of Manhattan carry an electric pulse, the air thick with the scent of street food mingling with the faint aroma of freshly brewed coffee wafting from the corner café. The skyline, a jagged silhouette against the setting sun, glimmers with the fiery hues of orange and pink, casting long shadows across the bustling streets below. I find myself caught in this vibrant tapestry, a small piece of the grand mosaic that is New York City. With each step, the rhythm of the city envelops me, the laughter and shouts of passersby intertwining with the distant wail of sirens and the honking of taxis that glide by like restless ghosts.

In this urban symphony, I'm paired with Noah—a man whose presence is as imposing as the skyscrapers surrounding us, yet whose laughter is as light as the air between us when our eyes lock. We've been thrust together in this whirlwind of creativity, our shared task igniting a spark that flickers beneath the surface, like a well-hidden flame waiting to blaze. Late nights in the conference room are punctuated with bursts of ideas, our voices overlapping like the chaotic dance of the city outside. It feels as if we're constructing a world of our own within these four walls, filling it with aspirations and dreams that shimmer brighter than the neon lights flooding the streets below.

As we sift through campaigns, designs sprawled across the table like discarded love letters, the barriers between us begin to dissolve. I glance up, catching him deep in thought, brow furrowed as he leans back in his chair, a pencil poised above a sketch. His dark hair tumbles over his forehead, and I can't help but think how amusingly disheveled he looks, as if he'd just stepped out of a novel set in the 1920s. In moments like these, my heart dances to a rhythm that's entirely new—a melody that makes me forget the chaos of our surroundings.

"Remember when we pitched that ridiculous idea about the skydiving squirrels?" he teases, the corner of his mouth curling into a smirk.

I laugh, the sound bubbling up like a fizzy drink. "You mean the idea that nearly got us kicked out of the meeting?"

"Exactly," he replies, eyes twinkling with mischief. "But it wasn't half bad. Imagine the headlines!"

Every shared joke strengthens the fragile threads weaving us together, drawing us into a tapestry of camaraderie. Yet beneath the laughter, a current of something deeper thrums, an energy that sends a shiver down my spine.

One evening, as the sun melts into the horizon, we find ourselves wandering the streets after a long session. The city's heartbeat thrums in sync with our footsteps, and I relish this rare moment of calm amid the chaotic rush of deadlines and expectations. We pause at a food truck draped in fairy lights, the warm glow inviting us to indulge in its offerings. The scent of sizzling meats and caramelized onions fills the air, wrapping around us like a comforting embrace.

"Noah, I don't think I can resist those," I say, my mouth watering as I point to a stack of glistening tacos piled high with vibrant toppings.

"Let's get a few," he replies, already stepping forward. The ease in his movements and the way he seamlessly engages with the vendor hints at his innate charm, drawing me closer, revealing glimpses of the man behind the professional façade.

As we munch on our tacos, the world around us fades into a soft blur. We share stories—little anecdotes that reveal the threads of our pasts. I recount the summer I spent in a small town in Vermont, where the air smelled of pine and freedom, and he speaks of family gatherings that turned into epic battles over board games, his competitive spirit flaring with each retelling.

"Who knew we had so much in common?" I muse, a smile tugging at my lips.

"It's surprising, isn't it?" he replies, his gaze steady on mine. "But I think it's more about how we see the world."

As we walk side by side, the city pulsates around us, but within our bubble, time seems to stretch and bend, allowing me to explore the nuances of his character. I learn about his younger sister, a spirited artist who dreams of leaving the city for a life of adventure, and I can feel his pride mixed with an undercurrent of protectiveness that tugs at my heart.

Just when it feels like we are sailing smoothly, the waves of uncertainty crash upon us. A major client meeting looms on the horizon, casting a shadow over our newfound camaraderie. The stakes rise, and the pressure begins to seep into our interactions. Noah becomes a flurry of energy, his focus narrowing as the deadline approaches. The lightness that once danced between us dims, replaced by the anxiety of impending expectations.

"Do you think we're ready for this?" I ask one night, my voice barely above a whisper as I trace the rim of my coffee cup, seeking comfort in the familiar porcelain.

He hesitates, the confidence that usually radiates from him momentarily flickering. "Honestly? I'm not sure. We've put in the work, but..." His words trail off, leaving a silence heavy with unspoken fears.

I feel the shift in the air, the delicate balance between us tipping precariously. Just as we begin to find common ground, the very foundation of our connection seems to tremble beneath the weight of looming uncertainty, and I wonder if we can withstand the pressure or if it will drive us apart.

The days blurred together like paint on an artist's palette, each one mixing into the next until we were drenched in the colorful chaos of deadlines and ideas. The city outside continued its frenetic dance, but inside the conference room, a different kind of magic brewed. Noah and I became a duo, a creative force navigating the ebb and flow of late-night brainstorming sessions and coffee-fueled mornings. The laughter we shared echoed off the sterile walls, a vibrant reminder of the connection blossoming between us, wrapped tightly in a cocoon of shared ambition and subtle glances.

As the skyline outside our window darkened into a deep indigo, the flickering lights of the city twinkled like stars scattered across a cosmic sea. Each late night found us hunched over laptops, crumpled sketches, and vibrant mood boards, our conversations flowing seamlessly from work-related chatter to the personal stories that peeled back layers of our guarded selves. The professional distance we once maintained melted away, revealing shared vulnerabilities that tethered us together.

One evening, as the rain drummed a soothing rhythm against the glass, I looked up from my screen and caught Noah staring out into the storm. His brow was furrowed, not in concentration, but in a quiet reflection that tugged at something deep within me. I set my laptop aside, feeling the weight of the moment, and asked, "What's on your mind?"

He turned to me, his eyes glistening like the city outside, a hint of apprehension flickering beneath his calm exterior. "Just thinking about my dad. He's been struggling with his health lately, and it's been tough on the family."

I felt a sudden pang in my chest, the weight of his words wrapping around me like the humidity in the air. "I'm so sorry, Noah. That must be really hard for you."

"It is," he replied, a faint smile tugging at his lips, though his eyes held a storm of emotions. "But we're managing. It just makes me realize how important it is to seize every opportunity, you know? To really live."

His words resonated deeply, reverberating through my own experiences. I shared with him the tale of my grandmother, whose laughter was the music of my childhood. "She always said life is a series of moments," I recalled, feeling a warmth in the memory. "The good, the bad, and everything in between. It's all about collecting them."

Noah's expression softened, the tension in his shoulders easing as we connected over our shared losses and the lessons they imparted. We sat in silence for a moment, the rain falling in soft symphony around us, a tender backdrop to our unfolding bond.

In the weeks that followed, we fell into a rhythm, a dance of creativity punctuated by our budding friendship. We delved into brainstorming sessions that felt less like work and more like an exploration of dreams. One day, while we were sketching out an idea for a campaign centered around community and resilience, I mentioned a local shelter that served as a safe haven for those in need.

"What if we used their stories? Highlighted real people overcoming adversity?" I suggested, my heart racing at the thought.

Noah's eyes lit up, and I could see the gears turning behind his warm gaze. "That's brilliant. It would create an emotional connection, something that resonates with people. It's about giving a voice to those who often go unheard."

In those moments, I realized that our partnership was blossoming into something beyond mere professional collaboration. It was a beautiful blend of shared passion and mutual respect, and the electric spark between us was unmistakable.

However, the looming deadline of the campaign presented a challenge that felt like a dark cloud overhead, threatening to overshadow our progress. Just when I thought we had found our stride, Noah began to retreat into himself. His laughter became less frequent, and the warmth of our conversations chilled as the stress of the project mounted. I watched helplessly as he juggled late nights, a strained smile plastered across his face while I yearned to breach the walls he was constructing.

One particularly challenging afternoon, I found him in the corner of the office, his hands running through his hair, a storm of frustration clouding his features. I approached cautiously, my heart pounding in my chest. "Noah, what's going on? You seem—"

"I'm fine," he interrupted, the sharpness of his tone surprising me. But the crack in his facade was evident, the tension radiating off him like heat from a summer sidewalk.

I took a deep breath, reminding myself that our connection was worth fighting for. "You're not fine. We're in this together. Talk to me."

For a moment, I feared he would retreat further, the distance between us widening, but he sighed, the weight of the world pressing heavily on his shoulders. "It's just—everything feels overwhelming. I want this campaign to succeed, to prove that I can do this," he admitted, his vulnerability a thin veil over his pride.

"I know you can. You're one of the most talented people I've ever worked with," I said, trying to inject a dose of encouragement into his spiraling thoughts. "But it's okay to feel stressed. We're a team, remember? We'll figure it out."

He met my gaze, and for a heartbeat, the storm in his eyes receded. "I just don't want to let anyone down."

I stepped closer, the warmth of his presence drawing me in. "You won't. We're in this together. And whatever happens, we'll figure it out."

Noah's features softened, and I felt the tension easing, the connection reestablishing its hold on us. We stood there, the buzz of the office fading into a distant hum as we forged a new understanding.

As the days passed, I vowed to help him navigate the storm, intertwining our efforts in a way that felt organic and effortless. Our laughter returned, echoing through the halls once more, a beacon of hope amidst the chaos. We resumed our late-night sessions, finding solace in shared meals and the occasional game of chess, which only added to the playful banter that characterized our growing bond.

Through the whirlwind of emotions, uncertainty, and unrelenting deadlines, I began to feel an undeniable pull toward him, a connection that went beyond the professional. Yet, the weight of the looming campaign weighed heavily on my mind, casting shadows on the bright moments we shared.

Days transformed into a dizzying carousel of ideas, our project evolving into a living entity, full of quirks and personality, much like the city itself. The buzz of creativity surged between Noah and me, manifesting in laughter that echoed through the dimly lit office long after the sun had vanished beyond the skyline. I often caught myself watching him as he animatedly discussed his latest concept, the way his hands gestured passionately, illuminating the depths of his thoughts. It struck me then how beautifully flawed we both were, wrestling with our personal demons even as we crafted something new and vibrant together.

The late nights gradually became a comforting ritual. We filled our spaces with half-empty coffee cups and pizza boxes that bore witness to our progress. Each brainstorming session morphed into something more profound, the tension in the air lightened by our growing camaraderie. I learned to read the subtle shifts in his expression, the fleeting smiles that hinted at vulnerability, as if he were slowly unraveling a tightly wound ball of string. I reveled in the way we could transition from discussions about marketing strategies to playful debates over whether pineapple belonged on pizza—Noah firmly believed it did, while I could only shake my head in disbelief.

As the campaign began to take shape, we crafted a narrative steeped in emotion and grit, rooted in the stories of those who had faced adversity head-on. Each client interaction revealed a new layer of resilience, illuminating the importance of their struggles in a world that often overlooked them. We poured our hearts into every word, transforming our project into a tapestry woven from human experiences, the kind that demanded attention and empathy.

Yet, just as we began to feel a sense of momentum, the specter of uncertainty loomed again, creeping into the corners of our otherwise vibrant world. A major client meeting approached, and with it came the weight of expectations. I sensed Noah's restlessness grow, like a pressure cooker teetering on the brink of explosion. His charm began to fade under the stress, replaced by a seriousness that made my heart ache.

One afternoon, as the clouds gathered ominously outside, a storm brewing in the atmosphere, I found him pacing the conference room. His usual enthusiasm was replaced by an intensity that felt palpable, every step echoing with unspoken worries. I watched him, a knot tightening in my stomach as the familiar urge to reach out and help surged within me.

"Noah," I ventured, my voice cutting through the charged silence. "You don't have to shoulder this alone. We're in this together, remember?"

He paused, turning to me with eyes that mirrored the turbulence outside. "It's just... what if it isn't good enough? What if I let everyone down?"

"Failure is a part of this process," I replied, stepping closer, feeling the magnetic pull between us intensify. "But so is growth. This campaign isn't just about meeting expectations; it's about telling a story that matters. And you've already done that. We've done that."

His gaze softened slightly, and for a fleeting moment, the tension in his shoulders eased. "I just wish I could be as confident as you. You're the heart of this project."

The compliment felt like a warm ember, igniting something deep within me. "And you're its soul," I countered, hoping to bridge the gap that seemed to widen between us with every passing moment of stress. "We're a team. Don't forget that."

As the rain began to pour, tapping rhythmically against the window, I felt the distance between us shrink, if only for a moment. But as we prepared for the meeting, the unease crept back in, tightening its grip on Noah. I knew we were on the brink of something extraordinary, yet it felt like a high-wire act—one misstep, and everything we'd built might come crashing down.

The day of the meeting arrived, and the atmosphere in the office crackled with a nervous energy. I watched Noah pace before the conference room, his breaths coming in sharp, measured inhales. He was dressed sharply in a tailored suit, the fabric hugging his frame, but the sharp lines of his attire couldn't mask the unease that radiated from him. I approached him, placing a gentle hand on his arm.

"You're ready for this. Just be yourself," I whispered, my words a small buoy in the storm of his anxiety.

He nodded, though doubt lingered in his eyes. As we stepped into the conference room, the lights above flickered, casting a warm glow over the polished table where our presentations awaited. The client sat across from us, a stern figure who radiated authority, his gaze piercing as he assessed us both.

Noah launched into the presentation, his voice steady despite the tremor of his hands. I could see him gathering strength as he spoke, his passion for the project igniting once more. I supplemented his points, feeling the rhythm of our partnership flow effortlessly, like a well-rehearsed duet. The tension shifted, the client's interest piqued as we painted a vivid picture of resilience, hope, and community.

As we concluded, the room fell into a heavy silence, the kind that both thrills and terrifies. The client leaned back, fingers steepled, and for a heart-stopping moment, I held my breath. Finally, a smile broke across his face, and I felt the weight lift from my shoulders.

"This is compelling," he said, nodding slowly. "You've tapped into something genuine here."

Relief washed over me, a tide of euphoria that felt electric. I turned to Noah, and his eyes sparkled with disbelief. As the meeting wrapped up, the client's praise felt like a warm embrace, reinforcing the bond we had forged through our struggles and triumphs.

Outside, the rain had subsided, leaving a sheen on the pavement that reflected the glow of streetlights, turning the city into a living watercolor. We stepped out together, our spirits buoyed, the air fresh and tinged with possibility. I felt a profound sense of camaraderie and something deeper igniting between us, a spark that had been patiently waiting to ignite.

"Can you believe it?" Noah said, laughter bubbling from him like a long-held breath finally released. "We did it!"

I grinned, the thrill of our victory surging through me. "We did it together."

Our eyes locked, and for a heartbeat, the world around us faded. The noise of the city dimmed, and it was just the two of us, standing on the precipice of something new. The moment stretched, filled with unsaid words and promises that shimmered in the space between us. I could feel the undeniable pull toward him, the warmth of connection igniting within my chest, teasing me with the thought of what could be.

As we walked down the wet streets, laughter spilling from our lips, I felt a surge of hope. It wasn't just about the project anymore; it was about the journey we were embarking on together, a dance through the chaos of life that was only just beginning. And as the skyline loomed above us, a reminder of dreams both realized and yet to come, I couldn't shake the feeling that the best was yet to unfold.

# Chapter 23: The Saboteur Revealed

The air inside the office hummed with a peculiar blend of excitement and anxiety, a cocktail that seemed to thicken with each passing hour as the campaign launch loomed closer. The glow from the overhead lights cast a stark brightness across the polished mahogany desks, illuminating the anxious faces of my colleagues, their brows knitted in concentration, fingers dancing over keyboards like frantic musicians striving to keep time with an increasingly chaotic score. It was an orchestra of sorts—each person contributing to a symphony that could either soar to magnificent heights or fall flat in an embarrassing cacophony. My heart drummed a restless beat in my chest, a reminder that I wasn't just a player in this ensemble; I was the conductor, striving to harmonize the chaotic energy swirling around me.

As the sun dipped below the skyline, painting the horizon with hues of fiery orange and soft lavender, I found myself alone in the conference room, the late summer heat making the air feel dense and oppressive. The shadows of the skyscrapers outside stretched long, merging with the dim light within, as I rifled through a mountain of documents scattered before me. My breath quickened with every revelation, every telltale clue that hinted at the unseen hand working against us. Sabotaging emails had become a regular torment, each one more destructive than the last, shredding the fabric of trust we had painstakingly woven among our team.

With each click of my mouse, I sifted through the digital debris of our recent campaigns, my heart racing as I pieced together a puzzle that, until now, felt insurmountable. The rhythmic tapping of my fingers became a mantra, grounding me amidst the uncertainty. I could almost taste the metallic tang of adrenaline on my tongue, spurring me to dig deeper. Each email bore the hallmark of someone who knew us intimately, someone who understood our weaknesses, and it sent chills racing down my spine. The thought that betrayal lurked so close felt like an unwelcome specter at a dinner party, lurking just outside the flickering candlelight.

The fluorescent lights buzzed overhead as I leaned closer to the screen, the glow illuminating my furrowed brow. I was on the brink of something monumental, a revelation just waiting to break free from the constraints of my exhaustion. My laptop screen flickered, casting ghostly reflections of my determination against the glossy conference table. As I scanned the lines of text, something caught my eye—a pattern, perhaps, or a connection I had missed. The sender's name, the tone of the messages, the timing of each email—they all pointed to someone I had never considered. The realization crashed over me like a sudden downpour, and I fought to steady my breath as dread settled into the pit of my stomach.

Just then, the door creaked open, and Ashton stepped in, his presence a welcomed balm against the tension that had been coiling around me. He was a constant in my whirlwind existence, a reassuring figure with his tousled hair and those warm, chocolate-brown eyes that seemed to hold the promise of clarity. "Still at it?" he asked, his voice a gentle rumble that reverberated through the room. He stepped closer, peering at the documents sprawled across the table. "What's going on?"

I gestured toward the screen, my voice a low murmur tinged with urgency. "It's worse than we thought. Someone is deliberately trying to sabotage us." I watched as his brow furrowed, his fingers brushing over the papers like he was searching for hidden answers, or perhaps a way to navigate the storm brewing between us. "I think I've found something," I continued, adrenaline pumping through my veins like a lifeline, guiding me through the fog of uncertainty.

Ashton leaned over, his shoulder brushing against mine, and I felt the heat radiating from him, grounding me as I detailed my findings. Each word spilled out, fueled by a mix of fear and determination. The air crackled with unspoken questions, tension simmering just beneath the surface. "It's someone inside the company, Ashton. Someone who knows us. Someone who has access." The weight of those words hung between us, a fragile thread tethering us to a reality that felt increasingly precarious.

The silence that followed was deafening, the world outside our bubble falling away as we both grappled with the enormity of the situation. Ashton's gaze locked onto mine, a silent agreement passing between us. "Who?" he asked, his voice low, barely above a whisper, yet charged with an intensity that made my skin prickle.

I hesitated, the names swirling in my mind like autumn leaves caught in a gust of wind. The realization that we were not only fighting an external foe but also battling the specter of betrayal from within made my heart ache. I took a deep breath, gathering my resolve. "I think it's Mia."

The name slipped from my lips, heavy and bittersweet, and I could see the flicker of disbelief in his eyes. Mia, with her bright smile and infectious laughter, was the last person I had imagined could harbor such dark intentions. Yet, as I laid out the evidence, detailing the moments when she had lingered just a bit too long, her questions laden with subtle scrutiny, I could see the pieces fitting together in Ashton's mind.

We spent the next few hours piecing together our plan, the camaraderie that had drawn us together now tinged with an undercurrent of tension. The shadows cast by the city skyline crept closer, wrapping us in a cloak of secrecy as we made our way through the dimly lit office. I could feel the weight of the confrontation ahead, each step echoing the rhythm of my racing heart. The air was thick with anticipation, and I knew that when we faced Mia, it would not only be about uncovering the truth but also about confronting the fragility of our own partnership, testing the limits of trust we had built amidst the chaos of deadlines and corporate ambitions.

As we approached her desk, I could almost hear the pounding of my heart in my ears, drowning out the sounds of the bustling office. I caught a glimpse of her, bent over her keyboard, the familiar rhythm of her work somehow a mockery of the storm brewing between us. I exchanged a glance with Ashton, and in that moment, I felt an unshakeable resolve settle within me. This was not just about saving the campaign; it was about reclaiming our narrative from the clutches of deceit, a chance to fortify our bond against the challenges that lay ahead.

The office buzzed with a frenetic energy as I steeled myself for the confrontation ahead. Each footfall resonated through the polished floors, the rhythmic sound mirroring the chaotic dance of thoughts swirling in my mind. My pulse quickened, a thrum that echoed the urgency of the situation, weaving a tapestry of unease and determination. As Ashton and I approached Mia's desk, a delicate veil of normalcy draped over the room, the steady click of keyboards and hushed conversations painting a picture of a bustling workplace. Yet, beneath this facade lay a current of tension that electrified the air, binding us to the reality that something was profoundly amiss.

Mia was oblivious to our approach, her focus locked onto her screen as if it held the secrets of the universe. She flicked her hair back with a casual toss, her laughter spilling into the air like the tinkling of wind chimes on a breezy day. I had always admired her effortless charm, the way she could lighten even the heaviest atmosphere with a smile. Now, that same charm felt like a well-crafted mask, concealing motives that had, until recently, seemed innocent.

As we stood there, my heart thundered in my chest, the uncertainty gnawing at my resolve. I shot a quick glance at Ashton, who appeared equally apprehensive yet ready, his brow furrowed in contemplation. The weight of unspoken words hung heavily between us, binding our fates together as we prepared to peel back the layers of betrayal that had ensnared our team.

"Mia," I said, my voice emerging steadier than I felt, "do you have a moment?" I kept my tone light, wrapping the inquiry in a veneer of casualness, hoping to disarm any suspicions she might harbor.

Her head snapped up, surprise flickering across her features before a smile broke through. "Of course! What's up?" she chirped, her demeanor deceptively bright.

Ashton leaned against the edge of her desk, his presence a steadying force beside me. "We need to talk about the campaign," he said, his voice calm but firm, a gentle storm brewing behind his eyes.

The atmosphere shifted slightly, a subtle tightening in the air as the undertones of our inquiry reached her. Mia's smile faltered for a fleeting moment, her eyes narrowing with curiosity. "Is there a problem? I thought everything was going smoothly."

The weight of the moment felt almost tangible, pressing down on me as I glanced at the documents I'd gathered. Each piece of evidence glared back at me, a reminder of the treachery lurking beneath the surface. "We've noticed some emails that don't align with our objectives," I began, choosing my words carefully. "They're damaging, and they seem to come from someone inside the company."

A flicker of surprise crossed her face, quickly masked by a well-practiced calm. "That's strange. I haven't seen anything like that."

The words fell from her lips with a casualness that sent my instincts on high alert. "They're aimed directly at undermining our efforts," I pressed, my voice growing firmer. "They mention sensitive information that shouldn't be shared outside our immediate team."

Mia's demeanor shifted again, a subtle transformation that reminded me of the way clouds could darken without warning. "You must be mistaken. I mean, there's always someone trying to stir the pot," she said, a hint of defensiveness creeping into her tone.

The back-and-forth felt like a dance, a waltz of misdirection where each step required precision. "We're not mistaken," Ashton interjected, his voice laced with authority. "This is serious. We need your help to find out who's behind it."

I watched her carefully, studying her reaction, looking for cracks in her façade. The vibrancy of her personality felt like a distant echo as I pieced together the puzzle, each clue leading us closer to a truth that threatened to unravel the very foundation of our teamwork. The silence that settled was thick, heavy with unspoken truths, and I could sense the shifting dynamics in the room.

"What do you mean, 'find out who's behind it'?" she asked, feigning innocence, her brow arching slightly.

I pressed on, refusing to let the doubts fester. "You've always been a pivotal part of our team, Mia. We thought you could help us figure this out." The words hung in the air, tentative and charged, as if each syllable could break the fragile equilibrium we had crafted over months of collaboration.

A flicker of hesitation passed across her face, quickly masked by a forced smile. "I wish I could help, but I don't have any insight into those emails. You know I'm busy with the upcoming launch."

The tension in the room was palpable, a taut string ready to snap at any moment. "Mia," I said, the weight of my tone pulling her attention back to me, "this affects all of us. If we don't get to the bottom of this, it could ruin everything we've worked for."

Her posture shifted slightly, an imperceptible change, but one I noticed nonetheless. "I'll do my best to help," she replied, her voice light but devoid of conviction. "Just keep me in the loop."

Ashton and I exchanged glances, the unspoken questions swirling in the air between us. There was something in her eyes, a glimmer of mischief or perhaps fear—something that suggested she wasn't as uninvolved as she claimed to be. As she turned back to her work, the moment felt suspended, and I couldn't shake the sense that we were walking on a tightrope, balanced precariously between revelation and deceit.

As the days unfolded, the atmosphere in the office grew increasingly charged. Each morning brought fresh emails, each one laden with insidious suggestions and veiled threats. The walls felt like they were closing in, and the energy that once inspired creativity now buzzed with apprehension, casting a pall over our team. It was as if a storm was brewing on the horizon, dark clouds gathering while we remained blissfully unaware of the tempest ready to unleash itself.

In the evenings, I found solace in my small apartment, the sanctuary that had become a refuge amid the chaos. The city outside thrummed with life—honking taxis, distant sirens, and the hum of pedestrians weaving through the streets. I would stand at the window, clutching a cup of tea as I watched the world blur into a tapestry of motion and noise, the bright lights shimmering like stars fallen to Earth. It was during these quiet moments that I allowed myself to breathe, the chaos of the office fading into the background as I pondered the storm brewing within.

Yet, beneath the facade of tranquility, a gnawing fear lingered, a whisper of doubt that threatened to consume me. I found myself replaying our conversations with Mia, her laughter ringing in my ears like a taunting echo. The more I reflected, the more I began to see the cracks in her smile, the subtle way her eyes darted when she felt cornered. What had once felt like camaraderie now transformed into a complex web of uncertainty, a tightrope act where every misstep could lead to disaster.

In the dead of night, as the city settled into a restless slumber, I often found myself staring at the ceiling, mind racing with thoughts and possibilities. I couldn't shake the sense that we were in a race against time, battling not just for the campaign but for the very integrity of our team. And with every passing day, the realization deepened: trust was a fragile thing, easily shattered and often difficult to rebuild.

As the week wore on, the undercurrents of tension within the office deepened, wrapping around me like an unwelcome embrace. Each morning, I entered the building with a palpable sense of dread, my stomach twisting at the thought of what awaited me in the glow of the computer screens. The emails had morphed into a steady stream of insidious whispers, casting long shadows over our project and turning my colleagues into wary strangers. I would catch glimpses of hushed conversations, furtive glances exchanged over conference tables, the camaraderie that had once buoyed us now eroded by suspicion and fear.

Mia's presence had shifted, morphing from a spark of light to an enigmatic figure, elusive and distant. Each time we crossed paths, her smile felt rehearsed, a mask expertly worn to conceal the turmoil beneath. I could sense that she was playing a part, perhaps not even fully aware of the role she had chosen in this tragic play of deception and betrayal. The simple act of sharing a cup of coffee had transformed into a tactical maneuver, each sip steeped in unspoken truths and guarded intentions.

Ashton and I convened nightly, our discussions echoing into the dimly lit corners of my apartment. The living room, usually a sanctuary adorned with soft blankets and scattered books, became our command center, the air thick with unresolved tension. With a pot of coffee brewing in the corner, we delved deep into the intricacies of our investigation, poring over the details of each email as if they held the keys to a locked door we desperately wanted to break down. We scribbled notes on a whiteboard, the scribbles and arrows forming a chaotic web that mirrored the tumult in our minds.

"Look here," Ashton pointed, his finger tracing the lines of a particularly damaging email. "The language is so specific, almost too familiar. It's as if they know exactly where to hit us."

I nodded, my mind racing with the implications of his words. "It's almost like they're watching us, waiting for an opening to strike," I replied, the chill of realization crawling down my spine. "But why? What could Mia possibly gain from this?"

That question haunted me as I lay in bed each night, the city outside alive with its own rhythm, oblivious to the turmoil unfolding in our small corner of the world. My mind wandered down dark alleys of speculation, imagining scenarios where Mia, once a friend and confidant, might have found herself in the company of shadows, entangled in a scheme far larger than I could fathom. I had shared my dreams with her, my ambitions, my fears, and the very essence of who I was felt at stake.

The night before the campaign launch, the weight of the impending confrontation hung heavily in the air, thickening the atmosphere in the office like a storm cloud poised to unleash its fury. I arrived early, the office still shrouded in darkness, the faint hum of fluorescent lights flickering to life one by one. I felt a sense of foreboding creep into my bones as I settled into my chair, my gaze falling on the city skyline that shimmered with the promise of a new day. This was it—today would be the reckoning.

As the sun climbed higher, the office gradually filled with the rhythmic sound of heels clicking against the marble floor, punctuated by the rustle of papers and the soft whir of computers powering up for the day. I exchanged nervous glances with Ashton, who had arrived shortly after me, his face a mask of determination tempered by uncertainty. The air buzzed with anticipation, a tangible electric current that seemed to surge through the very walls of our workspace.

When Mia finally entered, the room seemed to hold its breath. She sauntered in with a confidence that was both disarming and infuriating, her laughter ringing out like a bell in a quiet church. I felt a pang of nostalgia for the easy camaraderie we had once shared, a time when the air had felt lighter and our laughter had echoed freely. Now, her presence felt like a weight pressing down on my chest, suffocating the remnants of trust that still flickered within me.

"Mornin', team! Ready for the big day?" she called out, the enthusiasm in her voice seeming almost forced.

"Absolutely," Ashton replied, his eyes narrowing as he leaned forward, a subtle challenge buried within his casual tone. "But we need to talk about some of those emails before we launch."

The smile that graced Mia's lips faltered for just a heartbeat, and I seized the moment. "We know what's been happening," I added, my voice steady despite the whirlwind of emotions swirling within me. "And we need to understand why."

For a moment, the world around us fell silent, the soft hum of the office fading into the background. Mia's expression shifted, the easy laughter replaced by a steely resolve that sent a shiver of anticipation through me. "I have no idea what you're talking about," she said, crossing her arms defensively, her posture rigid.

"You can't keep pretending," Ashton pressed, his voice unwavering. "The emails are coming from someone who knows our processes inside and out, and that means it's someone on our team."

The room pulsed with tension, the air thickening as Mia's facade cracked, revealing a glimpse of the turmoil that lay beneath. "I didn't do anything!" she shot back, her voice rising with panic, a tremor lacing her words.

I stepped forward, my heart pounding with the weight of our revelations. "We want to understand, Mia. We're not here to accuse you; we just need the truth."

Her eyes darted around the room, searching for a way out of the conversation, a strategy to deflect the scrutiny weighing heavily upon her. I could see the conflict swirling in her expression, a battle between self-preservation and the friendship we had once shared. The walls of the office, adorned with motivational posters and bright colors, seemed to close in around us, a claustrophobic reminder of the truth we were fighting to unveil.

Finally, she inhaled sharply, her shoulders dropping slightly. "I—I didn't mean for any of this to happen," she said, her voice trembling with a mixture of fear and regret. "It was supposed to be a joke, a way to see how you all would react."

A flurry of emotions washed over me, disbelief battling against a strange sense of empathy. "A joke?" I echoed, incredulous. "You thought sabotaging our campaign was funny?"

"I didn't think it would get this far," she stammered, desperation creeping into her tone. "I wanted to test our team, to see if we were strong enough to handle pressure. I never intended to hurt anyone."

Ashton and I exchanged glances, the weight of her confession settling in the air like a dense fog. It was a mix of betrayal and an odd, twisted rationale that left us both reeling. "But look where we are now, Mia," I said, my voice steady despite the turmoil in my heart. "You've put everything we've worked for at risk. Our trust, our relationships—everything hangs in the balance."

Mia's eyes shimmered with unshed tears, the mask of confidence slipping away to reveal the vulnerability beneath. "I thought I could prove a point, but I see now how wrong I was. I'm so sorry," she said, her voice cracking, each word punctuated by the weight of remorse.

In that moment, I felt a wave of conflicting emotions wash over me—anger, sorrow, and a strange sense of understanding. Perhaps this betrayal was not born of malice but of misguided intentions, a misguided attempt to gauge our resilience. Yet, the damage had been done, and the scars would linger long after the echoes of this day faded into memory.

As the reality of her actions settled in, I felt the walls begin to shift, the tension transforming into something heavier—a collective realization that we would need to rebuild what had been shattered. The road ahead would be fraught with challenges, trust needing to be earned anew, but in that moment, as I stood in the heart of the chaos, I felt a flicker of hope ignite within me. The truth, once unveiled, could pave the way for redemption, a chance to rise from the ashes of this ordeal and forge a new beginning.

In the aftermath of our confrontation, we began the painstaking process of healing. Conversations flowed more freely, laughter returned, albeit cautiously, and a renewed sense of purpose settled over our team. We understood that trust was a fragile thing, built on shared experiences and moments of vulnerability, and it was a journey we would navigate together.

As the campaign launched successfully amidst the tumult, I felt a profound sense of gratitude for the lessons learned. Betrayal had etched its mark on our hearts, but resilience and forgiveness had emerged as our guiding stars, illuminating a path toward rebuilding our connections. The city outside buzzed with life, a reminder that amidst the chaos, there existed a vibrant world waiting to be embraced, one where the shadows of yesterday could illuminate the brightness of tomorrow.

# Chapter 24: The Breaking Point

The rain tapped insistently against the glass windows, each droplet racing to catch its neighbor in a gleeful competition, a stark contrast to the tension bubbling within me. I sat at my cluttered desk, the remnants of our last brainstorming session still scattered like confetti from a forgotten party. A vibrant array of sticky notes, coffee-stained napkins, and hastily scribbled ideas formed a chaotic tableau of our shared ambitions, each piece of paper a testament to the dreams we once spun together. The office, a modest space in a building that bore the scars of a time long past, held echoes of our laughter and whispered plans, but today, it felt like a battlefield.

Ashton stood across from me, arms crossed, his dark hair falling into his eyes like a curtain hiding a storm. The anger radiating off him was palpable, a tempest brewing behind the calm facade he usually wore like armor. I could see the clenching of his jaw, the way his fingers tapped rhythmically against his bicep—a dance of frustration that mirrored my own heart's erratic beats. How had we gotten to this point? A few days prior, we had stood shoulder to shoulder, united by a shared vision of success, but now, the air crackled with accusations and unspoken fears.

"It's not about the idea, Ava. It's about your timing!" His voice was sharp, each word punctuating the already fraught atmosphere. The mention of my timing felt like a blow, as if he were accusing me of recklessness instead of passion. I knew he meant well, but in that moment, the warmth I'd once felt towards him flickered like a dying candle.

My throat tightened as I leaned back in my chair, trying to find my footing amidst the rising tide of frustration. "And what about your grand plans? You're so consumed by what the investors want that you've lost sight of what we started this for! It was supposed to be about us—about our vision!" Each word poured out with the fervor of a desperate plea, an attempt to reach him through the haze of anger.

He shook his head, his eyes narrowing. "You think I don't want that? You think I'm just a puppet dancing to their strings? I'm trying to navigate a world that doesn't care about our dreams, Ava. This is how it works." The passion in his voice was unmistakable, a testament to his dedication, but the more he spoke, the more I felt the walls closing in, suffocating any ounce of reason left in our discussion.

With each syllable, memories of our late-night brainstorming sessions rushed back. The way we used to toss ideas around like confetti, giggling at the absurdity of our aspirations, the electric energy buzzing between us. We had been partners in crime, weaving together a narrative of hope against the backdrop of a gritty city that often felt indifferent to dreamers. But somewhere along the way, the pressure of reality had seeped in, twisting our enthusiasm into a fraying rope, each argument unraveling what we had built.

I could feel the tears threatening to spill, not from defeat but from the weight of it all. "Ashton, please. We can't let this tear us apart. I believe in us—this project, our vision. But we need to trust each other." My voice wavered, and I silently cursed the vulnerability that had crept in uninvited.

The silence that followed felt like an eternity. His gaze dropped to the floor, the anger fading into something softer, something almost pained. I could see the conflict playing out behind his eyes, the struggle between his ambition and the bond we had forged.

Suddenly, he turned, the tension shifting like a gust of wind. "I don't want to fight anymore, Ava. But every time we seem to get close, something pulls us apart. I don't know how to fix this." His words hung in the air, heavy and haunting, a fragile admission that felt like a chasm opening between us.

He strode out of the office, the door swinging shut behind him with a finality that echoed through the room. I sat in the remnants of our battle, the walls closing in around me as uncertainty wrapped its icy fingers around my chest. I could hear the rain intensifying, drumming against the window as if mocking my turmoil. In that moment of solitude, the office felt like a cage, the once vibrant colors fading into shades of grey.

I took a deep breath, forcing myself to focus on the rhythm of my heartbeat rather than the noise of my racing thoughts. The world outside continued to swirl in chaos, but I needed to find a semblance of clarity amidst the storm. The clutter on my desk, once a source of inspiration, now felt like a reminder of the fracture that threatened to consume us.

Sitting there, I realized how much we had invested in this venture—not just time and energy, but pieces of ourselves. Every argument seemed to peel away layers of trust, and with each passing moment, I felt the fear of losing Ashton overshadowing the hope that had once driven us. The line between ambition and trust had blurred, leaving a chasm filled with uncertainty.

As I gazed out into the rainy abyss, I resolved to fight for what we had built. We had come too far to let doubt extinguish the spark that had ignited our journey. I would find a way to bridge the gap between us, to remind him that our dreams were worth the struggle, that our bond was stronger than the pressures we faced.

I stood up, a newfound determination coursing through me. The rain continued to fall, but I refused to let it drown out the vision we had crafted together. I would reach out to him, find the words that could soothe the wounds between us, and reignite the passion that had once fueled our shared journey.

The echo of the door slamming reverberated through the office, leaving me in a cocoon of silence, punctuated only by the persistent drumming of the rain. Outside, the world seemed to swirl with its own kind of chaos, a blurred dance of color and sound that felt almost mocking in its vibrancy. I remained anchored in my chair, heart racing as the last words exchanged between Ashton and me replayed like a broken record, each loop digging deeper into my chest.

I forced myself to look around the room, trying to find some comfort in the familiarity of our cluttered workspace. The coffee mugs, emblazoned with quirky slogans that had once sparked joy, now stood as silent witnesses to our turmoil. The stack of papers, once a thrilling blueprint for our future, lay neglected, as if they too were caught in the throes of our disagreement.

The tension that had simmered between us for weeks felt like a thick fog, obscuring any clarity and vision I had. I could almost taste the bitterness in the air, each inhalation pulling at my resolve. How had we reached this point where ambition and trust seemed to clash like opposing forces in a cosmic battle? I closed my eyes for a moment, seeking a reprieve from the tumult within.

In the distance, I heard the faint hum of the city—a reminder that life outside continued, blissfully unaware of our struggles. The streetlights flickered on, casting a warm glow against the wet pavement, illuminating the vibrant colors of the storefronts across the street. The sight tugged at my heart, pulling me toward the comfort of the familiar coffee shop we frequented. Memories of laughter, late-night brainstorming, and stolen kisses danced in my mind. That was where we had dreamed—where everything felt possible.

With a sudden surge of determination, I stood and grabbed my jacket, the fabric soft against my skin as I slipped it on. I needed to break free from the confines of our office, to find solace in a space where hope still felt tangible. The rain greeted me with a cool embrace as I stepped outside, the city enveloping me in its familiar chaos. The scent of wet asphalt mixed with the sweet aroma of roasted coffee, a comforting reminder of the solace that awaited me just a few blocks away.

As I navigated the streets, my thoughts swirled like the autumn leaves dancing in the wind. I replayed our argument, the words I had chosen with such fervor now feeling like clumsy attempts at connecting. It struck me how easily frustration can morph into fear, how the very ambition that had once united us was now the source of our discord.

I quickened my pace, my heart pounding in rhythm with my footsteps. Each splash of rainwater beneath my feet felt like a countdown to a revelation, a reminder that I needed to find a way to bridge the gap between us. The coffee shop came into view, its neon sign flickering like a beacon of hope. I pushed through the door, the familiar warmth wrapping around me like a well-worn blanket.

The air inside was thick with the rich aroma of coffee and the sound of laughter, a cacophony of life that momentarily dulled the ache in my chest. I scanned the room, searching for a corner table that would offer both comfort and a view of the bustling street outside. Settling into a cozy nook, I ordered my usual—an espresso, sharp and invigorating, hoping it would kick-start my thought process.

As I sipped the bitter brew, I let the world around me fade into the background. The patrons engaged in animated conversations, their laughter bubbling like champagne, filled me with a sense of longing. I missed the ease of connection, the effortless joy we once shared, the way ideas flowed freely between Ashton and me like a well-rehearsed dance.

Pulling out my notebook, I flipped to a fresh page, the blank canvas inviting and daunting. I needed to find the right words, not just to express my feelings but to reach him—to remind him of the bond we had forged amidst the chaos. As I began to write, each stroke of the pen felt like a step toward healing. I poured out my heart onto the page, crafting sentences that danced with emotion and sincerity.

I spoke of our shared dreams, the late nights spent plotting our future under the city lights, the thrill of creating something new. I acknowledged the pressures that had seeped into our lives, the weight of expectation that had begun to suffocate our passion. But above all, I wrote about my unwavering belief in us, in our ability to rise above the turmoil and rediscover the spark that had ignited our journey in the first place.

Time slipped away, the café's bustle blurring into the background as I lost myself in my words. The rain continued to fall outside, each drop a reminder of the storm we were weathering together. My heart began to lighten, hope intertwining with the ink on the page.

As the last of the afternoon light filtered through the window, casting a warm glow on my notebook, I folded the page and slipped it into an envelope. I wasn't sure if I'd find Ashton at the office, but I knew I needed to share my thoughts, to reach out and let him know that despite the distance created by our recent argument, I still believed in us.

Stepping back into the rain-soaked streets, I felt a renewed sense of purpose. Each step toward the office was filled with the rhythm of my heartbeat, the anticipation of reconnecting with Ashton threading through my veins like electricity. The city bustled around me, a vibrant backdrop to my own personal journey—a testament to resilience amidst the storm.

As I reached the office building, I hesitated for a moment at the door, taking a deep breath to steady myself. The memories of our dreams rushed back, a powerful reminder of what we had built together. With newfound clarity, I pushed through the door, ready to bridge the gap that had threatened to divide us. I stepped into the space where so much of our journey had unfolded, determined to mend what had been frayed and reignite the fire that had once burned so brightly between us.

The office felt colder now, the flickering overhead lights casting uneven shadows that danced around me like specters, reminders of everything we had built and now stood on the verge of losing. I glanced at the empty chair across from me, its very absence echoing the void left by Ashton's departure. Each minute that ticked by seemed to stretch into infinity, the silence wrapping around me like a heavy blanket, thick and suffocating. My mind raced with thoughts of what I could have said differently, of how to reach the part of him that felt so far away now.

Resigned to the weight of my own thoughts, I rose and wandered over to the large window. The city sprawled before me, a living tapestry of neon lights and car horns, where life seemed to carry on unabated. Outside, people hurried along the sidewalks, their umbrellas bobbing like whimsical mushrooms in the drizzly dusk. I wondered how many of them were battling their own storms beneath the surface, masking their fears with smiles and hurried steps. It felt almost surreal, the contrast between the vibrancy of life outside and the tumult within me.

Just then, the sound of footsteps echoed in the hallway, growing louder until the door swung open. It was Mary, our ever-enthusiastic intern, her hair a wild halo of curls that bounced as she entered. "Ava! I was just—" Her words trailed off as she caught sight of my expression. "Oh no. What happened?"

I forced a smile, knowing it didn't quite reach my eyes. "Just a little disagreement with Ashton. Nothing I can't handle." I wished I believed that, but even I could hear the uncertainty in my voice.

Mary stepped closer, her eyes sparkling with the kind of optimism that often felt foreign to me. "You two are like the perfect team! It's normal to have bumps in the road. I mean, look at all you've accomplished together!" She gestured toward the whiteboard, where our ambitious project timelines and colorful brainstorming notes still hung like trophies, remnants of our late-night collaborations.

Her words reminded me of our collective aspirations, of the late nights spent sharing dreams and visions that once felt so attainable. "Yeah, I know," I replied, my voice softer now. "It's just... this project means everything to us. Sometimes it feels like the pressure is pulling us apart rather than pushing us together."

Mary nodded, her youthful enthusiasm undeterred. "But you're not just a team; you're friends, right? You can get through this. I mean, look at how much you care about each other." She flashed me a grin that was pure sunshine, infectious in its simplicity.

Her optimism stirred something within me. Perhaps I needed to remember the friendship that had blossomed between Ashton and me long before our ambitions intertwined. The laughter, the inside jokes, the moments of vulnerability—we had forged a bond that had weathered storms before. I glanced at my phone, half-expecting a message from him, but the screen remained dark and silent. "Thanks, Mary," I finally said, "I think I just need to give it some time. Maybe I'll try reaching out later."

"Definitely! And if you need anything—like a distraction or a coffee run—I'm your girl!" She bounded toward the door, her energy spilling over, leaving behind a hint of hope.

As the door clicked shut behind her, I returned to the window, my reflection merging with the blurred colors of the cityscape. I needed to find the right moment to reconnect with Ashton, to remind him that despite our differences, our shared goals were more important than the hurdles we faced. The thought sent a surge of determination coursing through me.

The rain continued to drizzle outside, a rhythmic patter that became a soothing backdrop as I pulled out my notebook once more. I flipped to the page where I had poured my heart, my thoughts spilling onto the paper in a chaotic but honest manner. This time, instead of simply describing our shared dreams, I began to sketch a plan—one that acknowledged our frustrations but also embraced our hopes. Each line felt like a step toward rebuilding the bridge between us, a way to carve out a path through the fog that had clouded our vision.

With every stroke of my pen, I envisioned our future: the coffee shop on the corner where we would sit, laughter spilling from our lips, plans flowing as freely as the drinks we shared. I pictured the moments we would spend brainstorming, ideas soaring higher than the buildings that surrounded us. It was a future steeped in camaraderie, where ambition was not an enemy but a friend that pushed us to become better versions of ourselves.

Hours slipped by as I immersed myself in the vision of our renewed partnership, each sentence fortifying my resolve. I would reach out to Ashton not with an apology but with an invitation—a chance to rebuild, to reaffirm our commitment to each other and to our dreams.

Finally, as the sun dipped below the horizon, casting a golden hue across the sky, I gathered my things and stepped back into the bustling streets. The energy of the city pulsed around me, and I felt invigorated by the vibrant life that surrounded me. I could do this. I could reach him.

As I approached the office building, I noticed the light spilling from the windows. Ashton was still there, and as I walked in, the familiar sounds of our space filled my ears—the soft hum of the computer, the rustle of papers, and the distant echo of his voice as he spoke on the phone. My heart quickened, a blend of anticipation and trepidation swirling inside me.

I stood in the doorway for a moment, gathering my thoughts, clutching the envelope containing my letter. I needed to approach this delicately, to tread lightly on the fragile ground between us.

Finally, I stepped forward, the sound of my footsteps breaking the quiet as I made my way to his desk.

Ashton looked up, his expression shifting from surprise to something softer, a flicker of recognition igniting in his eyes. "Ava," he said, his voice a mix of relief and wariness.

I held out the envelope, my heart pounding. "I wrote you something."

He took it, his fingers brushing against mine, a spark igniting at the brief contact. The moment felt electric, a reminder of everything we had shared. "I was just thinking about you," he admitted, his gaze locking onto mine, a warmth flooding through the tension that had simmered between us.

I took a deep breath, emboldened by the connection between us. "I want us to get through this. Together. I believe in what we're building. And I believe in us."

As he opened the envelope, I could see the tension begin to ease in his shoulders, the shadows of doubt flickering away like candlelight in the dark. "Let's talk," he said softly, and for the first time that evening, I felt hope blooming in my chest.

The path ahead might still be fraught with challenges, but standing there, amidst the remnants of our ambitions, I realized that together we could face whatever storms came our way. We were still a team, bound by dreams and resilience, and I was ready to reclaim that bond, one heartfelt conversation at a time.

# Chapter 25: A Temporary Escape

The sun dipped low in the sky, casting a golden hue across the rolling hills as I pulled into the gravel driveway of the bed-and-breakfast. A charming Victorian house stood proudly amidst a symphony of flowers—daisies, lavender, and the ever-present sunflowers swaying lazily in the warm breeze. My heart beat a little faster as I parked my car, the familiar thrill of anticipation mingling with a deep sigh of relief. The chaotic rhythm of my life back in the city felt miles away, trapped behind the steel and glass that usually surrounded me. Here, in this quaint oasis, I could almost hear the whispered secrets of nature, beckoning me to let go.

As I stepped out of the car, the scent of honeysuckle enveloped me, sweet and intoxicating. I took a moment to inhale deeply, letting the fragrant air fill my lungs and wash over me like a balm. It was as if every petal, every leaf had conspired to coax me into their world. I could feel the city's frenetic pulse slow to a gentle thrum, harmonizing with the distant sound of birds chirping, a far cry from the honking horns and endless chatter I was used to. I had craved this serenity, and now that I was here, I could hardly believe my luck.

The wooden door creaked softly as I entered the B&B, revealing a cozy lobby adorned with vintage furnishings and an inviting fireplace that promised warmth on cool evenings. The walls were lined with floral wallpaper, their delicate patterns bringing a touch of whimsy to the otherwise tranquil atmosphere. A sense of belonging washed over me, as if I had stepped into a long-lost haven where I could breathe again. My heart, which had felt heavy with the weight of expectations, began to lighten as I was greeted by Evelyn, the owner, a woman whose smile radiated kindness and warmth.

"Welcome, dear! You must be tired from your journey," she said, her voice soft like the rustle of leaves. Her bright, twinkling eyes scanned my face, offering a sense of reassurance. "Let me show you to your room."

As we ascended the creaky wooden staircase, I marveled at the little details that adorned the walls—old photographs of couples sharing laughs, wildflowers pressed delicately between pages of books, and the whimsical quotes that seemed to speak directly to my heart. Each step felt like a journey into a story I had yet to uncover. I followed Evelyn down the narrow hallway, the scent of fresh linen and lemon-scented cleaning products tickling my senses, leading me to a room filled with sunlight and a view that made my heart skip a beat.

My sanctuary was small but inviting, the kind of room where stories could unfold in quiet whispers. The bed was draped in soft, inviting quilts, and a small writing desk sat by the window, beckoning me to pour my thoughts onto paper. I dropped my suitcase on the floor and collapsed onto the bed, letting the weight of the world lift off my shoulders. I could hear the gentle rustling of leaves outside, the soft hum of a nearby brook creating a lullaby that wrapped around me like a cherished memory.

For the first time in what felt like ages, I allowed myself to relax. I wandered outside to explore the gardens, where vibrant bursts of color filled every nook and cranny. There was something magical about the way the flowers danced in the breeze, their delicate petals fluttering like butterflies. I knelt beside a patch of violets, their rich purple hues vibrant against the emerald backdrop, and reached out to touch them gently. It was grounding, the kind of moment that anchored me in the present and whispered promises of renewal.

As I meandered along the cobblestone paths, I reflected on the whirlwind of emotions that had consumed me lately. My life in the city felt like a never-ending chase—running after dreams that sometimes felt just out of reach, while my heart wrestled with feelings for Ashton that I had buried beneath layers of self-doubt and fear. The connection we shared was undeniable, but the walls I had built around my heart were crumbling, and I had to confront them head-on.

I plopped down onto a weathered wooden bench, its surface warm beneath me from the sun's embrace, and closed my eyes. The sounds of nature enveloped me, a soothing symphony of chirping crickets and rustling leaves. I felt a gentle breeze brush against my skin, as if nature herself were urging me to release my fears and embrace the possibilities ahead. In that stillness, clarity began to unfold, the kind that had eluded me amidst the chaos of my everyday life.

Happiness, I realized, wasn't merely a collection of achievements or accolades. It was about connection, trust, and vulnerability. I thought about Ashton—his laughter, the way his eyes sparkled with mischief, and the warmth of his presence that made me feel inexplicably safe. I had let my insecurities overshadow what we could be, and I knew that if I was going to reclaim the love I feared losing, I had to be brave. I had to confront my feelings and let him in.

With renewed determination, I returned to my room, where the golden rays of the setting sun spilled through the window, casting a warm glow across the space. I opened my journal, the pages blank and inviting, and poured my heart out in ink. Each word became a declaration of my resolve—a promise to myself that I would embrace the unknown, step into the light of possibility, and open my heart to the love that awaited me.

As I wrote, the chaos of the city faded into the background, replaced by the gentle whispers of hope and the sweet scent of blooming flowers. I was no longer merely an observer of my life; I was ready to be a participant, to reclaim my happiness and take the leap into the unknown. The journey ahead was uncertain, but standing at the precipice of change, I felt alive, ready to embrace the adventure that lay ahead.

Morning light spilled through my window, draping the room in soft, golden warmth. I blinked awake, cocooned in layers of fluffy blankets that seemed to whisper promises of comfort and peace. The fresh scent of blooming roses drifted in from the garden, mingling with the faint aroma of coffee wafting up from the kitchen below. It was a gentle reminder that I was far from the suffocating embrace of my usual life, and my heart swelled with gratitude.

I slipped out of bed, my feet sinking into the plush carpet as I padded across the room to the window. The view was nothing short of enchanting. Dew-kissed petals shimmered like jewels, each bloom a testament to the beauty of simplicity. My heart raced with an excitement I hadn't felt in ages. This was a place where time stood still, where the cacophony of my thoughts could finally quiet down.

After a quick shower, I dressed in a light cotton sundress that fluttered around my knees, its floral print echoing the very blossoms that surrounded me. I took a moment to examine myself in the mirror, my reflection a mixture of vulnerability and determination. The woman staring back was ready to shed the layers of fear that had clung to her for so long. I brushed my hair, letting the sun's rays kiss my shoulders, and then I made my way downstairs, the promise of breakfast guiding my steps.

Evelyn was already bustling about in the kitchen, her laughter like a melody that danced through the air. The kitchen was a haven of warmth and familiarity, where the smell of sizzling bacon and freshly baked pastries created an inviting aroma that wrapped around me like a warm embrace. She caught my eye and smiled, her eyes twinkling with mischief as she motioned for me to join her at the table.

"Ah, the lovely guest awakens!" she exclaimed, her voice a comforting blend of cheerfulness and warmth. "You're just in time for my famous blueberry pancakes. They'll change your life, dear."

As I settled at the table, I couldn't help but chuckle at her enthusiasm. The table was set with mismatched plates, each one bearing a unique pattern that told stories of family gatherings and shared moments. I watched as Evelyn expertly flipped pancakes, the golden-brown discs dancing on the griddle with delicious promise. The sunlight streamed through the windows, illuminating the space in a warm glow, while the cheerful clink of cutlery and the soft murmur of Evelyn's anecdotes filled the air.

As I savored each bite of the fluffy pancakes, I realized I was feasting not just on food but on the essence of connection that radiated from this place. Each forkful was an invitation to relish the moment, to embrace the present rather than fretting about the future. It was a lesson I needed, one that was slowly sinking into my bones like the sweetness of syrup pooling on my plate.

"Tell me, dear," Evelyn said, wiping her hands on her apron, "what brings you to this little slice of paradise?" Her eyes held a knowing glint, as if she sensed that I was on the cusp of something transformative.

I hesitated for a moment, contemplating whether to unveil the tangled emotions that had driven me here. But Evelyn's warmth coaxed the words out of me, and I found myself recounting the chaos of my life, the pressure of expectations, and the knot of feelings I had for Ashton.

"Oh, love can be such a tricky thing," she said, her voice a blend of empathy and wisdom. "But sometimes, the most beautiful moments come from the bravest choices. You must follow your heart, dear."

Her words resonated within me, igniting a flicker of courage I hadn't realized was smoldering beneath the surface. After breakfast, I stepped outside, letting the morning sun wash over me, rejuvenating every inch of my being. I wandered through the garden, trailing my fingers along the vibrant blooms, feeling their softness against my skin. Butterflies flitted from flower to flower, their delicate wings carrying them like whispers of hope.

Lost in thought, I settled onto a wooden swing that hung from an ancient oak tree, the cool breeze swaying me gently. I closed my eyes, allowing the sounds of the garden to envelop me—the gentle rustle of leaves, the distant chirping of birds, and the soft hum of life all around. The peace settled within me, urging me to dig deeper, to confront the truth of my feelings rather than hide behind the barriers I had built.

As I rocked back and forth, the memories of Ashton flooded my mind. His laughter, the way his eyes lit up when he spoke about his passions, and the moments of quiet intimacy we shared. Those fragments of joy brought a smile to my lips, but they were also laced with a pang of longing. I realized how much I had pushed him away, cloaked in my fears of inadequacy. The fear of not being enough had kept me locked away in a cage of my own making.

With a newfound resolve, I decided to confront my feelings head-on. I would return to the city not as the woman burdened by uncertainty but as one willing to embrace vulnerability, to open myself up to the possibilities of love and connection. The path ahead was daunting, but the thought of reclaiming that part of myself filled me with excitement.

I hopped off the swing and took a deep breath, filling my lungs with the fresh, sweet air of the countryside. It was time to indulge in the delicious freedom of possibility, to step outside the confines of my comfort zone. The garden seemed to mirror my transformation, vibrant and alive, inviting me to take a leap of faith.

As the sun began to dip lower in the sky, painting the horizon in hues of pink and orange, I made my way back inside. Evelyn was tidying up the kitchen, and her presence felt like a steady anchor. I wanted to thank her for her wisdom, for reminding me of the beauty of connection. As I approached her, I felt a flicker of excitement rush through me, a whisper of encouragement that promised I was on the right path.

"Evelyn," I said, my voice steady with conviction. "Thank you for everything. I think I'm finally ready to embrace what comes next."

Evelyn's smile broadened as she wiped her hands on her apron, nodding knowingly at my declaration. "That's the spirit, dear! Life has a funny way of nudging us where we need to go, but it takes courage to respond. I'd wager that courage is your next best adventure."

Her words hung in the air like the sweet aroma of the honeysuckle vines creeping along the garden trellis. I felt a rush of excitement at the thought of what lay ahead, my heart quickening in rhythm with the fluttering wings of the butterflies nearby. The sun was beginning to dip toward the horizon, casting a warm glow over everything, and I couldn't help but feel that my own transformation was just beginning.

The afternoon slipped away like grains of sand, and I reveled in the small moments—the soft laughter of children playing in a neighboring field, the distant sound of a train whistle echoing through the valley, and the gentle caress of the breeze rustling the leaves. Each sensation wove together a tapestry of belonging, reminding me that I was a part of something greater. I spent my time exploring the gardens, letting my thoughts meander like the brook that wound its way through the property.

The sun was beginning to set, painting the sky in breathtaking shades of orange and purple, when I decided to take a walk into the nearby woods. The path was well-trodden, lined with moss-covered stones and delicate ferns that swayed in the light breeze. As I ventured deeper, the sunlight filtered through the branches above, casting dappled shadows that danced along the ground, creating a magical atmosphere that felt straight out of a fairy tale.

Each step resonated with a newfound sense of purpose, my earlier fears melting away like morning mist in the sunlight. I paused to take in the grandeur of the towering trees, their bark rough and sturdy, each one a testament to the storms they had weathered. I felt a kinship with them—a reminder that resilience is rooted in embracing one's own story, no matter how tangled or messy it may seem.

As I strolled along, my mind drifted to Ashton. The thought of him brought warmth, but also a tinge of anxiety. What if he didn't feel the same way? What if I laid my heart bare and found it wasn't reciprocated? But I brushed those thoughts aside, recognizing that vulnerability was the first step toward genuine connection. With every crunch of leaves beneath my feet, I reaffirmed my commitment to be honest, to seek out the love that had been lurking in the shadows of my insecurities.

Eventually, I found a small clearing, a hidden gem surrounded by the embrace of trees. I settled on a fallen log, the earth cool beneath me as I took a moment to breathe, letting the sounds of nature wash over me. The gentle babbling of the brook nearby blended harmoniously with the occasional rustle of a bird flitting through the branches. I closed my eyes, letting the symphony of the wilderness lull me into a peaceful state.

Time seemed to suspend itself in that clearing, and for the first time in what felt like eons, I felt truly at peace. I envisioned the conversation I would have with Ashton, a blend of honesty and hope. I pictured his smile, the way his laughter rolled over me like a soft wave. I wanted to tell him how much he meant to me, how the connection we shared was a rare gift, a treasure worth fighting for.

After what felt like hours in the serene embrace of the woods, I reluctantly rose and made my way back to the bed-and-breakfast, the sun a fiery orb sinking beneath the horizon. The glow of dusk was a gentle reminder that darkness often paves the way for the light of new beginnings. As I returned to the warmth of Evelyn's home, I felt invigorated, ready to confront my feelings and embrace the love that awaited me back in the city.

That evening, as I settled down with a cup of herbal tea in the cozy nook of the B&B, I reflected on the journey that had brought me here. I thought about the late nights filled with self-doubt, the endless worries that had cluttered my mind, and the moments of joy that had flickered like fireflies in the dark. I was not defined by my fears but by my willingness to rise above them, to embrace love even when it felt daunting.

Evelyn joined me, pulling up a chair with a contented sigh. "You seem a thousand times lighter than when you arrived," she remarked, her eyes twinkling like stars in the night sky. "What's changed?"

I met her gaze, a smile breaking across my face. "I've decided to be brave," I replied, feeling the weight of my resolve solidify within me. "I'm going to tell Ashton how I truly feel."

Her face lit up, as if she were sharing in my joy. "That's the spirit! Love is worth the risk, dear. It's the only way to find out what's meant for you."

After our conversation, I retired to my room, clutching my journal like a lifeline. I poured my heart onto the pages, crafting a letter to Ashton that reflected my truest feelings. Each word felt like a release, a shedding of my insecurities as I committed my emotions to paper. The act itself felt liberating, a step toward embracing what I had always wanted but had been too afraid to claim.

As the stars began to twinkle outside, I nestled into the blankets, clutching my letter tightly against my chest. I drifted off to sleep with a sense of anticipation, my heart swelling with hope.

The following day dawned bright and clear, the sun rising over the hills with renewed vigor. I packed my bags, feeling a bittersweet tug in my chest at the thought of leaving this idyllic retreat. Evelyn appeared at the door, her presence as comforting as ever.

"Are you ready for the next chapter?" she asked, her voice full of encouragement.

I nodded, my heart racing with the weight of my decision. "I am. I'm going to embrace whatever comes next."

After a final goodbye, I stepped into my car, feeling the familiar rush of city life call to me. The journey back felt different; the trees whizzed by in a blur of green and gold, but my heart was steady. I was ready to confront Ashton, to let him see the true me—the one unafraid to love.

As I pulled into the city, my mind raced with possibilities. I parked outside our favorite café, the place where we first met and shared dreams over steaming cups of coffee. With the letter tucked safely in my bag, I took a deep breath, grounding myself in the moment.

Walking inside, I spotted him at our usual table, his brow furrowed in concentration over his laptop. The sight of him sent a thrill of warmth through me, and I knew I had to seize this moment.

As I approached, time seemed to slow, the bustling café fading into the background. This was it—the moment I had been preparing for. I could feel the weight of uncertainty in my stomach, but beneath it simmered an electric current of hope and courage.

"Hey," I said, my voice steady despite the storm of emotions swirling within. His head snapped up, and for a moment, all the noise around us faded into nothing. His eyes widened in surprise, then softened, a smile spreading across his face that felt like a light breaking through the clouds.

"Hey, you," he replied, his voice warm and inviting.

I took a deep breath, letting the moment settle around us. Here, in this small café, the world felt limitless. I was ready to step into my truth and share the love that had been waiting patiently for me to embrace.

# Chapter 26: The Heart of the Matter

The office buzzes with an undercurrent of muted conversations and the gentle hum of the overhead lights, a symphony of modernity blending with the echoes of ambition. I step inside, my shoes tapping against the polished wooden floor, each sound punctuating the air with a reminder of the weight that rests on my shoulders. The walls are adorned with abstract art, splashes of vibrant colors that speak of creativity and risk, and yet, they feel like a curtain veiling the truths hidden beneath the surface of our lives. I glance around, searching for him amidst the sea of familiar faces.

There, leaning against the glass-paneled wall, is Ashton. The sunlight spills through the large windows, framing him like a character from a classic novel, with tousled hair catching the light and a gaze that feels both inviting and intimidating. I can sense the pulse of tension between us, an electric charge that ignites the air, but it is tempered by something warmer—a flicker of understanding, perhaps, or the faint promise of hope. As I approach him, I feel my heart racing, a wild creature trapped in a cage of uncertainty.

"Hey," I manage, my voice a soft note in the cacophony of the office. He turns to me, and in that brief moment, I see a reflection of my own apprehension mirrored in his eyes. They are deep and dark, a pool of thoughts I long to dive into but fear the depths might swallow me whole.

"Hey," he replies, the corners of his mouth curving upward just slightly, as if to reassure me that we're still on the same page, though we both know we've been drifting.

We settle into the chairs that face each other, the gap between us an invisible chasm filled with unspoken words and half-formed thoughts. I take a breath, the air tinged with the faint aroma of coffee and the lingering scent of the morning's pastries, both comforting and unsettling in their familiarity. I can almost taste the tension, thick and palpable, and I know it's time to strip away the layers of pretense that have accumulated between us.

"Ashton, I—" My words stumble out, hesitant like a deer peeking through the underbrush, unsure of the way forward. "I've been thinking about us, about everything that's happened." I pause, searching his face for a sign that he's still with me, still willing to navigate this labyrinth together.

He nods, his expression softening, and I feel the grip of anxiety start to loosen, just a bit. "Yeah, me too," he says, his voice low and steady, like the steady rhythm of a heartbeat. "I think we need to talk about where we're headed. I don't want to assume things, and I don't want us to be lost in this... whatever it is."

I exhale, a rush of relief flooding through me. We're finally here, standing at the precipice of honesty, and I can see the glimmer of vulnerability in his eyes—a vulnerability I'd never expected to witness in someone so composed, so seemingly in control.

"I'm scared," I admit, my voice barely above a whisper. "I care about you, and I don't want to lose what we have. But I feel like we're both tiptoeing around each other, afraid to step too close."

Ashton's gaze sharpens, a flicker of understanding lighting his features. "I get it. I've been feeling that way too. But it's not just fear for me; it's this gnawing uncertainty. I want to be open with you, but sometimes it feels like we're playing a game, and I don't know the rules."

The honesty in his words resonates deep within me, unraveling the knots of worry I didn't even realize I had tied. "I think we've been holding back because we're scared of what might happen if we lay everything on the table," I say, a rush of honesty pouring forth like a long-hidden secret finally finding its voice. "But if we keep doing this, we might lose each other completely."

There's a silence that stretches between us, heavy with implications and possibilities. The office around us fades, the chatter of colleagues dimming into a distant murmur, and all I can focus on is the man sitting across from me—his brow furrowed in thought, the lines of concern etching deeper into his handsome face.

"What if we made a pact?" he suggests suddenly, the spark of an idea igniting his expression. "A commitment to be honest, no matter how uncomfortable it is. No more guessing games, just... truth."

My heart skips a beat, a melody of hope entwined with the rhythm of uncertainty. "I like that," I reply, feeling a warmth blossom within me. "It's scary, but maybe it's what we need to bridge this gap."

We sit in silence for a moment, each contemplating the weight of our unspoken truths. I can feel the air thrum with the promise of change, an awakening of sorts as the light filtering through the windows shifts, casting intricate shadows that dance across the floor. I'm struck by how vulnerable we both are, how this simple agreement—this commitment to openness—could forge a path into the unknown, a way forward into uncharted territory.

Ashton leans forward, his eyes locking onto mine with an intensity that sends a shiver down my spine. "So, what do you want?" he asks, his voice steady, inviting. "What do you hope for?"

I swallow hard, the weight of his question pressing against my chest, and for the first time, I allow myself to dream out loud. "I want us to be partners, in every sense of the word. I want to build something real, something that lasts. I want us to challenge each other, support each other, and grow together."

He nods, a small smile breaking through the tension, and I can feel the air between us crackling with possibility. We have crossed a threshold, and as we sit in that office, surrounded by the mundanity of our everyday lives, I sense the dawning of something profound. It's a shared understanding, a commitment to face whatever storms lie ahead—not just as individuals but as two souls intertwined, ready to navigate the heart of the matter together.

The glow of the afternoon sun spills through the expansive windows, casting a warm halo around Ashton and me. We've shed our masks, and the air feels charged with newfound honesty, as though we've peeled back the layers of expectation and are standing at the raw, unguarded core of ourselves. A world outside the glass walls buzzes with the mundane rhythms of office life, but inside, everything is different. Our moment feels sacred, cocooned in this bubble of vulnerability.

As I gather my thoughts, I watch him. His features, typically composed and confident, are softened by a hint of trepidation. There's a flicker of something profound in his eyes—a mix of hope and fear that mirrors my own. I can't help but smile at the thought that behind his often calm exterior lies the same tumult of emotions I grapple with daily. It's reassuring, almost endearing, to witness this side of him.

"Okay, let's talk," I finally say, my voice steady, as if I'm affirming a pact we've already made. "We've been dancing around this for far too long." The words feel liberating, an opening of floodgates I didn't even know I had. "I need to know what you want, Ashton. I need to understand how you see us."

He leans back in his chair, crossing his arms, and I can see the gears turning in his mind. "I've been thinking about that a lot, actually," he begins, his tone measured. "I want to be with you. I want to explore whatever this is, but I'm scared of messing it up. We both have baggage, and I don't want us to carry that into something new."

His candor catches me off guard. The man I've admired from afar, the one who commands every room he enters, is wrestling with insecurities like anyone else. It humanizes him in a way I hadn't expected, and I find myself nodding, understanding rippling through me.

"Baggage is a part of life, Ashton," I respond, a warmth blooming in my chest. "I think it's how we handle it that counts. If we can be honest about what we're carrying, maybe we can lighten the load together." The words spill from me, filled with a conviction I've been nurturing since this journey began.

"Right." His brow furrows slightly, and I can almost see the wheels turning. "But how do we do that? I don't want to throw everything at you and scare you away. You deserve better than that."

A light laugh escapes me, the sound surprising us both. "You're not going to scare me off. I'm tougher than I look. Besides, we're not in a horror movie; this isn't some dramatic plot twist waiting to happen."

He chuckles, the sound a welcome break in the intensity of our conversation. "Fair enough. But I still want to be careful. I can be a little overwhelming sometimes."

"Understatement of the year," I tease, playfully rolling my eyes. "But that's okay. We can figure it out together, one step at a time."

A moment of silence stretches between us, comfortable and inviting. I can see Ashton grappling with something just beneath the surface, a thought swirling like a leaf caught in a breeze. Finally, he speaks again, his voice softer, almost vulnerable. "I guess I worry that I'll let you down. You have this amazing ability to light up a room, and I don't want to dim that light."

His words resonate deeply, reverberating in the caverns of my heart. It's a weighty revelation, the acknowledgment of how our perceptions can shape our fears. "Ashton," I begin, my voice steady yet gentle, "you don't have to be perfect for me. I'm not perfect either. I just want you to be you. It's enough."

He meets my gaze, and in that moment, it feels like the world around us fades away, leaving only the two of us suspended in our shared understanding. I can see the tension in his shoulders ease, the walls he'd built around himself slowly crumbling.

"I want to try," he finally says, the sincerity in his voice sending a thrill through me. "I want to be there for you. I want to know you—really know you."

"Then let's start from here," I urge, my heart racing at the prospect. "Let's share everything—the good, the bad, the ugly. We can tackle it together."

Ashton nods, a slow, deliberate movement that feels like a promise. "I think I can do that. Just bear with me if I trip over my words sometimes. I'm not used to this kind of openness."

"I'll catch you," I promise, my heart swelling with affection. "And I might trip over my own words too. So let's just laugh it off when we do."

With a newfound sense of camaraderie, we delve into the details of our lives—the things that make us tick and the shadows that linger in the corners. I share stories from my childhood, the laughter that filled my home and the tears that followed a family upheaval, and I watch as Ashton listens intently, his expression a canvas of empathy. He speaks of his own experiences—of growing up in a world that seemed to demand perfection while feeling painfully inadequate.

The weight of our confessions lifts as we weave our stories together, the room filling with the sweet, rich scent of camaraderie, hope, and possibility. Each revelation draws us closer, each shared experience a thread stitching our hearts together. I see him opening up, layer by layer, like the petals of a flower unfurling under the sun.

"I didn't think I could feel this way again," he admits, his voice low, almost a whisper. "It's refreshing, but also terrifying. I've built so many walls, and now you're asking me to let them down."

"Trust me, it's not easy for me either," I reply, a soft laugh bubbling up. "But maybe we can create a space where it's safe to be vulnerable, where we can both let our guard down."

A flicker of hope ignites in Ashton's eyes, and for a moment, I can see the glimmer of a future shimmering before us. "I'd like that," he says, his voice steady, and I know we are both stepping into uncharted territory, hand in hand.

In that moment, with the sun casting golden rays across our shared space, I realize we've crossed a threshold. We're no longer just two individuals navigating the complexities of life; we are becoming a team, ready to tackle whatever lies ahead—together. The world beyond the office walls remains a chaotic storm, but within this sanctuary, we are crafting something beautiful, fragile, and fiercely real.

The sunlight begins to dip below the horizon, casting a warm amber hue across the office, and with it comes an inviting atmosphere that feels almost cinematic. The lively chatter of my colleagues fades into the background, leaving only the rhythmic tapping of keyboards and the distant whir of printers. It's as if the world has narrowed down to just Ashton and me, two explorers daring to chart the uncharted territory of our emotions.

"Let's grab some coffee," he suggests, breaking the comfortable silence that had settled between us like a soft blanket. "I think we could both use it." There's a spark of mischief in his eyes, and I can't help but smile. The casual ease of our interaction fills the air with a sense of lightness, and I find myself longing to extend this moment beyond the confines of our office walls.

"Coffee sounds perfect," I agree, my heart fluttering at the thought of spending more time with him. Together, we navigate through the labyrinth of desks and chairs, dodging the occasional colleague who greets us with curious glances. I wonder what they might think—if they could see the invisible connection weaving itself tighter between Ashton and me.

We step into the bustling café on the ground floor, a cozy nook adorned with local art and the rich scent of roasted beans wafting through the air. The atmosphere is filled with laughter and chatter, a cacophony of life that contrasts sharply with the seriousness of our earlier conversation. I glance at the menu, my eyes dancing over the options, but my mind is elsewhere, tangled in the threads of our conversation.

"What's your go-to order?" I ask, turning to Ashton, who's already scanning the menu with a contemplative frown.

"I'm a sucker for a vanilla latte," he replies, a hint of playfulness in his voice. "And you?"

"Classic cappuccino. Simple but effective," I say, a smile tugging at my lips. "It's like my life philosophy."

He chuckles, the sound warm and infectious, and I can't help but feel a flutter of excitement at the prospect of spending more time together. We place our orders, the barista flashing us a bright smile as she scribbles our choices on a paper cup. As we wait, Ashton leans against the counter, his posture relaxed, and I catch the subtle way he watches the world around him—an observer taking in the nuances of life, just like I often do.

"You seem to have a talent for bringing light into dark places," he says suddenly, his gaze turning serious as he meets my eyes. "You've made this whole ordeal feel lighter."

I feel my cheeks warm at his compliment, the fluttering in my chest intensifying. "It's easier to be optimistic when I'm with you," I admit, the words tumbling out before I can filter them.

"Really? I didn't think I had that effect on anyone." There's a teasing lilt to his voice, but I can see the sincerity behind it.

"You absolutely do. You've managed to break down my walls without even trying. I didn't realize how closed off I'd been until you walked in."

His expression shifts slightly, and I sense the weight of our unspoken truths hanging between us. "It's funny how life works, isn't it? Sometimes, you meet someone and everything changes."

With our drinks in hand, we find a small table by the window, the warm light enveloping us like a comforting hug. We settle into our seats, and I can't help but admire the way Ashton cradles his cup, the steam curling upward like a delicate ribbon.

"So, tell me more about your dreams," he prompts, leaning forward, his interest palpable.

I take a moment, sipping my cappuccino and letting the rich flavor wash over me. "I've always wanted to write," I confess, the words spilling forth. "To create stories that resonate with people, that spark something deep within them. I used to dream of having my own novel, something people would connect with."

Ashton's eyes light up, and I can see the enthusiasm bubbling beneath the surface. "You should go for it. I can see you crafting beautiful stories that leave a mark on the world. There's something magical about the way you speak about it."

His encouragement swells my heart, filling me with a sense of purpose I hadn't fully recognized until this moment. "It's just been hard to find the time between work and life. Sometimes, it feels like a distant dream."

"I get that," he replies, his expression earnest. "But maybe it's time to prioritize your passions. We spend so much time chasing things that don't truly matter. What if you carved out time for yourself?"

His words resonate deeply, and I nod, feeling the spark of inspiration igniting within me. "You're right. I think I've been so focused on everything else that I lost sight of what truly makes me happy."

Ashton takes a sip of his latte, a thoughtful expression on his face. "I want you to know that I'm here for that journey. I want to support you in whatever way I can. Whether it's reading drafts or just being your cheerleader, I'm all in."

His declaration warms me from the inside, a gentle reminder that I'm not alone in this endeavor. We share a moment of quiet understanding, the world around us fading as we sit cocooned in our little bubble of dreams and aspirations.

"Thank you," I say, my voice barely above a whisper. "That means more than you know."

The moment feels fragile, like a delicate flower blooming in the early spring, and I'm acutely aware of how precious it is. We continue to share stories, laughing and teasing one another, and the hours slip away like grains of sand. Time blurs, and for once, it feels as if the outside world has receded, leaving only our connection.

As the sun begins to set, casting a golden glow over the bustling street outside, I realize that this moment—this newfound clarity and camaraderie—is something to be cherished. With each laugh and every shared secret, we build a bridge over the chasm that once separated us, the foundation of trust strengthening beneath us.

"I never expected to find this with you," Ashton says softly, a hint of wonder in his voice. "But I'm so glad I did."

"Me too," I reply, my heart swelling with warmth. "I think we're just getting started."

In that instant, I know that we're standing at the precipice of something beautiful, ready to embrace the uncertainty that lies ahead. Together, we'll face whatever comes our way, armed with the knowledge that we are stronger when we lean on one another. The promise of tomorrow glimmers on the horizon, and I feel an exhilarating rush of possibility sweeping through me, ready to write the next chapter of our lives together.

# Chapter 27: The Launch

The office hummed with a vibrancy that mirrored the autumn leaves dancing outside the large windows, each gold and crimson hue promising change. I leaned against the cool glass, a swirl of nerves and excitement knotting in my stomach. The sun dipped lower in the sky, casting golden shafts of light across the sleek desks, the fluorescent lights buzzing softly like a hive of honeybees, hinting at the sweetness of success just within reach. The scent of freshly brewed coffee mingled with the faint aroma of cinnamon from a neighboring café, wrapping around me like a warm embrace.

Ashton stood next to me, his hands tucked into his pockets, his usually meticulous hair slightly tousled, as if he had spent the last few hours raking his fingers through it in frustration—or perhaps in thought. I admired the way he focused, his brow furrowing slightly as he practiced our lines under his breath. In moments like these, he was my anchor, steadying my wild heart with his calm demeanor. A smile crept across my lips as I watched him; he had that effect on me, somehow turning my jittery energy into something hopeful, something tangible.

The conference room door swung open, and a flurry of colleagues filtered in, all of us swept up in the shared anticipation of what was about to unfold. I exchanged glances with familiar faces—each one a testament to late nights and early mornings spent poring over spreadsheets and brainstorming sessions that turned into laughter-filled gatherings. We had poured our souls into this campaign, building it piece by piece, like crafting a mosaic from shards of glass, each colorful fragment representing our ideas, our dreams, our relentless pursuit of something extraordinary.

"Ready?" Ashton turned to me, his voice low, a teasing lilt playing at the corners of his mouth. He was so infuriatingly charming, and I felt that familiar flutter in my stomach. I nodded, my heart racing, not just from the weight of the moment but from the electricity that sparked whenever he was near. We shared an unspoken connection, one that had been stitched together through late-night brainstorming sessions and shared coffee runs, but today it felt heightened, more significant. Today, we were stepping into the spotlight, ready to unveil our vision to the world.

As we walked into the room, the atmosphere shifted. It was filled with the anticipation of innovation, a palpable energy that crackled like static electricity. The board members settled into their chairs, their eyes trained on us, some wearing expressions of skepticism while others glimmered with intrigue. A massive screen loomed behind us, the projection of our hard work—a kaleidoscope of ideas—waiting to burst forth and fill the space.

Ashton took a deep breath, his voice steady as he opened the presentation. I could see the slight tremor in his hands, but he spoke with the confidence of someone who had believed in this idea long before I had. He outlined the campaign, his words painting vivid pictures of our vision: a community-driven project that would not just engage our audience but transform it, allowing them to see themselves as part of something greater. My heart swelled with pride as I watched him, the passion in his eyes infectious, and I felt a surge of determination to match his energy.

When it was my turn to speak, I felt the weight of our collective hopes resting on my shoulders, but I welcomed it. I stepped closer to the screen, my fingers lightly brushing against it, a physical connection to the world we had created. The data danced before me—charts, images, testimonials. I spoke of the impact we hoped to make, how this campaign wasn't just about numbers; it was about building connections, about touching lives, about creating a movement that would ripple outwards and encourage others to join us. As I spoke, I could see nods of approval from some board members, their expressions softening as they began to connect with the story we were weaving.

The room began to fill with murmurs of agreement and encouragement, and I felt the tide turning in our favor. Ashton and I exchanged glances, our excitement bubbling beneath the surface, igniting the fire of our ambition. Together, we had crafted something that could resonate beyond the sterile walls of the conference room, something that could echo through the very heart of our community.

As the presentation unfolded, the connection between us deepened, each slide revealing not just the intricacies of our strategy but the essence of who we were as a team. Laughter erupted at just the right moments, breaking the tension, and I could feel the audience leaning in, captivated by our passion. The way Ashton leaned toward me, encouraging me to elaborate, made me feel seen, valued. It was as if we were dancing—each step in sync, leading us toward a shared vision.

Finally, we reached the concluding slide, the culmination of weeks of hard work and late-night brainstorming sessions. The last image flickered onto the screen: a vibrant community united, a tapestry of diverse voices coming together in harmony. The room fell silent, the weight of our message settling over us like a thick blanket. I could see the board members processing our words, their expressions shifting from skepticism to intrigue, from doubt to hope.

With the final click, I felt the air shift. A moment suspended in time, our fate hanging delicately in the balance. It was a moment where dreams and reality converged, and I could sense the excitement crackling in the room, sparking from person to person. Together, we had crafted a narrative that not only represented our aspirations but had the power to inspire change.

As we stepped back, the applause erupted, filling the room with warmth and acceptance. I turned to Ashton, my heart swelling with pride and relief, knowing that we had not just survived this moment but had thrived. The road ahead was still long, filled with uncertainties and challenges, but we had taken the first bold step toward something extraordinary. And in that shared glance, I knew we were not just colleagues; we were partners in this journey, ready to face whatever came next.

As the applause reverberated around the room, a giddy wave of relief washed over me, flooding my senses like the first sip of a perfectly brewed cup of coffee on a chilly morning. I could still feel the electric charge in the air, as though the very walls of the conference room pulsed with the excitement of new possibilities. Ashton's eyes sparkled with uncontained enthusiasm, and for a fleeting moment, we basked in the glow of our achievement, soaking in the approving nods and smiles that radiated from the board members. It was a small victory, but oh, how monumental it felt.

As the formalities concluded, we stepped away from the presentation space, the rush of adrenaline morphing into a heady mix of joy and disbelief. My heart raced, each beat echoing the thrilling realization that our vision was now more than just ideas whispered in late-night discussions; it was on the verge of becoming a living, breathing entity. I caught Ashton's gaze, his expression a blend of triumph and disbelief, and I couldn't help but laugh. "We did it," I said, the words tumbling out in an unguarded moment of vulnerability.

The post-presentation chaos unfolded around us like a well-orchestrated symphony. Colleagues were gathering their things, their chatter a blend of excitement and relief, punctuated by the occasional whoop of joy. The atmosphere was intoxicating. I wanted to bottle this moment and keep it forever—a token of our hard work, our sacrifices, and our audacity to dream big. But the clamor also brought me back to reality; we weren't out of the woods yet.

"Let's not get too comfortable," Ashton said, a playful glint in his eyes as he leaned closer, his voice low. "We still have to tackle the launch party tonight. No pressure." He grinned, and I felt that familiar flutter stir in my stomach again, a mix of nerves and something entirely more exhilarating.

As the afternoon waned into evening, we slipped into the rhythm of preparation, the excitement palpable in every corner of the office. I busied myself with coordinating logistics for the launch party, pouring over spreadsheets and confirming last-minute details. Each email I sent felt like a stepping stone into our future, a tangible action toward a dream that had begun as mere whispers in our minds. The décor would be a reflection of our campaign—bold, vibrant, and utterly engaging, designed to capture the spirit of what we had envisioned.

The city outside transformed as dusk settled in, the skyline aglow with hues of amber and violet. I glanced out the window, entranced by the sight of bustling streets below, where people were rushing home, their faces illuminated by the warm light of shop windows. The world outside thrummed with energy, a stark contrast to the steady hum of our office, yet somehow perfectly in sync with the anticipation brewing within me.

When the clock struck five, a flurry of activity erupted as our team members began filtering out, donning their best outfits, ready to transition from the workday to celebration. I glanced down at my attire, a carefully chosen dress that danced around my knees, its vibrant pattern mirroring the lively spirit I hoped to embody tonight. The reflection in the glass showed a confident woman, yet beneath the surface, I felt the flutter of self-doubt that always lurked in the shadows of my ambition.

Ashton approached, impeccably dressed in a fitted blazer and that charming smile that could light up even the most mundane day.

"You look amazing," he said, his sincerity washing over me like a soothing balm. "Ready to conquer the night?"

I chuckled, feigning confidence even as my heart raced. "If by conquer, you mean hoping the punch isn't spiked, then absolutely." We both laughed, and I could feel the camaraderie swirling around us, binding us in this shared experience. Together, we navigated the transition from colleagues to partners in every sense, our playful banter shifting effortlessly into moments of shared understanding.

The venue for the launch party was nestled in the heart of downtown, a chic loft overlooking the bustling streets, where the city's pulse thrummed beneath us. As we arrived, the space was already alive with color—streamers hung from the ceiling like rainbows in mid-air, and tables adorned with eye-catching centerpieces sparkled under the soft lighting. It felt as if the walls themselves were echoing our excitement, a fitting backdrop for the momentous occasion we were celebrating.

Guests began to trickle in, laughter and chatter weaving a vibrant tapestry of sound around us. I poured myself a glass of sparkling water, watching as familiar faces mingled, the air thick with excitement and anticipation. It was as if the city had transformed into a living canvas, the energy palpable, inspiring me to take a step forward into this new chapter of our story.

"Let's do a toast," Ashton suggested, his voice steady yet enthusiastic. We gathered a small circle of our team, our fingers brushing again as we lifted our glasses. "To new beginnings, hard work, and the amazing journey ahead." His words resonated, weaving a spell of unity and hope amongst us. As the clinking of glasses harmonized with the laughter around us, I felt a deep sense of belonging, a surge of gratitude for this team that had become a family.

As the night unfolded, I reveled in the camaraderie of our shared success, each conversation unfolding like petals of a flower, blossoming with creativity and ambition. Ashton moved seamlessly through the crowd, his charm radiating warmth, while I found myself drawn into discussions that inspired my own aspirations. We were more than just colleagues; we were a force of nature, an ensemble cast in the unfolding story of our campaign, and it felt exhilarating.

The music pulsed softly in the background, a gentle reminder that life thrived beyond the confines of our workplace. Each laugh, every shared anecdote deepened the bond we were building, and I marveled at how our campaign had woven us together, transforming us into something greater than ourselves. I felt like a storyteller, sharing not just our vision but the very essence of who we were—a tapestry of dreams, fears, and the relentless pursuit of something meaningful.

As the night deepened and the conversations flowed, I found myself standing by the window, the city sprawled beneath me like a vast ocean of lights. Each twinkling beacon represented a story, a life intertwined with the energy of the night. I took a moment to breathe it all in—the scent of the city, the sounds of laughter, the feeling of something truly magical in the air.

In that moment, I realized we were on the brink of something incredible, and though the road ahead was still uncertain, I felt a powerful resolve to embrace every twist and turn. The night was ours, a celebration of everything we had achieved and everything we were about to become, and as I turned to rejoin the party, I knew I wouldn't want to miss a single moment.

As I rejoined the lively throng of partygoers, I felt a renewed surge of enthusiasm, as if the very atmosphere charged my spirit with its electric energy. The music pulsed, weaving its way through conversations, wrapping around laughter and soft gasps of delight. Everywhere I looked, faces illuminated with excitement danced in the soft, twinkling lights that adorned the loft, casting a magical glow that seemed to elevate our spirits even higher.

I spotted a small group huddled near the bar, animatedly discussing their roles in the campaign, their voices rising and falling in harmony with the music. I drifted closer, eager to join the vibrant exchange. "What's the plan for the next phase?" I asked, leaning in, intrigued by the fiery energy that sparked between my colleagues.

One of my teammates, Chloe, a creative whirlwind with an infectious laugh, leaned forward, her eyes glimmering with ambition. "I think we should really lean into social media. Make it a challenge—something interactive. Get our audience involved!" The enthusiasm radiating from her was impossible to resist, igniting my own ideas. The prospect of engaging our audience in such an organic way was thrilling. I could envision it—a digital tapestry woven from our community's stories, a living testament to the campaign's heartbeat.

As I shared my thoughts, the conversation began to morph, each idea building upon the last, like a symphony crescendoing toward a glorious finale. The collective energy in the room swelled, a palpable current of creativity that set my heart racing. I felt like a conductor guiding an orchestra, each voice contributing to a harmonious vision of what we could accomplish.

Just then, Ashton appeared at my side, a playful grin spreading across his face. "I thought you might like to join the discussion," he said, his voice teasing yet warm. "Chloe has some fantastic ideas brewing. It sounds like we're on the verge of something spectacular." I could hear the pride in his tone, and my chest swelled with gratitude for the support he continually offered.

Before I could respond, a tap on my shoulder drew my attention. I turned to find Marcus, our CEO, standing there with a gleam of satisfaction in his eyes. "Incredible job tonight," he said, his voice steady and reassuring. "I could feel the passion in your presentation.

The board was impressed." My heart leapt at his words, a soothing balm to the nerves that had tangled in my chest all evening. "We've got a lot of faith in you two. I expect great things," he added, before slipping back into the crowd.

With Marcus's praise lingering in the air, I felt a surge of confidence wash over me, bolstering my resolve. I turned back to Ashton, our eyes locking for a moment that seemed to stretch into eternity. In that shared glance, I recognized an unspoken agreement: we would push the boundaries of our campaign, igniting a spark of innovation that would take us far beyond expectations.

As the night wore on, we mingled with colleagues and friends, celebrating not just our achievements but the relationships we had forged along the way. Each interaction felt like a thread weaving us tighter together, creating a tapestry of support and ambition that would carry us forward. Conversations flitted between dreams and ideas, each exchange a brushstroke on the canvas of our collaborative future.

I found myself lost in a discussion with Jenna, our social media guru, who was buzzing with excitement over the response our campaign had already garnered online. "You won't believe the engagement metrics! People are responding! They're hungry for this," she enthused, her energy infectious. "We've got to keep the momentum going."

I nodded, feeling the spark of inspiration light up within me once more. The thought of capturing our audience's attention, of building a community that thrived on connection and creativity, sent shivers down my spine. We were no longer just a team; we were architects of a movement, creators of a narrative that would resonate long after the launch party faded into memory.

As the clock crept toward midnight, the loft buzzed with the sounds of celebration, laughter interspersed with the clinking of glasses, each one a toast to our journey thus far. The anticipation of the unknown ahead felt exhilarating, a shimmering possibility shimmering in the dim light.

"I think it's time for a dance," Ashton suggested, his eyes gleaming with mischief. Before I could respond, he gently took my hand, guiding me toward the dance floor, where the music swelled, wrapping us in its rhythm. The world around us melted away as we swayed to the beat, our bodies moving in sync, a tangible reflection of the harmony we had created in our work.

With every spin and sway, I felt the worries and expectations fall away, replaced by an exhilarating sense of freedom. In this moment, we weren't just colleagues or partners in a campaign; we were simply two souls sharing an extraordinary night. I glanced up at him, our eyes locking once more, and I could see in his gaze a depth of understanding that went beyond words. He was right there with me, anchoring me in a world of endless possibilities.

The music shifted, a softer melody floating through the air, and as we continued to dance, I felt a connection deepen between us, a bond that transcended the boundaries of our professional relationship. "You know," I whispered, my heart racing, "I never imagined I'd find this kind of partnership in my career. It's more than I ever hoped for."

Ashton smiled, a warmth radiating from him that enveloped me like a soft blanket. "Neither did I. But I think we're just getting started." His words resonated within me, filling me with a heady mixture of excitement and possibility.

The evening continued, a blur of laughter, dancing, and heartfelt conversations. As the clock approached the witching hour, the energy began to ebb, and I found a quiet corner where I could catch my breath. The city skyline glittered outside, a panorama of dreams shimmering beneath the blanket of night.

I took a moment to reflect, to absorb the joy and triumph of the evening, feeling a surge of gratitude for everyone who had come together to make this dream a reality. I realized that while our campaign was a testament to hard work and creativity, it was also a celebration of connection—between colleagues, friends, and even with our audience. Each person in that room played a part in the narrative we were weaving, and I felt honored to be a part of something so significant.

As I glanced back toward the dance floor, I caught sight of Ashton, his laughter mingling with that of our colleagues. It was in that moment that I knew this was just the beginning. We had embarked on a journey filled with potential, and together, we would navigate every twist and turn, crafting a story that would resonate long after the music faded. With hearts full of hope and hands intertwined, we would embrace the adventure that lay ahead, unafraid to dream bigger and reach higher, fueled by the magic of what we could create together.

# Chapter 28: A Moment of Truth

The bar hummed with life, a vibrant pulse echoing the thrumming energy of the city below. I leaned against the cool, wrought-iron railing of the rooftop, the scent of fresh mojitos mingling with the salty breeze that danced playfully through the air. Below, the streets of Manhattan sprawled out like a patchwork quilt, each block illuminated by a chorus of neon lights, the rattle of taxis merging with the distant sound of live music from a nearby venue. Laughter and clinking glasses floated around us, a celebratory symphony marking our hard-earned victory.

As I took a sip of my drink, the coolness of the mint and lime was a brief distraction from the tumult of emotions bubbling just beneath the surface. We had just launched a project that had consumed us for months, the culmination of countless late nights and fervent brainstorming sessions. But as the revelry swirled around me, I felt like an imposter in my own joy, a fleeting specter haunting the laughter and gaiety that enveloped my colleagues.

The cacophony of celebration faded slightly when I spotted Ashton across the terrace, his smile bright enough to rival the skyline behind him. He leaned against the bar, effortlessly charismatic, his tousled hair catching the light, making him seem almost ethereal. Yet, in that moment, he felt like an island—an oasis of charm surrounded by the churning sea of my unresolved feelings. My heart thrummed with anticipation and fear, a delicate balance that threatened to topple me into uncertainty.

I stepped away from the railing, weaving through the crowd until I reached him. The din faded further as I found myself lost in the warmth of his gaze, the kind that seemed to know my thoughts before I spoke them. "Can we talk?" I asked, my voice almost swallowed by the laughter and music surrounding us. He nodded, his brow furrowing slightly as he sensed the gravity behind my words.

We moved toward a quieter corner of the terrace, away from the revelers. The view stretched endlessly before us, a sea of lights shimmering against the night sky. I drew in a shaky breath, the crisp air filling my lungs and grounding me in this moment. "I can't keep pretending that everything is perfect," I began, my voice barely above a whisper.

Ashton looked at me, his expression shifting from playful to concerned. "What do you mean?"

"I love you," I blurted out, the words tumbling from my lips with a force I hadn't anticipated. There it was, raw and naked in the open air, and I felt an exhilarating rush, as if I had just jumped off a cliff, soaring for a brief moment before the ground rushed up to meet me. "I've been so afraid to say it, afraid of how it might change things between us. I just... I didn't want to ruin what we have."

His eyes widened, a mix of surprise and something else—something deeper that I dared to hope was love. "You're not ruining anything. You're giving it shape." His voice was steady, yet soft, a melodic balm to my frayed nerves.

"Really?" I asked, my heart thrumming louder now, a drumbeat echoing the unease that had lingered for so long.

"Yeah," he replied, stepping closer, the distance between us shrinking until the heat of his body warmed my skin. "I've been feeling the same way. I just didn't know how to tell you."

The honesty hung between us like a fragile thread, shimmering with possibility. "So, what do we do now?" I ventured, my pulse racing as I took in his handsome features, the way his eyes sparkled with hope and understanding.

Ashton took a step back, his expression shifting to one of contemplation. "We face it. Whatever comes next, we do it together."

I couldn't help but smile, the weight of uncertainty lifting like the clouds that sometimes obscure the sun. "Together," I echoed, tasting the sweetness of that word as if it were the last sip of my mojito, refreshing and invigorating.

He pulled me into his arms, the warmth of his embrace enveloping me, and in that moment, all the fears and doubts I had carried faded like the last rays of sunlight. Under the vast expanse of the night sky, with the world shimmering around us, I knew that this was a beginning rather than an end.

But even as I relished the warmth of his body and the promise in his words, a flicker of worry crept back into my mind. The world below continued to bustle with its relentless energy, and our new reality would not exist in a vacuum. Would our connection withstand the pressures of life? The chaos of our jobs? The distractions that threatened to pull us apart?

But in that fleeting moment, none of those worries mattered. All that mattered was the warmth of his breath against my neck, the intoxicating scent of his cologne, and the unspoken understanding that we had crossed a threshold. The skyline glittered above us, each light a promise of the adventures that awaited, and as I leaned into him, I felt an exhilarating surge of hope, ready to embrace whatever came next.

The city, once a cacophony of noise, transformed into a backdrop for our dreams, a canvas on which we would paint our story. Each heartbeat echoed with the potential of what was to come, and I reveled in the thought that, together, we would navigate the challenges ahead, hand in hand, heart to heart.

The warmth of Ashton's embrace lingered like a soft melody, wrapping around me as the laughter of our colleagues faded into the background. The vibrant energy of the rooftop bar pulsated with a life of its own, each burst of laughter and clink of glasses painting a scene that was both celebratory and surreal. Yet, nestled within the delight of our success, I felt a new weight—a profound realization that love was not merely a spark ignited in the heat of the moment;

it was a choice, a commitment to journey together through the intricate maze of life.

As we stood entwined under the sprawling Manhattan skyline, the twinkling lights seemed to mirror the fluttering excitement in my heart. I felt like a character from a romantic movie, caught in a moment that transcended the ordinary. But as the initial rush of confession faded, reality settled in, casting shadows on the glowing surface of our newfound connection. What did it mean to love someone in a city that never slept, where ambition and distraction loomed large?

With the cool night air swirling around us, I pulled back slightly, wanting to gauge Ashton's reaction. His expression was a blend of surprise and joy, his eyes dancing with an intensity that ignited my own fears and desires. "Are you okay?" I asked, my voice laced with concern. The question felt necessary, even though I already sensed that we were stepping into something beautiful yet terrifying.

"More than okay," he said, his voice steady, yet the slightest tremor betrayed his vulnerability. "I just didn't expect to hear you say that, but it makes sense. You make sense."

His words ignited a warmth in my chest, a flicker of hope intertwining with the anxiety I couldn't fully shake. I had wrestled with this truth for so long, convincing myself that keeping my feelings hidden would somehow protect us both. But now, standing there with him, I realized that love couldn't flourish in the shadows; it needed light and air, the very elements that nurtured it.

"Good," I replied, offering a smile that I hoped conveyed the relief I felt. "Because I want us to be honest with each other, especially if we're going to do this."

A deep breath filled my lungs as I scanned the bustling scene around us. Friends clinked glasses and cheered, their faces aglow with excitement, but my focus remained solely on Ashton. The city felt alive, but so did the uncharted territory we were about to explore together.

"Let's not pretend this won't be complicated," I continued, my tone shifting to one of cautious optimism. "We both have our lives, our careers... our dreams. I don't want to throw all of that into chaos."

He nodded, his gaze unwavering. "I know. But maybe chaos is just part of life, right? We're both ambitious, driven. It's what brought us together in the first place."

I found comfort in his words, like a lifeline thrown to someone struggling against the currents. "I just want to make sure we don't lose sight of each other in the hustle. I don't want this to be another item on our to-do list."

The corners of his mouth turned upward, that playful smirk I adored making an appearance. "I promise not to treat you like a project, if you promise not to treat me like a checklist."

Laughter bubbled up between us, a welcome reprieve from the seriousness of our conversation. The tension that had been building began to dissipate, replaced by a shared understanding that we could navigate this new territory together.

As the evening progressed, we found ourselves lost in conversation, our laughter mingling with the sounds of the city. Each shared story wove a tapestry of memories, forming a narrative that felt rich and textured, as if we were creating a legend of our own right there on the rooftop. The bustling bar, once a mere backdrop, transformed into a sanctuary of connection.

"Remember that time you tried to convince everyone that we could build an app to predict the best pizza toppings?" I teased, leaning into him playfully. "I thought we were going to end up with a world where pineapple was the reigning champion."

He chuckled, shaking his head. "You say that like it's a bad idea! But really, we should've gone with anchovies. I mean, that's the real underdog story."

The banter flowed effortlessly, each quip and playful jab drawing us closer. But beneath the surface, I felt a deeper connection forming, one that anchored us amidst the whirlwind of laughter and revelry. It was as if we were weaving an invisible thread between us, stitching together our hopes, dreams, and fears in a way that felt both exhilarating and terrifying.

"Look at us," I said, catching his gaze. "We're not just celebrating a successful launch anymore; we're celebrating... us."

His eyes softened, a myriad of emotions reflected in their depths. "I wouldn't have it any other way."

In that moment, the weight of the city around us seemed to dissolve, leaving only the intoxicating promise of possibility. It was a feeling I wanted to bottle up and carry with me forever, a shimmering treasure tucked away for the times when uncertainty threatened to creep back in.

As the night wore on, we danced together among the stars, oblivious to the world around us. Our bodies swayed to the rhythm of an unseen melody, the beat of our hearts harmonizing in a way that felt both familiar and new. The city below continued its relentless pace, but up here, on this rooftop, we created our own oasis—a space where dreams could take flight and love could flourish against all odds.

Yet, as the clock ticked on and the laughter began to wane, a sense of reality seeped back in. Tomorrow would bring its challenges, the demands of our jobs waiting like silent sentinels. I glanced at Ashton, his expression shifting from playful to contemplative. "What happens when the excitement wears off?" I asked, my voice barely a whisper against the backdrop of the night.

He took a moment, his brow furrowing as he considered my words. "Then we remind ourselves of nights like this," he replied, his voice steady. "We'll create more moments that matter, even in the chaos. That's the key, right?"

I couldn't help but smile at his determination, at the way he turned uncertainty into a rallying cry. "Yeah," I said softly. "Together, we'll figure it out."

With that promise hanging between us like a delicate thread, I knew that this was just the beginning. We were on the brink of something beautiful and messy, a journey that would be as unpredictable as the city itself. And as we stood there, our fingers intertwined against the backdrop of a thousand glowing lights, I felt a surge of hope. The world may have its chaos, but within the embrace of our love, I sensed an unshakeable strength—one that would carry us through the storms to come.

As the night deepened, the city began to transform. The laughter that had once echoed through the rooftop bar softened into an intimate hum, the sounds of celebration now mingling with whispers and the clinking of glasses. The world beyond our little bubble continued to rush by, but up here, we were ensconced in a cocoon of shared moments—small glances and lingering touches that felt both electric and tender. I stole a glance at Ashton, who was deep in conversation with one of our colleagues, his laughter a rich sound that resonated in my chest. There was a magnetic energy about him, an aura that drew me in like moth to flame.

Yet, as the night wore on, I sensed the clock ticking. Reality waited for us just beyond the glimmering skyline, a reminder of the responsibilities that would descend upon us with the dawn. I felt the familiar tendrils of anxiety creeping back in, as they always did when the thrill of the moment began to fade. I clutched my glass tighter, the condensation slick against my palm, a physical manifestation of my swirling emotions.

In a burst of courage, I stepped away from the laughter and lights, leading Ashton to a quieter corner of the terrace where the city's sounds became a gentle murmur. The air was cooler here, a crisp reminder of the autumn that was settling into the city, the leaves outside beginning to shift from green to gold, echoing the changes in my heart.

"What's going on?" he asked, concern etching his features as he watched me closely. "You look a bit distant."

"I guess I'm just trying to grasp how all of this feels," I admitted, my voice laced with a vulnerability I hadn't planned to expose. "This—us—it's a leap. A wonderful leap, but still a leap. I want it to be more than just a fleeting moment in the whirlwind of our careers."

Ashton stepped closer, his expression softening. "And it can be. But we have to communicate, really communicate. I don't want this to be a secret we share, something hidden beneath our success. It should be celebrated."

His words sent a thrill through me. I realized that this connection we were forging was more profound than I had anticipated. It wasn't merely a relationship built on fleeting glances and shared victories; it was a promise to face the complexities of life together. I nodded slowly, appreciating the weight of his sincerity.

"Okay," I said, my heart pounding. "But what if the pressure of our careers pulls us apart? What if I get consumed by my work, and you lose yourself in yours?"

His laughter was rich, echoing against the backdrop of the city. "Then we create moments like this. We promise to find our way back to each other, no matter how far we drift. Love isn't just a feeling; it's an action. It's in the choices we make, the time we carve out for one another, even when life gets messy."

A smile spread across my face, lighting up my features as I watched the fire in his eyes. He had a way of transforming my fears into something tangible, something manageable. "You make it sound so simple," I said, rolling my eyes playfully.

"Simple doesn't mean easy," he countered, a knowing smile curling on his lips. "But we'll figure it out. Together."

As the night unfolded, the city continued to glow with life beneath us. Each streetlight felt like a beacon, illuminating the paths we might take. I could imagine a future filled with the kind of laughter that sparkled just as brightly, memories made in stolen moments between meetings, and coffee shared in the early hours of dawn.

A sudden gust of wind swept through the terrace, tousling my hair and sending a chill up my spine. I instinctively leaned closer to Ashton, seeking warmth and comfort. He wrapped his arm around my shoulders, pulling me tightly against him, and I found solace in his embrace, as if nothing could disrupt our newly forged bond.

"Let's make a pact," I said, my voice low, a conspiratorial tone creeping in. "For every late night we spend working, we'll take a weekend to explore the city. Museums, parks, street fairs… anything that takes us out of our routine."

He chuckled, his breath warm against my ear. "Deal. But we have to promise to turn our phones off. No emails, no notifications. Just us, living in the moment."

I nodded, excitement bubbling within me as we began to dream aloud, painting vivid pictures of escapades that would break the mundane rhythm of our busy lives. I envisioned wandering hand in hand through Central Park, the leaves crunching beneath our feet, or losing ourselves in the narrow alleys of SoHo, hunting for hidden gems in the form of quirky boutiques and artisanal coffee shops.

In the midst of our conversation, I caught sight of a shooting star streaking across the night sky, a fleeting moment of magic that seemed to echo the promises we were making. I squeezed Ashton's hand, my heart racing at the thought of our future adventures and the challenges we'd face together.

The celebration continued around us, the voices blending into a comforting hum, but within our little bubble, time felt suspended. Each laugh, every word exchanged, deepened the connection that had blossomed between us, a tender shoot breaking through the concrete of our busy lives.

But as the clock inched closer to midnight, the reality of our lives pressed in once more. I glanced at my phone, the notifications flooding in like an unwelcome tide, reminders of deadlines and meetings that awaited. A wave of anxiety washed over me, and I couldn't help but feel the familiar pull of responsibility tugging at the edges of our celebration.

Ashton seemed to sense my unease and gently turned me to face him. "Hey," he said softly, his eyes searching mine. "We've got this. I promise I won't let work get in the way of what we have. We'll support each other, remember?"

I took a deep breath, finding solace in his steady gaze. "You're right. We're a team now, in every sense of the word. We'll balance our lives, and I won't let the fear of losing what we have keep me from embracing it fully."

With that resolve, the weight on my shoulders lightened. I felt like I could take on the world, or at least the endless to-do lists that awaited. And as we rejoined our colleagues, laughter spilling from our lips, I realized that the night had transformed into something more than a celebration of our project. It was a celebration of us, a toast to our future—one where love and ambition could coexist, crafting a life that felt vibrant and alive.

The skyline twinkled in the distance, a reflection of the dreams that awaited us. I squeezed Ashton's hand, a promise that echoed in my heart as we stepped into the fray of the world below. Together, we would navigate the twists and turns ahead, crafting our story amid the chaos of life, love lighting the way forward.

## Chapter 29: Building a Future

The soft hum of the city enveloped me as I stood on the balcony of our apartment, a cozy retreat perched above the bustling streets of Charleston. The air, thick with the scent of blooming jasmine and the lingering aroma of freshly baked pastries from the café below, wrapped around me like a warm embrace. I leaned against the railing, my heart beating in rhythm with the distant jazz that floated through the open windows, each note a reminder of the life we were building together. Below, the cobblestone streets, slick from a recent rain, reflected the city lights like tiny galaxies scattered at our feet, illuminating the charm that enveloped this historic place.

Ashton joined me, his presence grounding yet exhilarating, like the perfect blend of sweet tea and bourbon. He leaned on the railing beside me, his shoulder brushing against mine, and I turned to catch the glint in his eyes, a playful spark that always sent a shiver of delight through me. "What are you thinking about?" he asked, his voice low, carrying the weight of curiosity laced with genuine care.

"Just... everything," I replied, a smile creeping onto my lips. The corners of his mouth quirked up, and I knew he could sense the whirlwind of thoughts swirling in my mind. This moment felt pivotal; it was as if the universe had paused just for us. I looked out at the historic district, with its pastel-colored houses and vibrant flower boxes, each facade a testament to the stories hidden within. I could almost hear the laughter of generations echoing through the air, blending with the soft rustling of the leaves in the breeze.

Ashton nudged my side gently, breaking my reverie. "You know we're in this together, right? Whatever it is you're dreaming about." His sincerity wrapped around my heart, and I felt the walls I'd built to protect myself slowly start to crumble. It was strange how love could make you feel simultaneously fragile and invincible, as though you were dancing on a tightrope, each step a balance of vulnerability and strength.

"I know," I said softly, the weight of his words settling comfortably within me. "I guess I'm just thinking about how far we've come. Remember when we first started this campaign? It felt like climbing a mountain with no end in sight." The memories flooded back, both exhilarating and terrifying. The late nights spent strategizing, the early mornings filled with adrenaline and doubt, and the moments when everything seemed to hang by a thread, like a fine spiderweb glistening in the morning dew.

He chuckled, the sound rich and warm. "And yet, here we are, standing at the peak, looking out over the landscape we've shaped together. It's beautiful." His words resonated deeply, echoing the uncharted territories of our future. I could almost envision the possibilities stretching out before us, like the vast ocean meeting the horizon, endless and inviting.

"But what now?" I mused, my fingers tracing the edge of the balcony. "What do we do with this success?" The question hung in the air, weighty and bright, igniting the fire of ambition in my chest. There was a world beyond this moment, a canvas waiting for us to splash our dreams across it. The potential was both thrilling and daunting.

Ashton turned to me, his expression shifting to one of fierce determination. "We build, love. We build a future that reflects us—our values, our passions, our hopes. We can blend our professional lives, our dreams of traveling, maybe even starting that nonprofit we always talked about." His enthusiasm was infectious, and I could see the flicker of ideas sparking in his mind, illuminating the path forward.

"I love that idea," I said, feeling my heart race with possibility. "Imagine creating a space where we can inspire others, where we can help those who feel lost or unseen." I could picture it—a bustling center filled with laughter, education, and a sense of belonging, a stark contrast to the quiet isolation that often accompanied ambition. It was more than just a dream; it was a legacy, a way to weave our lives into the fabric of the community.

The thought electrified the air between us, and Ashton's eyes glinted with excitement. "We could host workshops, mentorship programs, and even art classes. We could invite local artists to showcase their work, create a hub of creativity and support. We can encourage others to embrace their dreams." He paused, looking at me as if he could see the gears turning in my head, urging me to join him in this vision.

I nodded, feeling the rush of inspiration coursing through my veins. "And we could use our platforms to amplify voices that deserve to be heard," I added, envisioning a mosaic of experiences coming together, each piece adding depth to the larger picture. The thought was intoxicating; it felt like a calling, a purpose we were destined to fulfill.

"Let's make it happen," he declared, and in that moment, the air around us crackled with unspoken promise. It was as if the universe had aligned itself in our favor, and I knew we had the power to transform our dreams into reality. The warmth of his hand found mine, and I squeezed it tightly, a silent vow passing between us. We would navigate this journey together, arm in arm, heart in heart.

The city hummed beneath us, vibrant and alive, a tapestry of dreams waiting to be unfurled. I glanced out at the horizon, where the sun dipped low, painting the sky in hues of pink and gold, a breathtaking reminder that the best was yet to come. We had faced challenges, but we had emerged stronger, more resilient. I felt a rush of hope, and with it, the undeniable truth that our love was the foundation upon which we would build our future.

With our hearts intertwined, we stepped back inside, ready to start sketching the outlines of our vision. Each moment we shared in that cozy apartment, filled with laughter and deep conversations, felt like a step toward something extraordinary—a new chapter waiting to be written. The future shimmered before us, and for the first time, I could see it clearly, a canvas rich with potential, and it was ours to paint.

As the sun dipped lower in the sky, casting long shadows that danced across our living room, I felt the familiar flutter of excitement as we settled into a rhythm of planning. The old oak table, marked with the imperfections of countless meals and late-night brainstorming sessions, stood as our battleground for dreams. I spread out sheets of paper, the crispness of the blank pages urging me to fill them with our aspirations, while Ashton grabbed a couple of colorful markers, his eyes glinting with mischief.

"Let's do this the right way," he declared, tossing a blue marker into my hands. "No boring lists; we need visuals!" There was a childlike enthusiasm in his voice, infectious enough to sweep me into his whirlwind of creativity. I couldn't help but laugh as I watched him begin to sketch, transforming our ideas into whimsical doodles, his scribbles of houses, trees, and stick figures morphing into a landscape of possibilities.

"Are we building a town or a dream?" I teased, trying to suppress my giggles as he elaborated on his sketches. "Because I'm not sure if we're ready for city planning yet."

"Oh, come on! This is a brainstorming session," he replied, waving his marker dramatically. "Every great dream starts with a little chaos. Besides, I think I just created a skyline that rivals Manhattan." His grin was disarming, and in that moment, I knew we were on the brink of something beautiful, something that would blend our ambitions with our love.

I picked up a green marker, matching his enthusiasm as I began to draw alongside him. The rhythm of our pens scratching against the paper created a symphony of creativity that resonated through the room. "How about a community garden?" I suggested, my imagination sparking to life as I sketched a patch of rich soil, bursting with flowers and vegetables, a place where people could come together and cultivate not just crops, but connections.

"That's perfect!" he exclaimed, his eyes lighting up. "And we can host workshops on sustainable living. Teach people how to grow their own food. It'll be like an oasis in the city." The excitement in his voice sent shivers of hope through me, igniting the embers of my own dreams.

We lost ourselves in our doodles, ideas flowing like water as we scribbled out our visions for a future filled with purpose. I imagined creating spaces for artists to showcase their work, musicians to perform, and children to play, all intertwined with the community we longed to foster. Our laughter rang through the air, punctuating the creativity with joy. Each line I drew, every curve and color, felt like a promise, not just to each other but to the world around us.

As the night wore on and the golden hour faded into a deep indigo, our sketches began to take form, a beautiful tapestry of dreams woven together. The room was awash in the warm glow of fairy lights strung across the ceiling, illuminating our makeshift studio of aspirations. The comforting scent of vanilla candles flickered in the background, grounding us as we transcended the ordinary and delved deeper into the extraordinary.

But amid the laughter and light, a moment of stillness passed between us, a silent acknowledgment of the weight our dreams carried. It was easy to get swept away in the excitement, but we knew there were hurdles ahead. I bit my lip, hesitating as I considered the challenges that lay in wait. "Do you think we're ready for this?" I asked, my voice barely above a whisper, the doubt sneaking in uninvited.

Ashton paused, his expression shifting to one of contemplative seriousness. "We'll never know unless we try," he replied, his voice steady. "Every great endeavor comes with risks, and if we let fear dictate our choices, we'll miss out on the chance to create something amazing." His conviction washed over me, like a balm to my insecurities, reminding me that we had faced storms before and emerged, time and again, hand in hand.

"You're right," I conceded, a smile creeping back onto my face. "It's just—" I took a deep breath, willing myself to articulate the uncertainty that nagged at the edges of my heart. "What if we fail? What if all this effort doesn't pan out?"

He leaned closer, his voice softening as he took my hand in his. "Then we'll adapt. We'll learn from it, and we'll keep going. I'd rather try and stumble than not try at all. And I'll be right here with you, every step of the way." The sincerity in his words wrapped around my heart like a protective cocoon, banishing the shadows of doubt.

The fire between us flickered, growing stronger as our hands intertwined, a physical manifestation of our shared resolve. We could face anything together, the weight of our dreams grounding us while our hearts soared. I felt a sense of calm wash over me, knowing that regardless of the outcomes, our journey would be one filled with lessons, laughter, and love.

In that moment, surrounded by our colorful sketches and the soft glow of the candles, I felt an overwhelming sense of gratitude. For Ashton, for this life we were building, and for the dreams that danced just beyond the horizon, beckoning us closer. The night air outside was cool and inviting, a reminder that while our ideas ignited our spirits, there was a world out there waiting for us to leave our mark.

"Let's make a pact," I suggested, my eyes sparkling with mischief. "For every idea we scribble here, we have to take one step toward making it real. No matter how small." I squeezed his hand, my heart racing at the prospect of turning our dreams into tangible actions.

"Deal," he said, his smile infectious, igniting a fire of determination within me. "Tonight, we sketch out our dreams, and tomorrow, we take our first step." The energy in the room shifted, fueled by our shared commitment, and I could almost see the path unfurling before us, lit by the promise of a brighter future.

As the night deepened, we continued to create, the pages of our dreams filling with vibrant colors and bold lines. I felt the weight of possibility hanging in the air, a tapestry of our aspirations interwoven with laughter, love, and a shared commitment to forge a future that reflected who we truly were. The world outside might have been cloaked in darkness, but within the four walls of our little sanctuary, the light of our dreams shone brightly, guiding us into the adventure that awaited.

The following morning unfurled like a canvas splashed with vivid hues, the sun's golden rays streaming through our window, waking me gently from my dreams. I stirred, feeling the warmth of Ashton's arm draped protectively across my waist, a living anchor in the whirlwind of my thoughts. The scent of freshly brewed coffee wafted in from the kitchen, mingling with the lingering sweetness of last night's creativity, and I smiled, letting the moment wash over me. There was something profoundly comforting in this routine, the way our lives intertwined like the vines of the ivy that clung to the brick walls outside, resilient and full of life.

I slipped out of bed quietly, careful not to disturb the peacefulness that enveloped him, and tiptoed to the kitchen. The tiles felt cool beneath my feet, grounding me as I filled the kettle and watched the water come to a boil, its bubbles rising like the excitement building within me. Today was the day we would take our first step toward those dreams we had mapped out in colorful chaos, and the thought sent a thrill coursing through my veins.

As I poured the hot water over the coffee grounds, I glanced out the window at the world beyond our little sanctuary. The street was alive with activity—people bustling about, their conversations blending into a melodic hum. I spotted a couple jogging by, their laughter echoing in the morning air, while a dog barked enthusiastically at a squirrel, its owner struggling to keep up. In that moment, the vibrancy of the city felt like a heartbeat, pulsing with the promise of new beginnings.

Just then, Ashton entered the kitchen, his tousled hair and sleepy smile rendering him undeniably adorable. "Good morning, beautiful," he murmured, and I felt my cheeks flush at his compliment, a sweet reminder of the affection that wove through our everyday moments. He approached me, wrapping his arms around my waist, his warmth radiating against my back.

"Good morning," I replied, leaning into him, savoring the comfort of his presence. "I was just thinking about how we're finally going to start making our dreams a reality." My excitement bubbled over, and I turned to face him, my hands resting on his shoulders.

"We have a plan, and we're going to stick to it," he said, his gaze steady and reassuring. "Let's start by meeting with that community center we found online. They're looking for volunteers for their outreach programs." The determination in his voice ignited a fire within me, and I nodded, imagining the lives we could touch through our efforts.

After a quick breakfast, we donned our jackets, ready to brave the crisp autumn air. The streets, now dappled with golden leaves, crunched underfoot as we made our way toward the community center. The vibrant colors of fall created a picturesque backdrop, and I felt as if nature itself was celebrating our newfound purpose. The warm sun kissed our faces, a gentle reminder that we were on the right path.

As we arrived, the community center loomed ahead, a charming brick building adorned with ivy and local artwork. Its walls told stories of the people it had served over the years, and I felt a wave of anticipation wash over me as we stepped inside. The air was alive with energy; children's laughter echoed through the hallways, mingling with the aroma of homemade pastries wafting from the kitchen.

We were greeted by a woman named Clara, her hair streaked with silver and her eyes twinkling with kindness. She was the director of the center, and as we introduced ourselves, I could feel her warmth enveloping us like a cozy blanket. "I'm so glad you're here! We're always looking for passionate individuals to join our team. Our outreach programs are designed to help underprivileged families, and we'd love your help in expanding them."

I could see the fire ignite in Ashton's eyes as Clara spoke, his enthusiasm contagious. "We have some ideas for workshops and community events that could really engage the neighborhood," he suggested, his voice steady and confident. I felt a swell of pride watching him navigate this new terrain with ease, his passion lighting up the room.

Clara's smile widened, and she led us through the bustling center, showing us classrooms filled with eager children and activity rooms where families gathered for support. "We believe in creating a space that fosters learning, creativity, and community," she explained, her voice rich with conviction. "Every child should have access to opportunities that allow them to grow and thrive, and we rely on volunteers like you to help make that happen."

As we walked through the center, I felt a sense of belonging wash over me. The energy buzzed like static electricity, and I could see how our dreams could merge beautifully with the needs of this community. The idea of organizing art classes, financial literacy workshops, and mentorship programs felt not only attainable but vital.

When we reached the main hall, Ashton paused to take in the vibrant mural painted on the wall, a swirling explosion of color depicting children playing together, their laughter depicted in lively strokes. "This is incredible," he breathed, a hint of awe in his voice. "Imagine how much good we could do here."

I nodded in agreement, my heart swelling with the possibilities. "We can create events that bring people together, foster creativity, and empower families to connect with each other and with resources." My voice trembled with excitement as we brainstormed ideas, the weight of our dreams transforming into a palpable energy that pulsed through the air around us.

Clara watched us with a knowing smile, her gaze shifting between us, as if she could see the deep bond we shared—a connection that fueled our shared aspirations. "I can already see the impact you two will have here. Let's set up a meeting next week to discuss your ideas in more detail and get you started," she said, her voice warm and encouraging.

As we left the center, hand in hand, the air felt charged with possibility. I couldn't help but smile at Ashton, the shared thrill of embarking on this new journey palpable between us. "Can you believe we're actually doing this?" I asked, my heart racing with anticipation.

"Absolutely," he replied, his eyes shining with a mix of determination and excitement. "This is just the beginning."

As we strolled back through the golden leaves, the laughter of children and the hum of the city wrapped around us like a warm embrace. We walked in silence for a moment, savoring the beauty of what we were creating, each step echoing the rhythm of our hopes.

With each passing day, we would build a future where our passions intertwined seamlessly, crafting a legacy of love, community, and creativity. The tapestry of our lives would be vibrant, woven together with threads of laughter, empathy, and purpose. I felt an overwhelming sense of gratitude wash over me, a deep appreciation for the journey we had embarked upon together. This was our adventure, a shared story filled with beautiful uncertainties and glorious possibilities, and I couldn't wait to see where it would lead us next.

Milton Keynes UK
Ingram Content Group UK Ltd.
UKHW040638131024
449481UK00001B/40